Cover design by: Miblart

ANNARITE BORN

R.B. LEYLAND

For Jade, Cole and Aria. I cherish you, more than you know.

Prologue

A guttural howl pierced the still air, smashing the serene night into pieces. The entire town seemed to jerk awake in that moment, either in shock or disbelief, horror twisting in their gut as the sound sank in. They'd come. Deep in Annar territory that backed onto the mountains on one side and impassable woodland the other, the region of the Annarite General himself, they thought themselves safe. But none of this mattered as the howl ripped the town from slumber, alerting them to exactly who had arrived: The Hounds.

Men leapt from their beds, grabbing anything they could find to defend themselves; whilst their wives ushered screaming children towards exits. A bell began to toll almost instantly, calling for aid. But the Hounds knew their trade, and their trade was death.

Instead of tearing down doors and breaking through walls, they opted for the lazy way out - lighting fires wherever they could and tossing firebrands into the thatch of houses. Oblivious families were like rats in the inferno and the only thing they could do in their terror was flee out of the front door and onto the blades and spears of the waiting wraiths.

Men armed only with tools attempted to rally and push them back, but it was futile against the forged swords and mail of the rebel group. They butchered every living thing, and the ones they didn't find were inevitably burned alive by the flames that spread quicker than the citizens could run. No remorse was shown on the faces of the men they showed only the cold face. Calm. Efficient. Ruthless.

One man stepped into the firelight of the chaos and whistled once. His face was hidden by the black hood that matched his robes, but the men knew their leader. He knew the Annarites better than anyone and he wouldn't risk their lives against them, not yet. They melted into the night at his command, leaving the town lifeless and burning.

Only the cry of a single baby punctured the crackle of the flames.

*****

Aldred Sain stormed up the weatherworn path towards the screaming of his people. His tall, broad form was enhanced by the armour he wore, showing that a lord of battle had come. He and his men knew they were too late, but that didn't slow them as they sprinted past the grasping branches of the woodland, ignorant of the whips and scratches they incurred. Aldred felt a fierce pride in them matching his pace; they were the elite.

They crested the hill above the town of Satern and despite the urgency of the forced march, they froze, looking in dismay at the carnage below. Not a single building had been left untouched, emphasised by the smoke cloud staining the sky. The screams of the villagers could still be heard, carried on the foul wind that buffeted their faces. A growl of anger came from the group as they saw the dark figures disappearing into the gloom at their arrival, their grisly work done for the night. They'd all been duped; scout reports putting the Hounds in the south mere days ago.

"At the double lads!" barked the squad leader without waiting for the order from the General. He knew his work, and Aldred knew that.

They began the descent into the town, angling towards the east side where they knew the Aveni villagers would be coming to help. The Saternac region had only two villages, and although they weren't a close-knit community, they had no animosity. The sounds of devastation would have reached the Aveni as it had the guard at the Sain manor, and they would come.

Avoiding the treacherous rocks and tree stumps recently cut down to expand the village, they reached the bottom of the hill and formed a line out of instinct, each man hefting his shield and drawing his blade. This is what the Annarites were meant for, keeping the peace, protecting the land, and they all knew their worth. But all their training and God-given talents were for naught that night.

With their shields interlocked they pushed into the town, using the burning buildings themselves to protect the flanks of their wall and all eyes were alert, darting at every shadow. Aldred was in the middle of the wall as was his way.

"Cowards!" Aldred screamed, but he was greeted only with silence. He allowed his fury to boil over at the bodies strewn across the floor without ceremony. Man, woman and child were left in the streets, gruesome wounds telling the story of their deaths, and most covering their loved ones until their last breath, embracing them even though they knew it was hopeless. He knew his men felt the rage as keenly as he did and felt no shame in his own.

Tears pricked in the corners of his eyes, and he brushed them away furiously, but his men either didn't notice or didn't care. They moved systematically around the village square without hearing a sound except their own marching and breathing, the air getting hotter by the minute as the flames devoured the timber structures around them. Aldred decided it was enough.

"Dextri!" Aldred shouted over the cacophony to the guard's leader. A ball of muscle to his right responded instantly to his order with a barked acknowledgement. "Get the men to gather the dead. Treat them with honour, they were our people, and we failed them. I'll get some of the Aveni to identify them and we can get a memorial built for the fallen," Aldred said.

A pang of woe came upon him, and he bowed his head for a solemn moment until a sound so alien in the deathly surroundings broke through his reverie.

"A child" Aldred gasped, looking at Dextri wild eyed.

The General ripped off his helmet and began to run towards the sound, ignoring all cries from his warriors in his haste to locate the child's wails. Flames whipped around him, tendrils of smoke following him between the earthy paths of the dead village, mocking his attempts to hear and fouling his vision. His head spinning from the smoke's attack on his lungs, Aldred dropped to the ground and took a deep breath of the precious, clean air. His head cleared almost instantly with the oxygen and in that clarity, he heard the delicate whimpering that he'd been straining so hard to hear. Much closer this time.

Staying low to the ground and kicking specks of dirt and ash into his own face, preferring the stinging hits to the burning of his throat, he got to a haggard arch, barely recognisable as the door it once was. The darkened beams of timber had almost burnt through and collapsed, most of the wall coming down with it to the incinerated flowerbed below. Through that doorway the blaze was in full force, and yet that's where the cries were sounding. Aldred crashed through, his eyes darting around like minnows in a stream, taking everything in, missing nothing.

The scene that greeted him however, left him dumbstruck like nothing else ever had before. In the centre of the blazing building, in a wicker basket that should have long since burned, lay a baby. But it wasn't the baby that left Aldred in awe, it was the flames. Fingers of flame probed the area surrounding the child and found no purchase. It was as though an invisible bubble reflected the heat as it came close, extinguishing it with a flash of light that blinded Aldred, and resonated with a slight *pop.* Deciding in a heartbeat that he didn't want to test this invisible shield for too long, Aldred crept forward reverently before slowly removing his mailed gloves and reaching for the child.

The air thrummed as he came closer, amplifying all his senses; pressure mounting on the tips of his fingers as they brushed what he judged to be the beginning of the impenetrable sphere. His hands made progress into the protection as a numbness started to lance through his body. With a great effort of will he forced with all his strength, his body screaming in protest at the force he was exerting. A final desperate roar fuelled by adrenaline gave him extra power and he felt the sphere give. Unlike the pops and crackles that it gave repelling the flames, there was a silence as it moulded around his hands, then his arms, and then his entire body, a feeling of tranquillity and icy water flooding over his skin and allowing him into the area.

The flames were still devouring everything in their domain outside of the sphere, sending a wave of alarm through Aldred as he realised that he still had to get them out fast before they were both swallowed too.

Hastily bundling the baby into his arms, he noticed that his head was so full of red hair which seemed strange in one so young. The infant stopped his wails under the scrutiny and looked back into the blue eyes of the General observing him and smiled; then the bubble popped.

The heat buffeted them both instantly as the flames roared their triumph and attacked the part of the room that had, until that moment, been denied to them. The baby resumed his hoarse cries which spurred Aldred into action faster than any sound could.

Using every ounce of energy he had left and covering the child as best he could, he powered forward dashing for the closest exit he saw, broke through the shroud of smoke and plunged into darkness, heat scorching at his back. He stumbled further from the house towards the tree line before collapsing to his knees with a groan, coughs wracking his body as he tried to expel the smoke from his lungs. Eyes streaming and throat burning, he struggled to draw the breath he was craving. He began to panic. Placing the baby on the soft grass below him, he closed his eyes to bring the calm to his mind, but nothing could dispel his terror at being unable to draw breath.

His face contorted now, muscles beginning to spasm as the air he so desperately needed evaded him. He fell to the floor in a heap, the vigour he possessed mere minutes before passed as his body began to shut down and his eyes began to blur. Through the trees he could have sworn a figure began to emerge, hooded and stooped, dressed in pitch black robes.

One of Ezimat's reapers, he thought with a smile; knowing he would at least go to the god's hall with his forefathers. Aldred shut his eyes to the blissful darkness he knew would end in paradise.

Then a breath ripped through his throat, dragging him back from the precipice and into the world of smoke and pain. The air, although like nectar to Aldred's lungs, was like a firebrand to his throat and his eyes streamed at the stinging pain as he began to cough again. Once this fit subsided and he could breathe the needling air, he glanced towards the treeline, saw the hooded figure and jolted back to full consciousness, staggering to his feet attempting to pay his respects.

"Seeress," he rasped hoarsely, attempting a formal bow but giving more of a hunch in his state. He now knew how he'd been torn back from death's paradise and was grateful for the woman's intervention. He knew Seeress' were known to have powers beyond the realm of mortal men and had seen their healings on occasion.

"Thank you for your assistance. I feared I was for the afterlife there," he continued. Aldred was interrupted by the woman stooping down to gather the baby into her arms, cooing and soothing whilst kissing his brow. A chilling wind swept through the air clearing the haze and making Aldred shiver, such was the contrast between the heat and that biting breeze, out of place in the otherwise humid night. With that wind, the Seeress' eyes turned milky. She began reverently,

"He was born to it, and will live with that fire in his veins as it burns him onwards to greater things. Two others are by his side, one from this day forward, the other near his age day. *YOU* will raise him, not as your own but alongside your children

5

as a sibling. Betrayal sets his life course in motion, from one who is present from the beginning."

Aldred stood aghast at the prophecy having never heard of one spoken in all his thirty-two years, even about the royal household. In contrast to his mood, the Seeress smiled.

"Just an airway clearance spell, use them on all the young 'uns when they're born to clear the mucus, but you're welcome, all the same General," she said to his earlier thanks. "Putting your life on the line for a stranger's child, you Annarites aren't all idiots, eh?" she continued with a cackle, causing Aldred's awe to fade and mirth to appear in its place. An ominous prophecy and then joking within an instant.

"The babe if you please, Seeress. He's my responsibility now, be he a burden or a blessing. I will raise him amongst my own boys; my newest boy, Alkor, is within months of the same age, they'll get along perfectly. I would ask you to stay for a while, however... my men may need healing assistance if they find any left alive," Aldred said, knowing no matter his rank, he couldn't order a Seeress chosen by the Gods.

"It is why I came, Lord, saving you was just a bonus. Look after this one, Aldred Sain. I feel a hint of fate surrounding him to have survived this night." She gave the child a final kiss on the forehead and passed him over gently, making sure the blanket was wrapped firmly around his tiny form to keep his skin off the cold of Aldred's armoured steel.

"Shall we?" she said, gesturing back towards the flames and the destruction beyond.

Just then, a group of his men came around the corner, breathless and pouring in sweat with shouts of "He's here!" and "Dextri - got him!" relief evident at having found their General. Dextri came tearing around the corner, his expression livid.

"General! Forgive my confusion but you always drill into the men to stay with the grou..." he started. He paused as he saw the babe, anger vanishing from his face to be replaced by awe.

"You saved the babe, General. Please, forgive my insubordination."

"Forgive *me* Dextri. I had the chance to salvage some life tonight and I would have given my own if that meant I did that" he said solemnly.

Aldred watched as the rest of the men registered his quarry. Collectively they gasped. First at the sight of the Seeress, now hooded again, stood behind the General looking as ominous as ever, and then at the babe squirming against his wrappings, clearly full of life. A murmur went through the crowd, and many drew the circle of the Haldi on their heads to bring luck or ward off evil.

"The Gods must have a hand in this! A newborn survives the slaughter and flames, yet not a single adult does?" murmured one of them, unable to keep the tremor from his voice.

And a prophesized newborn to boot, Aldred thought, smiling inwardly. He waved his hands to quiet the group. It took some time given the man's last comment, any mention of the Gods in small towns like these drew a huge amount of trepidation and wonder.

"Spread the word, brothers. THIS WILL NOT HAPPEN AGAIN! This child will be a constant reminder that, although darkness exists in this world, so does light, so does hope! He will be a brother to my sons and will want for nothing in my household!" he said regally, the announcement sending rippling whispers through the group.

Even Dextri stood slack jawed at the comment but quickly recovered his composure as the seeress piped up behind him.

"And what, Aldred Sain, will the babe be named?" she said quietly, knowing full well he couldn't give the child his own name as a noble house.

Eyebrows raised amongst the soldiers as they waited for an answer from the General, his face unchanged and blank as he mulled over the question.

"Balzor," he said finally. "He will be named, Balzor."

Chapter 1

Glorious rays bathed the treetops as the sun reared its welcome head over the Bunta mountains, the birds greeting its appearance with an orchestra of singing as they rose from the bright green foliage in celebration. Around five miles from the mountain base, smoke could be seen coming from Saternac, the single town in the area.

After the devastating attack fifteen years previous, the people of Aveni had expanded their own town rather than rebuild over the ghosts of the past. That old wreckage was now the burial ground for the slain, a memorial valiantly dominating the area. As the Saternac region now only had one town, it made sense to rename the town after the region it lived in. It was now more protected than any small town in the kingdom. A ten-foot wall had been erected around its entire circumference, patrolled by town militia whose only weapons were a spear and a large horn. They were not warriors, but their horns would alert the Annarites stationed nearby. The warriors would be there within minutes thanks to the newly constructed road. It connected the outskirts of the newest buildings with the Sain Manor, which had the barracks attached and was only half a mile away.

The town also made good trade from the soldiers permanently stationed there, now a whole century rather than the usual squad of twenty. All expenses were paid for by Aldred Sain, who trained, equipped, fed, housed and paid the men who served him. The town grew to accommodate the extra needs of the men, with food stalls thrown up in the street outside the butchers that served mouth-watering shanks of meat seasoned with eastern spices from over the mountains. These were traded for with the mountain tribes, who sent delegations when the passes were free to the much more frequently used tavern that had sprung up to sate the insatiable thirsts of the warriors after a day's training.

It was these warriors that were stirring from their beds groggily, the sun being a source of irritation for a lot of them due to the pounding heads from too much wine. It signalled the start of their day which consisted either of training or patrols. Either way, a hangover was a bad thing to wake up to, the sun's stunning rays becoming a harsh glare for these men. Strutting through his father's halls like a peacock, drinking in the summer's warmth and relishing its light on his skin, was Alnor Sain. He was cocksure and bore the height typical of a Sain along with the bright blue eyes that went with it; but that's where the comparison ended. His hooked nose trailed his fat lips and short, greasy hair graced his head, which was pounding just like the rest of the warriors but was alleviated to the point of bliss at what he had overhead that morning.

He'd heard the scurrying of feet past his room as he slept off the effects of the wine and leapt out of bed to follow. Anyone willing to risk waking up his father in his personal quarters at that time of the morning must either be mad or have urgent news. His suspicion proved correct, and his stalking rewarded at what he'd heard; they were going hunting.

Over the years since the raid on Satern, the Hounds had been hitting small settlements all around the kingdom, taking select prisoners and burning everything before scuttling back into the night. They'd never been pinned down, with only one patrol coming across them by chance which ignited a quick and savage skirmish between the groups before they again fled to lay low. *Fifteen years!* Alnor thought. *Fifteen years they've escaped us and sown chaos through the realm!* But now his father's informants, numerous around the land and paid well for their work, had found what they thought was a camp. It was well hidden in the dunes that nestled around the Jarnad desert and had a skeleton crew which could only mean one thing: The Hounds were hunting too.

He could already feel the anticipation building in his bones at the massacre of the camp's small crew, their long wait for the rebels to return who would be expecting a warm welcome only to find a brutal death waiting for them. His thoughts were completely content as he whistled on his way out of the hallway which connected the personal rooms of the house. These rooms were only meant for himself, his father, his brother and esteemed guests.

He passed the final door before the archway that led to the stairs which was slightly ajar, deliberately ignoring the occupant of this room with a contempt he knew was justified. *Peasant boy,* he thought savagely. Balzor could always ruin his happy day-dreams. Alnor, however, couldn't walk past the room without needling the ruffian, so he kicked at the door to startle the pup with the sudden sound. As the lad wasn't even in his room, it only served to stub his toe and further sour his disgruntled mood as he saw the mess of the unmade sheets and clothes strewn across his floor. "Father takes him in and this is the thanks he gets," Alnor grumbled under his breath, spitting on the floor and slamming the door shut with a crash before exiting the hallway under the large archway. This led to a wide, stone staircase which dominated the entrance hall to the house; it sat on top of the kitchens which in turn fed the feasting hall behind them, underneath the living quarters of his family. Benches sat along the side walls of the hall, waiting areas for messengers or guests to either be ushered into to dine, or more frequently to his father's office, which was basically his command post outside of war.

However, it wasn't the elegant staircase or the mouth-watering smell coming from the kitchens that drew Alnor's attention, it was the magnificent tapestry that adorned the wall above the thick oak door that indicated the entrance. Despite his foul mood, he paused on the stairs and bowed his head in deference because nobody ignored or disrespected the Haldi.

The Haldi were the family of the Gods ruled by their patriarch, Ezimat. He was known as 'Old Ezi' by the common folk, not that Alnor would ever be heard to say it. He was the supreme leader. The God of the sky and the earth, above all deities - male or female. He had two sons who were the furthest from brothers as they could be; Sarnat was the God of chaos and battle, Exat, the God of wisdom and knowledge. One the God of warriors, the other the God of seers. Both were displayed in the tapestry behind their father, as was proper. Further back still were the female deities but Alnor paid them no heed. It was known to bring ill luck to pray to a deity that wasn't of your gender unless you were a seer.

Raising his head after his moment of pious reverie, he began his descent down the stairs, the succulent smell of bacon wafting across his nostrils and making his day bright again. A breeze kissed his bare arms as he reached the bottom and he realised the entrance door was slightly ajar, with a clacking of weighted practice swords echoing across the house grounds despite this being the warriors' rest day.

Frowning in puzzlement, Alnor strode to the door and wrenched it open, curiosity beating his hangover in a silent battle. Light streamed into the entrance hall as the door creaked open, dispelling the shadows with its ravenous beams and instantly warming the room. Allowing himself a moment to adjust to the harsh change in bright-ness, Alnor raised his hand to shade his eyes and squinted into the grounds. What he saw made him bare his teeth in anger.

On a patch of ground used for the warriors' training, just to the side of a plain building he knew held the practice gear and a bathhouse, two boys were sparring. Their youth was painfully obvious in the unpractised, clumsy swings, but they weren't com-pletely without training. It wasn't their age which made Alnor's eyes narrow however, it was their identities. One was clearly his brother, his cropped hair and tall height a mirror image of his own. If he got closer, he knew he'd see his father's eyes and easy-going smile, although his brother had inherited his mother's stubbed nose rather than his father's hooked one.

The second boy on the other hand was the source of Alnor's irritation. His long, braided hair glistened in the sunlight, its red hue giving his head the image of being alight. He was a good deal shorter than his opponent and not quite as broad. "Balzor," Alnor hissed. Deciding instantly that he would prefer to ruin the peasant boy's morning more than getting bacon, he stepped out into the grounds and closed the door behind him. The bacon could wait.

*****

Balzor swung his sword in an overhead arc towards his brother's head, yelling excitedly with the anticipation of the blow landing. Instead, he was rewarded with a jolt coursing through his arm as Alkor Sain met the attack with his own makeshift blade resulting in a resounding clack. Spinning away with a flourish, Alkor grinned gesturing with his free hand in a taunt.

"Come, little brother, let's see if you can beat a Sain," he goaded, eyes mischie-vous as he needled his friend. Balzor felt a lurch in his gut, but he didn't take the bait. He knew it was a joke, but using the same phrase that usually came from the slimy mouth of Alnor Sain? It was a low blow, and he knew it.

Moving in slowly and deliberately rather than the rushed assault Alkor had clearly been counting on, he unleashed a flurry of attacks which Alkor desperately parried, giving ground and trying to disengage without leaving himself open. In the end though, Balzor was not to be denied. He feinted towards the left, drawing Alkor's blade from his defensive stance to try to take the opening Balzor had exposed, but he was ready. Flicking his blade quickly, he knocked the rushed attack aside and swiftly brought it up to his brother's throat, ending the bout and leaving both boys out of breath from the exertion, chests heaving.

"Not a peasant now am I, rich boy?" Balzor teased between gasping breaths, before realising the pain in his side wasn't just from his straining lungs but from the point of Alkor's sword digging into his ribs.

Seeing that Balzor had finally noticed this fact, Alkor let out of a guffaw of laughter as his friend's face changed from triumph to dismay in seconds. "Always gotta win, you bastard," Balzor said grumpily, lowering his sword and stepping back. "Least this time I would've taken your head off too," he said, causing Alkor's laughter to intensify, Balzor soon joining in good naturedly. Kneeling and placing the practice blade on the dusty floor, Alkor started to re-tie his boots.

"Round two, if you're not too gassed that is?" he said before rising with a smug look on his face, picking the sword up in the process. That smug look abruptly changed to one of alarm. This was the only warning Balzor received before a fist crunched into his temple, igniting a savage pain in his head and sending him sprawling to the ground.

"You think you're good enough to spar with a *Sain*, peasant boy?" hissed a voice he knew and hated – Alnor Sain. For some reason only known to him, Alnor had detested him since birth and had never accepted him into the family like Alkor had, despite the younger Sain's pleas to do so.

"Leave our brother alone, Alnor!" Alkor shouted, a slight tremor in his voice betraying the fear he felt at standing up to his older brother. They'd both been on the receiving end of Alnor's temper before and he didn't relish the thought of the bruises that would inevitably come.

"OUR BROTHER?!" Alnor raged, spittle flying from his mouth and his blue eyes bulging giving him a demented look. "This. Is. Not. Our. Brother!" he screamed. Each word was punctuated with a ruthless kick to Balzor's ribcage, causing him to curl up into a ball in utter terror, crying out in pain and detesting his weakness. Finishing his tirade, Alnor turned to his brother, dusting off his hands at a job well done. "You'll do well to remember that you're a Sain, Alkor. Hanging out with this turd will only tarnish our name, whether father took pity on him or not," scorn oozing from his voice as he looked contemptuously at the sorry figure on the ground, red hair now stained with dirt.

"I think I'll take my chances, *brother,*" Alkor replied defiantly, sounding much steadier this time and standing with his head held high. Alnor's eyes bored into him for an uncomfortable amount of time, then he snorted and turned away.

"Suit yourself, I'll just have to make enough glory for both of us," he shouted over his shoulder as he swaggered away, laughing cruelly. Balzor hawked up a mouthful of blood and spat it onto the floor in a congealed mess before trying to rise despite the pain he felt.

"Bastard," he said, gritting his teeth against the discomfort lancing through his body. Alkor moved to help his brother, but he brushed him off angrily.

"I just don't see why he hates me so much! He's of age now and I'm not even classed as an adult until next month. You'd think he'd grow up!" Balzor said furiously. Alkor took a moment before he answered, using the time to dust off his friend's back.

"Listen, Balzor, he's just a bully. He hardly even likes me and I'm his own blood! He doesn't like the fact that our father had to take you in, or that he practically treats you as one of his own. The top and bottom of it is that you're not a Sain, despite us accepting you into the family. Coming of age only inflames the idiot's arrogance that he's better than everyone" he said simply. As quickly as it ignited, Balzor's fury was quenched, and was replaced by complete bitterness.

"That's just it," he mumbled. "I'll never be one of you, not matter how hard I try. I'm just the peasant boy to take pity on." With his head drooping low and clutching at his injured ribs, he shuffled off into the sunlight towards the bathhouse, the day seeming suddenly gloomy despite the sun's joyous rays covering the land. Shaking his head sadly, Alkor watched Balzor go, stooping to pick up the practice swords before following his friend to the bathhouse.

✶✶✶✶✶

The bathhouse doubled up as an armoury, filled to the brim with things the warriors would need. From the leather and weighted swords used for training the century, to the chainmail, axes, swords and shields needed to do their job should the need arise. Benches surrounding the large rectangular room offered places to change or rest after training, with trunks underneath the benches for specific warrior's armour and weapons separate to the basic gear supplied by the General, which was what Balzor had been using.

Unstrapping the sweat stained leathers, he let them hit the ground with a thump making the pristine floor look unkempt. Balzor sighed, trying to release some of the sorrow he felt clamping on his chest because of Alnor's tirade. His voice reverberated around Balzor's head, hammering home the same undeniable truth – he wasn't one of them. He had no family, the makeshift home that had always been his felt alien to him and that solid realisation hit his core.

"Nobody would ever miss me," he muttered sullenly, throwing the practice sword to the ground next to the leathers in a childish attempt at rebellion. As the echoes of the sword hitting the floor faded, he caught the sound of a foot scuffing the floor behind him. Determined to get a real hit in this time, he spun around and instantly swung his fist with the momentum of the spin. Before he had time to register who it was, the man ducked the punch, rose fluidly and slapped Balzor on the side of his face, causing his ears to ring and his eyes to shudder in their sockets.

"You'll have to be quicker than that lad, even against that piss stain Alnor," he said, a hint of a smile tugging at his lips.

"Dextri!" Balzor exclaimed, a grin splitting his face in two. He threw his arms around the boulder of a man before he could protest, earning himself a gruff laugh but a shove; Dextri never was one for affection, even when they were children.

"Hey, lad!" he said. "You've grown."

"I didn't think it was possible but so have you" Balzor accused, and he had. Dextri had always been a monster of a man by normal standards, towering around six and a half feet tall and fathoming a tree trunk rather than a human being. If it was at all possible, he'd grown even larger, his shirt straining at the seams to contain his bulk and even his bald head made his weathered hat bulge. His cheerful demeanour hadn't changed though, and his broad smile still brought crinkles to the corner of his eyes.

"S'what the army does to you. A good shield wall will put meat on your bones and fire in your belly! You'll know soon enough. Although my nose is twice as bent as the last time you saw me, damned Kerazar grunt hit me with a broken axe haft!" he said grumpily. Balzor didn't even look at his nose, his mouth had dropped open and his eyes were like saucers.

"You were in a shield wall against the Kerazar?!" he blurted, amazed.

The kingdom of Annar and the kingdom of Kerazar were bitter enemies, although fighting hadn't escalated in years. Despite the kingdoms sharing a border, the ideology of each monarchy couldn't have been further apart. The Kerazar only traded in strength of arms. Any too weak to defend themselves were either killed or made to serve a higher lord, a slave in all but name. Whereas the Annar, its strength was used to protect its people, making sure they could live their lives in peace and prosperity despite their lack of martial prowess.

"Aye lad, but that's a story for another time," Dextri deflected, despite sulky protests from Balzor. "For now, you'd better tell me what all that was about. And leave nothing out," he added firmly.

Balzor's enthusiastic demeanour evaporated at the question, and he retreated into himself sitting down in morbid silence. Sighing, Dextri punched the defeated lad's shoulder to get his attention, then raised his eyebrows at him. He wouldn't take no for an answer. Balzor knew that look from his childhood so took a deep breath and began reluctantly, his tale gathering speed as he went on.

He started with Alnor's apparent hatred of him that had only grown with time, then of the not so irregular punching matches they'd had, moving onto Alkor's pity of the whole situation which ended with him storming off like a child. "I guess I just hate that I'll never be fully part of their family, despite Alkor being my brother and Aldred being my guardian," he finished lamely, raising his hands in exasperation.

Dextri, who had remained standing for the entire tirade, sat down at the last comment, his muscled frame filling out the rest of the hard wooden bench and making the legs creak with anxiety at the added weight. "Balzor, let me tell you something that I figured out early on in life. Your family doesn't have to mean the bearers of your blood or the members of a household; my Da was a bastard. Used to beat me, my sister and my Ma up after a tankard or two of ale every night, 'til I got older and put him on his arse and sent him packing! Then just before I went into the army and met the General, my Ma met a travelling baker and is still with him to this day. Morale of the story is -

it's the people that stick with you through thick and thin, the ones who'd die for you without a moment's hesitation, they're the ones that matter. Blood don't mean shit. Although Alnor scorns you regularly, Alkor more than makes up for that with the love he so clearly has for you, just like a brother. Aldred has also given you every chance he has given his own kin – you'd be a fool to discount that over a single bad egg. So, chin up and shoulders back. Learning to fight better would help so you didn't keep getting flattened by that peacock... I can help you there," he said, his serene manner evaporating as he gave Balzor another shove. "And pick that armour up, you lazy arsehole!" he barked. "I know I've been gone a couple of years, but I'm back now and with it the standards will be too. You and - " he dragged Alkor from his hiding place behind the door, "This little eavesdropping toerag, better be ready at first light tomorrow. It's about time you learnt how to fight like men. You're going to wish you'd never been born," he said, eyes glinting maliciously. Releasing Alkor, he marched out of the room without so much as a backward glance.

"Good to see you too, Dextri!" Alkor shouted at his retreating form. They could've sworn they heard him laugh.

*****

Any thought of their old friend and mentor giving them special treatment vanished as the door to Balzor's room crashed open, and Alkor was thrown into a tangled heap on the floor at the foot of his bed. Dextri strode in purposefully, surveying the room with distaste and glaring at the two lads as they looked shell shocked at each other at the treatment.

"I told you first light, pups. It's first light and I've dragged one out of bed and found the other still snug in his dreams. Get your scrawny arses ready and meet me on the field and be quick about it! Balzor, this room is a shithole. Tidy it!" he said, storming out the room.

Balzor leapt out of bed and threw on the nearest clothes he could find, smoothing the crinkles out of them as he swept any mismatched garments off the floor.

Alkor scrambled to his feet and dusted himself off, tutting at the messy state of his friend's room but helping his manic tidying by making the just-vacant bed. "He's keen. Must be putting us into the century's training regime to bollock us like that. He's obviously seen the state of your sword skill and thinks we could do with starting proper training early," Alkor mused as he tidied, glancing sideways at his friend before ducking, a shoe narrowly missing his head. Grinning, he continued, "At least it looks like they're trying to keep us in the same century. Father would've sent us directly to the legion otherwise, to be sorted where they see fit. It looks like they're gunna train us together brother!"

Throwing the last shirt adorning the floor into a half empty trunk at the foot of the bed, Balzor breathed a sigh of relief. "Come on then, we better not keep Dextri waiting," he said, letting Alkor out in front of him with a gesture and closing the door behind them.

As they emerged onto the practice field, shielding their eyes from the sun's glare, they froze, suddenly unsure how to proceed. Usually they practiced alone, when the warriors were off duty, but seeing twenty warriors in full gear sparring or honing their bodies into a tool with relentless exercise seemed to throw the boys for a moment.

The century had four patrols of twenty men out at any one time, forming a defensive square around the entire area and making Saternac the safest inland county by a long way. The other twenty were left in reserve to replace one of the patrols on their return, which was usually once every fortnight.

Balzor and Alkor were still standing there uncomfortably as Dextri noticed their presence and strode confidently towards them, slowing the whole field almost to a halt as the group watched with anticipation, the clacks of their practice swords going eerily silent after the echoes and grunts of the men.

"Well, lads. Look what old Ezi dragged out to us, way past schedule, might I add!" Dextri said, earning himself a roar of laughter from the group. "Round the field young 'uns, ten laps! The rest of you, give them thirty seconds head start and then follow at whatever pace you like. Every time you pass the little lords, give them a crack to speed them up!" he said. After a few seconds he looked expectedly at the two brothers who looked dumbfounded to hear the challenge.

"They really will hit, so I'd get going if I was you!" he warned them, giving them a slight nudge. Not needing any more encouragement, the men had already downed their gear and were ready for the chase, relishing the thought of showing the boys the real world as they knew it. This, more than anything, spurred the brothers into action and they tore off for the first lap, shooting furtive glances behind them as if not fully believing that the warriors would actually chase them.

Their thin belief was shattered when the men behind them roared and broke into a run, most of them sprinting to the limit of their endurance to reach the lads with an excitement borne only from a chase. The two boys had thought themselves fit, having spent years exploring the woodland around the estate and even going as far as the mountains sometimes. But after a few minutes of the hunt, the lads began to tire of the pace and the warriors drew closer and closer. Sweat poured off Balzor's brow and he panted like a dog, dragging himself along in an effort to stay ahead. Glancing over at Alkor, he saw that his friend wasn't faring much better, tongue lolling out of his mouth and breath becoming laboured.

The first hit he received was the worst, shocking Balzor's body out of the fatigue daze he'd felt himself in and sending a sharp pain through his lungs as they expelled even more air from his body when he so desperately needed it. Inevitably, the rest of the warriors caught up, one by one dealing out crushing blows to their ribs or, occasionally, a heavy slap around their ears. Dextri waited until the last guard caught up before he shouted a command to call it off, watching the delighted guards congratulating each other on a job well done with a smirk on his face.

Balzor had his hands on his knees, doubled over attempting to catch his breath through bursts of pain from his winded lungs, Alkor knelt on the floor next to him retching at the last hit to the stomach.

Shaking his head at the sorry pair, Dextri walked over to them, arching his eyebrows at the display. "To be honest lads, you evaded them for longer than I thought but you need to do better. Despite your tender years, you're already destined for command in one of the cohorts due to your birth and status, but men won't follow someone they don't respect, and respect must be earned. Every morning at first light I want you running laps down here for fitness, lifting your body weight for strength and rolling those trunks over there for stamina. Swordplay is only half the fight. If you get winded, you might as well offer up your neck for the blade because you're as good as dead. Now, stand up straight, catch your breath and nurse your pride. It's time to spar," he said, striding over to the rack outside the armoury, grabbing two swords and tossing them to the panting duo. "Get your own shields from inside, then meet me over there," he ordered, gesturing to where the rest of the guard had resumed their own duels.

Both boys groaned at the prospect, but the venomous look from Dextri had them moving quickly, both wincing at the stabbing pains from the forced movement. "As if the kicking from Alnor wasn't enough, the guard's just put bruises on top of my bruises," Balzor muttered, observing the different shields in front of them. Alkor chuckled dryly but didn't reply, intent on his own choices.

After a moment he reached out, selecting a plain round shield with a worn iron boss in the centre, rimmed with iron to protect the edge from blows. Balzor noticed Dextri glaring with obvious impatience at his own deliberation, so chose a similar shield to alleviate the scrutiny. The pair trudged towards Dextri with a growing feeling of dread, certain they'd be humiliated in front of the men, again.

Although none were Annarite born, the General's own century were known for their impeccable skill and dedication to their training; most were second generation Annarites like Alkor, but they were destined for either the King's elite cohort or running districts for the crown, just like Alkor's father did.

It was with mixed feelings of delight and disappointment when Dextri announced they'd start by practicing their stances and sequences - basic training for any soldier - and things they'd been taught casually years before. They lasted ten minutes before Dextri heard Alkor's audible sigh, which he'd exaggerated for Balzor's amusement. That amusement rapidly faded as Dextri's head whipped round sharply and he stormed to square up to Alkor, his anger evident.

"Something boring you, pup?" he hissed into his face, causing Alkor to go a deep shape of red and take an involuntary step backwards in alarm.

Alkor, realising he'd lost his composure in full view of the guard, responded with a hard voice. "We've known these sequences for years; they're the first thing you taught us as children. I thought we'd be doing actual training or at least advanced forms."

The men had gone back to their sparring, but this confrontation had made the closest pairs stop and watch in anticipation, feeling the tension coming off Dextri and growing with every word. "Listen to me pup and listen well. No man, even a sword master, is EVER too good to perfect the basics. Thinking you're better than these sequences will get you killed quicker than an arrow to the brain. Out in the real world, it's a no rules game, so your training will be a no rules game - except for one: you do not question me! Your father has told me to train you earlier than most. He wants you ready for the future and he wants you both to be better than the rest! With that in mind, he's given me complete authority to train you no differently from the other lads. If any of them question this authority, we know what would happen, right lads?" he shouted, raising his arm up in the air, erupting a cheer from the guard.

"Defend yourself!" he barked, flying at the boys with a speed usually unseen outside of battle, rapping both boys smartly on the shoulders as they stood slack jawed at their trainer's tirade. The stinging pain of the practice blade jolted them out of their astonishment and soon had them crouched low behind their shields, points of the weighted blades resting menacingly on the rims. They'd had it drilled into them to stand side by side with your brothers, never breaking the wall, shoulder to shoulder until the death. Linking up, they raised defiant eyes to Dextri, standing proud next to one another, ready for an attack. Their confidence was their undoing.

Dextri moved lightning fast, feinting quickly to the left then, as the lads reacted, simply darting to the right around what they now realised to be a flimsy defence. Not having the room to manoeuvre due to how close they were, the boys tried to break their wall and turn to meet the threat, much too late. Dextri's sword crashed into Balzor's wrist as he attempted to block, causing him to cry and involuntarily drop his sword. Alkor, unperturbed at his friend's speedy defeat, shot forward to engage Dextri without hesitation and launched a series of attacks which were easily deflected by the now laughing man.

Alkor's inexperience and youth showed in moments, as Dextri swept the lad's weapon wide and bulled into the gap using his colossal strength behind his own shield to knock him to the floor in a heap. He kicked Alkor's sword out of his hand with ease before snorting in contempt. "A shield wall will only work in numbers. Any attempt at flanking by an enemy will be its undoing and will sow instant panic in the ranks, usually resulting in a rout and the loss of the fight. In a melee like this, footwork is the key and to stop moving is to die; defend each other's backs and trust the men around you. Now get off your arses and run more laps, using the time to think about holding your tongue and doing as you're told next time. Neither of you are too good for sword work," he mocked, bringing about another round of jeers from the men.

Red faced and ashamed, the boys rose gingerly from the ground and, whilst averting their eyes from everyone, put their gear away and set off without a word to run around the field again and again without complaint. They'd learnt their lesson and wouldn't disrespect authority again – at least where they could be heard.

✶✶✶✶✶

Finally, Dextri's booming voice echoed over the field to end the torment they were forcing their legs to endure, and they collapsed to the floor breathing heavily. Dextri strode casually up to the pair with a huge grin on his face, clearly enjoying the moment and the scowls that they were both throwing his way. "How was morning training, little lords?" he cackled, glee rolling off his frame as his huge shoulders rose in tempo with his laugh. Both boys glared at him with as much force as they could muster but didn't have the energy or the breath to retort, which only made Dextri laugh even more. "You got what any other recruit would get on their first day's training in the Sain guard. If anything, I didn't hit you as hard in your little attempt to defend yourselves. Pick up your bottom lips and hit the baths; the lads are washing up after lunch, but I think you need to recover for the day," he said, grinning broadly as they muttered curses and rose from all fours covered in dust and sweat.

Still sullen at the earlier humiliation, they sloped off towards the bathhouse, wanting to wash away the grime of the morning and hopefully their shame with it. As they walked through the door, they jumped out of their skin as a roar of twenty men greeted their arrival. The guards were all sat on their benches, some clapping and whistling but others punching their fists in the air cheering hoarsely.

"Happy first day pups," one guard said, clapping them simultaneously on their backs. "Don't take Dextri personally - on the field he's a harsh taskmaster, but he's our leader and a better leader you'll find nowhere, right lads?!"

Livius' comment was met with a cacophony of cheers and shouts. "He's the first man on the field and the last one to leave, his skill is second to none and he's seen more than any of us combined. Heed his words and trust he does everything to make you into someone to rival your father's skill. You'll learn a lot from him so less of the bitching, eh? It'll keep you alive one day."

With that last comment, the boys' glares finally subsided, and they looked sheepishly at their feet. Balzor had thought Dextri was unnecessarily harsh, but he soon realised from the goodnatured insults being tossed around between the guards that this was just common practice amongst soldiers. Taking a deep breath, Balzor forced himself to smile at Livius, giving Alkor a nudge to urge him to do the same.

The guards were unstrapping their armour and talking casually, the hubbub giving the room a natural light mood which matched Livius', although his face wasn't as comely as his personality. A hideous scar stretched from one side of his face to the other splitting the bridge of his nose and narrowly missing his eyes. But his eyes shone brightly, and his crooked smile barely left his face even when he noticed Balzor's scrutiny and raised his eyebrows to let him know he'd been caught despite thinking he was being stealthy in his observation.

"The bastard would've killed me too if Dextri hadn't turned the blade before it took my head off," Livius laughed clearly amused by the mortified look on Balzor's face.

"I – um... I mean, no." Balzor stammered, heat suffusing his face and his nervousness causing Alkor to chuckle.

"Don't worry lad, it's not bothered me for years. The women in the village kinda like it too. They say it makes me look more rugged," he said shrugging. "Got it from a Kerazar berserker in the early days of the war when we were mopping up the remnants of a cattle raid. Dextri gutted him seconds after, so I owe the man my life. Anyway, story time's over children, get to the baths, I gotta go and see me Ma' tonight," he finished, leaving Balzor's open mouth to close, killing the questions that had struggled to be born.

Knowing the man wouldn't say any more at that time, the lads nodded to him and shuffled through the room to the inevitable jabs at their running speed or sword skills. As they reached the doorway at the opposite side of the room, a tiny, rat like man shouted, "No servants to wash your balls in there, little lords," which was followed by jeering laughter again when the man settled back down, looking very proud with his comment. Alkor flipped him the finger and they left the room, grumbling but content.

Entering the other room, the boys looked around in dismay. They'd known it wasn't going to be an iron bath with heated water but had expected more than a stone flagged hole in the floor filled with water, basically a pool. Balzor was the first to exhale and begin to strip down, untying his red mop of hair from the braids and letting it hang loose before looking at his brother with a resigned look and jumping in. To his evident surprise and delight, the pool was warm, and he came up to the surface spraying a great plume of water from his mouth and shaking himself like a dog. "It's warm!" he exclaimed to Alkor, who didn't take much more persuading, throwing off his own clothes with a whoop and followed his friend in.

Washing the morning's labour off his skin and letting his earlier childish sulking wash away with it, he let himself relax and reflect on the day. After a few moments, Alkor broke the daydream.

"I don't think this'll be so bad after all, brother," he said, voice echoing off the flagged room. He breathed a sigh of content, his head leaning on the side and looked across to Balzor, letting his toes just rise from the water, the shock of the cool air outside making him submerge them again instantly. Balzor didn't answer immediately, and they went back to silence for a while until he finally responded.

"We give them no reason to doubt our courage. No 'little lord' comments will barb us, and no amount of training or pain will break us."

Alkor raised his head off the side, Balzor seeing the iron determination etched into his brother's face and feeling the intensity of his gaze. "We'll be the best, whatever it takes. No matter who stands in our way," he said, clasping hands with his brother and feeling the weight of the moment. Their training had begun.

Chapter 2

Alkor awoke to a soft tapping on his bedroom door, wrenching him unwillingly from slumber. He managed a groggy mumble, and the door creaked open revealing Balzor's face looking as tired as he felt. Creeping inside the room, Balzor closed the door quietly behind him as Alkor sat up in his bed resting his head on the wall behind it as he rubbed sleep from his eyes.

In direct contrast to Balzor's own room, Alkor's was perfectly organised, he thought with relish. His bed was on the far wall facing the door, an old tradition so the sleeping person would always be facing the entrance should they be attacked, and none of his clothes from the previous day were dotting the floor. Instead, they'd been hung up in his extravagant teak wardrobe which lay next to his bed beside an equally extravagant bedside table which had legs of solid silver.

Alkor rolled out of bed to begin making the sheets, so he missed the hunk of bread flying through the air; It collided with his head with a dull slap, causing Balzor to chuckle.

"Breakfast," he said, holding his hands up in resignation at his friends tired glare. "Eat and get dressed. We'd better be the first down there today, I don't fancy the wrath of Dextri so soon."

This prompted Alkor to speed up his bed-making, he bent down for the bread on the floor, groaning as his muscles alerted him to their pain. "Hurts like a bitch, doesn't it?" Balzor laughed. "Don't worry, it gets easier as you move. Now hurry up, I'll see you down there!" With that, he spun on his heel and left the room, closing the door quietly.

Knuckling the remaining sleep out of his eyes, Alkor tore a piece of the bread off with his teeth and chewed quickly. Despite his surly mood at being woken at that hour, he too wanted to get down there early, so dressed promptly and wolfed down the rest of his bread before opening the door and leaving the room.

His attempt to be quiet was thwarted as the door slammed before he could slow its momentum, so he abandoned silence in favour of speed and sprinted through the corridor, barely slowing to apologise as a wideeyed, plump lady named Nerva with a tray of pastries shrieked in surprise as he barrelled down the stairs, making her almost drop them all.

With her curses ringing in his ears, he leapt off the bottom step and ran out of the main entrance and into the grounds beyond. Instantly blinded by the eager sun and buffeted by a wall of heat, the usual early morning chill was already burnt from the air and he felt sweat immediately break out on his forehead, not relishing the day to come. He arrived with not much breath to spare, seeing Balzor already stretching for the morning run.

"About time!" Balzor exclaimed. "Dextri will be down in a minute and the other lads will be right behind him. We need to already be running before they do, or we'll definitely take the hits! Come on!"

Balzor's eagerness to prove himself was always lost on Alkor, but he walked over to begin his own stretching catching his breath all the while. When he felt ready, he gave Balzor a shove as he was stretching his hamstrings, causing him to fall into the dirt. Leaving him red-faced and furious, Alkor took full advantage of the head start to charge around the track just as the guard came from the bathhouse. He whooped as he heard the pounding of feet behind him and knew his friend had given chase, regretting the outburst as soon as it left his body. Alkor wasn't fully recovered from the headlong rush from his room and it wasn't long before Balzor regained lost ground, although it looked like he'd put in a serious effort to get alongside him. Ezi knows they were unfit!

Both boys were panting by the time the guards made their way to the start of the track, whistling and jeering at the lagging pace. Not even bothering to loosen up, the guards set off after the youngsters, contempt showing in their faces as they began to gain on them almost immediately, Livius in the lead. Cupping a hand to his mouth, Livius bellowed, "Best if you speed up, pups! Don't wanna let on that you really ARE just children."

Balzor glanced back scornfully and gave the guard the finger before putting on a burst of speed and leaving Alkor in a cloud of dust. Alkor could hear the guard laughing as his coughing slowed him down even further. By the time he'd cleared his throat enough for a real gasp of air, the distance had closed dramatically. He tried to summon his own energy for the race, but his legs were already starting to cramp from the abuse of the day before.

The whistles and taunts got louder as the pack behind him realised their prey was flagging. "Faster little lord, faster!" somebody urged sarcastically, cackles emitting from the group. But try as he might, he couldn't keep up the pace and the first punch landed soon after. The jolts of pain were a masochistic relief, his brain registering that each hit meant he didn't have to force himself to run any longer, but the humiliation of being caught so soon began to pummel him more than any fist could. This only grew as he looked up to see Balzor powering forward in grim determination, though he only lasted another minute before the guards caught up and delivered their hits, some panting themselves at the pace he set for them.

As the last guard gave a scathing slap to the back of Balzor's head, causing his fiery hair to bounce in retaliation, they heard Dextri whistle signalling an end to the run and a begin to sequences, or in the guards' case, sparring. Good natured insults and jibes were thrown at the lads making even the seething Balzor crack a smile before they reached the armoury, strapping on their gear and picking up swords, the run forgotten during the familiar process.

Veering off the more open ground in the centre of the track, the guards paired up and began to spar, starting slowly and picking up the tempo as each strove to strike the other first. Balzor and Alkor stood shuffling their feet, unsure about what to do as Dextri finished strapping on his own gear before wheeling around on the lads.

"Well, what are you waiting for? Sequences!" he said, prompting them to step apart and begin the basic forms from the day before. Neither of them dared roll their eyes or mutter under their breath. Every slight infraction or pause was picked up by Dextri's keen eyes and they were made to practice the move until they'd gotten it right.

After one such infraction, Balzor felt a prickling on the back of his neck as though he was being watched. Initially he ignored the feeling but after a few seconds, he couldn't resist a quick look, seeing a guardsman arrogantly lounging on a practice post and sneering at their attempts.

Alkor caught Balzor looking and followed his gaze, spitting on the floor as he saw what had caught his attention. "That's one of Alnor's lackeys, Petra. Probably best to steer clear of him for the moment. Despite looking like a weed, he's crazy fast and skilled with a blade, more so than Alnor that's for sure," Alkor said to his friend as Petra turned away with a snort.

Balzor looked away from the young guard, hating the way his stomach churned with fear at the thought of another beating so soon. Gritting his teeth at his cowardice, he threw himself back into the sequences, feeling a huge satisfaction as Dextri gave them both a grudging nod.

After an hour of sparring in the summer heat, sweat sheening their bodies and dust sticking to their faces, Dextri called for a water break. Livius strolled over to them his familiar crooked smile on his face as he said cheerily, "Better than day one today, eh pups? No arse kicking or extra runs so you must be doing alright! What's up with his face?" he gestured towards Balzor, who was brooding with his chin resting on his hand, his long braid almost trailing the floor as he sipped water from one of the wooden cups left floating in the water barrel.

Alkor shrugged and kicked his sullen friend's foot. "Cheer up, whatever it is, it can't be..." Balzor interrupted to say, "Who's that guard over there, Livius", causing Livius to frown and look at the young man facing away from them, his short, cropped hair common amongst soldiers but his small size contradicting his occupation.

"That there's Petra," he informed them. "Seems to be very friendly with your mate Alnor," he added with a sly look at Balzor, snorting at the lad's reaction of distaste. "As far as I know, he's a good lad. Keeps himself to himself mostly but never causes any trouble and follows orders well enough. Anyway..." He trailed off his sentence, raising his cup to them and trundled off back to the other guards.

Alone again, Alkor dropped his cup back into the water barrel, causing a slight splash in the still drink, the sound seemed to wake Balzor as he stood up and did the same. "I told you he was friends with Alnor," Alkor murmured. "Steer clear, brother!".

Trying to stifle the grim sense of foreboding that seemed to have settled on Balzor, Alkor struck up a conversation about a travelling musician who was supposed to be on at the Tavern, upselling his talent in an attempt to excite Balzor about the thought of a drink that night. When even the thought of good music and ale did nothing for his friend's mood, he changed tactics.

"Look, it wasn't as if we didn't know Alnor had friends in the guard. He's trained with them for Ezi's sake! Granted, most of them know he's a fool but there was bound to be a few that didn't. There's nothing we can do about it so man up and train harder. Make it so they can't do anything about *you* either," Alkor exploded.

This seemed to shock Balzor into a half-hearted grin and a sigh. "You're right brother, you're right," he said, dropping his own cup into the barrel as Dextri's whistle blew again.

The guards stepped back onto the field, facing off and instantly beginning to spar again but Dextri halted the lads before they could begin their sequences. "Not this time, pups. It's time to start putting some meat on your bones! Both of you are to do the training course, one starting on the task ahead of the other and you finish when you reach the same task you began on. And no slacking!" he said, pointing over to the corner of the field in the shade of the trees.

Tree trunks of varying sizes were strewn across the field - some for rolling and some for standing up and throwing back down – all for building strength, and all worn smooth by years of use. Beside them was a large wooden frame with different attach-ments hanging every few feet. One was a plain rope meant solely for climbing to the top beam where short wooden handles stuck out. These were meant for manoeuvring yourself over to the other corner of the frame where a ladder-like structure allowed for climbing down. The problem was, each rung was much too far apart to just step down, so you had to let go of each one and grab the next. If you missed, you kissed the ground and nursed more than a few bruises. Last, but certainly not least, was a clear patch of smooth ground with a pile of rocks next to a wheelbarrow. You were to choose the weight and then expected to walk it round the patch until you could move no more.

Alkor cringed at the thought of the exertion, his body already sullenly antici-pating the extra punishment it was going to endure. He looked dismayed but Dextri all but dared him to complain with the glint in his eyes, promising more pain if they didn't comply. Lips clamped shut, the boys trudged off towards the course, risking a string of curses, some more creative than others, under their breath as they were out of range of the taskmaster. When they reached the row of trunks, they split as per Dextri's instruc-tions - Alkor going to the much larger trunks for rolling and Balzor going to the ones meant for flipping.

Always eager to prove himself, Balzor went for one of the wider trunks, clearly much too big for him, but the challenge of it with so many guards around was too much to ignore. He bent his knees, gripping the trunk where the worn grooves were and using them as handles.

Alkor began to push his own log but slowly to watch, trepidation growing at the task Balzor had set himself.

Balzor caught him looking before he began, winked and started to lift. To Alkor's surprise the trunk rose off the ground, despite Balzor's face turning beetroot red and his eyes almost popping out with the effort. He looked like he was straining every muscle in his body, but the trunk defied his efforts to lift past his abdomen. Nearby guards whose attention had been drawn by Balzor's attempt, began to snigger.

Come ON Balzor Alkor thought, silently willing his friend to throw the trunk to the heavens to land at Ezimat's feet. With an effort that could only be borne from humiliation, Balzor wrenched the trunk savagely up, using his legs to power it higher until it was stood pointing proudly to the sky, before using the momentum to send it crashing back to the floor, defeated. Staggering slightly from the endeavour, he took a moment to recover before turning to look smugly at the sniggering guards, who rolled their eyes and continued to spar now the entertainment was over.

Realising with a start that he hadn't even half finished his part of the course, Alkor rushed his own trunk to the finish point and back again, using much of his energy for speed and cursing himself for gawping at his friend. Seeing his friend selecting rocks and putting them into the wheelbarrow, he moved himself to one of the lifting logs close to him to allow a conversation without Dextri thinking he was shirking the task.

"Don't let the guards goad you Balzor, they were in our shoes once. The novelty will wear off in a few days," Alkor advised, receiving a non-committal grunt from his friend in response as he carried on loading the wheelbarrow. Sighing at his friend's dark disposition, Alkor chose a log and heaved.

Balzor soon finished loading the rocks, taking care not to overdo the weight again, lifted the handles and set off at a steady pace around the flat area. Sweat dripped from his nose leaving minuscule spots on the bone-dry dust at his feet. Alkor moved over to the logs shaking his head, and carried on watching Balzor out of the corner of his eye. A focus borne of determination was clear though he was profusely sweating within minutes. He put his tongue back into his mouth more than once wanting to avoid looking like the pup the guards accused them of being.

Alkor succeeded in flipping the log over - albeit one of the smaller ones than his friend - and was waiting at the cleared ground for Balzor to finish. He came back around and dropped the wheelbarrow with a crash, flexing his cramping hands and running his forearm over his dripping forehead, a smudge of dirt now inked across it. "Have fun," he said to Alkor with a sly grin, indicating a slight uplift to his mood.

Before Alkor could pick up the wheelbarrow, the delicious sound of Dextri's whistle entered their ears and they turned to see him striding over the field towards them. Balzor was massaging his arms in a hope they'd stop aching and Alkor was more than a bit glad that he could have a break before doing the same thing.

"Tidy up the rocks and get cleaned up pups, you're escaping the frame today. Only today though, d'ya hear? Your father wants to see us lad," Dextri said, directing his last words at Alkor whose stomach had dropped.

Meeting Balzor's eyes, he knew his friend felt the same way: Aldred Sain wouldn't stop a day's training without a reason.

"Wipe that look off your face; by the sound of it he and your brother are off to hunt some rebel group. Probably just a lecture on 'How to be a Sain' whilst they're away," he said mockingly but without malice. Dextri was his father's most loyal friend.

"Balzor, tidy up these rocks for your mate here whilst we go. Maybe you can both go and see this musician I heard you gossiping about like ballroom dandys." This drew grins from the lads and the last of Balzor's sombre mood evaporated.

"C'mon lad, let's get it over with," he said, and the pair left Balzor stacking the rocks.

"Gossiping like dandys, pah!" Balzor snorted, wincing as his abused body let him know it was hurting. Despite the aches and pains, he stacked the rocks in good time, and with a smile at the thought of the night ahead, went to get washed up.

✶✶✶✶✶

"Enter!" boomed the commanding voice of Aldred Sain. The door opened promptly and Dextri strode in, Alkor following behind. Seeing his older brother lounging casually on a seat, Alkor grimaced at his smug face.

"Decided to make an appearance, little brother?" Alnor drawled, leaning further into the back of the chair as if bored of waiting. Alkor rolled his eyes but before he could make a response Dextri stepped forward, loosely covering the distaste and addressing Aldred directly, making a point of blanking the arrogant older sibling.

"You wanted to see us, sir?" he said, snapping an informal salute and bringing the room's attention to the General.

For the first time in weeks, Alkor saw the toll his father's role had taken on him recently and was shocked at the changes wrought on his face. Although he still had the air of confidence around him, his once golden hair had streaks of grey and his usually clean-shaven face was infested with patches of stubble.

As he rose from his own chair though, it was clear that it hadn't affected his vigour. He still boasted the wiry strength and height typical of a Sain, and his posture hinted at a lethality hidden in the man. But it was his eyes that riveted Alkor in that moment. They were as piercing and intelligent as they'd always been and when a smile split his features at the sight of his youngest son, Alkor knew it hadn't affected their connection.

"My boy!" he bellowed. "I hope the lads aren't pissing their breeks in fear of you yet. Dextri?" Allowing himself a small smile, Dextri replied.

"Not quite, sir. He's still not outran them yet, let alone beat them!"

Alkor scowled at Dextri as his brother snorted at the comment but let the barb pass as his father's laugh cut through the comment and he moved to clasp Dextri's arm, embracing him. Alnor saw his chance to get his own hit in on his brother, taking Aldred's laugh at Dextri's comment as permission.

"Hardly going to beat the best squadron in the Annarite legion when he can't even beat that common termite, Balzor" he scoffed.

The mood in the room darkened instantly as the two old friends broke the hold and Aldred turned to face his first-born whose face paled at the cold fury emanating from his father.

"You use common as a dirty word, an insult. Dextri here is as common as they come but could put you on your arse in an instant. Who do you think feeds us? Builds our houses, forges our swords? These common 'termites' you so casually disdain.

A true lord, a true Annarite knows that the Haldi choose them to protect these people, to allow them to thrive. Not to count themselves above them. This is the reason we fight the Kerazar. This is what it means to be a Sain! They treat their common folk as mere slaves, to only be released by death. They believe when Sarnat gives a man these powers, they should use them to take what they want, to destroy. Is that what you believe my son? Is it?" hissed Aldred, the low volume of his voice made even more terrifying by the rage that laced his words.

Alnor had shrank further into his chair as he spoke and shook his head quickly at the question, averting his father's steely gaze which was all but burning a hole into his son's face.

After a moment, the General took a deep breath and turned away, rubbing his temples as he faced out of the window behind him, calming himself. Dextri had seen his old friend's temper flare more times than most so he knew not to push the moment. The seconds passed agonisingly slow and even Alkor, who usually revelled in his brother's discomfort, began to feel uncomfortable.

During the awkward pause, Alkor took the time to survey the room realising quickly that nothing had really changed in the years. His father had always been a plain man; the only furniture was a desk adorned with a mess of reports from scouts and maps of the kingdom, a large chair for the General on one side of the desk, and three less comfortable chairs on the other for visitors. His father's huge war axe hung on the wall at the side of the window - veteran of many battles and the reason his father had risen so high before getting command of his own district. Alkor could only imagine his father and Dextri obliterating a shield wall and carving through Kerazar ranks.

In direct contrast to the grisly weapon, a small painting of a woman hung next to it. The sight of it made Alkor's breath catch in his throat. Hello mother, he thought, drinking in the features of a woman he couldn't remember. She had died when he was very young and with his father rarely speaking of her, the only thing Alkor had to refer to was this painting. He saw his own nose on her face but the likeness ended there. Most of his features were of a Sain through and through, except the small, stubbed nose. His mother was the direct opposite. Her long, dark hair trailed in curls past her shoulders and chocolate brown eyes stared at him from the frame, dimples on her cheeks showing as she smiled.

A clap of hands startled Alkor back to reality. His father sighed and took his seat and with what seemed a great effort, smiled.

"Apologies; it's been a hard week preparing and I've had little sleep. Forgive

29

me, my son," he said wearily, losing the fury from his earlier tirade.

Perking up instantly, Alnor sat up straight before replying. "It is me that should apologise father; I should never have made a comment like that outside of jest. I am nothing like the Kerazar."

Now it was Alkor's turn to snort in contempt which earned him a furious glance from Dextri, silencing him instantly. Nodding his acceptance of his son's apparent heart-felt response, he again clapped his hands.

"Onto business then! Dextri, Alnor, you already know this part, but Alkor is still in the dark, so I'll be brief. The century stationed at Saternac is going hunting. I've had a report from a reputable source of a large rebel camp hidden in the dunes on the outskirts of Jarnad. We'll be meeting up with the King and his Century before moving towards the camp and wiping out the remnants of what I think is the Hounds. Once they're mopped up, we'll be moving to the frontier to help with the effort against the Kerazar. The King believes his men need the boost of seeing their leaders in the thick of things, and I can't say I deny that. With you and Balzor only just coming of age and beginning training, you'll be staying here," he explained, overruling the instant protests from his youngest son. "I've no doubt of your bravery, even now. But you need to stay here, train hard and run the estate in my absence. You'll get your fair share of battles in your lifetime, don't worry," he said, slightly mollifying his sulking son, laughing as Alkor huffed and nodded.

"And next on the list..." Aldred said, turning to his friend and looking him straight in the eyes. Dextri shifted warily before saying "Go on..."

"I also need you and your squad to stay here," Aldred said quickly, his confident facade breaking slightly as he cringed inwardly at the reaction he knew would come from his friend.

Dextri's eyes bulged, and he took a step forward before catching himself. "Sir! My place has always been at your side, for years. The lads too. We're a brotherhood, a family. Don't order us to stay behind, I implore you!" Dextri protested.

Holding up his hands to placate his friend, which only served to knot Dextri's eyebrows together stubbornly, Aldred continued. "Dextri, Alnor's coming with me, and Alkor has only just begun his training. I need someone I can trust to hold the fort whilst

I'm gone. Alkor isn't of age yet and nowhere near ready to lead a squad in my absence – don't look at me like that Alkor, you know it's true. Keep to your training and obey Dextri's commands like they're my own, the same goes for Balzor. Dextri, my friend, you're the only one I can trust to train my son properly AND keep the area safe whilst I'm gone. Will you do it willingly? I can order it, but I sincerely do not want to."

At this, Dextri's face hardened before he blew out a held breath and relaxed. "I'd do anything you asked Sir, you know that. Just don't get yourself killed whilst I'm not there to have your back, d'ya hear?" he joked, getting a dry chuckle in response from the General, who rose again to clasp arms with him.

"Never my friend, never. Thank you" Aldred said sincerely, before clapping Alkor on the shoulder. "Leave us now, we still have much to prepare before we leave in the morning and not a lot of time," he said, seeing the alarm spike in his son's eyes at the comment.

"So soon?!" Alkor sputtered, the announcement hitting him like a bolting horse. Smiling sadly, his father let his hand fall from his shoulder and nudged his son.

"I'll miss you coming of age, don't think that information hadn't crossed my mind. We'll celebrate in true Sain style as soon as I return, but for now, duty calls, and we must answer," he said. The words did nothing to soothe Alkor who adopted a neutral face rather than show his father his hurt. "Go with Dextri, we have work to do. I'll see you in the yard at dawn," Aldred said, the General in him overriding his paternal instincts.

He nodded at Dextri, who saluted and steered the boy out of the room without much resistance. Aldred put his palm on the door before sighing deeply. He didn't see the cold stare Alnor aimed toward him at the gesture which quickly morphed into an innocent expression as the General turned and moved back to his chair. Eyes lingering slightly on the painting as he passed, he resigned himself to a long night ahead as he wondered when he would see his youngest son again.

*****

Balzor took no time at all washing the day's sweat from his skin and roughly drying himself before dressing quickly, all the while ignoring the ribald comments asking him where his boyfriend had gone. He'd pay the insults back in time, he thought - even the good-natured ones. His head was full of thoughts scuttling around like spiders on his brain; worrying about what Aldred wanted only adding to the many worries already heaped on to him.

Deciding that to wait was just adding salt to the wound, Balzor put on his boots and ran a hand through his hair, tying it in a ponytail, before rising from his space on the benches and leaving the bathhouse to whistles and more laughter. He stopped short of actually running across the grounds to the manor but his long strides came very close. The sun was sitting low in the glistening sky indicating more time had passed than he'd initially thought so he sped up, almost at a jog now. It was this rushed pace that caused him to collide with a wall of muscle coming out of the manor's front door, knocking him back two steps. He started to mumble an apology sheepishly but was interrupted by a bark of laughter. Looking up, he saw that he'd collided with Dextri's huge bulk, his smile showing that it was forgotten.

"Not been to the tavern in a while, eh lad?" Dextri chuckled, waving off Balzor's clumsy apology. "Your mate shouldn't be too long, his father kept us longer than we thought," he added, laughing again at Balzor's obvious ache to ask what was said. "Ask Alkor, lad, it's not my place. You'll know tomorrow at any rate. Me and the lads are off to the tavern ourselves tonight; it's tradition that the new lads buy the ale so bring your purse, pup!" he said, making Balzor roll his eyes but smile, nonetheless. Dextri punched his arm and stalked off towards the bathhouse, his monstrous frame silhouetting against the falling sun, Balzor's arm already bruising.

Head reeling at what could be so important to stop an entire squadron training, Balzor trotted through the great door into the entrance hall, the candles inside dancing as the breeze tickled their flames. The mouth-watering aroma pleasing his nostrils alerted him to his hunger, slowing him slightly as he deviated from his direct route to the personal quarters and followed his stomach. Instead of bounding up the stone staircase, he jogged past its dominant steps and the worn wooden benches along the walls. Behind the staircase was another huge oak door that led to the Lord's feasting hall; this was rarely used, usually to entertain guests and for the few guards who didn't frequent the tavern. However, it was the smaller, more used door directly underneath the staircase that Balzor wanted. He opened it slowly, the creak of used hinges mixing with the familiar worn wooden handle and extravagant smell telling him this was what aroused his hunger: the kitchens.

The slow-moving door was in direct contrast to the pace set in the room by the plump, middle aged lady who cooked the meals, her tatty grey hair stuffed into a bun. Although facing away from him, Balzor knew she would have bulky leather gloves on her hands and her tongue sticking out of a smiling mouth, waiting for the timing glass to finish to cook the meat to perfection.

An assortment of pots and pans lined the first wall Balzor saw, hanging from the wall with obvious gaps between for their brethren which were filled to the brim with boiling water and vegetables bubbling away happily on top of a small set of hot, metal plates. In turn, they were sat atop a large metal structure with a thick door, its handle coated with a generous amount of some animal leather to allow the cook to touch its piping heat and access the inside, which was where the delicious smell was coming from. Inside there were two compartments, one for a mixed quantity of glowing logs and coals, heating the second compartment, which usually held succulent, spiced meats for the table. There were rumours this new type of oven cost a fortune, though the design seemed simple to him. It used stored magic instead of embers to heat the food - which seemed ludicrous to Balzor - but it worked, nonetheless.

The centre of the room was reined by a rectangular, marble tabletop across which different sized knives and utensils merged with vibrant colours of fruits and vegetables, arranged in small piles ready to be put into the bowls eagerly awaiting being filled.

He'd hoped he could sneak in, snatch something for the road and sneak out - but his hopes were dashed as the woman ripped open the oven door, grabbed an oval tray out of the heated compartment and, with a practiced movement, butted the door with the tray to slam it shut causing the meats juices to slosh dangerously.

Turning to the tabletop, her eyes narrowed as she saw the sly, red-haired youth standing shiftily by the door. "You know the rules, young 'un. Nobody eats before it's ready, not even the General!" she ordered, putting the tray down with a thump on the table. She took off her gloves with the opposite forearm, pinching them between her sides to avoid the heat on her bare skin, before wiping sweat from her brow with the back of her hand.

His lips puckered at her words drawing a sweet laugh from the lady, her small round mouth revealing chubby dimples on her cheeks. "But Nervaaaa..." he whined. "We've not been to the village in weeks and there's a musician on! Just this once?"

Whilst he sulked, she'd chosen a broad cutting knife and began to slice the meat, the crunch of the crackling revealing the huge hunk of meat was pork, glazed with Nerva's speciality of honey and sugar. Balzor's eyes widened at the sight, and he instantly began to salivate as the sticky outer layer was cut. Nerva's eyes glinted mischievously as she saw his realisation at what was on offer; she knew it was a favourite amongst most of the household.

"What's in it for me?" she said, acting aloof to his eager reaction.

"Anything! I'll run errands into town or find one of those small poetry books you like from the market?!" he begged. This was a standard occurrence for them both, she knew he and Alkor liked eating early. It had begun as a game between them that had gone on for years, usually resulting in one of the lads getting her a small present every now and again. She loved the lads like her own and would never have denied them the food early anyway, but it was almost a tradition between them now, so she entertained it.

"I'll tell you what - this time, I'll allow it" she said, holding her hand up to forestall Balzor's excited rush towards her. "But... it's a favour in the bank. I don't need anything yet but I'm sure I'll think of something."

Allowing herself a small smile at the nodding boy in front of her, she placed a generous amount of the dripping pork on to freshly made bread making two sandwiches for the lads. She laughed a surprised laugh, her cheeks going a slight pink as Balzor kissed her and gave her a hug, before waving him away with a roll of her eyes. "Now get gone. I'm not just here for the good of my health, I've got men to feed!" she barked, picking up the knife again and pointing it at the sandwiches.

"Thanks, Nerva! I knew we could count on you!" Balzor yelled over his shoulder, mouth already full of food. She shook her head with a smirk as the door creaked closed behind him before getting back to work.

He took his time around the staircase, savouring every morsel of the succulent meal. *Nerva's too good for this place,* he thought as he chewed slowly, appreciating the flavours. Swallowing his last bite and seriously considering eating Alkor's and denying all knowledge, he set off quickly before his consideration became a reality. Rounding the corner, he saw the only thing that could've darkened his mood: Alnor. Only the fact that he was followed closely down the stairs by his father saved another fist fight, this time instigated by Balzor. Instead, he opted for the sane route.

"Sir!" he saluted, snapping to attention whilst slyly hiding the pilfered food from the General.

Aldred chuckled wearily at the hasty salute. "Two days in and saluting quicker than most of my guard! And off duty too. At ease lad, there's no need for that here," he said, face looking tired but still jovial. Balzor eased his posture but kept the sandwich hidden.

"Heard you boys are going to the tavern tonight? Don't be too late. I want you both in the yard at first light. See you then," Aldred said, casual conversation laced with veiled authority. Balzor nodded and snapped another salute before walking away quickly.

"Oh, Balzor?" the General called, causing him to turn. "Make sure Alkor eats some of that food you're attempting to hide," he finished with a smile, causing Balzor to grin sheepishly and lift the sandwich in the air as a mock salute, before running off up the stairs. Oblivious to Alnor's distaste at the exchange, Aldred chuckled and walked towards the kitchens gesturing for his eldest son to follow.

When Balzor arrived at his friend's room, the door was slightly ajar, and he could see a flicker of light inside. Cautiously, he inched the door open to see his usually cheery friend sat on a floor littered with clothes, chin resting on his knees and leaning against his bed, sheets askew. He took in the situation and seeing a stray boot near the door, he aimed and kicked it at his friend, earning himself a sulky glare.

"Father's leaving again. This time, he's taking the golden son and most of the Century with him. We're left with just Dextri's squad to complete training and help me run the estate in their absence. What fun we'll have!" Alkor blurted, angry tears in his eyes.

Balzor knew his friend was angrier about the lack of time spent with his father over the years, but to mention it was to incur his displeasure. Instead, he wordlessly

35

passed over the still-warm pork sandwich which was enough to bring a smile to any face. It didn't bring a smile to Alkor's face, but he ripped off a piece and chewed grumpily, causing Balzor to laugh at his friend in delight.

"Why the long face then, brother? Your arsehole sibling is leaving. We'll continue our training and the squad staying with us is the one with Dextri and Livius in it! Yeah, your father's going with them, but the General always does his duty. The next time he goes, we'll be side by side with him! Now finish your pork, get dressed and let's go and get royally pissed as a send-off!" he said, a huge smile on his face at the news. He'd honestly thought he'd be left alone at the estate and Alkor would go too, so for him, this was great news.

"When you say it like that, it doesn't sound so bad," Alkor admitted, shovelling the last bit down. Taking a shirt from the floor, he gave it a quick sniff to confirm it was clean, dragged it over his head and took a deep breath dispelling the bad mood at the thought of good music and ale.

"Now THAT'S more like it!" Balzor encouraged, and with a swagger only a seventeen-year-old that was promised alcohol could muster, marched out of the room. Alkor quickly made his bed, his personality not allowing the mess even then, before running out of the room and slamming the door behind him.

"Come on, brother!" Balzor shouted, bounding down the stairs and whooping in excitement. Alkor laughed aloud as he joined his friend, taking the stairs two at a time and whooping even louder. In the kitchens, Aldred Sain smiled at the sound.

Chapter 3

The cobbles of the snaking road into town gleamed in the sun's final rays. Still baking hot to the touch, the two boys started sweating with only a brisk walk. Balzor ran his arm over his forehead, the perspiration sticking his hairs to his skin and causing a streak of red.

"This heat is stifling, let's take the trees," he complained, before moving off the path into the undergrowth, Alkor following without hesitation.

The woodland might as well have been a well-travelled road to the lads; they knew each hulking oak as old friends, many of their branches having supported their weight at one time or another. They liked to boast to anyone who'd listen that they knew every nook and cranny of the vast forest, right up to the base of the mountains. So, walking effortlessly over the gnarled roots, the lads made their way into the town in the comparative shade of the evergreens.

As the trees started to thin out, the pungent smell of wood smoke filled their nostrils, and they knew the village was nearby. Within a minute, the soft glow of the wall's torches filled their view, outlining the sharp edges of the weathered logs against the faint light, some supporting twisting vines that hugged the wood like a lover. The familiar sight warmed their hearts as they practically bounced over the undergrowth into the lights caress before following the wall around to the main gate and re-joining the road.

The militia peered curiously at the lads over the wall, before realising who they were and hailing the duo as they materialised from the trees. Saternac was a close-knit community; most people knew each other so any newcomers were treated with an instant distrust, despite having good intentions. The two guards at either side of the gate – brothers both named Richard which gave them the nickname the two dicks, out of earshot of course – waved them through on sight and the lads entered the town. They speared towards the centre of the town eager to reach the revelry. A large building on the outskirts of the market blocked their way and, once they heard the unmistakable sounds of bellows and hammers being rung, they knew they'd reached the forge.

Knowing the market and the tavern lay beyond, Alkor rushed around the corner only to be dragged back roughly by Balzor. Giving his friend a furious but questioning glance, he stopped. Balzor put his finger to his lips and gestured at him to listen.

"... the last of the mail is repaired and will be delivered by my lad first thing tomorrow morning. Again, apologies for the delay, old friend, but with the new child coming, Martha needs all the help she can get around the house," said a voice they recognised – Lortmund the blacksmith.

The understanding voice of someone they knew brushed off the apology. "Nonsense, Lortmund, one blip doesn't erase all your earlier work, eh? The General does need that armour in the morning, though. I'll send your lad back with payment with two lads from my squad. We've been safe here for a long time, but you can never be too certain."

Alkor started at the voice and turned round alarmingly to Balzor, who grimaced and mouthed "Dextri". The lads thought they'd avoided their taskmaster until later and by avoiding him, shirked buying the drink he'd been promised.

Balzor indicated to Alkor to take the route around the back of the forge, and they crept away with the utmost care, Dextri's voice fading away to be replaced again by the steady pump of the bellows. They broke into a jog at hearing this, knowing the sounds of the forge would cover their heavy footfalls. A quick check behind them as they rounded the opposite side revealed the hefty shadow of Dextri against the orange hue of the forge embers, facing away from them. Seeing this, the friends set off in haste towards the tavern, cringing slightly as they crossed the open ground and imagining Dextri's booming voice dragging them back – it did not come.

As they dashed through the worn paths that served as streets, ignoring the exclamations their speedy passage caused and stallholders pausing to shake their fists as they packed away their wares, they came to the centre of town. The large building was one of two in the area, flickering lights peeking through the crack in the doors and sounds of a lyre gracing their ears, but the other structure drew their attention away and the delicious smells of cakes and bread assaulted their senses – the bakery.

They stopped outside the building, its door wide open, with a man kneading dough at a table. "We're closed for the day, come back in the morn," he shouted without looking up from his work. "Oh, it's you lads", he finished, glancing up at the pair.

"Good evening to you too Traf," Alkor said sarcastically, a sly grin on his face.

The baker put down the dough and looked at them quizzically. "You're never too old for a clout, young'un," he warned, raising his flour covered fingers to point at Alkor, earning him a laugh from both lads.

Alkor stepped inside and clasped hands with Traf, Balzor following suit, careful to keep his hair out of the dough. "Is Grifa about? Musician's on in the tavern tonight!" Balzor asked. Grifa was Traf's son and one of the small group of friends he and Alkor had.

"He's not lads, sorry. Sent him up to Torizo last week, the baker there's a good friend and has asked me to take an apprentice of his for a while, so Grifa has gone to bring him back for us. I'm sure you can do without him this time," Traf said with a small smile, knowing the sorry state his son had been in in the past after drinking with the boys.

Alkor rolled his eyes at the comment using the conversation to creep slowly toward a tray of lemon tarts he'd spied. Being fooled by the lads in the past, Traf was not one to repeat past mistakes. He lurched forward, clapping Alkor around the ear and causing him to cry out in surprise.

Balzor barked a laugh at his friend's obvious attempt earning himself his second furious glance of the night from Alkor.

Traf chuckled at the look, before waving his hands. "Begone, both of you. I've still got work to do without you two toerags trying to steal my wares; Dola's itching to go to the tavern and I'm a man who gives his wife what she wants!" he said ushering them away from the tarts and out of the bakery, slamming the door behind them.

Laughing amongst themselves, they turned around towards the tavern, excitement rolling off them in waves as they got nearer. The dim orange light streamed through the misty glass windows, the window frames looking tired as they supported their cargo. Tattered white paint flaked off the walls but it did nothing to curb the enthusiasm. They were nearly at the creaking door when suddenly a bearlike grip on their shoulders stopped them in their tracks. They winced as strong fingers dug into their collarbones.

"Thought you could get out of giving old Dextri a drink, eh pups?" whispered the dreaded voice. "Now I think we'll make it two!"

The pair groaned at Dextri, caught at last. They good naturedly threw off his hold and stepped to open the swinging door to paradise. A wall of sound greeted them as they broke the threshold, both boys grinned. Despite the sweltering heat of the day, a roaring fire burned in the corner of the room surrounded by the older villagers, their weathered bones enjoying the lick of heat as the logs crackled and popped in front of them. They were sat on straight backed chairs almost as old as themselves, enjoying the revelry around them but happy to observe rather than participate.

In comparison to the secluded corner, the rest of the room was alive with voices, dancing and drinking. Hard, wooden tables and stools were dotted around the centre and a space had been cleared between two supporting pillars for dancing. Just in front of the pillars was a raised stage where a lyre player was working his magic, people stamping their feet along with the beat a young drum player was setting. After a few moments of frantically looking around, the lads were dismayed at the lack of room in the tavern.

Balzor hung his head with Alkor following suit. Dextri took one look at the dejected pair and guffawed. "It's a good job I had the sense to send some of the lads down early, eh? We'd never have gotten a space otherwise. Ah, right on cue!" he said as a piercing whistle cut through the jovial atmosphere.

Craning their necks, they looked over and saw Livius' crooked smile across the room, his arms waving like a madman. Now delighted, the boys made to move over but were stopped by the colossal hands yet again.

"Didn't I say you pups owe me a drink? Might as well get one for the lads too whilst you're at it. Bring a full jug and cups with whatever you're having," Dextri said, already beginning to stride past the lads with a short laugh at their disgruntled looks. "Or TWO jugs, if you're joining us!" he shouted over his shoulder.

The lads silently agreed that paying for the drinks but having a seat was a good trade and resigned to it and made their way to the bar. Alkor used his typical Sain height to bull his way through the crowd, leaving Balzor to mutter apologies to the victims with his best innocent face. He didn't mind this, though, as being in the throng of sweat and ale unnerved him slightly so an apology was a small price to pay to get through it quicker.

Reaching an open space next to the bar, they waited impatiently for one of the staff to notice them, Alkor drumming his fingers on the stained bar whilst Balzor enjoyed the vibe of the night. A sharp pain in his side caused Balzor to lurch out of his daydream, spinning angrily and looking for the culprit who was standing directly behind him, a large smile on his face. A coating of dust sat atop his shaven head, and the tang of molten metal was strong on his clothes. He wasn't much taller than Balzor but he made up for it with how broad he was, the veined muscles in his arms drawing envious looks from the younger females in the vicinity.

"Now then, lads, long time no see! Haven't seen you in town in weeks! Where've you been?!" he said in a booming voice.

"Far away from you, thank Ezi," Balzor said grumpily, massaging his side. Alkor, on the other hand, clasped the monstrous youth on the shoulder and grinned. "Ignore him, he's not had a drink yet. Father came home, so it's been pretty hectic back at the house; not had a chance to get out until tonight. Want a drink, Svein?" he asked, indicating toward the bar. Svein was part of the foursome, their group of friends with Grifa, the baker's son, being the other.

"My da' wants me in the forge tonight mate. Big order for the guard for the morning and we've still got a bit to do. I only came 'cause I saw you creeping under our window to avoid Dextri earlier," Svein said with a bark of laughter, the lads looking sheepish but laughing all the same.

"I'm sure one drink won't hurt - Lortmund won't even know," Balzor taunted, not that Svein needed much persuading.

"Fuck it! One," he conceded with a grin. "Though me ma'll murder me if I have a hangover in the morning. Ah, just in time!" he added, with a meaningful look at the bar.

They turned around and Balzor's mouth dropped open in shock because, in front of him, was the most beautiful girl he'd ever seen. Although in a plain dress with chocolate hair tied up in a scruffy bun, he couldn't take his eyes off her. Her green eyes sparkled as she looked at him, cheeks slightly red and a small smile playing on her rosy lips. Alkor, looking at his friend to order, sniggered at the gormless expression on his face and had to order for them.

"Ale... jugs... er... two," Balzor stammered.

"Two jugs of ale and nine cups please, miss," Alkor ordered, coming to the rescue, struggling to keep the glee out of his voice at his friends mesmerised look.

"Not a problem, two secs," she replied, glancing shyly at Balzor before averting her eyes and preparing the order.

"When you've finished gawking, that's the Seeress' granddaughter. Only came into town last week. But if you think you can handle her..." Svein said, trailing off and waiting for a reaction from his friend. Balzor seemed to snap out of his trance and clamped his mouth shut, cheeks turning red.

"The Seeress' granddaughter?!" Alkor laughed, eyebrows raised at his friend whose face was still a shade of beetroot.

"This Seeress' granddaughter has a name, Mr Sain," the girl said reprovingly, slamming the jugs down on the stained bar in front of them.

Now it was Balzor's turn to snigger as Alkor stammered a mortified apology. Svein chuckled at the back of them both but kept his counsel for once. Stricken at being caught out, Alkor covered himself by asking an easy question: "How do you know who I am?"

"Well, there aren't many who come in here who have your height and arrogance lord," she said innocently, her eyes showing jest in her words. "Plus, your brother was in a few days ago, and you're only slightly less ugly than him," she added.

Alkor's mouth dropped open at the comment. The other two lads were unable to contain their laughter at the barb. Balzor grabbed the jugs, shoved them into his friend's chest and passed the girl their silver, a thrill going through his body as their fingers brushed during the exchange.

"Well, nice to meet you too," Alkor retorted grumpily, managing a small smile before jerking his head towards Dextri. Svein grabbed some of the cups and inclined his head at the girl, still grinning stupidly at Alkor's humiliation before sloping off towards the guards.

Alone now, Balzor began to sweat. Even with the huge crowd of revellers behind him, without his friends to hide behind, he stood self-consciously, not knowing what to say or do. Giving her what he really hoped was a smile, he picked up the other cups and made to follow his friends.

"Aria, by the way," she called, causing him to willingly turn back to her, looking puzzled. "My name, stupid. Can't have you calling me Seeress' granddaughter forever, can we?" she teased, causing Balzor to blush again and her to giggle slightly.

"I'm... I'm Balzor," he stuttered back. Smooth Balzor, first words to her and you trip over them, he thought sourly.

His response made Aria smile warmly and he was struck senseless again, her smile lighting up the dimly lit room. He couldn't help but smile back, severely hoping that it didn't come across as goofy as he felt in that moment. Aria opened her mouth to say something, but before she could, a banging on the bar interrupted her; a man was demanding more ale. Balzor threw an annoyed glance at him as Aria gave an apologetic look and shrugged her shoulders before hurrying away.

He stared longingly after her until another piercing whistle dispelled him and he turned to see Dextri waving impatiently at him, a knowing smirk on his face. Sighing softly to himself, he shouldered his way through the throng of people. Banging the cups down on the table, he sat down grinning sheepishly to himself. Leaning back against a wall, he good naturedly endured the hooting and catcalling that Alkor and Svein directed his way. Even Dextri joined in slightly, until a voice drawled, "When you've finished taking the piss outta the young'un, my throats dry!" Balzor looked up gratefully and saw the slashed face and crooked smile of Livius as he thumped himself down next to them, gesturing at Alkor.

"Won't fill itself, little lord," he said gruffly, causing Alkor to scowl but pick up a jug and pour the drinks, Svein laughing again.

A short, wiry man with cropped hair and a long, pointed nose reached forward as soon as Alkor finished downing a cup in one and smacking his lips appreciatively. Balzor recognised him from training, remembering he was one of them that pulled his punches, slightly to the relief of the lads. It was only this that kept Alkor's lips glued together, in slight annoyance nonetheless, as he refilled the cup for the man.

"Seems I'm the lord and you're the wench tonight, pup," the man said gleefully, igniting another round of laughter at the table. Alkor's face darkened.

"Aye 'lord,' it seems like it. Do be careful you don't breathe as you drink, that snout of yours may snort up the ale," he retorted, leaving him slack-jawed as the table erupted in laughter, but promptly joined in appreciating the comeback.

"Touché, little lord," he said. "Name's Devar, but these bastards all call me Beak, for reasons you've already mentioned." Alkor grinned broadly and clasped arms with Devar, Balzor rising to do the same.

"You already know Livius and Dextri obviously, now you know me. This sack of shit here is Ingvar," he added on, pointing to the last man at the table.

Ingvar was of the same build as Devar and had an unkempt mop of black hair which stuck up at erratic intervals, giving him a crazed look. Smiling stupidly at the pair, showing he had a few missing teeth, he clasped arms with the lads.

"What Devar failed to mention, is that I'm his much prettier older brother," Ingvar exclaimed, which the lads now realised was obvious, despite the differences between them.

"Right, ladies, introductions over, little lords finally poured the ale," Livius said, picking up his cup and raising it into the air with a cheer, the rest of the table hurrying to follow his example.

It didn't take long for Balzor and Alkor to feel part of the group and as the night wore on the 'little lord' comments became less and less although the insults became worse, the consumption of ale elevating the banter. Alkor had matched most of them cup for cup, but Balzor had slowed dramatically after the first two or three, his head swimming already.

Feeling slightly out of place in a group of warriors, Svein made his excuses after the first cup and sloped away with promises of pain from Dextri if the quality of the goods was compromised by his ale addled brain. Although none of the group got up dancing, the table wobbled dramatically as the song's tempo increased, Livius' legs moving to the beat.

"Why don't you dance instead of spilling all of the ale, you great buffoon?" Dextri complained to Livius, only serving to enhance Livius' jig as he now knew it annoyed his friend.

Given the ale was already sloshing over the sides, Dextri picked the half full jug off the table, raised it to his lips and preceded to glug its entire contents in one. Finishing off with a large belch and slamming it down on to the now still table, he looked at the shocked faces around him before shrugging, although not apologetically. "It was going to get spilled, lads. I did the world a favour just now... alright, alright. I'll buy the next round," he said hastily, the glares from the group burning holes in him.

Taking his silver out of his pocket, he made to rise. Balzor rose with him and reached out for the silver. "I'll go, don't worry!" he said to the knowing looks and sly grins. Though from his earlier performance, he had no idea why he'd volunteered.

"Make sure you bring ale back and don't just speak to your new friend," Dextri jeered, bringing out the hoots and catcalls again as Balzor downed the contents of his own cup before going to the bar with the empty jugs. His earlier eagerness to get the drinks subsided as a quick scan of the area let him know Aria wasn't there. It was with a glum look on his face that he ordered another two jugs with the bare minimum of communication, paying the owner with a nod and a forced smile before sloping back over to the table.

As he got closer to the table, battling his way through the line dancers that had sprung up at the new tune, he heard Dextri's voice over the sound of the lyre. "... shot straight up, all eager. My guess is it's to – ah, here he is now!" Dextri said, his polite voice making Balzor narrow his eyes in suspicion.

It was only when he stepped around the table that his breath caught, and the riveting green eyes caught his again causing him to blush as Aria came into sight.

"As I was saying, miss - he'd jumped up all eager at getting the ale. My guess was he wanted to come and see you again," Dextri finished, bringing out the dark beetroot shade in Balzor again as he slammed the ale on the table and sat down, embarrassment eating at him which was clearly Dextri's intention. Only the sweet laugh and the next comment reversed the situation completely.

"Well, we must have just missed each other. I was coming here to find him," Aria said, turning to look at Balzor.

Alkor guffawed as heat suffused Balzor's face alerting him to the deep shade of red he must have achieved on his cheeks.

"He didn't want any more ale anyway, did you mate?" Alkor said slyly, nudging him in the ribs and bringing out grins in the rest of the group.

Instead of needling Balzor more, they had the great satisfaction of seeing the silence stretch uncomfortably for a few more seconds, Aria's smile faltering at the prolonged pause. This, more than anything jerked Balzor to action. "I'm assuming you don't want to spend the remainder of your night with this rabble. How about I walk you home?" Balzor said, slightly too timidly for his liking.

The grins from the group grew wider, anticipating and waiting for the response. "I'd like that," she said, a smile on her face, eyes twinkling as the hooting began again, causing the pair to blush. Balzor rose triumphantly.

They began to make their way towards the exit, not a word spoken between them, but shy looks being thrown back and forth. *Come on, man. Pull yourself together!* Balzor silently berated himself. He could still hear the guards in the back shouting ribald comments. As they reached the swinging door, Dextri's booming voice shouted, "We aren't saving any ale for you!" Holding the door open for Aria, he gave Dextri the finger and hurried out into the still warm night with her.

Although his head had stopped swimming, the night air soon made him remember the ale he'd drank, and he felt some of his confidence return. He also realised he had no idea where the Seeress actually lived. "Which way?" he asked Aria, feeling the invisible ice crack with the first word finally being uttered. "It's just on the outskirts, near the trees," she replied, and began walking slowly in that direction, Balzor falling in at the side of her.

He was torn between beginning a conversation with her and not wanting to seem too keen. He went for the former. "So... what brings you to Saternac? Besides seeing your grandmother?" he probed, hoping to get a bit of insight on her life.

Seeming to jump at the chance, Aria launched into it without hesitation. "My Ma' and Da' thought it was best to come back here. See - we've been living in Torizo as far back as I remember; my grandfather on my father's side was a cloth merchant, and my mother's a damn good seamstress. When they married, she began to make dresses for the highborn women there and the business flourished. Personally, I could never make a handkerchief, let alone a dress, so they gave up on me pretty early," she laughed.

Balzor laughed easily with her, which enticed her to carry on. "It was only in the last year or so it was clear that I'd inherited my grandmother's gift. It traditionally skips a generation, but when I began to have dreams regularly, I realised they were more than that. A particularly graphic one was my mother being hit by a moving merchant cart in the city. When I warned her minutes before it was going to happen, she wasted no time ushering me down here, despite my father's protests." She laughed, "Seeing the future in dreams is a touchy subject."

Taken aback by this, Balzor couldn't hold his shock. "You're a Seeress?!" Aria seemed to retreat into herself, looking slightly hurt at the surprise and partial fear on Balzor's face. Cursing himself for not choosing his words, he backtracked slightly.

"I mean, I didn't realise it came so young. Every Seer or Seeress I've ever seen seems ancient," he joked. Instantly mortified, he backtracked again.

"Please don't tell your grandmother I said that," he said in alarm, but Aria just giggled, the sound a salve to a wound Balzor didn't know he had. She waved her hand to show no offence was taken and they settled into a content silence, Balzor not trying to break and just enjoying her company.

They strolled slowly down the empty streets, dim lights peeking out at them through the house windows, shadows from the occupants going about their nightly routines dancing into the path. The sound of shouting and music had almost faded from their ears when Aria broke the silence next.

"So now you know my short story, what about yours?" she asked as they reached a fork in the road, one straight to the exit of the town and the other leading down a wooden path lit by torches dug into the ground and surrounded by stones. Eying the path warily, Balzor hesitated. Aria's laugh tinkled again as she took his hand and pulled him along. "You're supposed to be walking me home, maybe I should walk you?" she teased, nudging Balzor with her shoulder playfully as his face burned with embarrassment.

"I was just thinking about what to say, that's all," he recovered, trying to save himself. Aria rolled her eyes and grinned, accepting the explanation, if not agreeing with it. Coughing out an awkward laugh and realising protesting would only make him look worse, he took a deep breath and began. "I live up at the manor with Alkor and his family; I have all my life. When the attack on the original village landed, Aldred found me in the aftermath and took me in. Nobody in this village, originally Aveni, knew who my parents were. Most of them had friends but it seemed none knew them. It was presumed they'd died in the savagery and were written as nameless on the memorial," he began sadly, Aria squeezing his hand, trying to comfort him as he talked. "Honestly, it's okay. I was only a baby at the time, I've grown up with the Sains as my family and they've treated me well, mostly," he said, thinking of Alnor but not wanting to share that just yet. She already thought him to fear a wooded path, best not let her think he was a complete child. "Anyway, as Alkor is such a close age to me, we grew up doing the same things. We used to love exploring the forests together. We know every area of the woodland all the way up to the mountains!" Balzor boasted, raising his free hand in to the air to enhance his point.

Aria smiled, leaning into him slightly. "But you feared the path to my grand-mother's house? Shame on you."

Balzor laughed unashamedly and gave her a playful shove back. "I told you, I was gathering my thoughts," he laughed, unable to keep a stupid grin from his face.

"Mmm, sure!" she mocked. "So, you played in the trees and grew up in a Lord's manor. Anything else?" she added, eyes glancing playfully under her lashes at him as he bristled at the implied insult, but smiled, nonetheless.

"We practised with the weighted weapons whenever the guards weren't around. Dextri relented eventually and taught us the basics but then went to the fron-tier with the General at the King's call; that was around a year ago. They only got back last week. Alkor's kinda pissed that Aldred is going again so soon, but at least this time Dextri's staying," he said, feeling as though he was babbling.

Aria didn't seem to mind one bit and kept the tirade of questions going. "Ah, so you want to be a warrior then. Part of the Saternac century?" she continued.

Balzor almost answered instantly but they rounded the corner of the treeline, and an old cottage came into view. Lanterns dangled from sticks at the entrance, the dwelling surrounded by a rickety fence that looked in need of repair. But, despite that, it looked like any other cottage. The shutters were ajar revealing the same dim light as any other in the village. He could see a painting hanging above a large fireplace. Rows of flowerbeds adorned the windowsills, some much more exotic than he was used to.

"Herbs," Aria explained, seeing Balzor examining the house and dragging him to a stop at the open gate. "You didn't answer my question," she said, releasing his hand and leaning on the gate.

Pulled back from his scrutiny of the house, he answered. "I guess so. Alkor and I started our official training a couple of days ago, so it seems that's the way we're to go. Defending people from the evil that this area suffered all those years ago is what I've always dreamed of doing," he said determinedly but was cut short as the door to the house creaked open.

Aria turned to the sound, thankfully not seeing Balzor blanch at being caught by the Seeress with her granddaughter. "Coming, Gran," she said over her shoulder to avoid the bark of her name she knew was heading her way. Reaching up on to her tip

47

toes, she kissed Balzor's cheek whose attention was drawn from the Seeress to the now burning brand where she'd kissed him. "Thank you for walking me home," she said, smiling shyly as she began to walk away.

Balzor raised his hand to his cheek, knowing he was smiling like a fool but not being able to help it. Her reply stopped in his throat though when he looked up to a woman he'd rarely seen in the village. She looked so normal, standing at the backlit door waiting for her granddaughter to come home. Even her hard eyes held a twinkle at seeing the kiss, and he could've sworn she smiled slightly when he met her eyes, though he looked away abashed. Raising his hand to wave, he scurried off down the path.

As Aria passed her grandmother, averting her eyes and hoping to avoid the inevitable questions, the Seeress kept looking into the night. Seeing the youngling hurrying off into the trees resonated deep into her core. She felt a touch of destiny about that moment, her eyes turning milky as she saw what was to come. She smiled.

"So, the wheels begin to turn," she murmured.

*****

Balzor couldn't recall any of the trip back to the tavern, his mind being somewhere else entirely. His spirit was soaring, and he felt like wings carried him down the moonlit path and across town where a lot of the lights in the houses were now doused as people went to their beds. Only when the sounds of a spent night began to reach his ears did he stop his daydreams and come back to reality. A pained groan, followed by a retch and a wet splatter, made Balzor peer into the shadows. What he saw made him emit a bark of laughter as the figure rose from his prone stance, spitting on to the floor and wiping his mouth with the back of his hand.

"Not a word," grunted the ale-stained Alkor as he staggered towards him, clearly aiming for the swinging entrance door again.
Balzor raised his hands in surrender but couldn't keep the grin at his friend's state off his face. As Alkor swayed his way to the door, he froze. Raising his hand up to his mouth again, he gave a pitiful moan and dashed back into the shadow, throwing up the rest of the night's contents.

Shaking his head and chuckling, Balzor left his friend to it and went in. He was greeted by a chorus of loud cheers from the corner, the roar in complete contrast to the now quiet tavern. The lyre player jumped out of his skin and gave the culprits a scowl before carrying on packing his things away, but the owner shook his head and smiled. The guards were his best customers, after all.

Livius rose as Balzor entered and announced he'd better check on the other pup, catching the door before it closed and rolling his eyes at the stench of sick as he left.

"Go on young'un, did the Seeress scare you off so soon?" Dextri roared, slamming his cup on to the table amid jeers from the rest. He picked up a jug and the look of disgust on his face showed that they'd emptied the lot as promised.

"She said I'd better come and look after you lot seeing as you clearly can't handle your ale," Balzor retorted, dropping down on to Alkor's vacant chair with a thump.

His arrival barely even stirred Ingvar who was snoring with his head resting on his arm, his spare hand nursing a cup of ale like a lover. Devar was clearly drunk, blurred eyes gazing stupidly at Balzor as he still grinned at Dextri's comment. Only Dextri seemed unperturbed by the night's antics.

"Hey, Olsten. What say we get some more ale over here?" Dextri demanded to the innkeeper.

Shaking his head slowly, Olsten finished wiping a cup with a cloth and set it down. His apron was stained with some sort of gravy from the stew and sweat bathed his crinkled forehead, dripping down his nose to be caught on the apron that his rotund stomach held proudly.

"Unless you're staying at my inn tonight, Dextri, the bar's closed." This response brought out a loud amount of booing from Devar as Balzor gingerly prised Ingvar's fingers off his full cup and then up and downed the contents, before replacing it in Ingar's hand which was still clawed around the empty space.

"All right, all right. We'll be off then. Thanks for the night old friend," Dextri replied, thumping his hand down onto the table with a loud bang, jerking Ingvar out of his sleep. Ingvar scowled and brought his cup to his mouth. Balzor stood quickly and danced away as Ingvar realised the ale was gone and lunged for the obvious culprit, furious at the theft.

Devar, who had seen the entire exchange, laughed loudly when his brother missed the lad and went sprawling onto the floor. Balzor ran out of the door with Ingvar on his heels, Dextri and Devar following behind egging Ingvar on in the chase. The innkeeper sighed softly, walking over to wipe the table. His best customers indeed, he thought as he cleaned, whistling a tune from the night.

Outside, Livius was supporting a barely conscious Alkor, grimacing as the lad's head lolled against his shoulder, a mixture of drool and ale dribbling onto his shirt. Ingvar caught up to Balzor fast, sending him sprawling in the dirt and kicking dust into his face, laughing as he spluttered and tried to rise.

"Think you can keep up with the big boys, eh pup?" Dextri cackled to Alkor, who tried to soberly respond but just managed a groan, hammering Dextri's point home. Dextri threw Alkor's other arm over his shoulder and assisted Livius carrying the drunken youth through the village letting Devar stop his own brother from terrorising Balzor. When they reached the gate, it had been closed for the night, but the two Richards were still there and opened it without a fuss knowing the guards by sight and joined in the laughter at the youngest Sain's sorry state.

As soon as the gate slammed shut behind them, Devar and Ingvar began to sing, barely coherent enough to let them know what song it was, let alone join in. The road was pitch black now. The slight glow of the town's torches only enough to light up a few feet beyond the wall, the drunken voices echoing off the wall and bouncing back to them, doubling the pain as they heard the racket twice. Although dark, the trees around the road seemed friendly, branches overhead hiding the moon's gaze as it lit up the night. Sounds that the night was alive reached Balzor's ears. Squirrels dropping their hard-won nuts and the clamour that followed as another found easy pickings. An owl hooted above, causing the squirrels to scatter for cover.

His thoughts drifted back to earlier in the night, the tingle when she held his hand, and the blaze on his face where she'd kissed him goodnight. Even the Seeress herself didn't seem so foreboding anymore.

With the sounds of the makeshift song from the brothers and his fanciful daydreams, the walk back seemed to pass quickly, and it wasn't long before the manor came into view, illuminated by the silver rays of the moon. Dextri cut the brothers off short with their song, getting resentful glances from the pair.

"Well, do you want to explain to the General why he's being wakened in the night by his drunken men when we've an early start tomorrow? Hmm?" Dextri hissed, the comment instantly sobering them up and quieting them down.

They crept up through the grounds, Ingvar still humming softly and drawing livid glances from his brother, but he was too drunk to care, only stopping his tune when passing the bathhouse and realising how close they were to the house. Devar sighed in relief.

When they reached the base of the steps leading to the manor, Livius released his hold on Alkor and let Dextri take the load; Dextri grunted at the extra weight. Like children hiding from their mothers, they waited in silence as Livius crept up the steps and opened the door, cringing at the slight creak. It was like a scream in the silence. Checking the entrance hall, Livius waved Dextri and Balzor up, both supporting the now unconscious Alkor, and disappeared inside. Devar and Ingvar waved their farewells and snook off to the barracks block around the side, still trying to be silent but failing miserably as one tripped and cursed loudly. They carried their burden up the stairs, Livius as lookout and having the job of holding the doors. They passed through unseen, a great feat in itself, and entered Alkor's room, throwing him fully clothed onto to the bed and hurrying out.

Livius scurried off back down the staircase as soon as Alkor was down but Dextri pulled Balzor to one side. "Whatever you do, DO NOT be late in the morning. The General will skin him alive if he needs to be dragged out of bed," Dextri warned. His whisper carried menace but the hint of humour.

"You're loving this, aren't you?" Balzor said.

Dextri chuckled quietly as they reached Balzor's door. "Of course, pup, why wouldn't I be? Goodnight!" he announced, leaving as quickly and quietly as they'd come.

Opening his own door and glad Dextri hadn't seen the mess inside, he went in. Stripping off his clothes, he flopped onto the bed, still unmade from the night before. He lay in complete silence, listening to the sound of insects chirping through his open window.

A sound of wood scraping followed by a loud retching indicated Alkor coming back to the living realm. Balzor chuckled to himself as he rolled onto his side, hearing the sound of a good night getting its revenge on his brother. His own night, though, was much better and for a much different reason. He drifted off to sleep with thoughts of twinkling green eyes, a dazzling smile, and a tied-up bun of messy brown hair.

Chapter 4

Rearing its unwelcome head, the sun announced the new day. A soft tapping on Balzor's door stirred him from his dreams. Opening his eyes, he found Nerva's head peeking through the door which was slightly ajar.

"I thought you'd need a wake-up call since it was gone midnight when I heard you louts creeping around last night," she said disapprovingly, yet there was a slight smirk on her face at his sorry state. "You can wake the other one up. I've got breakfast to make!" With that she left, leaving the door open slightly, beckoning him out of his bed.

Shaking his head and knuckling sleep out of his eyes, he threw his legs out of bed and began to dress drowsily. He didn't envy the state he knew Alkor would be in, feeling as tired as he did. Only the thought of Nerva's bacon spurred him on, knowing it would help cure them both. Running a hand through his hair and not bothering to comb it, he tied it back and splashed his face with the almost empty basin next to his bed. Feeling somewhat refreshed, he left to wake his friend, getting a mischievous enthusiasm at the thought.

However, when he reached Alkor's room, the door was wide open. In contrast to its usually spotless image, clothes lay strewn across the ground and his bed was a crumpled heap. Puzzled, and poking his head further in to double-check he wasn't there, Balzor spun on his heel and made his way to the staircase. He heard Alkor before he saw him and knew exactly what he was up to.

"Pleaaase Nerva! The room's still spinning now," Alkor whined as Balzor walked into the kitchens, grinning widely.

"Don't start," Alkor said grumpily to Balzor in the same tone as the night before. He laughed, but didn't say a word turning instead to Nerva who had the same I-told-you-so smirk on her face as she gave him earlier.

"This time no begging or favours. If you'll feed us first so we can get down before the General, we'll make breakfast for you tomorrow, and you can have it in bed," Balzor offered, urgent to get something to soak up the ale for his friend.

Nerva, looking astonished and amused, declined. "Although it's a very lovely offer, I wouldn't trust you two in my kitchen if I was starving. This one's a freebie only because I don't want anything to sour the General leaving. And his youngest son being sick on his shoes will do just that," she said, with a small chuckle.

Relieved, Alkor's shoulders sagged as he put his back against the wall and slid down it with a sigh, leaving him sat on the floor. "If you didn't already know Nerva, you're Ezimat sent," Alkor said, making Nerva laugh again. "Yes, well" she said, cheeks tinged pink and busied herself with the breakfast.

They sat in companionable silence with the sizzling of bacon, a sound that was music to their ears. The aroma soon filled the room making the lads mouths water slightly with Alkor even sitting up eagerly, despite his pounding head. Nerva threw an apple each at the boys, Balzor deftly catching his whilst Alkor just sat helplessly as it hit him in the mouth, yelping as it did.

"Eat those whilst you wait, you look like you need a bit of fruit in you!" Nerva berated them. Alkor massaged his lip and Balzor struggled hopelessly not to laugh at his friend's misfortune.

Balzor bit instantly into the apple but Alkor looked at it in distaste before pocketing it for later when Nerva wasn't looking. After a few more minutes, the sacred bacon was done. Nerva had to swat both of their hands away as she put it onto a piece of bread for them, since the pair kept trying to swipe an extra rasher. Once they had their prize, Nerva took the tray out of their reach, placing more pieces onto a clean tray and began to cook more. "Now get out to the yard and sober up you pests. I've got to have this ready for when the General leaves; he won't be happy with delays. Go!" she ordered, leaving the boys scrambling out of the kitchen with thanks uttered around a mouthful of bread.

They left the entrance hall to sit outside in the crisp morning, the slight chill doing wonders for their ale addled brains. Sitting on the top step, they crunched away at the sandwich, content, Alkor already feeling the food working its magic. Just as Alkor swallowed his last morsel and belched loudly, Dextri strode around the corner looking like he'd slept a full night and not touched a single drink.

"Morning, pups! How's the heads?" he called, already knowing the answer given Alkor's dishevelled look. "Looking at the state of you both, I'd say training's going to be especially brutal today," he added.

The pair looked aghast at Dextri, who cackled after the comment. "You didn't think you'd be getting a day off, did you? You only did half a day yesterday, so you'll damn well work it off today!" Dextri barked before stalking off into the house, leaving the lads crestfallen and wishing they hadn't drank so much the night before – especially Alkor.

Within moments of Dextri disappearing, Livius, Devar and Ingvar came into view. Ingvar, at least, looked on par with Alkor. The other two, though, looked more like Dextri, shrugging off the night's drinking without flinching. All three guards took one look at Alkor and burst into laughter, throwing mocking comments his way as they passed on their way to breakfast. The rest of the guards walking behind them were insulting him, angling at the fact that Alkor couldn't handle his ale. Balzor, delighted at being ignored in the tirade, received a dig in the ribs from his sulking friend after the guards had passed.

They sat for a while, enjoying the feel of the breeze in the slowly heating air. Alkor closed his eyes against the light whilst Balzor just took in the scene, enjoying the morning. The clip-clopping of a horse's hooves, coupled with the squeaking of an ungreased axle, announced the arrival of a cart. It stopped suddenly at the side of the armoury and the huge bulk of their friend Svein dismantled himself from the reins and leapt down, hailing them both. Hauling themselves to their feet, they trudged down the steps to meet him, Alkor huffing and sighing, feeling truly sorry for himself. Svein stayed with the cart, untying ropes from the bundles and beginning to unload them against the armoury wall, the weight of the repaired armour seeming nothing to him.

As they got closer, Svein dusted his hands off and moved to clasp arms with his friends, shaking his head in mock disapproval at the green shade to Alkor's face. "Looking at the state of you, it's a good job I left after one," Svein laughed, resuming his task with Balzor moving to help him. Alkor, however, chose one of the bundles already stacked against the wall and sat on it, head in hands. "I take it he tried to match Dextri, did he?" Svein murmured to Balzor, who laughed and confirmed this was the case.

Another couple of jibes from Svein directed at Alkor brought some life back to him. "The only reason you're not in the same state, brother, is because you spent the night trying to woo the serving girl!" Alkor retorted.

Balzor sputtered a number of unintelligible things as Svein raised his eyebrows, shock on his face, though he looked impressed. "Don't tell me you went for the Seer-ess' granddaughter?!" Svein blurted, throwing the last of the armour down and letting out a guffaw.

"That Seeress' granddaughter is called Aria," Balzor said coolly, instantly defensive against Svein's mocking tone.

"Oooh! First name basis already, are we?!" Alkor teased, hangover forgotten in his friend's discomfort.

Svein grabbed Balzor and shook him slightly, laughing and puckering his lips at him, causing Balzor to grimace and shove him away. "Come on, lover boy, tell me everything!" Svein said, the stupid smile still on his face. Irritated by the attention, but also knowing they wouldn't let it slide, he began. He started from the beginning despite Alkor's complaints.

"You'll get my version or none at all," Balzor said, finger in the air to forestall any arguments. Alkor made to protest but a quick hush from Svein quieted him. Svein loved gossip and knowing things he shouldn't was a skill, according to him. Motioning for him to carry on, Svein leant on the wall expectantly, so Balzor continued. He told them of how she'd come to find him and of Dextri playing polite whilst trying to embarrass him at the same time. He talked of the walk home, her holding his hand, the kiss on the cheek and of the Seeress herself being at the door.

At this, Svein whistled softly. "You're a braver man than me. If I'd have seen the Seeress there, I think I would've bolted," he said with a dry chuckle.

"She didn't seem as ominous as I remember, no dark cowl over her head or anything. Even her house seemed relatively normal" Balzor said, feeling slightly honour-bound to defend her. "Except the flowers on the windowsill were herbs," he added, before Svein could ask more.

"And you say Aria has the gift too? You're playing with fire, mate." Alkor laughed. Balzor rolled his eyes but smiled along with him.

Tramping feet coming out of the entrance to the manor saved Balzor from any more details as the squadron came out from their breakfast, making their way over to the trio and starting to sift through the sacks containing their newly repaired armour. Barely acknowledging the lads, they began throwing chain mail over their heads and striding into the armoury for the rest – equipping themselves as a machine of war.

Dextri followed in the tracks of the guard, bellowing in his best parade ground voice. "Commanding officer present!"

Every man, in various stages of undress, stopped what they were doing and snapped to attention. They knew training was over and were back to army regulations so when the General strode out of the manor, fully dressed as a god of war, they saluted, slamming their feet down in unison to emphasise the respect. Aldred Sain's armour gleamed in the morning sun, the light reflecting in all directions, almost as if the source of the light came from the man himself. He carried his open-faced helmet under his arm, the blue plume on top an indication of his rank. His huge battle axe thrown casually over his back was held by an oiled leather strap over his chest. Svein gawked at the sight, barely even sniggering as Balzor and Alkor hastily saluted late. Dextri frowned at them, but they were saved by the General's voice.

"At ease, gentlemen, but increase the pace. I need you all ready to move out in five minutes," he said casually but with underlying authority. This prompted an instant scuffle as men jumped to obey the order.

Aldred beckoned to the two lads and Svein jumped at the chance to come face to face with the General for the first time in years and went with them. As the trio walked over, Dextri whistled behind him to Ingvar and Devar who were just strolling casually out from breakfast with Livius, knowing they weren't going with the party. At the whistle they broke into a jog across the grounds reaching them at the same time as the boys.

"Great work on the armour, Svein. Please give your father my thanks for the speedy repair. There's extra silver in there for getting it here on time," Aldred said, leaving the young blacksmith dumbfounded at being addressed directly, and by name.

"Th- Thank you sir!" he stammered, as Dextri pressed the weighty bag of silver into his palm with a roll of his eyes.

"These two will ride on the cart with you back to the village. It's a lot of silver to carry, even in these parts," Dextri said, indicating to the two brothers.

"I can wait for the column sir, there's no need," Svein said, hoping to travel with the warriors in their war glory. Aldred smiled at the obvious eagerness of Svein but shook his head.

"We're on foot 'til the village lad. The horses are stabled there, remember? Lortmund would curse me if you were away that long," he explained to a crestfallen Svein, who nodded glumly and brought a rare laugh out of the General. "Maybe next time you'll be with us, eh lad?" he said, clapping him on the shoulder and instantly perking him up. "Go on now, young 'un," Dextri prompted, gesturing for Ingvar and Devar to jump on the cart.

After a quick salute to the General, they hopped up alongside Svein as he snapped the reins on the mules who brayed in irritation but began to drag their burden back towards with town. Waving at his two friends, he whipped the reins again to increase the pace and disappeared down the road.

Business completed, Aldred turned to the remaining two boys meeting their eyes with his own piercing gaze. "Hopefully this ordeal will be over quickly. I haven't had my fill of home yet," he began gravely to which Alkor snorted softly in agreement. The General's gaze hardened, eyes turning to ice. "This isn't the time for sulking, Alkor. You're no longer a child and you cannot act like one in my absence. There's too much at stake," he berated his youngest, who stood shocked at the outburst.

Alnor came out of the entrance door, also fully armoured. but not looking anything like the grand image of his father and paused slightly behind the General, smirking smugly at his younger brother being scolded. Aldred saw the hurt on his son's face but kept his hard composure. "You're to come of age within weeks, your training has begun and you're being left in a position that realistically you're not yet ready for. Use Dextri for guidance and trust his counsel. I've every faith that you'll become the man I *know* you are. Greater than I could ever be," he said, face showing no emotion as he gave his son the rare praise he knew was needed. Alkor squared his shoulders in pride at the acknowledgement.

Turning his body slightly to include Balzor, he continued. "This advice is to both of you, not just Alkor. I know I haven't been around as much as regular fathers, and I know I could have done more. But you'll soon understand that duty to the Kingdom *must* come first if we're to defeat the darkness in this world. Darkness that this town has seen first-hand, many years ago. Being a Sain means that we stand as a bulwark against that darkness, whatever the odds. Watch each other's backs and remember you are *both* Sain," he said, the last addition sending a warmth through Balzor and easing a hidden pain that had always been a thorn in his heart.

Balzor saw the disgust flicker on Alnor's face at the comment and he frowned sourly, hatred burning in his eyes. *Didn't think he'd like that one,* Balzor thought to himself as they saluted the General, who smiled warmly as he returned the salute in a gesture of respect before turning to Dextri.

"I sent Petra to tell the men on patrol to meet us at Torizo, so don't expect him back for a while," Aldred said, receiving a nod from his friend as they clasped arms.

"Just don't get yourself killed without me, Sir," Dextri replied gruffly, an age-old joke between them.

"Never, old friend." He laughed, releasing his grip and ramming his helmet on to his head.

"Annarites!" Aldred bellowed. "At my command."

Trained to perfection, the men fell in to marching column behind the General and his eldest son within seconds, Dextri and the two youths stood to the side. Alnor threw a withering look at them, returned in kind, despite Dextri studying the exchange and missing nothing. "March!" came the General's command, and the Annarites instant-ly responded, the column of metal snaking down the road, the two Sains at its head. The remaining three watched the column leave. Livius strolled over picking the remains of Nerva's bacon out of his teeth before standing with them.

"Makes you ache to go with them, doesn't it?" Livius said longingly, getting a grunt of agreement from Dextri. As the two lads said, "Yes," in chorus, Dextri whirled on them. "You'll never get to be part of the legion if you keep standing there gawking, GET THOSE LEGS MOVING!" he yelled, but the boys stood there in confusion at first.

Dextri lowered his voice and leant forward dangerously. "This time, I'll be on the hunt too," he warned. This, more than anything, jerked the pair into action and brought a chuckle from Livius. They shot off around the track and Dextri turned to Livius to join him in his mirth. Looking back down the road and seeing his comrades without him left a bitter taste, and he could tell Livius felt the same; but orders were orders. Taking a deep breath and glancing at his friend with eyebrows raised, who smirked and nodded back, they took off after the lads.

"Run, little Lords!" Livius bellowed, increasing his pace to match Dextri who laughed aloud. "Maybe this won't be so bad after all," Dextri mused, as the distance closed and his fist crashed into Balzor, sending him sprawling. "Not so bad indeed," Livi-us agreed as he dropped Alkor simultaneously. On the floor, both boys scowled.

*****

As a rule, Annarites marched in a column three men wide when on foot. However, the connecting road meant the third person was almost marching in the trees, so they marched in two's which left Alnor and his father leading the column alone. The sour mood in Alnor's gut soon evaporated at leading a force of men in full armour. He anticipated the eyes of the village taking them in and admiring them as they saddled the horses, the maidens batting their eyelashes as they rode out to war. Daydreaming like this, Alnor's march was more of a strut and the guards behind rolled their eyes at the cocky Sain in front, but said nothing.

Aldred chose to ignore his son's swagger at first, reminiscing that he'd once been young but the irritation needled him. He started a conversation to cover the growing itch. "How are you feeling about leaving, son?" Aldred asked without break-ing stride. Alnor missed a step at the question, almost falling over his words to answer quickly. "Excited, father. I can't wait to cross blades with the Kerazar dogs," he replied, his swagger enhancing at the words. Accepting the words with a nod, Aldred resumed his march, satisfied.

Within moments though, the swagger began to grate on him, to the point ignoring it became impossible.

"Cut that out," he snapped. Alnor looked shocked, his eyes questioning the rebuke. "You're a man of my legion, and we don't walk like peacocks going into war; we walk like warriors!" he said.

Alnor's ears burned with embarrassment at the public scolding from his father and he knew the guards were laughing. He also knew that any type of answering back would earn him much more than words, so he clamped his lips together and nodded, marching with his shoulders slightly slumped.

Aldred felt a slight remorse at his anger so tried to mask over the reprimand. "We've all been young and eager once, son. But now, because of who you are, you must mask the base instincts and not look forward to bathing in admiration, however good it may feel. We are Sains, and expectation is higher of us because of it. Confidence is fine but arrogance distances the men from us," he said, trying to explain the outburst.

Although still ashamed, Alnor squared his shoulders slightly and hid the irrita-tion behind a cold face, nodding. "Understood, father," he said, a little too abruptly.

The town's walls appearing as they rounded the bend stopped Aldred from responding to his son as a hailing from the town gates interrupted them, and a small boy tore off into the town to alert his friends. They entered the town just as a crowd was gathering, cheering at the arrival of their beloved Annarites, staying off the road to allow passage. Children ran across the road in front of them, daring each other to get as close as they could to the famous General. He laughed at their attempts and feinted a swipe, though never connecting, at any who came within range.

To Alnor's obvious disappointment, there weren't many girls swooning over the column - only the wives and partners coming out to greet their leaving husbands - giving them small tokens to hang around their necks and tearfully kissing them goodbye. Many of them had only returned recently, to leave so soon cut the hearts of more than a few families, but they knew the stakes and they all remembered the past; that devastation could not be allowed to happen again.

Aldred reduced the pace to allow the warriors to say their farewells, knowing the men would be grateful at the brief pause. He flipped a small coin at one of the children running around him and sent him hurtling off to the Stable Master to make sure the horses were ready. They were located behind the southern gate, beyond that led the road to Torizo. The men knew the General's patience would not last forever so with tight embraces and passionate kisses, not caring who saw, they began to break apart from their loved ones.

The child came back, baring her teeth in a feral smile and announced the horses were ready along with five days of rations in saddlebags for the men. Aldred inclined his head, flicking another copper at the girl who caught it deftly and turned to look smugly at her friends who were gazing enviously at the easily earned coin. Alnor hid his distaste, knowing his father would pick up on it quickly and drew a few coins from his own purse, scattering them amongst the other children who scurried around frantically on the dusty ground. Aldred laughed at the squabbling children and nodded approvingly at his son, whilst their mothers scowled at the cause of the disruption and ushered them back to their morning chores.

They moved through the town quickly after that, reaching the stable in good time, the crowd following behind to keep their loved ones in sight for as long as possible. The large wooden building was more of a barn than a house, the bottom floor packed with stalls for the horses and large bundles of hay from the outlying farms leant casually on the outside walls. Above the barn was an imitation of the apartments in Torizo and other cities, a sturdy staircase hugging the right side of the structure and taking you to a door, which was being closed by a rushed looking Stable Master.

Aldred took off his helmet and unstrapped his great war axe from his back, tying them both to his horse as it was led out by the Stable Hand. The horse, Moonlight, whinnied at seeing its owner and pushed its nose into his face at being reunited. "Whoa, girl," Aldred said, easing the horse's excitement with a chuckle, lest it spread to the rest of them.

The other warriors followed suit, happily copying their General and taking off their helmets which had baked their head on the march. Some men preferred to keep their weapons with them and mounted up with scabbarded swords leaning across their thighs, belts loosened to allow movement. Whatever their preference, all men were ready to ride within minutes.

The Stable Master approached the General, wringing his hat in his hands nervously. "Sorry, Lord. We didn't think you'd be so early coming or else we'd have had the horses already waiting for you," he said anxiously, but Aldred waved off the man's unease.

"No need to apologise, Gerald. We're much earlier than I expected myself. Applaud yourselves on a quick service!" he said, Gerald's relieved look at the remark making him smile. "But now, we must be off. Duty calls." Gerald stepped back from the group.

"Ezimat be with you, General." he said, bowing at the group and drawing the circle on his head for luck. Everyone did the same.

"And with you, Gerald," he replied, the response expected.

Pleasantries aside, he focused more on the task at hand. "FORM UP," he bellowed. The unit responded like an extension of his will, the southern gate creaking open in expectation of them leaving, beckoning them onto the road. "Advance!" he said, and dug his heels into Moonlights ribs, urging the horse forward.

Caught up in the moment and being surrounded by the villagers, Alnor cheered and punched a fist in to the air. The villagers loved the idea, and most of the warriors followed suit immediately, the cacophony causing birds to erupt from the trees in alarm and look indignantly at the leaving group. Aldred Sain rolled his eyes and sighed. He was young once, too.

*****

The trees flew past steadily at the slow trot the General set for the group. Because of the earlier start, his father clearly felt no impatience to push their horses unnecessarily and so Alnor let his imagination wander as the leaves whipped by lazily. He itched to increase the pace, but didn't dare do so without his father's permission so resigned himself to the steady plod of hooves on the dry road. He thought himself lucky that he wasn't at the back of the group where the dust was kicked up, the men at the back choking, despite their efforts to cover their mouths.

To pass the wasted time, Alnor satisfied himself by thinking of his younger brother back at the estate, left behind as he went onto glory. Even his father's comment to the peasant boy couldn't penetrate his thoughts as he realised that, by the time they returned, he would've experienced war, where his little brother would have only played at it. Then, Petra would bring the rest of the guard, and he'd finally have a like-minded fellow alongside him - not that he'd ever converse with Petra within the General's ear-shot, but it would be nice to talk to someone who also didn't swoon over commoners. Idly chatting, the hum of the guards' voices lulled Alnor into a daydream, imagining the day where he would finally command in his father's place, Alkor and the whelp bowing at his feet, having to obey his every whim. The miles were gradually eaten up as his mind fantasised, and it wasn't long before the trees began to thin out, giving way to the shrubs and bushes that propped up the hills bordering Torizo. Thin grassland covered the small rolling landscape like bristled hair for the hills, small gaps in between the parched ground overrun by dandelions and small weeds. The sun beamed from directly above now, indicating midday had come, with Torizo still not in sight.

It seemed his father suddenly began to chafe at the pace and dug his heels in further causing Moonlight to surge into a trot at the command, startling the rest of the squadron out of their inactive march. They matched the General's pace without command, conversations stopping and the group focused once more. Alnor stopped his speculation, glancing sideways at his father's face, which revealed nothing. His impatience boiled at the silence knowing his father had noticed his interest and feigned ignorance. In the end, he couldn't wait.

"Why the increased pace, father? I thought the King was only meeting us in the morning, on the West Road?" Alnor asked his father. His father gave a relieved sigh before speaking. Had he been waiting for Alnor to break the ice?

"Courtesy demands we get there first, son. We've got two groups of patrols out that we need to convene with first so hopefully your friend Petra has got the message there in time," he said, clearly trying to gain some familiarity by adding Alnor's friend into the discussion.

The ruse worked, as Alnor perked up at the mention and nodded enthusiastically. "Petra is a good warrior father and an even better scout. If anyone could get those patrols to us in time it'll be him," he bragged. "But... if we don't get there before the King, will he really take offence?" he added, biting his lip showing his nervousness at the implication.

Aldred laughed loudly, discounting the nervousness of his son and waving his hands. "No, son. He wouldn't take offence. But the King is a very competitive man, and it'll warm my bones to beat him to the meeting point knowing he had a huge head start," he said jovially. "No offence will be taken but respect will be given, if we can win," he added.

Alnor grinned at his father's enthusiasm infected by his mood and suddenly gaining newfound confidence. "Well, father, let us not keep him waiting. Hyah!" he said, snapping the reins of his horse with the sound and forcing it into a canter, the guard again jerking at the increase in pace, Aldred forced along with them. He didn't seem annoyed, however, barking laughter at his son's eagerness and raising smiles from the closest guards at their general's excitement. "There's life in your old dad yet," he taunted his son, digging his heels in knowing his men would relish the pace.

Racing ahead of the group, Moonlight advanced to a headlong gallop, chomping at the bit to be the leader of the herd. Alnor's momentary shock at his father's sudden speed dissolved quickly as he matched the madness, whooping and enjoying the wind tearing through his hair, tears leaking out of his eyes, though they dried rapidly. The miles were swallowed by the group, hooves crashing into the crisp dirt, leaving a huge cloud of dust dancing in the wind at their passage. The horses couldn't keep up the breakneck pace for long so, at a particularly steep uphill climb on the road, the General raised his hand to slow the party, first to a trot, then to a walk. "Squadron! Dismount!" he called as they crested the top of the hill. Some men sighed with relief at the command. They trusted their General, but still worried about lame horses too and with a long way to go, this could not be afforded. They knew they could change their horses in the cities along the way, especially whilst travelling with the King, but the men were fiercely loyal to their mounts and were loath to part with them easily.

"We'll take a small rest here. Tend to the horses and yourselves, we leave in half an hour," Aldred said, kicking his feet out of the stirrups and dismounting allowing the rest of them to do the same.

Men instantly grabbed their water skins, taking small gulps themselves before pouring some into a container for their horses who eagerly lapped it up. Some even went as far as to remove their saddles, grabbing tufts of grass from the side of the road and rubbing their sweaty mounts down, the horses nickering in content at the attention. Alnor, knowing his father was watching did both these things. A small nod of approval from Aldred brought a blossom in Alnor and finished rubbing his horse down just as his father started.

"Here, father, let me," he said, moving towards Moonlight and beginning to help.

Not wanting to show any favouritism in front of his men, Aldred inclined his head and they rubbed the horse down silently. A few of the men saw Alnor's attempt and began to call out for help themselves too laughing amongst themselves. "Why have a dog and bark yourself?" one of them jeered, men around him sniggering.

Scowling, Alnor knew it was no use to try and defend himself as it would only open himself to more ridicule; something he wasn't willing to happen in front of his father from men he one day hoped to lead.

"Woof, fucking woof," he called back. The men erupted in laughter at him playing along and even his father joined in.

Crisis averted, Alnor thought, mentally carving the man's face into his mind for future reference, all the while smiling and laughing along with them. Sitting on the ground as their horses nibbled at the grass around them, the men chatted idly, some eating the small things their wives had given them as they were leaving, some digging into the typical army issue rations of dried beef and cheese.

Aldred himself was chewing on a small piece of beef whilst lying on the floor, his arm propping up his head. Alnor was a mirror image of his father, minus the beef and twiddling a blade of grass in his spare hand. Once again, Alnor struggled to open a conversation with his father. He was so sure it had closed the invisible rift between them after their reckless ride and jokes. Not knowing what to do, he stayed in silence, worrying over what subject to choose. Luckily, his father saved him from the torment.

"You did well back there," he said. Alnor looked up from his twiddling. "With the men. Asserting authority or reprimanding them would've only distanced them from you. Joking with them and allowing small comments to pass by will bring them closer, not quite friends but hardly taskmasters either. It's a tight balance, and you did well".

Alnor inclined his head to his father at the praise. "It means a lot, coming from you," he said. "Over the years, duty has come first, which is understandable and, of course, necessary but I hope this journey can allow us time lost. I just wish Alkor was here to share in it with us." He wished nothing of the sort, his brother and the peasant boy would only serve to taint the moment. He knew that what he actually said would appeal to his father's sentiments more.

Aldred smiled sadly. "I'm glad you understand the reasons for my absence, and I hope you know that it's one of my biggest regrets - hardly seeing you grow. Alkor, too, must feel the same. Maybe after this, we can remedy the situation," he said. Pushing up off the floor, he knocked his son's arm, causing his hand to slip and his head crashed into the floor.

The shock on Alnor's face was enough to set his father laughing once again as he offered his hand to his son to help him rise. Before he was on his feet, he was laughing too, the connection he so badly craved beginning to form. "That's enough rest, this isn't a holiday!" Aldred barked, making men leap to their feet grumbling as they began to mount up again. "At the trot, we need to get to Torizo by morning! We'll camp on the West Road and wait for the King if he's not already there. Squadron, advance!" Once again Alnor fell in at the front of the column, his shoulders now proud and his thoughts excited at the prospect of spending some real time with his father. The sun was beaming triumphantly in the sky when they reached the western fork in the road the day after, the city of Torizo rising royally from the hills directly to the East. Its walls were built around six hills, towers ranging the length, men constantly atop the ballista positioned within them- ready to use them at a moment's notice. In between the towers, the wall had a jagged top, giving the appearance of windows for archers to appear, loose and fall back behind the cover of safety.

Each hill that the wall defended had different purposes. One, by far the most notorious, was what people liked to call The Nest. This was filled with inns and taverns, theatres and bath houses. It was where travellers and merchants spent all their hard-earned money on pleasures of the flesh and more than enough of the citizens did too. Alnor and his father had enjoyed many-a-night carousing there in Aldred's younger days, and he remembered them fondly and with only a little embarrassment. The others were less interesting, filled with barracks, houses and markets.

Only one other held value. It boasted a huge temple dedicated to Ezimat, surrounded by beautiful gardens with trees that had been brought from faraway lands, too many years ago for any to remember. Acolytes tended the gardens and lived in the temple, accepting offerings from visitors in the name of the Supreme God. It was widely argued that the city had sprung up *because* of the temple, a Priest of Ezimat had seen the God there and the land was sacred. Others disagreed as there were temples to Ezimat everywhere but both sides agreed with one thing: it was built by the High Priest Torizon, one of the original disciples of the God. Hence, Torizo was named. As it came into view, the men stared wistfully at its walls; more than enough of them had spent nights in The Nest to know its allure.

Seeing the look in their eyes, Aldred chuckled. "After the work is done, your reward will be a night there lads, paid for by yours truly!" he shouted. They all cheered, nudging their friends excitedly. "But not tonight. We camp here; it seems we've beaten the King to the meeting point. Either that or the Nest calls him, too," he added mischievously, causing a round of hoots and jeers as they dismounted and began the process of tending to the horses again, this time leaving the saddles off.

Some of them broke off to unravel their packs having drawn the shortest straw to carry the two man tent, which was rolled tightly around small posts that made its frame. Both men in the pair had their own jobs - one tended to the horses, and the other put up the tent. Only when both jobs were done could they get wood for a fire or eat food. In enemy territory, they were also required to dig a trench around the camp, piling the excess dirt as a make-shift barricade, but they were far into Annarite territory, so the rules were lax.

Soon, campfires crackled in the centre of a small circle created by four or five tents each, closer friends naturally gravitating around the same fires. Travellers and merchants rolled past the fork in the road, hailing the soldiers and trying to sell their wares, mainly food and ale. The warriors happily obliged, but only *after* the General and his son had bought their own - the General always led by example, after all.

Soldiers nominated to take the first watch listened sullenly as their comrades began to drink, some pleading with their mates to bring them a wineskin to join the festivities from afar. But even in Annarite territory, Aldred Sain was vigilant; he would not stand for drinking on the job. The sulking watchmen settled in as the sun began to set, its orange lips kissing the horizon as it crept towards its slumber.

Content with a belly full of ale, Aldred was on his back alone, arms crossed behind his head and thinking fondly, though sadly, about his late wife. The ride to Torizo always brought the same memory - his Lorelai chastising him regularly to update the road between the village and the city. He smiled as the familiar echo of her voice listed all the pro's and none of the cons to the idea. "Carts could be easily pulled, bring us more trade. Even your bloody guard could reach the city in under a day to pass messages; not to mention the fact you can't march in a real column!" She'd been right, of course. She always was.

Fireflies darted through the crisp evening air, dancing with the sparks that the flames spat out, creating a whirlwind of flashes against the fading light. He hadn't realised how much his sense of duty would impact the lives of his sons. With no mother to fill in, they'd raised themselves with the rough company of warriors the closest thing to a family they had.

Aldred sighed. Duty had always come first; it had to if he wanted his sons to live in a world where they could laugh and love rather than scrape and kneel to the darkness of the Kerazar. *One last stint, then I pass the duty on to someone else,* he thought wearily, knowing he was lying to himself. He and the King had vowed all those years ago to stop the darkness spreading until their dying breath. The King felt himself personally responsible, it was his family who'd birthed it.

Shaking his head to clear the unwanted thoughts, Aldred let out another deep sigh and took another swig of ale. Grimacing at the sour taste and the luke-warm temperature, he glanced around him and once he saw nobody was watching, threw the remaining contents on the floor. *If the men think I can't handle my ale, I'll be the point of jokes for days,* he thought, chuckling to himself and dragging himself from the dusty ground. Usually, he'd do a round of the fires, judging the mood and lifting spirits but, this close to home and half-drunk with their friends, he let it be. His joints creaked as he stretched his body, a testament to the ordeals he'd put it through and coupled with age, though he didn't like to admit the latter.

He strode through the centre of the camp, waving away the invitations to share different fires good-naturedly and came to where his son was currently armwrestling over a fallen log with Terva, a bear of a man with a huge moustache, and losing miserably. Sweat poured off his son's face, dripping off the hooked nose he'd inherited from his father as he forced with all his might against his opponent, but Terva's arms might as well have been made of iron. Aldred might not have even bet Dextri against him in an arm wrestle; a fair fight sure, but not one of strength. Terva relished in the warriors' cheers, being as brazen as to take his eyes off Alnor to look around and grin stupidly at the General, before slamming his son's arm down on to the log causing splintered pieces of wood to gouge lightly into both the men's skin at the force exuded.

Aldred laughed and clapped as his son massaged his arm and glared at Terva, who was sucking a bloody knuckle or picking a splinter with his teeth - Aldred could not decide. Terva grinned at the young man's baleful stare and spat the splinter out of his mouth triumphantly, holding out his other arm. Alnor snorted and clasped it.

"Too much ale would make anyone think they're Ezimat" he said dryly, earning himself a roar of laughter from the group.

Aldred nodded proudly at his son knowing that his absence through the years had not made his heirs soft. Alnor grinned back, and more of the guarded look he could see in his son's eyes faded.

"I'm going to relieve the watch on the East Road, draw straws between you for who relieves the others. No drinking anymore if the unfortunate man to pick the short one is you," Aldred said to the groans of the group, each man dreading the battle to stay awake after ale they knew they shouldn't have drunk.

The General clapped his son on the shoulder and walked off towards the watch.

He'd chosen that way not only because the King would come from there but because he could see the city walls. Although he'd always disliked cities himself – the sheer size and amount of people there made his head spin – he loved to look upon them. The feat to build a wall so high that stood for so long had always amazed him, but give him a small town to live in and he was content; he was never a man for castles or palaces. The landscape had scattered hills and patches of brush everywhere, bundles of trees placed haphazardly between them all, but he knew the general direction of the sentry.

Seconds before the sentry came into view he heard a cry in front of him, followed by the pounding of feet heading in his direction. In one fluid motion he'd drawn his sword and set his stance, instinct taking over from the years of training etched into his mind. He waited, heartbeat pounding in his ears to the rhythm of the footsteps, a slight breeze drying the sweat from his cheeks. Suddenly, a gangly youth with an abnormally large pair of ears tore around the nearest copse of trees, skidding to a stop at the bared blade. His eyes looked shocked as he scanned for the threat that his General seemed to see. However, the General let out a sigh of relief and lowered his blade. The youth visibly relaxed, though he didn't stop shaking.

"Report, Mortey!" Aldred barked, causing the man to jump again. We'll have to sort his nerves before his first fight, Aldred thought cynically. He sheathed his blade hoping to ease the tension still in the air.

"S-s-Sir, it's the... King! The King is on... the East Road," Mortey stammered, pointing his twig-like arms in that direction. Alarm shot through Aldred, he'd let the men get half drunk, expecting the King in the morning. His thoughts racing, he had to order quickly.

"Mortey, get back to the camp pronto. Tell every man to don gear and form up on the East Road, lining opposite each other," he said urgently. "And tell those bloody merchants to make sure they cook more food before the King arrives. He won't thank us for eating our fill if there's nothing left for him!" The urgency was lost on Mortey, who still stood gaping at the sudden change in the General, though he'd stopped shaking at least.

"WELL! What are you waiting for? Get a move on man!" Aldred shouted exasperatedly, and the lad sprang into action like he'd been hit by lightning, sprinting off in the camp direction, yelling at the top of his voice that the Royal party had arrived.

Shaking his head and hoping he'd never been that green once, Aldred set off at a jog towards the horses. He would meet the King on the road and hopefully buy the camp more time. The horses were picketed at the base of a hill just South of the camp. The long blades of grass blowing gently in the breeze made perfect grazing for the animals and was still close enough to the men. Barely slowing his pace, he nodded at the two guards nominated to watch the horses who jolted up from the ground they'd been lounging on, ashamed to be caught red handed. He ignored the nickering of other horses, his eyes darting around, looking for Moonlight amongst the stable. Relief flooded through him as he heard Alnor's voice from behind.

"Father," Alnor called, and Aldred turned to see his son waving, two horses saddled and ready to ride, Moonlight was one of them. Leaping up on to the magnificent beast's back, he shot his son a grateful glance and dug in his heels, Moonlight diving forward with relish at the command.

Alnor mirrored his father and they left the two guards standing in a cloud of dust, stunned, within seconds, the muted sounds of hooves slamming into the dirt fading on to the road.

Chapter 5

A fine breeze coupled with the setting sun announced the end of a hard day's riding. The brooding walls of Torizo loomed about the royal party, casting a shadow over them and making the earlier breeze decidedly cooler. The party, considerably less regal than they'd looked two days ago leaving Grea, still had shining armour – though the bright red cloaks gracing their backs had mud flecked on their hems. The heat of the day had seen most of the men hang their helmets from hooks on saddles, their hair stuck to their scalps with sweat. The King never did care about the looks of his men; he was only concerned with whether they could stand toe to toe with the best and win. His son, however, cared a great deal about appearance, and on this excursion nearly three quarters of the guards were Prince Krinar's.

Sitting at the head of the column, Krinar glanced at his father, the look noticed by the King. He gave him a hard look, feeling the crinkles at the corner of his eyes itch as he did so. Like the other men, he'd opted to remove his helmet, but his short, cropped hair couldn't stick anywhere. At his order, they'd slowed from their steady canter as they drew alongside the colossal walls, eager to hit the taverns of a city many of them hadn't seen in years.

"Shall I give the order to enter the city, father?" Krinar queried uncertainly.

He didn't answer immediately. His eyes scanning the hills towards the West Road, he perked up suddenly and pointed towards a seemingly random hill. "There, son. What do you see?" the King asked, needing his son's keener eyes to be sure. Age came to them all.

Krinar narrowed his eyes against the incessant dust, focusing in on the direction the mailed arm was pointing. At first, a puzzled look dropped onto his face, but he kept looking rather than face his father's displeasure. A few seconds passed and the King was beginning to feel impatient. One simple question, and the lad couldn't even do that.

"I don't..." Krinar began, before halting as a glint pierced his eye. The sun was reflecting off something rapidly criss-crossing downhill. "I'd say the only thing that can cause a glint like that, Father, was water or a man in armour running down a hill. But for what?" he said, the same puzzled look ingraining deeper into his expression.

King Malker sighed. His old friend had beaten him again. Raising his voice to a parade ground level, he bellowed his command. "No lodges in Torizo, tonight. We camp with General Sain!"

Muffled protests were heard in the column's midst, but a hundred men hid the culprits; even his own son quickly masked a look of dismay at missing the city's known pleasures. A spike of irritation flashed through King Malker though he let none of it show on a cold face. He hoped his son's guards were more disciplined against the rebels, even with some of his own veterans steeling the younger groups nerves. He felt the years keenly these days and he needed these younger men blooded, to fight when he was not able to, his son at the head. He'd had his first-born when he was just of age - much too young for the heir to the throne - but at the now overripe age of fifty, he was glad to have a full-grown son to do most of the leg work. However, a King still has to show his strength and he was far from dead; plus, some time away from the Queen wouldn't go amiss. He hadn't had a good fight in years.

Excitement suddenly broke through the King's cold façade, and he dug his heels into his eager mare, breaking into a full-blown gallop within seconds. The flailing column jerked awake at the change of speed and the once glorious red cloaks were left in disarray as they each reacted at differing speeds - a jester's group to be enjoyed by the guards on the walls, although they wondered why the King would pass a perfectly good city this late in the day.

Three miles were eaten up by the King before he finally slowed to let the column catch up, Krinar looking only slightly ruffled compared to the flustered group. He was used to his Father's random mood changes and adapted quickly to them but the veterans scowled openly; they didn't like the King going off alone, even in friendly territory. King Malker laughed at the open annoyance of his men. He knew each one as intimately as his wife, as a shield brother should.

"Look, brothers! The General has already sent men to meet us! Surely his camp will have fires and ale to warm our bellies!" he said, gesturing down the road at the small plumes of dust bouncing up from the racing figures of two horsemen.

At this, his son's guards cheered their King, but his own guards merely rolled their eyes and smiled. They knew their King's way of deflecting their concern for his safety and they let it be.

Despite the secure feeling of the royal party, cemented by regular patrols from

Torizo and the General himself, Krinar despatched four men to intercept the galloping riders. Considering their current mission, hunting rebels who had penetrated this far all those years ago, it was fresh in everybody's mind that nowhere was completely safe, so the precaution seemed apt. The King grated at such mollycoddling as though he was a defenceless babe, but he would make a fool of himself to override his son's valid command. That, and his men would burn disapproval at his disregard for his own safety, especially after his headlong rush moments before, he settled into his saddle to wait.

Puffed up at their own importance at being chosen to meet the riders, four of the red cloaked men somehow found a way to swagger as they rode. It wasn't a shock for them to be picked, they knew the prince trusted them more than most, especially Varnan, a grizzled, grey-haired veteran of many battles with scars to prove it. He could count on one hand how many teeth remained in his mouth and his nose was bent at an odd angle from some fight or other. An uglier man couldn't be found, and his soul mirrored his face. He had an aptitude for choosing violence over anything, against friend or foe alike, and he revelled in what he was – Prince Krinar's war dog. Men trod lightly around him, but in a fight, they wanted nobody else at their side.

When the two riders ahead curbed their mounts to a stop and waited, the other three glanced at Varnan to see his reaction before reacting themselves. Baring his few teeth, he slowed his mount and motioned for the three to surround the messengers before riding directly up to them himself. Seeing the pair sat motionless, their piercing blue eyes staring at him from a cold face with a hooked nose, he sneered. Father and son, maybe. He didn't care. The attempt at a cold face wouldn't impress him; he'd had more women than one man had years, and the other was well past his prime though he'd never say that in front of the King, as they looked of similar age.

"In the name of the King, you'll surrender your weapons and be escorted back before delivering your message. These are troubled times, and you can't be too careful, you understand?" Varnan's voice drawled, full of fake deference expecting to be obeyed. So, when both men sat as still as stone, challenge glinting in their eyes, Varnan felt a rush of rage though nothing showed on his face. He kneed his mount forward, at a *very* slow walk, conveying menace through every soft footfall of the horse on the parched road.

"I said..." he began as he got closer and reached for the older man's blade.

Before his hand had reached the man's hip, he moved lightning fast and grasped Varnan's wrist, twisting it around with a savage jerk, then delivered an ear ringing slap that almost unseated him and left his whole head shaking as he recoiled in the saddle, his face a mask of outraged shock. Varnan heard his men shout and begin to loosen blades, before a voice barked out.

"Sheathe those blades or I'll sheathe them in your hearts. Don't you know any man who tries to disarm General Sain usually loses his life, not just his pride?"

Hearing the voice, Varnan went pale. He shook his head to clear the throbbing from his ear before turning to the older man. General Aldred Sain sat looking impassively back, confidence coming out of his pores that his name alone would turn most men to jelly. Which it did - even Varnan - who now recognised the crest of rank hanging over the shoulder of the man. Nobody but the General would dare to wear that to meet the King, unless it actually was Aldred Sain.

"S-sir! I humbly beg forgiveness at our folly," he said bowing, ignoring the looks of annoyance he got from the other three at including them in his misfortune. "May we escort you to the king?" His voice had changed instantly as he found out who the man was, his fake drawl switching to a fawning purr which disgusted even himself. *You can never be too careful around powerful men,* he thought. He breathed a sigh of relief as the General nodded his acceptance, turning his horse expertly on the spot and leading the way back to the royal party. He noted the exchange in his head though. Even the mighty must fall one day.

*****

Alnor kept glancing at his father, failing to gauge his mood. He'd been shocked when his father had humiliated the man, seemingly for nothing more than doing his job, but he'd sat impassively so as not to shame the family image. Strength was certainly the picture his father had painted with his actions, maybe bordering on stupidity to slap the King's guard so nonchalantly, but Aldred Sain just sat on Moonlight, completely the General. He'd heard his father and the King were close friends at a younger age, but whether the bond had lasted through the years was another matter. It was with a slight worry, masked mostly by the excitement he felt at meeting the King, that Alnor cantered towards the much larger royal party amid four red cloaked guards.

The sun was almost below the skyline now, its eyes finally closing for a night's rest, its lazy rays reflecting off the armour of two hundred men. Dust spiralled beneath the horses' hooves and settled lightly on the shrubs dotting the roadside, to be spun back into the evening air by the devious wind.

Irritated that his father hadn't given him an inkling of his plans when he did reach the King, he turned his attention to the grim-faced man at the head of the party. Unsure of who the man was, he was subtle in his study, taking in the man's clearly broken nose and empty mouth, coupling it with his riding skill and noting him down instantly as a born warrior. Whether he was Annarite or not wouldn't be distinguishable until he saw the man move, but a warrior for certain. He'd heard that some men who weren't Annarite were as skilled with a blade as their God-chosen brothers but, in his experience, that was something that lesser men told their friends, so they didn't feel inferior. He'd certainly never been bested by any of the normal men in his father's guard - not since his training at least - and he'd trounced those men over and over to make sure they knew they couldn't contend with him now. To try this ugly man would be a delight on the march, wiping that scowl off his face would give him great pleasure.

That warm thought was replaced with anxiety as the ugly warrior began to slow his horse, the royal party now only a hundred yards away. Lines of red cloaked men faced them, expressions hard as stone as they watched from pure bred horses of the Royal stock, and armour that shone in the dying sunlight. However, it was the two men in the centre of the line that caught Alnor's attention. They were the reason his father had ridden out here himself. The only thing that gave the King away was the age difference between the men - both looked the perfect image of a Royal, regal stature and self-assured looks painting them out from a mile away but with an age difference of around twenty years. *King Malker and Prince Krinar* thought Alnor in awe, and he glanced towards his father once more, seeing a slight smile on his face finally replacing the cold expression he'd worn since they left camp.

Alnor breathed a sigh of relief. He wouldn't have to try and explain the stoniness emanating from his father and he began to relax. As they reached within a few paces of the King, the ugly man held up a fist to stop the group and bowed his head to the King.

"Sire, this is..." he began.

"I know who they are," the King snapped, startling the man to stop his introduction and look with alarm at the men surrounding him, trying to decipher what he'd done to offend.

"Re-join the line, Varnan" said the prince, and the ugly man bowed his head and gestured to the men to follow. A sulky expression made his features even more hideous, something Alnor hadn't thought possible. He and his father were left facing two hundred men and the King of Annar and his heir to the throne.

Despite the cool wind on his skin, Alnor began to sweat under the scrutiny as the silence stretched over the seconds. He looked for the third time at his father, this time fearful that he'd try to keep the hard persona in front of the group. He and the King stared at each other, jet blue eyes meeting bright grey in a war of intensity; two titans sizing each other up, deciding who was the strongest. The smile was gone from his face, and the King was tight lipped at the scrutiny from his General.

Sweat began to drip from Alnor's armpits and trickle down his side and an eternity seemed to have passed in those few seconds. It was a relieved gasp that escaped from his mouth - thankfully not loud enough for his father to hear - as the man finally put his fist to his chest in a salute, and bowed as deeply as being mounted would allow.

"Greetings, your majesty," Aldred began as he rose from his bow. "It has been years since your face graced my eyes and I'm glad to see you in good health. May you always stay so, Ezi willing, and lead our kingdom to greatness!" His face was solemn as he said these words, but Alnor was sure there was an amusement in his eyes that wasn't there before.

Looking back to the King, his face was a mirror image, the same twinkling now replacing the intensity of moments earlier. It was a huge shock, however, when the King suddenly burst into laughter, Aldred following suit instantly. They rode the last few paces toward each other and clasped arms in the warrior's way, a familiarity that seemed to shock most but not all the warriors there, Alnor included.

"Aldred Sain, you old dog. How've you been?! And you can stop all that Your Majesty. We were spanked by the same maid as boys when you were just Aldred and I was just Malker," the King said, still chuckling at the facade.

"Whatever you say, your greatness." Aldred replied with a smirk turning his mouth up, the King emitting a bark of laughter again.

"It'll be good to catch up, old friend," Malker said. "I assume the warriors in your camp are hurriedly donning armour and pretending they're not drunk? I hope you left enough for us!"

Alnor stood looking aghast at the pair, chatting in the midst of the royal guard like they were farmers in a tavern. The prince was grinning at the look on his face and Alnor grinned sheepishly back and bowed his head, Krinar inclining his own in return, then kicking his mount out of the line to join his father.

"And this must be Alnor, General?" the prince said, raising his own arm to clasp Alnor's who reacted eagerly to the honour and going red at his father's raised eyebrows at the speed his arm left the reins.

"It is, sire," Alnor replied, speaking quickly to mask his embarrassment at looking like an over excited child. "It's good to finally meet you. And excellent to see you again, sire," he finished, turning to the King and bowing his head.

He had met the King a few times during his childhood. It usually signified his father having to leave again so he never relished his visits. Krinar, however had met Alnor's father several times and fought at his side once, which made Alnor secretly jealous. This journey would change all of that. He'd become a man in more than just name. It was this familiarity that enlightened Krinar at the General's humour with the King and also, it seemed, to the General's tendencies.

"I see my man's face over there is a tad red, General. Did he even get close to your sword?" he asked with a wry grin. Varnan's eyes widened behind the prince at the comment, a flash of anger crossing his face at the obvious trap he'd been sent in to. Aldred Sain laughed and lifted his hand in apology. Varnan responded with a tight smile, which looked like a pained grimace at best.

"You know my ways, Krinar. He barely reached my saddle, let alone my sword," Aldred answered with a smile. The King and the Prince roared with laughter; the older warriors of the guard joining in. They'd all been led into the same trap at some stage with their General, it was almost an initiation back in the day. The younger guards of the prince's party, however, passed confused looks between each other, nervous smiles on their faces so not to look like fools.

"Come! Merchants have stopped at the roadside for my warriors, let us see their faces when instead of the General, they suddenly have the King and his heir to feed," said Aldred, baring his teeth in a feral smile. Dragging Moonlight's head around and digging in his heels towards the camp, he gestured for the King and his son to fall in beside him. Alnor hurriedly ensured his place in that particular line, oblivious to the sniggers of the men behind him at his obvious attempt to get close to the prince.

They led the party at a leisurely pace towards the first mound where the King had spotted Mortey careening down the hill to alert the General. The sun was finally setting, taking the heat from the day and making the cool breeze suddenly cold, leaving the men wishing for their fires. To the relief of most men, the biting wind died down suddenly as they rode between the hills, the grassy mounds blocking most of the gusts, only for them to return stronger when they reached a break in the mounds. The moods were still high as the camp's fires came into view, rising even higher as the procession walked through two armoured lines of men.

"They actually managed to do it!" the King shouted voice strained from trying not to laugh. "I've never known a group of half-pissed warriors manage to don armour and form line perfectly in such a short time! They deserve a congratulations at the very least." The nearby men in the line relaxed their salutes disgustedly but chuckled nonetheless, as they slowly clicked on that the ceremony was a waste of time and they'd been the butt of a joke.

"At ease, lads, back to your fires," the General said, and they began unbuckling their mail good naturedly, throwing ribald insults between each other. Some produced wineskins that they'd hidden underneath and continuing with the night there and then. As they reached the camp, the King's men and Sain guards mingling together at this point, the merchants went wide-eyed at seeing the red cloaks that could only signify the royal guards. No-one believed the gangly young warrior that had come into camp yelling nonsense that the King was coming, it seemed too soon. Their wagons immediately became a flurry of activity as they filled cups of ale to the brim and heated some of the more expensive wine as a gesture of goodwill to the King and Prince, begrudgingly pouring one for the General and his son at the narrowing of eyes they received from the Sains.

Smells of freshly cooked spiced meats wafted from further into camp and a merchant that usually only produced unflavoured pork was red-faced and struggling to lift a huge suckling pig to roast over a fire for the new arrivals. All in all, it had turned into more of a party for the King and his men rather than a war band gathering to rout rebels from Annar territory; but although the General and the king had dismounted and given their reins to another, the men knew they were still expected to act like warriors.

They rubbed down their horses before picketing them with the others and continued to draw lots at who would take the next watch; even this far into Annarite territory, they were vigilant - the General would accept no less.

Alnor sat with the prince and his men, including the ugly Varnan, at a fire away from their fathers. He yearned to spend time with his Father, but also needed to step out of his shadow, to be his own man and he knew that Prince Krinar was the way to do that. A lot of the men were near his own age and completely devoted to the prince. Alnor fitted in better there, understanding the humour between them; swapping stories that didn't involve 'the old times' was invigorating and the fact that the prince never belittled him, despite the huge difference in social standing, made him feel like a new man.

"So, Alnor, don't you have two younger brothers? What are they like?" Krinar said. A spark of rage kindled in Alnor's stomach at Balzor's inclusion in his family which he smothered with a placid smile before anybody noticed.

"One brother actually, sire, and one my father adopted as survivor of the attack on Satern. Alkor's rash, true, but will be a fine man one day; Balzor, however, is a toerag," Alnor said thinly, getting a round of laughter from the small group, Krinar included.

"It is to be expected my friend. The blood of peasants is of different stock from the likes of us; that's why I choose my men carefully. To root out the roughness from my guard, so to speak," Krinar said loftily, wholly believing the words he was saying.

Alnor felt the words resonate with him and nodded eagerly, these views were in line with his own. He'd only ever talked like this with Petra. Only Varnan didn't nod and instead looked like a dog with his hackles raised. Krinar waved his hand at the sullen man, dismissing his scowl.

"Being a peasant doesn't diminish *your* value, Varnan. Stop pouting," he said, Varnan settling back down with a grumpy mutter, causing Krinar to roll his eyes at Alnor and change the subject. Alnor chuckled, earning him a glare from the sulking veteran which he ignored, as he listened to the prince tell them about his own siblings, all girls and at least 5 years younger.

"You should be thankful you have brother's, Alnor. Sisters are all about lovely dresses and tea parties, I'd have relished a brother to spar and sup ale with!" Krinar said.

"BrothER!" Alnor emphasised, his voice slightly angry, alarming him and forcing him to add more. "Balzor isn't my brother, sire. However much he wants to be a Sain." He thought he saw a gleam enter Krinar's eye at the comment, but it was quickly masked.

"Apologies my friend, you'd already mentioned that," Krinar said, sounding anything *but* sorry. "Still, Alkor sounds very similar to how I remember your father. He'll be a great man one day, as you are," he added. Alnor flushed with embarrassment at the compliment, muttering thanks he received a sneer from Varnan as a result, making him flush a deeper red than before.

The fire was beginning to burn down in front of them and the camp was dulling from a celebratory mood to a chilled vibe, men staring into flames and nursing the last of their ale as merchants shut the flaps on their wagons and retired to their caravans for the night, purses fat with silver. Watches ended and the disgruntled men kicked the next in line up from beside the fire, sour at missing the night but delighted at making their wine-soaked friends take the next watch, struggling to stay awake with stomachs full of ale and food.

Alnor watched the sparks from their own failing fire rise feebly into the sky to join the now visible stars which, in turn, gleamed brightly next to the toenail-shaped moon on an otherwise black sky. He was content and began to wish for a way to excuse himself to his blankets. As if reading his mind, after a few minutes silence, Krinar clapped his hands making the men around the glowing embers jump and chuckle dryly. Looking pointedly at the fire with his father and the General, who were in the process of clasping arms and retiring themselves, he stood, and the men surrounding the fire hastily stood with him.

"I think it's time we called it a night, lads. It's been a long day, and my bed is calling me," the prince said. The men murmured a chorus of "Aye" and "You're right there" as they trudged off into the gloom to find their tents. Krinar clasped arms with

Alnor, slapping his other hand on to his shoulder as they released arms.

"We'll talk more on this raid, you and I," Krinar promised. Alnor formally bowed.

"Of course, sire, I bid you good night," he replied.

The prince inclined his head and turned and Alnor realised with a start that Varnan was still present, still sneering at him for his fawning over the prince. Alnor scowled at the older man, who smirked and shook his head.

"Come, Varnan. I've absolutely no idea where my tent was erected, I assume next to yours somewhere?" Krinar said, laughing at his ignorance.

"Yes sire, if you'll follow me," Varnan said, throwing one last contemptuous look at Alnor before slowly walking away.

"Until tomorrow, my friend," Krinar threw over his shoulder as he followed his pet.

Alnor's mind still buzzed at the night, and the prince had called him friend. *Friend*! He kicked dirt over the last of the sizzling wood, extinguishing it completely. Smoke hissed for a moment before he smothered it fully, knowing his father wouldn't shirk from berating his son if a fire broke out in the very area he was sat that night. Turning towards where his father previously sat, he saw one of the other men doing the same, his father and the King nowhere to be seen.

It's alright to berate me when he doesn't even put out his own fire, he thought whilst walking drunkenly towards where their tent was pitched. The wind was bitterly cold now the night had set in, the warmth of the day now dissipated. The once friendly hills looked ominous in the moonlight and, if it wasn't for other men in the vicinity, Alnor would've shivered. As it was, he settled for increasing his pace to reach his blankets quickly, nodding briskly at them as he passed, but not stopping at offers of more wine or games of dice. He'd drunk with a Prince tonight, and he didn't want to drop himself down the food chain again; he liked being at the top.

As he reached his tent, the flap was slightly open, but no light came from within. His Father's snores could be heard, signifying a long night of tossing and turning until he finally succumbed to sleep. Aldred Sain sounded like a bear in his sleep, and it was no surprise that even his closest friends had brought padded earmuffs to block out the sound. He would have to get his own after tonight, no matter the cost. Kicking off his boots as he lifted the flap, he grimaced at the standard issue tent that they'd brought. Just enough room for two rolls of blankets with a small gap between, it was what the common soldiers brought on campaign. His father had said they'd all have them; to help move quickly and unencumbered from wagons but he couldn't imagine the prince in such quarters. He took off his shirt, shivering now nobody could see his weakness, and dove under the blankets attempting to cover his ears best he could.

But despite the breathing of the tent as the wind blew, and the bass of his father's snores reverberating through the thin floor, his mood couldn't be dampened. He had supped with a Prince who had called him his friend.

*****

Prince Krinar stalked through the camp with Varnan at his back mulling over the night. Varnan was filling him in on things he'd missed - even he couldn't see everything. From the cringing look on Alnor's face, it was evident that the lad adored him, but Varnan had watched him like he'd asked, so he endured the report.

"So, it seems we've already ensnared him, sire," Varnan finished quietly. He glanced around again to ensure nobody was listening, although this didn't matter as these were loyal men - not to his father, to him! But you could never be too careful, and Varnan was more his man than any other.

"You've done well, Varnan. Get some rest," Krinar interrupted, nodding as he bowed and stalked off into the night. He knew he didn't give Varnan the respect he deserved, but a man like that needed to be kept on a tight leash. *Let him off that leash every so often, and he'll be satisfied* Krinar thought. He opened the flap to his tent which was double the standard size to envelop the fold up bed he'd brought, complete with a table at its base for private meals. He couldn't be expected to eat at the fires *every* night after all, and enough of his men could spread the load evenly between them. He'd known from the casual small talk that night that Alnor shared his views but had suppressed them for reasons unknown. It was his aim to bring those views out, he needed the man on his side. Another noble son in the fold would bring much more legitimacy.

As he settled down into his cushioned bed, he knew he only had to tease those views out of him to slowly bring him over to the cause without the lad realising what had happened. He needed to think it was his own choice, or it could never work. Smiling wickedly into the darkness, he drifted off into an easy sleep, mind clear and resolute. The plan was set.

Chapter 6

The sun's slender fingers grasping through the half-open tent flap signified dawn had come. Alnor groaned groggily, knuckling his fists into his eyes trying to blot out the unwelcome light. How much had he drunk last night? His head felt like he'd been kicked by a horse and by how dry his mouth was, he might as well have been drinking sand. Reluctantly freeing one hand from its efforts, he groped blindly to where he knew his water skin lay and unstopped it, drinking greedily. As the water quenched his thirst, his felt his parched tongue decrease in size by at least half.

Opening his eyes fully, the dim dawn light still sent a painful jolt to his head. He realised his father wasn't in the tent and his bed was made. The man could never sleep in and now Alnor felt obliged to emerge from the tent as well. Before stoppering the water skin again, he poured a generous helping over his face, the shock of the cold liquid jerking him awake further. He dragged on his shirt, left messily on the floor from the night before and almost threw up when bending over for his boots before going out into the crisp dawn air.

The sun wasn't as bountiful as the day before, so his face felt the cold keenly. There were two men heating water over the fire in a large cauldron. There was one for each group of six and they shared carrying it between the mounts throughout the day; anything larger would have needed pack horses or carts which would hinder the speed needed to hit the Hounds before they knew what was happening. It would be porridge for breakfast, as usual.

Nodding to both men, who, to his chagrin, barely even inclined their heads, he walked away in search of his father and hopefully a better breakfast from one of the merchants. Porridge was a necessity in a camp, but if there were better helpings then he might as well take them. As he strolled through, he saw many men with their heads in their hands, clearly regretting their ale consumption the night before. He smiled broadly at these men as they forced themselves to see who was passing, the looks given in return made him smile all the wider. If they couldn't handle their ale, they shouldn't drink so much! The throbbing in his own head had subsided slightly - though not completely vanished - so he felt the need to belittle those who hadn't recovered, as was his right. Some men just gave him the finger, others ignored him completely, but some chuckled and accepted the taunting, knowing it was deserved.

Within a minute he'd already passed the tents of his father's men and gone into the realm of the Royal Guards. Not many in this camp were even awake, let alone out of their tents to prepare breakfast. His father held an iron discipline in his men, something that clearly lacked amongst the prince's - not that he'd ever dare admit it. The smell of baked pastries rode on the wind, blowing towards his nostrils from the east. He followed it like his life depended on it.

Before he reached the smells origin, he heard muted laughter and the sound of crackling logs as though adding to the hunger of the flames. He turned directly towards the sound, having to step over taut tent lines to avoid the tips of pegs which were both full of morning dew that glistened in the light. He left the town of tents, entering a small encampment of merchant's wagons. The sight in front of him was unrealistic at best.

King Malker and the General stood leaning on a wagon, crumbs of pastry on their shirts and licking their fingers. They were pleading with the merchant's wife for more of the delicacy. Pleading! The merchant himself sat on a tree stump he carried around with the wagon, if the worn marks on the rim were anything to go by. His balding head already covered with a sheen of sweat and his straggly beard ready to blow off his face in the morning breeze. He was laughing and holding his hands up helplessly towards both men, conceding defeat to his wife's scowls at having to give up their breakfast for others.

The plump, grey haired lady with her rosy-red cheeks glared at Alnor as he came around the corner then set herself to work kneading more dough, muttering sullenly. Alnor was infuriated at the sight – whoever heard of a King begging a merchant's wife. He hid it well as he stalked up to his Father and the King with a sickly smile on his face, forever acting the doting son. Bowing to the King, a bow he had to hold for a few seconds before he was noticed, and nodding to his father *after* the King had acknowledged him, he petitioned the plump merchant's wife for a pastry of his own and took the explosion of air from her as an unwanted agreement.

The crinkles of his smile faded from Aldred's face, if not quite from the King's, he looked firmly at his dishevelled son and frowned. "From the look on your face, ale doesn't agree with you Alnor," Aldred said sternly. Although the King didn't react, Alnor thought he saw amusement in his eyes.

"If we were leaving today, what kind of example would you set the men? Them being drunk is one thing, but you must be ready to give orders at a moment's notice, even in familiar territory. *Don't* let it happen again."

In the space of seconds, what Alnor would've hoped would be a nice breakfast with his father and the King, turned into scolding that made him look like a child. He strangled his response, knowing to answer in anger would only drive a wedge between them, making his life even harder in the long run. "I apologise father. Meeting Prince Krinar for the first time and seeing the King again went to my head, as I think it did many of the men, though that's no excuse," he said, trying to be as humble as possible given the situation.

Surprise crossed his father's face before he hid it, and a glance at the King showed a slightly curious look directed at Aldred. Aldred recovered quickly and nodded at his son in acceptance of the apology. "See that you don't," he said, finalising the conversation, regretting that he no longer knew how to hold one with his son.

Alnor, scrabbling to rectify the morning's mood, bowed to his father. "When you say *if* we were leaving today, what do you mean? I thought we were leaving as soon as we met the King?" Alnor asked, gesturing at Malker as he mentioned his name.

"We would be lad, if your friend Petra had brought the men on patrol. As it is, we've seen neither hide nor hair of him or any of the patrols, so we'll wait one more day before moving out," Aldred said disapprovingly - he hated delays. Even the King had a hard look on his face, but he kept his counsel. It was the General's son, not his, and it was his lead that he followed.

"He will come, father, Your Majesty. He's a good man. A good soldier. If he's not here, there is a valid reason for it. I'd wager my life!" Alnor said, voice close to begging.

As he rose quietly from his stump, the merchant stared aghast having dined with three of the most powerful men in the land, the King being one! He crept behind them, staying in Alnor's field of view long enough to throw the youth a look of sympathy, before disappearing through the wagon door at the side. His wife left three more flaky pastries on the step of the wagon and hid out back with her husband. The troubles of great men were not their concern.

Aldred stayed quiet for a moment and King Malker interceded, to Alnor's blatant relief. "Now then, Aldred. If your lad says the man's reliable, I believe him. He seems a decent judge of character. We'll wait one more day before we move out. They can catch us on the road otherwise; patrols move much quicker than a contingent of two hundred and fifty men," Malker reasoned. Alnor threw him a grateful look, which was noticed by his father.

Slightly peeved that the King had stepped in but wanting to save face, Aldred shrugged and leaned back on the wagon. Alnor moved to pick up the pastries, passing them out between them and picking slight pieces off, his appetite gone in his father's tirade. He ate every morsel though and refused to look like he was sulking.

"Right," his father began, rubbing his hands together briskly and brushing the crumbs off his shirt, making a content sound in his throat. "Go and wake the rest of the men, son. We won't waste the day. Get them to pair up and spar for an hour then we'll set up a run to Torizo's walls and back. The first one back gets three nights off watch! What do you say?" Alnor, keen to regain ground lost on his night's drinking, nodded enthusiastically and brushed off his own shirt.

"Of course, Father. By your leave? Your Majesty," Alnor said, giving both men short bows, before walking slowly out of the clearing, resisting the urge to massage his temples. Thunder still sounded in his head, but he couldn't let it show. He stopped behind the wagon and rested his head on the side wall, as he was about to leave, he heard his father start to talk.

"I told you, old friend. The lad just isn't a man. If my father gave me half as much grief as I just gave him, I would've given an earful back. For Ezi's sake, I even gave the order last night that men *could* drink and he still sulks like a child. He's good at hiding it mind, but not good enough. I blame myself; I was never there, even after his mother died," he added, voice lowering slightly at the mention of his late wife. He'd never gotten over her, and part of the reason he put duty before all else was to fill the void that she'd left in his soul. Malker clapped his hand on his general's shoulder, giving him a slight shake of sympathy. He knew his friend wouldn't take sympathetic words but sometimes the gesture was enough.

Behind the ring of wagons, Alnor seethed at what he'd overheard and stomped away in the direction of his men. He'd work them hard today and he himself would work harder still. He'd show his father that he was the man that he didn't think he was! As the proud, angry young man stalked away, a dark shape crawled silently from beneath the merchant's wagon, ignoring the rest of the General's conversation with the King. Varnan had got what he needed, and his face twisted into a hideous smile. Aldred Sain was making this easy! Not bothering to shake the droplets of water from his cloak, he shadowed the young lad's footsteps, taking care not to leave a trail for anyone to connect his being there. He knew his work, and the prince valued him for it. Knowledge was power, even if the knowledge was attained in a less than honourable way. With that in mind, he veered off towards the prince's tent, ready to divulge such knowledge to his Lord, knowing it could only bring their plans to fruition sooner.

*****

The air whooshed out of Alnor as he hit the floor bodily, having been knocked on his back by Terva for the third time. He wore a moronic grin every time he offered a hand to help him up. Alnor waved the offer of help away, rolling onto his hands and knees and attempted to hide the wheezing sound coming out of his throat. He felt lucky that it was still relatively early, the morning dew having left the ground damp and not yet given into the dust that was trying to claw its way free. The reason he refused was his father's gaze.

He'd noticed him come around the corner of the outside ring of tents; it was that momentary lapse in concentration that had allowed Terva to flatten him once again. It wasn't that he was ashamed of being beaten by Terva – after all, the man was a formidable warrior and a second born Annarite like himself - but he couldn't give up with his father watching. So, forcing himself to his feet and putting on a grin to match the ox in front of him, he settled into a stance once again.

His eyes took in the lumbering form moving towards him, knowing the slow, dopey look of the man was completely an act to mask his first move and keep his opponent on edge. True to form, Terva suddenly darted forward, his huge bulk looking odd moving so swiftly, but Alnor was ready. Their practice swords met with a crash that sent a jarring feeling shooting down his arm, numbing his shoulder as he stopped the strength of the larger man. Years of training and instinct kicked in and he whirled out of the contest of force, using his smaller size and speed to advantage and pressing the attack.

Terva still had the stupid grin on his face as he turned to match the onslaught, throwing in counterattacks when an opening presented itself, which Alnor turned away with minute taps rather than meeting them head on again. It was one of these attacks which gave Alnor his tiny window to strike. Feeling his father's gaze on his back, he performed a flurry of attacks intended to put Terva on the back foot, knowing the man resorted to strength in desperation. When the typical overbearing strike came from Terva, Alnor didn't block it. Instead, he took a large step to his left and dodged the attack completely hoping Terva would be unbalanced. Sure enough, the strength of the intended blow carried Terva a slight step past Alnor and before he could recover, Alnor swept the man's legs out from under him and placed the tip of the sword under Terva's chin after he crashed heavily on to his back, driving the wind out of him. Even then, his stupid grin stayed on his face as he swatted the sword away and raised his arm, which Alnor took, dragging the man to his feet.

"I've gotta let you win sometimes, kid" Terva said, massaging the base of his back with one hand, trying to catch his breath.

Alnor let out a bark of laughter and punched him on the shoulder. "I'll give you a breather, old man," Alnor said slyly.

"You'll need it to try and beat me to the walls and back." Terva groaned, he hated running. Although he wasn't fat, there was only so much speed a ball of muscle can reach before his weight inevitably slowed him down; maintaining a steady pace was easy, winning a race wasn't.

Alnor accepted the practice sword off Terva, taking that and his own to a small pile next to a sagging tent, the unofficial storage tent for their gear. Most of the men there had finished their bouts and placed their own weapons on the pile already. They were stretching their legs ready for the run. Alnor knew he was one of the fastest there, it wouldn't be too much of a challenge for him to outstrip the others and get back to camp first. With this in mind, he decided to spice things up a bit.

"Right lads! Last three to get back to camp take the full night's watch. First three get as much ale as they want. And *I'll* be paying!" he said, getting a mixed response.

Most of them cheered, knowing it'd be a close run for the first three. Others, Terva included, scowled. They knew they weren't quick enough for the free ale so it'd be a fight as to who took the watch.

Alnor glanced towards his father, seeing the shadow of a smirk on his face at the challenge he'd set. The General inclined his head at his son and moved off back into the tents. That, more than anything, let Alnor know his father approved.

With a warm feeling in his belly, he made his way over to the road, the procession of guards following him in anticipation of the offer of free ale. The dew had evaporated so every footfall created a slight puff of dust which the wind devoured greedily and swept into the air. Men at the back of the run would get the worst of it just like men at the back of a mounted column. It prompted most of them to wrap cloth around their nose and faces, choosing the extra heat to breathing in remnants of the wind's meal.

The rest of the camp was only just stirring, bleary eyes peering out tent flaps at the insane group who were joyous despite the hangovers. These men either couldn't handle their ale, or hadn't stuck to the same arduous training regime that the Sain Guard had, Alnor thought. Only the older men had surfaced properly - the same men that had shared the fire with the King and the General the night before. It seemed the King's guard had more discipline than the prince's. Some of them rose curiously, and when Terva let them know of the bet, they joined the ranks eagerly, willing to risk the night's watch on a chance of the General's son paying for their drunkenness.

Tying his own cloth around his face, Alnor stopped in the centre of the road, men arraying themselves to either side of him. The unfortunate ones had to line up behind them thereby losing a slight start advantage, or stand off the road at the side, which would force them to dodge the random shrubs that lay off the path providing they couldn't get ahead, of course.

It came as a shock when the ranks opened slightly at the side of Alnor, and his father stepped into the gap, the shadow of a smirk giving way to a full-blown grin at his son's astonished face. "You didn't think your old dad would let all the pups have the fun, did you?" Aldred said to the chuckles of the men. "Besides, it'll be nice to have you buying my ale tonight, son!"

Alnor laughed, but it was cut short as he and his father were barged aside by an already running figure. Terva's laugh boomed over his shoulder as he began the race early, determined not to come last. "Snooze ya lose, pups!" he shouted, which was the cue for the rest of them, Sains included, to roar a challenge and set off after the ox of a man who led the race. It didn't take long for most of them to pass Terva who scowled each time someone did, muttering curses into his self-made mask. Alnor spent the first few minutes keeping pace with his father, feeling obliged but restrained. Glancing to the side, he saw the General had barely broken a sweat, so he picked up the pace. Aldred matched his son, amusement written on his face, then sped up slightly more. He laughed aloud when Alnor allowed a surprised look flit across his features, evidently shocked at the older man's apparent ease at keeping up with him.

"As I said riding on the road, son, there's life in your old man yet!" Aldred taunted, before breaking into a sprint with a whoop, a lifetime of training and war keeping his body fit despite his age, allowing him to break through the leading group.

Kicking himself, Alnor barrelled forward through a group of startled guards, who were still recovering from their General forcing his way through them, then began his pursuit, intent on his prey. Soon, both men were lathered in sweat and surrounded by men of similar dispositions, all fighting for the first three spots. With the hulking walls getting closer and closer, the excitement sparking between the leading group was growing, but their strength was ebbing. The sun had climbed through the now brilliantly blue sky, the hills no longer a buffer to the heat, and its earlier comforting rays soon became a hindrance and sapped the endurance of men who had put everything into the race much too soon.

Aldred and Alnor both felt the lag in speed, but the Sain pride kept them going and allowed them to stubbornly creep away from the dismayed guards who'd thought their fitness was second to none. Sain pride could only carry them so far, though, and as they cantered into Torizo's blessed shade, guards at the gate staring incredulously at the haphazard string of sweaty, panting men, they began to lag themselves. Merchants queuing to get into the city dodged out of the way, grumbling about people with too much time on their hands. Slapping the weathered stone, clammy hands leaving an ingrained handprint on the dry, cold surface, both Sains turned for the return lap. What they expected to see, was the same men they'd just broken away from; what they saw was Terva's grinning face just passing the group, shocked faces mirrored down the line.

"Slow and steady wins the race lads!" he mocked, passing a laughing Aldred and a bewildered Alnor. The men in the group that was previously leading attempted a burst of speed, anger fuelling energy at the mockery, but that just depleted their last reserves. The steady pace that Terva had set himself had won out over the headlong rush and he knew it. A moronic grin plastered onto his face. Terva hit his own meaty hand on the wall and spun on his heel, eager to catch his superiors after their assumption that he'd be a mile behind.

The once leading group tried to good-naturedly hinder the huge man, but he barrelled through them with a roar and sped up slightly. Breathing heavily now, the Sains tried to catch their lost breath which allowed Terva to gradually gain ground on the duo. Blazing beams of light scorched the top of their heads as the sun reached its zenith, the final of the morning dew burning away, making the dust clog the air and stick to sweat like a beggar to a silver piece.

In direct comparison to Terva and the Sains, the larger men of the group were now gaining on the leading group who had just got to the walls themselves. Realising what it was all about, the bewildered guards at the gate started to cheer and egg them on. The small line of merchants waiting at the city were now laughing rather than grumbling as the guards who thought themselves the elite, were being gained on by the older giants at the back.

"Who needs youth when you've got experience, eh lads? Go an' get 'em!" one of the merchants shouted, fist pumping the air as Terva ran past the man, basking in the encouragement. But a lifetime of training and a body created for war soon recovered and Aldred Sain stopped his laboured gasps and began to breathe easier again.

Throwing an apologetic look to his son, who struggled to regain his wind, he began to creep forward and into first place. Alnor was secretly distraught at his father beating him, but the main worry was that Terva would catch him. *That* would be weeks of taunting from the bearlike man, he'd never hear the end of it. Focusing on techniques drilled into him, he tried to calm his breathing. *In through the nose, out through the mouth. In, out* Alnor thought, ignoring the footfalls behind him. Though the exercises were working, it wasn't a secret Seeress healing. So Alnor had to settle for a battle of determination, one that he wasn't willing to lose. Terva was right alongside him now, but the strain of the race was beginning to show, even with his slow and steady pace.

As they began to reach the first of the hills, both men were blown and only sheer will kept them putting one foot in front of the other. It grated on them both to see the General seemingly out for a stroll in front of them, slowing his speed as to not humiliate them too badly. The contest was now between Alnor and Terva. At that point the men in the groups behind were just fighting to not be the last three, knowing that they'd never catch up and gain the prize they'd originally wanted.

It was almost five miles to the city walls from the camp and five miles back. All

Alnor could think was that five miles seemed a lot shorter on horseback. Though most of them could comfortably jog across five miles of rough terrain in full kit, the headlong rush at the start had crippled them. So, coming into the last mile of the race, they were greeted by hoots and jeers from the camp as they saw the bedraggled group come through the hills.

Alnor focused furiously on the camp, intending to spar with the culprits the day after. It was that focus that brought a bright red cloak into view at the forefront of the group, with his hands behind his back and wearing a slightly amused face. Recognising the Prince instantly, Alnor gritted his teeth and put on another burst of speed. To lose was one thing, to lose in front of a Prince was another. Terva growled something under his breath but didn't waste any precious air on insults as he tried to match the younger man's speed and failed.

"I'm still third, pup. You'll buy my ale tonight!" he shouted as the end of the race was nigh. It was that lack of concentration that led to disaster. As Aldred crossed into the tent line, with Alnor close behind, they heard a yell and a crash behind them. Around a hundred paces from the end, Terva's shout had made him miss a small rut in the road and had sent him sprawling into the dust. The men behind howled in triumph at seeing a race they'd thought lost open up again, the two hundred pace gap suddenly seeming like a step as Terva rose and began limping furiously.

"He's not going to make it," Aldred whispered to his son, a slight regret in his voice despite it being a friendly race. Alnor shook his head and made his decision.

Tearing towards Terva as fast as his tired body would allow, he threw the man's trunk like arm over his shoulder, grunting as his body protested at the extra weight.

"You'd better not drink too much you great fucking lummox," Alnor said, his voice strained as the pair staggered towards the tent to the angry bellows of unfairness from behind them. The men at the tents were screaming encouragement and laughing as the pair crossed the tent line, Terva shaking his fist at the victory.

"Oh, my hero!" Terva fawned mockingly, crushing Alnor into a bear hug.

Alnor sputtered and choked as the man's disgusting sweaty chest hair scratched his face, the men around them laughing all the harder. Even the men who were sulking as they arrived back at camp had their bad mood dissolved at seeing the young Sain struggling to break free. Wrestling himself from Terva's grip, Alnor aimed a swift kick at the man, connecting brutally with his testicles, bringing out a chorus of "oooohs" from the spectators, followed by even more laughter at Terva's swearing as he doubled over.

"It's alright, the ale will take the sting off," Alnor said, spitting out bits of hair from his mouth and rubbing the sweat disgustedly off his face.

"I'll be drinking double, after that," Terva gasped, still massaging his offended area.

Alnor laughed and threw the man's arm over his shoulder again. "I suppose we can start now, to numb the ache," Alnor said, still chuckling. "Coming, father?" he asked over his shoulder, all the while trying to act like he couldn't see the prince walking towards the merchant's carts, like that wasn't the reason he wanted to go there.

"I'll meet you there, I need to change out of these clothes first. Gone are the days where I drink all day and survive," Aldred said with a smile, before walking off in the direction of the tents.

The rest of the men dispersed now that the fun was over and Alnor staggered towards the merchant's carts with his hulking load over his shoulder and Terva kept reminding everyone he almost beat a Sain. Alnor didn't care and even played along with the jest; it didn't matter to him, the prince *had* seen him win, after all.

*****

Aldred walked slowly through the camp, subtly massaging his legs in the pretence of warming up his hands. He knew most men wouldn't be fooled; the day was sweltering, but they pretended not to notice. The excitement of the free ale had made his men stupid causing them to wear themselves out too quickly. Even he himself had burned out too early but recovered fairly easily. It seemed he needed to make his men run more often; in enemy territory becoming blown could mean losing your life and possibly those of your entire squad. He chuckled dryly to himself, even when in a casual, fun race with his son he couldn't switch off the General in him.

When Alnor had run out to help Terva, Aldred had felt a fierce pride even though he'd had to be prompted into action. If it was something Aldred would use this time with his son for, it would be to force him to become his own man; too often he was looking for approval - either from certain senior men in the guards or Aldred himself.

In the past couple of days, the prince had been at the forefront of those Alnor was trying to impress which made Aldred extremely wary. He'd never mention it to the King, but the prince seemed to have a darkness, hidden behind a jovial nature and the pleasures of rank. He'd seen the way the act of nobility slipped with Krinar in the past, and scorn had crept through. Usually with people of a lesser rank. Aldred would watch that relationship and hopefully nurture his son to follow in his own footsteps rather than the prince's — not that he could openly announce to his son that he didn't want him to emulate the heir to the throne. Even secretly, insulting the prince could lead to bad blood when he finally became King; maybe not for him but for his own sons. A slight to the King isn't quickly forgotten.

Shaking his head and clearing thoughts of duty, he broke into the clearing where his tent was based and stripped his sweat-sodden shirt off his back. A slight wind kissed the perspiration on his chest, but it barely did anything to cool his body. The fire was completely burnt out, red charcoal glaring out of the remnants and struggling to put heat into the air despite being beaten.

Breakfast – plain porridge hanging over the fire – was a congealed mess of sludge mixed with berries but seeing it made his stomach growl with hunger all the same. He fetched his bowl from the tent and shovelled his share into it, digging in instantly. Being older than both Terva and Alnor, he needed a proper stomach lining if he was to match their drinking habits; he couldn't be out-drank by his own son! Stopping short of licking the bowl, Aldred grabbed the nearest water skin to the fire and swilled the bowl, put the stopper back on then went into his tent.

He sighed at seeing his son's messy roll of blankets; making the bed - even a makeshift one in a tent - was a great way to gain a positive look on the day. If you complete one job, one you literally *could not* fail at doing, you started the day winning at something. It was an outlook Aldred had had since he was a boy and tried to instil it in his children but, since he'd missed half their lives, he couldn't dictate everything they do - not without them resenting him at least.

He splashed some water from Alnor's water skin over his face then threw on a clean shirt, hanging the sweaty one up to dry and air out. Airing out was good enough when women weren't around, men weren't meant to smell like flowers. Striding out of the tent feeling refreshed, he stretched his limbs with a slight groan then set off the way he came. He kept his walk as slow as when he came into the camp, nodding to men who'd returned from the race cursing their luck. They saluted him best they could whilst massaging pulled muscles and Aldred waved their attempts away with a wry smile. *That'll teach them to forget their training for the sake of a few cups of ale!* He thought.

He soon located his son, the sound of Terva's booming laughter rebounding off the tents near the merchant wagons. Coming closer, he heard snippets of the conversation and smiled to himself. "... and the pup thought he could beat me easily, but the big man doesn't give up so easy, oh no!" Terva boasted, arm still around Alnor who was rolling his eyes good naturedly. In his other arm, a cup of ale was already half empty and after a hasty salute to Aldred, tipped its remaining contents all over Alnor's face. Alnor shoved Terva off himself, sputtering all the while and furiously wiping his face.

"Oops, sorry kid! Good job I'm not paying for the ale, eh?" Terva guffawed, to the glee of everybody in the group.

Rather than explode and make himself look like a child, Alnor casually ordered Terva another drink and performed a mock bow as he passed it over. Terva snorted but raised the cup in thanks before taking a huge gulp. Throughout the exchange, Alnor kept shooting glances towards the prince, who was lounging against one of the wagons nonchalantly but taking everything in. He, like the rest of the group, was chuckling at the display. Whether he could see the glances was unclear, but at seeing the General enter the clearing, he straightened his pose and bowed formally.

"General! Please, come and sit. From what I hear you won the race with ease? That deserves a drink, and I believe your son is paying?" He added with a smirk at Alnor, who sighed dramatically then looked at his Father and grinned. Aldred made a show of raising his eyebrows to hurry his drink along then sitting on the logs, tapping his foot in mock impatience.

Krinar sat down next to the General, instantly throwing his arm over his shoulder and talking like an old friend. Although he didn't wear his unease openly, Alnor could see this was more of an act than anything, since his father shifted uncomfortably despite his open smile. To disengage his father, Alnor raised the newly filled cup that the eager merchant had given, prompting his father to rise and accept it from him with an almost inaudible sigh of relief. If he felt slighted by the timely rise, Krinar didn't show it as he rose with him and struck up a conversation easily.

"My father did say he'd be around today, General" he began. "I think, although he doesn't mention it, he's missed having an old friend around. It's the same old faces in the same old city these days..."

"That's three times in one sentence you've used the word 'old' in relationship to me, son!" boomed a voice from the far side of the clearing, making Krinar flinch.

Turning, Aldred saw King Malker enter the circle of wagons with two men at his flanks, two men that he knew well from campaigning in his younger years.

"Sire, you didn't tell me you still kept such shitty company," Aldred said, a mischievous look on his face. "Ezi knows these men should be at their hearths with grandchildren by now." King Malker roared with laughter at the jest as the two men pushed past in outrage.

"And you? I'm surprised after running this morning that you can walk with those old sticks you call legs!" said a small wiry man, who wasn't quite bald. The little hair he did have was pure white. His apparent age didn't dull his look of a warrior though; scars ridged his arms, melded into the lean cords of muscle that ran down them.

His companion in comparison, had more hair than a woman. He wore it tied back and hung over his shoulder, a trailing blaze of white down his back. It was blatantly obvious they were twins, despite the differences in hair. They moved in on the General and embraced him, the action seeming much less forced than Aldred's embrace with Krinar earlier. As they broke apart, Aldred beckoned for Alnor to come to him.

"Bayar, Neve, this is my son. Alnor, the bald one is Bayar, and the woman lookalike is Neve. Don't let Bayar hear you call him bald, though, it's a sore subject," said Aldred, dancing away lithely as Bayar aimed a punch at his ribcage. Alnor laughed and nodded to the men, receiving a cheerful nod in return.

"Introductions out of the way, let's get pissed!" Malker shouted over them, already getting the merchant's attention for more ale and wine.

The merchant, who was happy enough serving regular soldiers, was now flustered knowing he'd spend the day serving the King, his General, and their heirs. He shouted at his wife to get more wine.

"And make it the good stuff!" the flabby man said over his shoulder, prompting a cheer from the two twins.

Alnor soon felt excluded from the group. Most of the men in the clearing had known each other for many years, and though the prince hadn't been around as long as the older men, he'd fought and drank with them, so it was easy to fall in as they bantered and laughed. He ached to join them, to feel the bond that these men so clearly had, but he didn't find the opportunity to in the jovial conversation. So, he settled back to bide his time, trying hard to keep the resentful feelings from showing on his face. The hopes of bonding with his father had been dashed for the day, as had his excitement for drinking with the prince again.

Letting his thoughts wander, he sipped his wine in what he hoped wasn't a sullen way and daydreamed about his first skirmish with the rebels. He'd never killed a man and the only blood he'd drawn had been in fist fights; bloodying somebody's nose wasn't quite the same as spilling their lifeblood on to the soil. It was something he'd anticipated for years, something he began to yearn for as he caught snippets of the conversation around him about old battles or duels fought in the capital.

"... Almost the same as when Alnor hit the deck today before the race." Alnor jerked back to the conversation at the mention of his name. He'd found his way into the fold, Terva his saviour, thanks to his mocking over losing three duels in a row. Looking at the man's stupid grin and coupled with his glazed eyes from the mixture of ale and wine, Alnor couldn't help but laugh.

"I was lulling you into a false sense of security you stupid oaf. If you recall, it was I who flattened you after that?" Alnor challenged the drunken man.

"Everybody gets lucky sometimes, kiddo," Terva grumbled, causing the group to chuckle and breaking the ice for Alnor to enter the fray.

Despite his instinct to instantly engage the prince, he thought it more respectful to speak to the King first. "Sire, how did you and my father meet? He hasn't told me the story," he asked, hoping the story wasn't a long one. Aldred barked a laugh but let the King tell the story.

"Well, the Sains weren't always a noble house in this land," Malker began, amused. "But they were well thought of - a respectable family of warriors whose sons always distinguished themselves in our legion. Then your father came along and started his official training. Within days it was obvious he was Annarite born, so he got pushed on to harsher training, that only an Annarite could stand. The problem was, this training was held in the grounds of the palace, where the King's personal guards spar. My sister Edi, she saw a dashing new recruit who'd shown untold potential with unnaturally blue eyes, and she fell in love. You can imagine my reaction when I found them kissing behind the stable!" he snorted.

The General choked back a laugh and held up his hands in defeat. "In my very meagre defence sire, I wasn't aware exactly who she was at the time... not that it would've stopped me," Aldred said slyly, getting a guffaw out of the twins.

Terva wasn't even listening, choosing the moment to refill his cup. Alnor stopped gaping at his father, seeing a totally different side to him.

"*You* kissed the King's daughter on palace grounds?!" Alnor blurted out, bringing the group's focus onto him and causing him to mumble an apology at the interruption; the King just laughed before carrying on. Krinar was watching his father intently, slight surprise on his face.

"Your Father wasn't always the dutiful General, lad. He was a rogue for years! But, back to the tale. Seeing this, I challenged him to a duel, not to the death of course, the kingdom needed warriors, but to regain the family honour. Realising who I was when I announced my second name, your father almost shit in his pants, although he had to accept," Malker finished with a grin. Gesturing at Aldred to continue, he took a generous swig of his own wine and smacked his lips.

"After that there isn't much to say. I put the heir to the throne on his arse, promised not to kiss his sister again and we became best friends," Aldred stated with a shrug, causing the King to choke on his wine with an early breath of outrage.

After a moment of spluttering and coughing, Bayar pounding on his King's back whilst trying not to laugh, the King took back over the story.

"It wasn't quite like that, but I'll let you have your moment showing off to your son," he said in mock sternness. "Plus, I hadn't ascended by that time, so you had an unfair advantage," he protested.

Aldred shot the King a look, which seemed to confuse him, but he stopped the train of conversation there. Alnor, his curiosity causing him to almost dance a jig at the exchange, asked the most obvious question.

"Ascended, sire?"

Understanding dawned on Malker's face at about the same time resignation dawned on Aldred's.

"Even to your own heirs, you kept the secret my friend?" Malker said softly. "Every man around this fire knows. They've all been with us since the start and kept their oaths. Why should I be any different?" Aldred challenged.

Malker sighed and raised his hands to ward off any insult to his friend's honour, coughing to clear his throat again.

"Your heirs would find out eventually, but I'll tell you now, Alnor. I'm sure most of this you already know, lad, but I'll explain it all to put it into perspective, so bear with me," Malker said. "This must never leave your lips to another, except your brother and you must impress onto him the seriousness of keeping it secret. If the wrong people knew we were vulnerable at an early age, they'd come for us; some people only respect strength, any weakness in my family would be exploited."

Nodding solemnly to urge the King on didn't work. Malker's unwavering gaze bore into Alnor for a short, uncomfortable moment before Alnor swore not to divulge any information, lowering his eyes in shame at the slight delay in doing so. This seemed to satisfy the King, who began after another quick gulp of wine.

The men around the fire listened intently now, although the merchant mumbled an excuse after a look from Malker and scuttled away out of earshot.

"As you know, Annarites receive their talents at birth. They're stronger and faster than ordinary men and are low in numbers. It's openly known that Sarnat chooses these people himself, seeing in their thread of life that they'll be great warriors, just as Exat chooses his Seers and Seeress'. What we don't know, is why he chooses these people. Maybe he sees they will be great before they are born? We'll probably never know. If an Annarite has offspring, these are what we call second generation Annarites. These are numerous since most men have many children; you yourself are amongst this group. You're still faster and stronger than ordinary men but not quite on the level of the Annarites born into it. With me so far?" Malker said, glancing at Alnor.

Alnor was disgruntled at being openly told he wasn't as valuable as his father but wore an earnest look on his face as he nodded.

"Well, there are also the True Annarites. These men are chosen by Ezimat himself, with huge potential to lead, but they're not *destined* to do so. Almost every leader we know about is True; we're faster and stronger than even the best Annarites, but we must ascend first. At the start of our lives, we're just ordinary people," Malker explained, pausing for a second to drain the last of his wine.

Krinar took the moment to chuckle lightly and dive into the explanation himself. "No Annarite is ordinary, but I see your point father" he said lightly.

Malker inclined his head, his eyes flashed in anger at being interrupted, and disapproval emanated from the entire circle of friends except Alnor of course. Sensing the mood of the group, Krinar rose and gathered the mostly empty cups.

"My round I see. My apologies for the interruption father," he said, bowing slightly before leaving the circle and moving towards the merchant's wagon and the jug of wine. As though nothing had happened, the King moved on.

"Ascending doesn't just happen to anyone - it's a sort of awakening in yourself to power that's always been there, but out of reach. It usually happens at a point of great pressure, which is why some people might never ascend. This is the reason I took the throne over my older brother; he didn't ascend, even with our regime that practically forces our family to do so. The Kingdom of Annar must have an Annarite on the throne, so he's now my advisor - albeit reluctantly – despite living out of the royal coffers," he said. Nods and chuckles came from the men who were clearly familiar with his older brother.

Krinar came back around the corner with a tray of more wine at that moment, making the narrative stop for as Alnor leapt up to help the prince unashamedly, taking the tray and distributing the drinks. Thanks from the men and a warm smile from the prince made it worthwhile in Alnor's opinion.

Muttering his own thanks, the King took another sip and sat back with a sigh of contentment and praising the vintage of the wine. Terva, being the man he was, drank most of the cup in one gulp and refilled it instantly from the porcelain jugs to the side of him. His eyes were already glazed over and Alnor felt himself praying the big man would pass out soon. He had more than enough silver to pay for the day's drinking but was reluctant to part with more than he had to, especially for Terva.

With the King seemingly finished with his story, he was leaning back on his elbows enjoying the falling sun's rays, eyes closed. Alnor however had questions, and lots of them.

"Sire..." he prompted nervously.

Nobody wanted to disturb a moment of peace for a King and Alnor breathed a sigh of relief as Malker sat up and looked at him intently with his grey eyes, waving a hand to indicate Alnor to continue.

"When in your training did *you* ascend?" he asked.

Instantly the King's eyes darkened, and Alnor struggled not the flinch at the sudden change. He hadn't realised what an imposing presence the King had until that point - even his Father's piercing blue gaze had never sent that kind of chill through him. Luckily, the King's demeanour was aimed at the question, not at Alnor himself. When he didn't speak, Alnor took the hint and succumbed to the uncomfortable silence despite his eagerness to know more.

The twins began muttering furiously amongst themselves, bickering as only siblings did. It seemed they too feared the mood of the King in that moment. Terva's head had drooped, his square chin resting onto his huge chest, relaxed arms now spilling the wine as he fell inevitably to sleep. Krinar was looking at his father intently, as if he too was as eager as Alnor for the questions to continue. *Surely he knows the story in its entirety* Alnor thought, confused. The prince's gaze never left his father's.

Clapping a hand onto his friend's shoulder, Aldred shook the King slightly to break the gloom that had enveloped the warriors, whose day was jovial before that fated question. Malker glanced at Aldred, gratitude plain on his face at the break into what was surely an evil thought train. Taking a deep breath, Malker smiled and drank the rest of his cup before rising.

"That is a question for another time, young Sain!" his voice boomed with a forced laugh, jerking Terva awake with a start. Aldred rose alongside the King.

"For now, I think it's time for my bed. I can't drink as well as you young pups these days, the hangovers ruin my body for a week! What about you, old man?" Malker said, turning to his friend with an impudent smile on his face. Aldred laughed at the look the King was giving him and nodded his head.

"You're right there - age has come to us both, Sire!" he said, smiling genuinely and using the hand clapped to the King's shoulder to throw his arm around his friend. The King shoved off the rough embrace with a growl, the twins joining in with

Aldred's laughter. It was clear those two didn't say much, but their attentiveness wasn't affected by lack of contribution. Terva agreed reluctantly that he too should probably sleep before they began their march in the morning and sloped off. The sun hadn't even begun to set yet, and the prince never even made to rise as his father looked at him.

"We'll be marching at first light, son, and at a risk of sounding like a nagging mother, an early night wouldn't go amiss," the King said, trying to ease the words from sounding like an order.

Krinar laughed and looked pointedly at the sky. "The sun hasn't begun to bed down for the night, Father. I think I'll stay a while longer," he said, with a more than insolent grin.

He was subtly mocking his father at the early end to the day but not subtly enough. The King didn't miss the mockery, and the dark mood suddenly returned, fully focused this time on his son. Krinar didn't even flinch, keeping the same grin on his face as though totally missing the atmosphere. How he did that, Alnor would never know. He wouldn't have been surprised to see the sun dim at the intensity of the glare between father and son, but Krinar sat impassively, staring back.

After a few moments, the King growled in anger and walked away, leaving Krinar with a broad smile at the exchange going in his favour. Seething in frustration, Aldred turned towards his own son with a sharp glare that would turn most men's blood to ice, daring him to do the same as the prince.

A sharp intake of breath made the General lose his glare to a shocked grimace, as Alnor did his best to mimic the insolent grin of Krinar, even going as far as to lean back onto his elbows lounging. He felt a stab of worry at his father's reaction, hoping the progress they'd recently made wouldn't be ruined by trying to save face for a Prince he barely knew. But he had to know more, so stuck with it.

Aldred regained composure quickly as he always did, bowing slightly to the prince and nodding coldly to his son before stalking away in the same direction as Terva. Alnor sighed in relief as the footfalls receded, convinced for a moment the General would come back and drag him away by his ears. Krinar chuckled softly at the double exchange.

"Fathers, eh? Always think they know best when they themselves did these things at our age. Ignore them Alnor, and your life is much more fun," he chuckled.

Alnor laughed dryly, taking a huge gulp of wine to cover his discomfort. He rose, carrying the one remaining jug of wine to the prince before topping both cups up and sitting down on the same log as him with a thump.

"So... can I ask why your father didn't answer the question?" Alnor probed, feeling like it was worth the ire of the prince to hear the seemingly forbidden story. Expecting to be rebuffed, he was surprised when Krinar instantly launched into it.

"It *is* a sad story but being all those years ago I figured he'd be past it. Somebody, and still to this day my father hunts them, sent an assassin after my father and his younger brother. Nobody knows who or why, and since the Kerazar formed years later it can't have been them, but someone had a grudge. The assassin found them - my father at sixteen and his brother at thirteen - walking through the palace gardens in the evening with their sister, Edi - the one your father kissed," Krinar added mischievously with a laugh.

The laugh that came from Alnor's mouth sounded sickly and fawning even to him, so he tried to cover it drinking more wine.

"It's obvious your father survived though, so why does it still haunt him?" Alnor asked

The innocent question made Krinar laugh again, but darkly this time. "My father, who'd started training a few months before – earlier than the common eighteen - tried to fight the assassin off. His brother tried to help but with little to no experience in fighting, he was soon knocked out. It was obvious the man was much more skilled than my father and he had weapons where my father did not. When the inevitable came and he was knocked to the ground, Edi jumped between the blade and my father to save him. It pierced her heart, killing her instantly. Ascending was inevitable then - for me it was a build up over days that I could feel coming until I finally erupted. When we ascend a huge energy wave emits from somewhere inside us, and when my father screamed, this energy knocked the man off his feet. What he didn't bank on, however, was his brother ascending at the exact same time. The double shockwave was said to have ripped trees from the ground. The guards found them repeatedly stabbing a congealed mess of blood and flesh, the remains of the man sent to kill them," Krinar finished, the story dampening even his natural energy.

Alnor was staring wide eyed at the prince, mortified that he'd pried the information from him. "Sire, I'm so sorry. I had no idea the pain it caused your family," Alnor apologised in a pleading voice.

Krinar brushed off his apology with a wave of his hand. "No need, my friend. Natural curiosity takes us all!" he said, downing his wine and frowning at the empty jug.

He looked towards the merchant's cart, but the man and his wife were nowhere to be seen so he settled back, disgruntled. "The worst thing to come of it was his younger brother. Ascending too early can be fatal which, fortunately in this case it wasn't, but it did drive young Elart completely mad. He soon had a view that all men who weren't Annarite didn't deserve to be free and lived only to serve him. He was banished when he turned seventeen after he was found torturing a common family for forgetting to bow to him in the street," Krinar continued with a subdued tone, though his face was lit with energy again.

Alnor gasped at the revelation, which got a laugh from Krinar. "Don't be so surprised, friend. His views were already considered, in a less violent way. The kingdom of Annar takes tax from men, farmers and businesses. Call it a good life and say it's for the protection of its armies, but the Annarites in charge are still above everybody. It just looks better from the common persons view to give them free rein of their lives, taxing them for working is just a roundabout way of making them slaves without them actually realising it. Elart wanted to use the Annarite force to bully his way through life. You heard my Father earlier - *the kingdom of Annar must have an Annarite on the throne*. Even he thinks we should be above the rest, although he doesn't word it that way," he explained.

Trying to wrap his mind around all the information, Alnor was reeling. He'd never thought of it that way, but it made sense. Something suddenly clicked within him. "Krinar... when you say Elart was banished...?". He left the question hanging.

This time, Krinar's laugh was as dark as it could go. "You made the connection? Elart. King Elart of the Kerazar – is my father's younger brother".

Chapter 7

Alkor cursed as the nib of his pen snapped, spattering ink over yet another dispatch that needed a Sain signature to release funds to keep the household and its warriors running.

Slamming the pen down with a frustrated breath, he leant back into his father's chair, aware of the importance of his role in the house now that he was the only Sain left. Being aware of the importance, however, was not the same as loving the tedious afternoons of paperwork and reports from all over the kingdom. Every scout his Father had out still sent reports back, either by pigeon or by courier, and each had to be pieced together to create the huge picture that was the ever-changing Kingdom of Annar. Scouts was sometimes an honorific word since half of the reports he received were from men working in other households, taking Sain money to divulge information that noble houses thought safe within their walls. *Spies,* Alkor thought with disgust. However necessary they were, he'd never like such men who were without honour and could be bought at any turn.

Rising from the sturdy chair, he turned to glance at the portrait of his mother hanging next to the ever-empty mantle where his father's axe lived... This was something he did regularly through the afternoon, it was the only representation of his mother that he could put a face to a name. He ached to remember *something* of his mother, the brush of her hands on his cheeks or the smell of her hair, but he was simply too young at the time. With his father and brother rarely speaking of her, looking at this picture gave him some comfort that she'd been there, that she still lived in the house.

A short rap on the door jerked him to the present and it creaked open without his command to enter. People didn't have the same respect for him that they did for his father. The short, balding man who entered the room was foremost among those people. A plain grey shirt covered his sagging chest and his rotund belly, and his small, dark eyes darted at the broken pen nib with disapproval. Ink-stained fingers held another minute stack of papers that required Alkor's attention, the sight of which made him groan and rub his eyes vigorously.

"Master Sain - you really must be careful with those warriors' hands. Heavy pressing will break more nibs than we can order if you keep this up! I'll have to draft this order again," he sniffed, sweeping the ruined, mottled page off the desk and tucking it into his already straining belt.

"You're extremely good at keeping this estate running, Yuri, but don't you ever rest? It seems every afternoon is full of purchases or revenues," Alkor said, disgruntled at having to remain indoors as his brother continued to hone his skills without him.

Balzor had settled into what Alkor thought was a perfect routine; waking up in the morning and training with Alkor, practising their sword skills and running laps then when he had to leave for the torture in the house, Balzor kept turning his body into a machine of war. After he'd spent his day exercising and sparring, Balzor washed himself and went to the tavern with the rest of the men, with or without his brother. Alkor would trade an afternoon doing this paperwork for an afternoon making his own body stronger and drinking with his friends. Yuri kept him busy well into the evening on most nights so his comradeship was limited to the nights he could slip from the man's grip.

His brother rarely drank more than one cup before going on nightly walks with Aria after she finished her shift, Alkor thought with a wry smile. He was totally besotted with the girl after a mere fortnight of knowing her. Jokes flowed freely on the training field about the love addled youth until the colour of his face matched his hair from either rage or embarrassment. A chuckle escaped Alkor's lips at the memory as he signed his name yet again on some paper or other.

Yuri cocked his head in confusion. "Is something funny, Master Sain?" he asked, his squeaky voice grating on Alkor's ears and bringing his amusement to an abrupt end.

Alkor shook his head and handed the papers back with a grumpy look on his face. Yuri smiled at the young lord's reaction.

"Your father has just that face after doing these jobs, though he accepts they need doing. You are so alike; it's like working with a younger Aldred, Master Sain," Yuri observed, still smiling at Alkor's face.

Alkor forced a smile onto his face, knowing the man was just doing his job, and was exceptional at it. "Yuri... do you ever wish you could just sign your own name instead of asking for permission from a younger, much less experienced man like me, just because of my name?" Alkor asked, genuinely interested.

The reaction wasn't what Alkor expected. Yuri gave a frightened squeak and pulled the papers into his chest and taking a step back, instantly repelling the notion.

"Oh no Master Sain, that is unthinkable. To have another man take total control over the coffers without a Sain *ever* looking? Eventually you'd begin to think I was skimming off the top, or spending frivolously and terminate my position here which I like very much," Yuri started, quickly shaking his head as he spoke, causing his tiny eyes to rebound off the sides of his skull.

Alkor let out a deflated breath, wishing the man had just accepted to make his life easier. Then, he brightened up as another idea struck him.

"How about a small deal then?" Alkor asked, trying hard to keep the eagerness out of his voice. It would not do to let the man know how much he wanted him to accept the offer.

"A... A deal, Master Sain?" Yuri almost whispered tentatively, edging forward again slightly.

"More an arrangement of sorts," Alkor said. "My father's gone on a mission to bring the Hounds to justice and, in his absence, has left an untrained youth to manage an estate that I don't have the faintest clue how to do. I need to dedicate myself to my training or else he'll return to find that same untrained youth rather than the man he wishes to see. I propose that we write a small contract allowing you to sign your own name on anything minimal, such as supplies or maintenance, then every third day we'll have our lovely meetings like this to sign off on anything major. I'll let you decide what's major or not. Sound fair?"

Alkor was reassured by the fact that the short man licked his lips with nervous energy, but didn't instantly recoil like before. "That sounds... reasonable Master Sain. Although if your father returns unhappy with the deal?" Yuri said, still obviously jittery about the situation.

"How about we enter a clause in the contract that any displeasure will be dealt with by me, on Sain honour?" responded Alkor. "My father would never tarnish that; plus, if he was here, he'd know it was the right choice. My training won't be impacted, and I'm completely assured that you can run this estate better than I ever could." Alkor could feel his pulse racing, imagining the turning of the man's brain as he considered it.

A strange clicking noise sounded in Yuri's throat and a broad smile appeared on his face, never seen by Alkor's eyes. Yuri nodded enthusiastically.

"It *would* save a lot of time on both our ends, Master Sain. I swear you won't regret this," he said, eagerness in his voice.

Alnor laughed, rising and shaking Yuri's hand. He'd never understood the strange man's fascination with letters and organisation, but if that was his nectar, who was he to complain?

"Also, there won't be any need to skim off the top, you'll be rewarded from Sain coffers without that," Alkor added, a mischievous look on his face as Yuri jumped again and stammered that he'd never do so. Laughing again, Alkor raised his hand to show he wasn't speaking true. Yuri stopped his protests but looked decidedly more uncomfortable than he had been moments before.

"I jest, Yuri. You've always been loyal to my family. If there's anything you need, all you need to do is ask. If you ever feel slighted, do not be wary of voicing that to me. I will see you right, by Sain honour," Alkor said formally, knowing the words bound him, jokes aside.

Yuri understood the weight of the words and bowed his head at the gesture. "I will draw up a contract soon, which will of course come under the major things you need to sign. Thank you, Lord," he said, backing out of the room, head bowing again.

 Just before the door closed, Alkor stood. "Oh, and Yuri?" he shouted, making him open the door again and peer in pensively. "You just called me Lord," he said with amusement in his voice.

The man rolled his eyes and closed the door. Alkor sat down again, this time with a sigh of contentment and his heart soaring. He was free!

✶✶✶✶✶

Balzor put the wheelbarrow down with a grunt, tired muscles screaming in positive protest as the weight dragged them down. He had learnt to relish the pain over the past fortnight. The first few days he'd awaken barely able to move in pain from torn muscles and tired legs, but after that faded, his body began to endure the punishment better, especially with his mind. He knew every jolt of pain was taking him a step closer to being fitter and stronger. He gritted his teeth and straightened his back, using the back of his arm to wipe sweat from his forehead and congealing the dust there, giving him an odd stain.

Scratching his face, the stubble growing there irritating him as it had for days, he considered shaving the itching hairs. Hating them for the discomfort, he also knew he wouldn't shave it just yet. Aria had made a comment the night before about it making him look rugged and had a twinkle in her eye as she said it. Anything that made her eyes sparkle like that was worth keeping in the world, in Balzor's opinion. He looked around the training yard. Most men were sparring, but Balzor was still a raw recruit and had to earn his place there. A couple of early thrashings by Livius had engraved that into his mind, he'd stopped trying to spar until he was ready.

He sighed and began to remove the rocks from their steed. Dextri would have his hide if he didn't ensure everything he used was back in its proper place. He'd learnt that from a very young age, way before his training began when he and Alkor used to steal the smaller practice swords and pretend to be great warriors. Dextri would box their ears if they weren't put back exactly where they'd gotten them from. He grinned as he imagined Alkor in his father's stuffy office with the annoying but efficient Yuri taxing his time every afternoon since his father left. Balzor had the better deal in that situation, that was for sure. Sometimes being a Sain *didn't* pay off.

Rocks now in a neat pile next to the barrow, he broke into a steady jog around the field again. Four times round, then one turn on each apparatus then drop to the floor and do as many push ups as he could do until he collapsed on his face. Maybe after, he'd try his luck sparring again, despite his earlier kickings. One win was all he needed to needle Livius all night at the tavern; Ezi knows he hadn't even scored a hit on the man yet.

Balzor was surprised at how quickly his fitness had improved; he could easily run the laps required now, completing them without the guards catching him that morning, although Livius had *just* caught Alkor, who protested after the strike saying he'd crossed the line first. Either way, he'd taken a hit. Dextri had taught them better ways of conserving their energy whilst running and techniques to recover their breath directly after. Both lads had been surprised at how technical something as simple as running could be.

Thoughts in total daydream mode, it took him a few seconds to register the footfalls close behind him and he cricked his neck as he spun round in alarm, expecting the guards to be trying to sneak a hit in. His eyes widened and a smile broke on his face as he saw an ecstatic Alkor sprinting behind him, and he slowed down to allow his friend to catch up.

"I thought Yuri would've had you there for hours yet!" Balzor exclaimed as Alkor pulled alongside him, a wide grin threatening to tear him ear to ear.

"Let's just say we came to an agreement," Alkor said, relating the exchange with Yuri to his friend whilst finishing their laps. Balzor whooped in elation.

"Now there's no reason for me to spank you every time we spar, brother!" he said, Alkor frowning at the comment as they crossed the line of their final lap and slowed to a stop, stretching tired muscles so they wouldn't cramp.

"Put your money where your mouth is, lover boy. Best of three bouts, loser buys the ale *and* gets to brag about it all night. *Especially* to Aria" he retorted.

Balzor cringed at the threat but couldn't back down after he'd begun the banter. "Deal!" he finished, spitting on his dusty palm and shaking his brother's hand, who pulled his face and wiped his own on his pants, making Balzor snort.

Later Balzor blamed being tired from the day's training for his loss of two to one, not that it mattered. He spent the entire walk in to town sulking and shooting furtive glances at Alkor, who obviously replayed the fights over and over again to anyone who'd listen. Thankfully, the mocking stopped as they neared the town gates, the two Dicks waving them through without a second glance.

The group had been there almost every night for two weeks, despite the gruelling regime Dextri imposed on them. The fact Dextri joined them helped; the man could hardly reprimand them whilst doing the exact thing they were.

Alkor's eyes took on a look of glee as the inn came close, and Balzor wasn't sure whether it was the free ale or the humiliation of his brother to his new fancy that made him look so happy. He decided it was both.

Dextri led the way through the town, clasping hands with stall holders he knew and nodding to ones that were mere acquaintances. Everybody knew Dextri of course, nodding and smiling back as they packed their wares away for the night. Ingvar and Devar followed behind, Livius with Balzor and Alkor at the back, trying to re-ignite the story of Balzor losing as they sent sly looks to the red-haired youth that were returned with open scowls.

As they walked through the doors to the inn, Balzor let out a bittersweet sigh of relief as Alkor's eyes darted furiously around for the messy brown bun that could usually be seen on entering. She wasn't there. Balzor began to laugh at Alkor's disappointed face, replacing the jovial features. It seemed it was the humiliation he was looking forward to, not the ale. The laugh was short lived, however, as he realised he wouldn't see her himself tonight either, humiliation or not. Alkor saw the expression on his friend's face and the laugh was returned as Balzor struggled to stop his sulkiness showing.

"Get the ale in, lover boy! If I can't take the piss out of you tonight, I can at least drink on your purse," Alkor teased, jumping to avoid the punch aimed at his midriff with a laugh before sitting down at their usual table.

Sighing, Balzor walked towards the innkeeper, who was busy pouring wine into a jug for Dextri and the others. He grimaced at the thought; he'd tried to do a night on wine and suffered greatly the day after, despite his early finish to escort Aria home. He'd stuck on ale after that. On the plus side ale was cheaper, and if he kept losing bets, he needed the cheapest he could get, even if he was now getting paid a recruit's wage. Drinking every night soon blew that away, as he was finding out. As Dextri scooped up his wine and left the silver on the bar, the others carrying the cups behind him, he snorted at the misfortune of the lad.

"Lost another bet, eh pup? You'll soon learn," he guffawed. Balzor turned crimson as the rest of them laughed with him.

Before he could form a retort, they'd walked to the table, where Alkor had again launched into the sparring tale again, to Livius' delight. Scowling, he moved to the bar and was greeted by Olsten's smirking face, he'd heard the entire exchange.

"It's a good job you drink ale, lad, or you'd be well and truly beggared by now," he chuckled, mirroring Balzor's earlier thoughts.

As he busied himself getting a clean jug, Balzor yearned to ask about Aria, but reined himself in before he seemed like a love-struck puppy. He could have a night with his friends and not moon over a girl, couldn't he? Shaking his head, he got out his meagre silver and counted out the coins, leaving an extra one reluctantly as Olsten put the full jug down. Giving Balzor a wry smile, he scooped up the coins before he could reconsider.

"She's not here today. The Seeress needed her, and the local innkeeper doesn't say no to a Seeress, even if it means he works the shift himself," Olsten explained, seeing the glum look on the youth.

Olsten laughed and waved Balzor away to the table which he went back to, albeit not as downtrodden as before. Plonking himself down on the spare seat, Balzor grabbed two of the cups and filled them to the brim before taking a generous swig of his own. He *would* have a good night without thoughts of her intruding, he thought, rolling his eyes good naturedly as Alkor finished the tale for the fourth time that night.

Livius was loving it as per, but Devar and Ingvar pointedly steered the subject away, to Balzor's gratitude, not that they did it for his benefit - four times is enough for anyone - but he was grateful, nonetheless. He drank quickly, much quicker than usual. It seemed he held back to not embarrass himself with Aria there, but he had no such reserve that night.

As more customers began to fill out the tavern, merchants wetting their throats after hawking their wares all day, and farmers quenching their thirst after back breaking work tilling the fields, Balzor's head began to feel fuzzy. His resolve crumbled quickly as his thoughts traitorously strayed to those green eyes and that tinkling laugh. He *would* have a good night, but thoughts of her were always inevitable. He would go to see her later, he decided. After one more jug of ale.

✶✶✶✶✶

"Can we just go over it again?" Aria asked for the tenth time. Her grandmother sighed in exasperation, rubbing her temples with her bony hands.
She was every bit the Seeress tonight, but Aria was testing her patience. Sometimes she wished she could just be Aria's grandmother instead of her mentor, that times would go back to the easy-going nature of a trusting young girl. But now, Aria was beginning to learn the craft and that meant ensuring perfection with something as serious as this. With a deep breath, she began anew.

"This is the last time, so ensure you listen girl! There are rumours all over the land that when a Seeress or Seer die, they pass their skills on to their chosen heir. We know this is rubbish. We can feel the power inside us from a young age if we have the gift, whether we know how to use it or not. Yourself, for instance, already have a slight aptitude for healing, even though I'm very clearly alive. But the rumour isn't totally without merit; every rumour comes from a slight truth. It is tradition for the mentor to bind her life to the one who will succeed her, to cement the passage of knowledge. It is very rarely needed, since the entire population of *any* kingdom revere Seeresses, but there are always discrepancies. The purpose of this binding spell will tie my life force to yours, but not yours to mine. This means when I eventually die, the spell will unravel, and you can take my place. But it has the reverse effect if you yourself die; if this should occur, my life force will flood into you and ensure that our line continues. The fact that the power stays in the family line makes this easier to do since it's the way of the world for a granddaughter to outlive her grandmother," she said. "Unless, of course, you decide to ask me to repeat it again, in which case, I might kill you myself," she added, stern eyes boring into Aria's, only the slight twitch of her mouth betraying amusement.

Aria laughed readily, enjoying her grandmother's temper. She'd seen people of all stations wilt under that glare in the past, but when it was aimed at her, it was always tempered with affection. She became serious quickly, however, as the look suddenly hardened. This wasn't a trifle spell or the healing of a minor cut on one of their many cats; this was a real binding spell. Clearing her head of any intruding thoughts, she focused her will and straightened her back.

"So, how do we begin?" she queried the Seeress – she was her grandmother no longer.

"Give me your hands and open your mind to mine. I will guide the binding; you just need to lend me your strength and ensure you stay focused. Don't try and halt what will happen midway-through, it could be disastrous for us both," the Seeress commanded, her palms facing up, already knowing her orders wouldn't be denied.

Aria placed her hands into the waiting palms and closed her eyes, finding that it helped her concentrate on the task at hand. She always had trouble completely opening her mind, knowing that to do so, she had to surrender control completely. If it was anybody except her grandmother in control, she didn't think she'd be able to do it. Being family created a bond that automatically forged trust, and her grandmother hadn't once broken that trust in Aria's eighteen years.

Unseen by Aria, the Seeress nodded. She could feel the iron concentration in her granddaughter and had to supress a strong feeling of pride to regain her own focus. The girl was an extraordinary apprentice, absorbing information quicker than any she'd ever taught, though it still felt slow to her aging bones. The small lie that every Seeress performed this binding on her students barely made her feel any guilt at all; only Seeress' whose gift passes through their lineage ever even thought of it - let alone performed it. A seeress of her standing had taken many apprentices before, but this was the first time she'd worked with her family. She knew that Aria's fate was interlocked with the Balzor boy, who sent a tingle down her spine every time he escorted her home.

It showed a flair for the romantic, moonlit walks under the canopy of trees and arms wrapped around each other, the boy throwing furtive glances towards the house in nervousness at being caught out. Even at that distance, she could feel something inside of him, ready to erupt, something that Aria held the key to. Fear lanced through her calm demeanour as she thought of her Aria getting hurt, whether it was intended or not. This is why she told the little lie. To keep her safe, to keep her alive. Taking a deep breath, she steadied her own nerves, knowing none of them showed on her. "Let us begin".

✶✶✶✶✶

Balzor whistled as he reached the now familiar fork in the path that led to the Seeress' cottage through the wooded path.

The torches burned lower than usual tonight, the only need to keep them burning longer was to light the path for when Aria came home. It gave the path a foreboding look, daring him to enter. Trees, usually friendly to Balzor's eyes, seemed to droop lower to deny him entry and he had second thoughts about going unannounced. But ale coursed through his veins, and it gave him a boost of confidence, confirming something he'd hoped wasn't entirely true: he was drunk.

He must be mad turning up at the Seeress' house trying to court her granddaughter with a belly full of ale. The over-confidence brushed aside his rational arguments, and he stepped towards the path, leaving the sounds of the inn behind him. The jeers that hit his back as he left the inn still rang in his ears – they'd known he would succumb to his lovesick thoughts after the third jug was ordered. He wouldn't be surprised to find out that bets had been wagered over it.

Still whistling a tune with his thumbs tucked into his plain warriors' pants, he firmed his resolve and moved under the grasping branches, even going as far to step closer to the trees nearest to the wall in an attempt to regain their apparently lost friendship. His boldness cost him his footing as a root caught his foot and tossed him onto the ground, the idiocy of tucking his thumbs into his pants prevented a cushioned fall. His face hit the worn path hard. It took him a moment of dazed silence, in which he imagined the leaves chuckling in the breeze, to recover.

He pushed himself to a seated position and rubbed his hands along his cheeks, brushing off the stray patches of dirt and sincerely hoping it wasn't ingrained into his skin. Turning up drunk looking like a beggar would be enough to make even Aria annoyed with him, let alone the Seeress.

As he rose unsteadily to his feet, still scrubbing his face furiously, he aimed a kick at the root in a childish tantrum. The kick connected and the root was surprisingly soft, seeming to give way to his temper and flexing rather than the expected pain.

Cocking his head in confusion, he crouched and looked closer at the root. He recoiled. What he'd mistaken for a root was in fact two legs interlocked with another, but they faced entirely the wrong way to belong to the same body. His eyes traced up the legs to two separate bodies whose faces he recognised. Their eyes were glazed over and mouths open in horrified surprise, their throats yawning revealing a mess of congealed blood. It was the two Dicks.

Shock reverberated through Balzor to his core, the safety of the walls and the sinister look of the trees a distant memory. They were dumped next to each other unceremoniously, and he saw scuff marks in the dirt indicating they'd been dragged there to avoid notice. Their spears were missing, though one of the brothers seemed to have enough time to draw his sword before having his windpipe slashed brutally. The sword lay on the ground next to him, limp fingers not having the power to grasp it any longer after his blood had soaked into the dirt, taking his life with him. Struggling to think, he snatched up the fallen sword, heart pounding loudly in his ears, the thud like a drum in the silence of the village. He needed to get back to the inn, warn Dextri and raise the alarm. Murder in Saternac was unheard of. The walls must have been breached, the two Dicks being the unsuspecting first line of defence eliminated.

A sudden realisation of where he was stood, where he had found the bodies, hit home - on the pathway to the Seeress' house.

He was running before the word had formed in his head, panic dispelling the effects of the ale and lending him energy as his training took hold. *Aria!*

✱✱✱✱✱

117

Power surged through the connection Aria had formed with her grandmother, making her hair stand on end and her eyes open involuntarily. Her instinct was to hide from such raw energy, not fully believing that half of it came from her own body. It was thought Exat let Seers and Seeress' draw power directly from himself, using their souls as a conduit. Aria could believe the assumption, as the feeling of purity that washed through her was almost certainly divine.

Her open eyes locked with her grandmothers who was staring intently at Aria, as if trying to gauge her reaction at her first real touch of the power. She'd felt tiny surges before as she healed but had never been able to harness it properly herself, and never on this scale. Holding her grandmother's eyes, she struggled not to smile in the ecstasy of the moment, knowing it would ruin their focus and remembering her earlier words of disaster. *Concentrate, Aria!* She thought to herself furiously, feeling her attention swaying.

"Concentrate, Aria!" the Seeress said, her voice empty and commanding. Aria jumped at the sudden break in the silence, feeling the link jolt as her mind wavered from the task at the repeated words. Calming her nerves, she let herself relax and forced her eyes closed again. Almost at the point of capacity, she tried to further open her mind to the link and felt a moment's satisfaction as the power increased ever so slightly. That satisfaction was short lived however, as the power didn't stop increasing.

She felt a stretching of her senses, feeling like an almost full water skin trying to be filled more and beginning to bulge at the seams. She grunted at the initial discomfort but remembered her grandmother's words. She couldn't pull away now; it became harder to do, as the power continued to increase. It poured through the link and panic started to creep in as she filled to the point of bursting, the discomfort starting to become pain. Eyes flying open and searching for her grandmother's, she found them still gazing intently at her, no panic on her face and seemingly in no discomfort, let alone pain. Something was wrong, she could feel it. She tried to open her mouth to talk but only succeeded in emitting a small gasp followed by short bursts of breath as she tried to draw air from lungs suddenly filled with power.

Crashing to her knees, she tried to wrench her hands away to break the link — damn the consequences. But her grandmother had knelt with her, her old bony hands having strength despite their age, keeping Aria's hands locked and the link secure. She tried to shake her head, but found her neck locked in place and all she could do was keep her eyes on her grandmother's, pleading wordlessly for help.

More and more power ran through the conduit eagerly; it picked up speed and became an unstoppable avalanche. It rose from her lungs and clenched her heart, filling her stomach and rising through her oesophagus and clogging up her throat, stopping breath entirely. It kept on rising until it reached the back of her tongue, and she attempted to retch, finding that frozen as well. It had control of her entire body, all nerves electrified as they twitched, shaking her muscles and joints. Her hair stood up vertically, giving her the impression of something dragging her into the air from above. The only place for the power to go was back out, and it came to the front of her mouth and made her teeth rattle. Just as it left her lips she collapsed to the ground and let out an ear-splitting scream of agony. Before the scream ended, the door burst open.

★★★★★

Legs stronger from the constant laps at the Sain manor, Balzor sprinted without reserve down the path in the dim light, a slight breeze making the flames flicker as the last of the oil-soaked rags burnt out. Fear grasped his heart as he flew towards the house, each second feeling like an eternity at the thought of Aria in the same state as the two brothers he'd left lying in the trees' cold embrace. The same fear fuelled him to greater speed, and he felt relief as he rounded the final oak and saw the lights in the windows, not a herb on the sill out of place. He leapt over the gate using his spare hand as a lever to help him clear the fence, then he stopped dead.

Eyes scanning around, looking for any discrepancies in what he was used to, he tried to catch his breath; his heaving chest didn't subside, and the feeling of unease didn't leave him. Knowing he needed to report to Dextri, he tried to catch any danger quickly; he could feel a pulsing in the air, getting stronger and stronger. Dread filled him as a terrified scream echoed from the house and the pulsing seemed to intensify before stopping entirely.

As soon as the high-pitched wail pierced the air, Balzor was moving again. He didn't hesitate as he put his shoulder into the Seeress' door. The door flew off its hinges, hitting the floor with a huge bang and Balzor glanced left and right in quick turns of his neck.

On the right was a normal kitchen; pans hung from hooks on the ceiling and a fire pit in the corner, a break in the floorboards as cobbled stone surrounded the pit. A pot dangled over fire, steam rising lazily from the contents which smelled delicious. On his left knelt the Seeress, with the still form of Aria on the floorboards next to her, unconscious. Berating himself for even noticing the smell of the food, he started towards the prone form.

At the bang of the door, the Seeress looked up menacingly and rose quickly. Balzor felt a wave of *something* crash into him, sending him flying across the room, landing next to the fire and singeing one of his braids as he rolled away, patting his hand to stop the sparks progressing into his hair.

He rose quickly, but was stopped mid-rise, his muscles somehow locked into place with an unknown force. It terrified him even more than the sight of the Seeress stalking towards him, a nightmare in itself.

"And *what* do you think you are doing, breaking into my home with a drawn blade?!" she hissed as she reached within striking distance of Balzor.

Balzor stuttered but found he couldn't find the words. "The bodies... Aria... screaming..." he mumbled in fear, trying to gesture at Aria but still being locked into place. The Seeress waved her hand in anger and the bonds seemed to release Balzor all at once, sending him crashing to the floor again but she wasn't done there. Her eyes had narrowed at the mention of bodies, and she reached down to grasp his tunic, surprising strength in the old woman.

"Bodies, boy? Explain!" she demanded.

He fell over himself trying to tell her quickly and her eyes widened further and further as the words tumbled out. When he fell silent, she released him as though an afterthought and moved back to Aria, lifting her granddaughter's head off the hard floor, placing a cushion from the bottom of one of three wicker chairs surrounding a small wooden table under it.

"Seeress, is she okay? I heard her screaming and...?" he let the question trail off as those hard eyes fell on him yet again, rendering him silent.

"This is the business of Seeress', young man. You will clear your head of all thoughts of what you've seen or heard here," she said, her voice ringing with authority. Balzor nodded, his eagerness to agree making him cringe inside. A Seeress wasn't to be questioned.

"Please, Seeress, I have to know," he said, gesturing helplessly at Aria on the floor, her usually messy bun ripped out, hair disturbingly straight. Her eyes softened slightly, seeing the genuine worry for her granddaughter. She felt the need to reassure him, despite his bulling through her door without ceremony; he'd thought Aria was in danger, after all.

"I will care for my granddaughter, Balzor. You need to warn the town," she said lightly.

Balzor took a half step towards Aria, biting his lip as his head and his heart warred with each other. Her composure hardened as the seriousness of the situation broke through her mellowing mood.

"Go, boy!" she snarled, making Balzor jump out of his skin and with one last look at Aria, tear off through the door at breakneck speed.

Turning to her granddaughter, she found a cover to keep her warm. She knew Aria didn't need healing; it was her body reacting to the huge influx of power for the first time, but she'd monitor her, just in case. The town could care for itself for one night.

✶✶✶✶✶

Dextri howled with laughter as Alkor stumbled back from the bar after his second attempt to acquire another jug of ale. Halfway through the third one he and Balzor had shared, Dextri received a look he had seen too many times from Olsten – no more for those two. But it was fun to watch Alkor try his luck, nonetheless. Balzor had taken the news with surprisingly good grace, downed his last cup and rose to announce he was going to see Aria.

Underneath the jeers and catcalls that inevitably followed, Dextri had a grudging admiration for the lad's nerve. He himself wouldn't have gone to the Seeress' house without good reason, let alone to steal kisses from her granddaughter with a belly full of ale. Alkor however had sulked ever since and kept trying to convince Olsten he wasn't too drunk; his stumbling and slurring of words had been their source of humour for the past fifteen minutes at least. Dextri thought he might give the lad some of their wine on the next jug, just to end his torment.

Sitting down in the middle of Ingvar and Devar with a thump, his bottom lip jutting out like a child, Alkor dropped his purse on to the table.

"I even offered to double the price, and he still told me to piss off with that smirk on his face. One of you will have to go for me," Alkor muttered sullenly.

Livius barked a laugh at him, causing the lad to jump slightly. "And risk Olsten pausing our consumption too? Fat chance little lord! I might let you have a little cup if you're a good boy," he said, patting Alkor patronisingly on the head and making Alkor take a swipe at the hand, almost knocking Ingvar's cup from his hand.

"Now, pup, I'm all for giving Livius a smack, but if my wine hits that floor because of you, you'll follow it promptly," he warned, making his brother snort. "And you brother, don't snort so hard, you'll dislodge your cup with that beak of yours." Devar's snort turned into a breath of outrage as the rest of the group hooted in delight.

It seemed Alkor had decided to see if Olsten had changed his mind yet again and tried to rise. Dextri's hand clapped his shoulder and forced him down, denying the lad his drunken shame one last attempt, despite the hilarity of it.

"Sit down, lad. One more cup out of this last jug of wine and a small one at that! Training will be hard enough tomorrow with the hangover you'll already have; let's not add to it, eh?" he said, voice slightly laced with authority to portray he was serious.

The lad nodded eagerly and Dextri chuckled and rose from his bench with Livius, moving toward the bar Olsten was scrubbing. The night was halfway done, but most of the tenants had already left for their beds. Pots of stew with crusts of bread discarded in them were left strewn around tables with chairs left pulled out ignorantly. Even the old boys in the corner had retired, the brazier left to burn down, not needed in the snug autumn night.

Dextri loved autumn, when the trees changed colour and lost their leaves. The regions infuriating dust began to hide back in the ground, giving way to moisture. Winter was a step too far, the ground becoming rock solid and the skin-biting winds; Summer not a step enough with the dust and the burning heat; Autumn was the perfect mixture of both. Spring was the same, he supposed, but he had a discomfort of treading on plants or flowers that were trying to grow whereas in Autumn they were on the way out anyway.

Olsten put the rag he used for his bar down and started to pour the wine, already knowing what his lone customers were going to order. Dextri chuckled.

"How do you do it Olsten? Tidy up after everybody in your own establishment, instead of cracking a few skulls and forcing them to do it? I know you're more than capable," he asked the innkeeper, who laughed without pausing his pouring or spilling a drop.

"It's easy, Dex - people like you pay me good money!" he replied, making Dextri chuckle again. After a slight pause, he continued. "To be honest, I've begun to enjoy it. Being the place where people come to relax, to be with friends, and to see where it all takes place, it's a small joy. I take all the joys I find these days - plus, the company's better than nothing. Even if it is you lot," he said slyly, glancing up at Dextri, who gasped in mock disbelief.

"We're bloody lovely company if I do say so my- "

Interrupted by a huge bang, Dextri span around, hand instinctively grasping for a sword that wasn't there and his mouth dropped open. Hooded men were pouring through the entrance to the inn, masks covering the bottom half of their face. They were brandishing drawn swords whilst studying the room intensely, like predators smelling blood but not knowing its location. One man's eyes stopped at their small drinking party, pinpointing them and raising his blade at the young man in the middle of the group. The blade was coated with fresh blood, droplets sliding down its edge in relish, as though trying to make room for more to be spilled.

In the second it took Dextri to take this in, Livius had risen from the bench and kicked it toward the intruders, fouling their legs before bellowing "Run!"

Ingvar and Devar leapt out of their seats and thrust the younger lord away, Livius' plea spurring the room into action as the men dashed forward, intent on their prey. Outnumbered and without weapons, the guards attempted to throw any furniture behind them as they too made for the kitchens and the rear exit. Thinking fast, Olsten grabbed a bottle of a mountain-brewed spirit and smashed it on the floor beneath the wraiths, passing Dextri a lantern from behind the bar and then ducking into the kitchen for cover.

Understanding instantly, Dextri let Alkor and the others dash over the sodden floor before tossing the lantern on to the spirit, engulfing it in eager flames that checked the hunter's advance. One of them wasn't so lucky, unable to stop before the flames licked up his legs and began to devour him.

Seeing his chance, Dextri dashed forward and swung a savage punch at the man as his mouth opened to scream, shattering his jaw and knocking him to the ground. As though his jaw was a minor inconvenience, he tried desperately to put the hungry fire out before it spread further, dropping his sword which Dextri promptly picked up before fleeing after the others, leaving the unfortunate man to burn.

Olsten was gesturing frantically at the back door and Dextri dashed through it before it slammed shut behind him, cutting off the man's mangled screams - the fire had claimed its bounty. Both men followed in their friends' footsteps, knowing their weapons were out of reach in the Sain manor and rushing towards the only place that seemed likely to have more: Lortmund's forge.

"You owe me a new inn," Olsten accused between panting breaths.

The man had never been the fittest and it already showed in the short sprint, his attempt at humour straining his lungs even more. A chorus of shouts and the sound of heavy footfalls announced that the hunters had picked up the scent and carried on the chase. Curtains twitched in cottage windows, curious eyes peeking and becoming fearful at the sight of drawn swords charging past them.

"If we survive the night, I'll even make sure it's stocked with wine!" Dextri promised. The forge came into view as they rounded the corner, their figures illuminated by the ever-present lights in the building.

Dextri heard Alkor shouting, hoping to get the attention of the blacksmith inside over the noise of his work. The fact he was still there working gave Dextri a feeling of relief; if Lortmund had retired for the night he would've locked the sturdy doors, which he insisted would stop anything short of a battering ram.

Risking a glance over his shoulder, alarm coursed through his body as he realised they were only a few paces behind. He forced his ale riddled body to speed up. He cursed inwardly at dulling his senses with wine. The huge blacksmith come through the door as Alkor reached it, gesturing behind at the dark figures then disappearing back into the forge with him. Ingvar and Devar hurried in behind, but Livius waited, shouting encouragement to the rest of the men.

In a story of heroes and valour, Dextri and Olsten would've made it to the forge just as the rest of the guards acquired weapons and then fought off the invaders before parading around the town; but in the real world, it wasn't to be.

Olsten cried out as his foot found a rut in the path, sending him sprawling on the ground at the mercy of the leading blade, whose wielder howled in triumph and lunged. Dextri spun, bracing hard onto his right foot and leaping backwards, swinging his own stolen weapon, parrying the death thrust with inches to spare. Off balance from the attack, the man stumbled into Dextri who roughly shoved him back and smashed the hilt into his nose with a crunch. Blood sprayed over Dextri's arm as his face exploded into a mess and he fell back with a cry.

The man behind him cursed as he collided with the falling warrior, checking his speed so as not to fall onto Dextri's blade. The small break in the chase was all Dextri needed to drag Olsten back to his feet and get him moving again, but the man was finished. His ankle was either badly sprained or broken, and he was leaning heavily on Dextri when he stopped and pushed the towering man away.

"Go, friend," Olsten sighed, already turning back towards the pursuers who'd helped their comrade to his feet and began to advance more cautiously. They knew they had their prey, losing men to stupid headlong rushes was a waste.

Face covered in blood and mask askew, the injured man led the group, teeth stained red as he bared them in anger at his humiliation. Dextri shook his head, turning back and planting his feet defensively; he wouldn't leave a man behind. He could hear shouting at his back and knew the rest of them would be too late, but he could buy them time. Cuffing his broken nose one last time, the leading man threw his head back and howled, the rest joining in the piercing noise that destroyed Saternac's world all those years ago. The Hounds had evaded the General and come to hunt again. Dextri opened his arms wide in challenge and prepared to die.

✶✶✶✶✶

Ears pounding in the silence to the rhythm of his feet, Balzor tore down the wooded path, pitch black now the torch's burnt out, the trees denying him even the moonlight's caress. Relief tinged with concern coursed through his body at seeing Aria unharmed but in such a strange state. He tried to put her from his mind and half succeeded; he knew the Seeress knew her work, but it didn't stop him worrying.

It was in this half state that he ran towards the inn with almost as much speed as he'd ran to Aria. He could hear shouting but couldn't yet tell if it was panic or glee that prompted it, so he didn't slow. Reaching the entrance to the path, he relaxed slightly as torches still lit the streets and windows emitted a soft glow that complimented the night. His relaxation was short lived, however.

Turning into the streets leading to the main square, he looked aghast at the flames licking at the lower walls of the inn, men tearing out of the back like rabbits to escape the heat. He saw three men run away past the bakery and towards the forge, two larger men follow in their wake. One of the men was bigger than most, and only Dextri had that predatory movement in his run for a man that size. Balzor breathed easier again at seeing his comrades escaping, but even more figures detached through the front of the inn, hooded and covered like demons from the underworld. He shivered at the thought of that dark place on a night like this and drew the circle on his head to ward off evil.

The pursuing party set off after his friends, swords bared glinting off the fire's light in anticipation. Balzor growled and set off towards them, intending to catch them unawares when two more figures came out of the same door - one dragging the prone form of another so badly burned it was a wonder he wasn't ashes. He was breathing raggedly and the man lumbered him to the side on to the cool grass, lowering him down to the floor, his head swinging side to side with indecision at leaving his injured friend alone. It was this that alerted him to Balzor's presence, stood in the gloom with a sword and a stricken look. If his age wasn't a dead giveaway, the lack of hooded attire was.

His friend suddenly forgotten, the hooded demon rose intently, drawing his blade with precise slowness and locking eyes with the startled youth. He growled. Balzor stood rooted to the spot, unable to flee or to call for help. Shame ate at him as he realised the simple truth: he was petrified. All the tales he'd listened to and boasts he'd made came to naught in that moment as the man advanced with a sinister look and death peering from his eyes. Seeming to read Balzor's thoughts, the man laughed and raised his sword quickly, spotting an easy kill on a boy not yet old enough to have been blooded. Balzor could just see the slight crinkling of the man's eyes, indicating his eagerness. As the sword came down, its trajectory towards Balzor's throat, the fear snapped and instinct kicked in.

At that moment, Balzor could have kissed Dextri. His body had thrown itself into one of the cursed forms, both hands grasping the sword and deflecting the blow whilst stepping back to disengage and gather himself. The shock of being parried by someone who was merely a statue a second before stalled the man's next attack, giving Balzor the much needed few moments to shake the fear away and harness it rather than letting it control him.

Intending to get the measure of his opponent, the man came on again launching a fresh series of savage blows which Balzor blocked or dodged without too much effort. Narrowing his eyes, the only visible part under the hood, the man adjusted his approach. He came slower now, feinting one way then the next and the dance began. More than once he leapt back just in time as the man's blade whistled past his throat or almost severed a limb. Only the fear of shame kept him there as jolts of fear ran through him and the instinct to run screaming at the back of his mind.

The clanging of swords and the crackling of the ever-growing fire soon attracted attention. Lights winked on in the square and worried faces peeped from cracks in the curtains, vanishing almost as quickly as they realised the situation. Knowing that these scared villagers might soon pluck up the courage to help the youth in front of him, the man began a furious assault in his desperation to end the fight quickly. Panic swelled in Balzor's bones as he felt his body start to slow down, the effects of the ale and constant training taking their toll.

His sword darted up to meet the intruder's and, too late, he realised the feint. Unable to do anything else, he bunched up his legs and dove backwards just as the man's blade scored a cut right where his head was seconds before. He crashed to the floor, driving the remaining air from his lungs but miraculously keeping hold of his weapon. He rolled quickly to the side, just evading as steel sank into the ground just beside him. The man was laughing now, knowing his prey was beaten and enjoying playing with his food. But it wasn't instinct that came to Balzor's aid in that moment, it was fire.

With a huge pop, the inferno of the inn belched a torrent of sparks as the walls began to collapse in on themselves, and being on the floor saved Balzor from being engulfed in them. The man wasn't so lucky. Diving out of the sky as though alive, the sparks found purchase in the many folds of his hood, not setting alight but making him flinch away from the sudden heat as it created tiny holes in his clothing before settling on his skin.

Rolling back the way he'd just come, Balzor used his body to crush the sword between himself and the ground, kicking out as he did and forcing the man to release the blade. In a final desperate attack, he swung his own blade and by sheer luck he felt it sink into the soft flesh of his neck. Time seemed to freeze. He looked into his opponent's eyes at the precise moment he realised he was going to die, making a futile effort to stop the blood leaking out of the gaping incision the wild attack had made. Legs weakening almost instantly, he crashed to his knees and began to make a sickening gargling as his body tried to draw precious air.

As the man began to sway, Balzor struggled to rip his vision away from the grisly scene but found he couldn't, feeling obliged to observe the final moments of a life he had torn away. He collapsed to the ground and the light went out of his eyes as his head connected with the floor, bouncing off it once before settling, gazing lifelessly into nothing. He lay there, death stare aimed at Balzor who lay only a pace away, mouth open in shock, his hand dragging off his hood as he tried to stem the flow of his life leaving his neck.

Balzor was numb, staring back at the corpse and taking in features that were before hidden by the shadowed hood. When he was a wraith, Balzor felt a single-minded determination to strike him from the world, to preserve his own life and the life of others. But now, seeing the grizzled grey stubble adorning a small jawline, crinkles clinging onto his eyes - the evidence of too much laughter - Balzor saw the horrible truth; he'd killed a human being - one that could have sons, daughters, parents, a wife.

With the realisation he hadn't before considered, he recoiled in disgust, breathing uncontrollably as he struggled to rein in his erratic reaction. Dragging himself to his feet, he rested the palms of his hands onto his knees and drew in the air deeply, coughing slightly as the smoke took its chance to tickle his chest, ever ready to taint the oxygen.

Failing to regain any composure and beginning to panic that his lungs had betrayed him, he tried a different approach. He screamed as explosively as he could manage, expelling any remaining air and ripping his throat with the intensity of it. It cut through the crackling of the fire and the groans of the burnt man and flew off into the night, echoing as it ricocheted off the trees that seemed to shed their dislike of him at its contact.

But it wasn't the scream that snapped him back into focus and allowed him to draw beautiful air into his body, it was the response. His blood turned cold, and the seriousness of the situation hit him like a galloping horse as he heard a dreaded sound. The sound made by only one group in the realm, the one his parents must have heard minutes before they were murdered in their homes.

He heard a howl, taken up in chorus as others voiced their own cry. The Hounds had returned which meant the General was lost or he had been duped; either possibility felt absurd to his stricken mind. He took one last look at the man he'd killed then sprinted towards the howls, hearing the desperate clash of blades. He knew what was to come. He would kill again.

*****

Livius had sent the others for anything they could find to fight inside the forge, Lortmund going with them and shouting for Svein to help. He was urging Dextri on when he saw Olsten stumble and slam to the ground, Dextri pivoting gracefully and parrying the blow before hammering his sword hilt into the man's face, sending him staggering into his entourage and checking their advance.

Right on cue, Alkor returned with the others on his heels, tossing Livius an unfinished shield and a smaller blacksmiths hammer, shrugging as if to say, "Take what you can get".

Without waiting to see what Ingvar and Devar had procured, he sprinted back towards their pursuers as they howled their war cry, announcing their identities. Dextri invited them to come as it was obvious Olsten could not escape.

"We're coming, Dex! For Saternac and the Annar! Up and at 'em lads!" Livius bellowed, the rest taking up the cry and roaring.

Knowing their best chance was to hit Dextri before the others reinforced him, the Hounds advanced. Two of the central men locked shoulders whilst the side two took a step out to hit him from the sides. They came quickly, attacking almost simultaneously to throw him off balance and end him in the first strike, but Dextri was ready.

He leapt to his right, twisting absurdly to dodge the centre swords and parry the right one. Lightly pushing the blade was the best he could accomplish though and he hissed as it scored a shallow line across his chest; the sharp pain dispelled the last of his intoxication as he spun back with a crazed swing in anticipation of the blow that was coming.

Too late, he saw the thrust aimed at his midriff, his counter-swing throwing him past the point of return. He tensed and readied himself for the fatal blow, already planning the backswing that would at least return the lethal attack in kind. Before the point slid home, something collided heavily with Dextri's shoulder, sending him flying to the ground. He rose almost as quickly when he heard the pained yell that turned into a growl of anger and defiance, tinged with fear. Ingvar had thrown himself at Dextri, barging him out of the way and taking the intended blade in his place.

The cry of defiance signalled an act of heroism greater than Ingvar's sacrifice as he grabbed the sword at the hilt, dragging it further into his own body, making the assailant's eyes widen beneath the hood. Ingvar used the closer quarters to drive the end of a butcher's knife into the man's neck so hard it almost severed his head. Devar saw the exchange and cried out in dismay, charging into the fray as two men from the back line made to finish the kill. He too had acquired an unfinished shield using it to batter into the men as Dextri saw his chance and dragged Ingvar out of harm's way.

Alkor arrived to overlap shields with Devar but neither of them had weapons. They were pushed back instantly, with the imminent threat of being flanked. Livius, Lortmund and Svein arrived with a great roar to bolster the miniature wall. Svein and his father were swinging their massive blacksmith hammers with ease above the heads of the wall - Livius using only his shield to cover the men and forgoing the use of his smaller hammer.

"Olsten! You need to get Ingvar to the forge," Dextri ordered, placing a now sweating Ingvar lightly to the ground as he grimaced in agony.

Olsten didn't look much better, barely able to limp on an ankle that was surely broken. He staggered and almost fell to the ground, catching himself on a bracing at the last moment and shaking his head.

Lights began to wink out in the houses around them, as though darkness would hide them from the savagery happening metres outside their domains. There was a muffled scream from inside the house Olsten had caught himself on, indicating residents hadn't fled as that light too, went out. Dextri used the sword to chop at the bracing being used as Olsten's crutch, dismembering it from the house and handing it to him. He set it beneath his sweat-ridden armpit, using his free arm to drag Ingvar.

The group moved at a snail pace backwards, going as fast as Ingvar could be dragged. Dextri, Lortmund and Svein swung their weapons over the heads of their comrades, knowing the odds were grim but attempting to keep the attackers at bay as they tried to break the flimsy shield wall. Devar was spitting and cursing foul things, enraged by the wounding of his brother on a night that was so peaceful under an hour before. Livius had the same look as always, the crooked grin on his face taunted the Hounds to come and die, daring them to step into the blacksmith's range. Alkor was whitefaced but determined, weathering the hail of blades, refusing to be broken. *Sain to the core* he thought proudly. Olsten panted heavily in sequence with Ingvar's pitiful whimpers and each step racked his body with agony.

An age passed before they felt the heat of the forge on their backs. This was the only source of light in the street now and it put them at a disadvantage. The attackers could see them clearly, the glow illuminating them whilst the Sain guards struggled to make out their opponents in the gloom.

Olsten shouted weakly that Ingvar was inside, but the hunters saw the plan of their prey now, pushing all the harder, making it impossible for them to disengage and bar the door. They wouldn't have had much time for respite as leaving the villagers to the mercy of these men wasn't the reason the guards trained like they did. They were too late before; never again.

As they reached the forge's walls, Lortmund and Svein lost the ground they needed to manoeuvre, and the men could finally close in on the wall. Though this enabled Dextri to begin thrusting and swinging his blade more, he felt despair begin to creep in despite his efforts to keep it at bay. The Hounds began to scent their victory and pushed harder, Livius' smile hidden behind a glare. He passed the smaller hammer to Svein, who looked at it quizzically then drew it behind his head and flung it towards the men.

The unexpected missile smashed into the same nose Dextri had broken before. This time it pulverised his face and he collapsed to the ground in an explosion of chipped bone and shattered teeth. His comrades stepped over the unconscious body without hesitation, renewing their onslaught. They were no longer afraid of the colossal hammers breaking their heads like pumpkins and knew the shield wouldn't last forever.

Step by step they were forced back until Dextri's back hit the wall, and he could do nothing but brace into Alkor's back to keep him from falling, his sword now useless. Olsten was at the door, throwing small ingots and tools over his friends and being a nuisance without any significant effect. Dextri felt a wave of regret that he couldn't save his best friend's son, knowing they would all die here. He knew it was always his fate to die in the fight, but Alkor was destined to do better.

Feeling a paternal fondness in his breast, completely out of place in the brutality of the night, he felt a growing rage at the thought of losing the chance to watch him grow. He roared in anger, the sudden sound causing the boy to jump as the corded arms bunched up behind his back.

"Push, you brutish blacksmith bastards! We don't die here today. PUSH!" he bellowed, Livius echoing his cry at full throttle as Lortmund and Svein braced their own huge bulk and forced with everything they had.

The unexpected burst of strength from the Annarites threw the attackers, their confidence wavering as they were bulled back a step. Livius, Devar and Alkor using their shields as a buffer whilst being pushed by the avalanche of muscle behind. They pushed forward a step, then another, until Dextri judged there was enough room for the hammers.

"On my mark, we disengage. Lortmund, Svein, be ready to swing those hammers," Dextri murmured, keeping his voice low so as not to alert the Hounds.

"Oh, you want the 'brutish blacksmith bastards' *now* do you?" Svein retorted sarcastically, causing Lortmund to roll his eyes and Dextri to snort.

"Just do as you're told big lad, eh? Be ready!" Dextri said, continuing the slog away from the walls.

If it was possible, the attacks intensified as the Annarites continued to defy the odds, men from the back rank now adding their bulk to the front. It became a war of pushing, with the odd bang of a sword on shield; that the shields had lasted this long was a commendation to the quality of the metal rims surrounding them and Dextri vowed to pay Lortmund more after this.

Alkor was sweating, his youthful energy barely intact as the adrenaline of the situation coursed through his body but he didn't have the full strength of an adult just yet. His arms began to feel wobbly at their constant use. He was thankful for Dextri's bulk at his back, knowing he would've been overwhelmed much earlier without the machine of a man.

Through the chaos, his eyes caught a flicker in the shadows of an alleyway, as though a dark smudge had just twitched; he looked closer and his inattention almost cost him his nose as the man in front of him finally broke through the rim of the shield, the point of a sword almost kissing his face and causing an eruption of splinters as he wrenched the sword free. Before the man could react, Alkor punched his shield forward into the man's face, creating two bloody gouges in his cheeks as the two-pronged broken shield became a weapon. The man recoiled and was forced back into the pushing match as it continued. Shadows twitching again, Alkor swore he saw a flash of red dart out. A cry rose from the back of the Hounds and the pressure relaxed briefly as Alkor saw a man collapse to the ground wailing in pain.

The short moment was all that was needed, as the man in front took an involuntary step back and Alkor stepped into his place, exposing his own but revealing the side of the enemy to his left. Dextri reacted first, stalling the forward push and stabbing his sword between the man's ribs, twisting cruelly before ripping the blade out. He grabbed the back of Alkor's collar and dragged him back into the line, the enemy wavering slightly as two of their men were dropped. Their back line was frantically glancing around, unsure why their comrade had dropped and unable to get any information out of the inconsolable man. Alkor saw the flash again and this time he smiled. The flash of red was braided.

Balzor darted out of his hiding place in the shadows, hamstringing another man and dropping him, this staying in the open as he screamed, "Saternac!" at the top of his lungs.

Dextri picked his moment perfectly. "NOW!" he bellowed, signalling the beginning of the end for the Hounds.

The remaining men at the back line turned to confront Balzor, who suddenly went from assassin in the shadows to half-trained boy against two warriors, but Dextri's order let chaos rein.

With one final shove, Lortmund and Svein took a step back, and brought their hammers down with the strength that only working a forge could give a man. Livius and Devar, knowing their intentions, had stepped back with them, creating the opening for the hammers to work. They crashed down onto the exposed shoulders and backs of the leading rank, dropping them with a crunch as their bones were obliterated.

Dextri now had space too, stepping around Alkor to confront the last man in the front rank. Alkor ignored him completely, darting to his left and bludgeoned his way to support Balzor, attacking with his shield, making the Hounds stumble before they could overwhelm his brother, giving Balzor a chance to chop his sword into one man's head, killing him instantly.

Devar charged forward before the other man could recover, knocking him to the ground and slamming his shield continuously into the back of his head, bursting his skull into fragments and crushing the soft brain underneath. That left one man standing. His eyes darted toward the alleyway that Balzor had emerged from.

"Oh no, friend. You won't be leaving this street," Dextri said, his voice soft and dangerous.

The man attacked desperately, intending to wound and run, but Dextri was a master at his craft. He parried the initial swings easily, stepping inside the man's guard and slamming his shoulder into his chest, knocking him to the floor. Refusing to admit defeat, the man tried a last swing and regretted it instantly, as Dextri's sword deflected it then swung back to sever his sword hand at the wrist. The man's screams reverberated around the otherwise quiet night until Dextri kicked him brutally in the stomach and cut them short.

"Who sent you?" Dextri said above the man's quieter cries.

He stopped, breathing heavily and clutching his one hand to the ruined stump, but firming his resolve and not answering. Dextri laughed darkly, sending shivers down Alkor's spine; it wasn't a sound he expected to come from the usually caring man. He pressed his foot down onto the man's bleeding arm, who writhed with intense agony.

After a few seconds, Dextri removed his foot and set it back onto the floor.

"Now, would you like to rephrase that?" he asked, mock politeness entering his tone.

"My father will rip you apart" the man spat, his voice peculiarly familiar to Alkor, who for some reason was reminded of his brother, Alnor. He shook his head in dismissal, which seemed to anger the man further.

"The world is going to change very soon, old man. Old regimes and ideologies will be thrown out, and the ones chosen by the Gods will rule with an iron fist, above all laws. Weakness will not be an option. The weak made to serve and the strong in their proper place!" he snarled, his voice rising higher, the words laced with feverish passion.

Dextri laughed and turned to Livius. "So, the Hounds are Kerazar, Livius, who would've thou – "he began, then reacted instantly as the man on the floor rolled for his fallen sword.

It was an obvious choice and Dextri had clearly expected it. He parried the blow with contempt and sank his blade through his heart to the hilt without mercy. The man gasped loudly as the sword sheathed itself inside of him, his eyes bulging as his remaining hand lost all its strength and the weapon dropped to the floor with a clang. His body slid off the blade as Dextri put his finger on the man's forehead and pushed lightly, prolonging the death in a last act of cruelty. Any Kerazar was less than human in his eyes and deserved any form of pain they got.

Hitting the floor with a dull thud, the light went from his eyes and his facemask fell askew. Stunned silence ensued as a face they all knew was revealed. Balzor and Alkor stood gaping at the body, and Livius blew air from his mouth in a burst.

"Well, Ezimat's balls..." Livius said.

Lying on the floor with blood seeping from the corner of his slightly ajar mouth, was Petra.

Chapter 8

Doors creaked open slowly, wide whites of fearful eyes the only thing that the warriors could see in the gloom. After the fighting had stopped and familiar guards were witnessed, doors were thrown open emitting light to the town again.

Blinking at the sudden glare, the men squinted at the families clustered in the small homes, cowering around children in the fake security of togetherness. Some began shouting questions, none of which received answers; others began to cheer half-heartedly before fading back into silence as the forlorn atmosphere absorbed their attempts. The shock of betrayal lanced them to the core and most of them struggled to recover. Even Balzor and Alkor, who barely knew Petra, were aware that defection to the Kerazar almost never happened, especially with someone so close to the King or the General. These specific guards were hand-picked; they were the best and the most loyal.

Devar recovered first, letting out a strangled cry and tearing off towards the forge shouting his brother's name. The agonised cry brought the rest of them out of their appalled trance, Dextri reacting as soon as it had left Devar's lips.

"Balzor!" he barked, causing the lad to jump out of his skin as he ripped his eyes away from the dead traitor's face. "Get the Seeress, explain and ask her *very* nicely to come to Ingvar's aid. Without her, the wound is almost certainly fatal, so be quick about it."

Balzor saluted and sprinted back down one of the dark alleyways that he'd emerged from earlier, making Dextri shudder slightly. The lad hadn't hesitated in the slightest using the shadows to his advantage, rendering two assailants unable to walk and currently passed out from the pain. They could be questioned later, but first they had work to do.

"Livius, Alkor, rouse the village and spread the word. Bucket teams will be useless at this stage, the stream outside the walls is possibly unsafe and the fire will have its claws too deep into the inn but get anything combustible out of the area. Do *not* let it spread. Lortmund, Svein, round up some of the local lads, make sure they have good eyes. Get the wall lit up and some faggots over the side, anyone approaching will be denied entry without express permission from me – even if he says his name is Ezimat! And if it wasn't obvious, get those gates barred," he finished, satisfaction settling in as his orders were carried out without question. Even some of the villagers volunteered and followed the guard to help.

Soon the bell was ringing but people were slow to react, still cowering from the fighting moments before. It was only when the villagers who resided close to the forge began knocking on doors and assuring their neighbours of their safety that they began to come out tentatively.

Livius ground his teeth at the pace but knew no amount of shouting or cajoling would speed up the process, so kept his counsel and began to dampen any thatch in range. Alkor began dismantling the stalls, the sudden cracks and curses indicating they were being broken down rather than dismantled.

Worry about that later Alkor thought after he used the base of his foot to snap off the legs of one stall. *Stalls can be rebuilt in an hour, a life cannot.* His train of thought stayed along that road as he winced, imagining the reprimands from the owners; the fire didn't slow its devouring of the inn, the roof flexing as the upper walls held on by a hair's width. The heat from the inferno was excruciating, sweat dripping down Alkor's back as he dragged the closest of the now destroyed stalls out of range of the eager sparks. Disgruntled villagers appeared to help move their own broken equipment with only minor grumbling; at least this way they kept the materials.

Once ensuring everything was running smoothly, Dextri moved back to the forge to check on the two brothers. Fervently hoping that Balzor hadn't been waylaid, he entered the unusually quiet forge to a scene he felt he was intruding on. Ingvar was alive, just. He was breathing raggedly, eyes calmly shut with perspiration beading on his face, rested in Devar's hands atop his knee. His usually erratic hair was plastered to his head and a blood-stained rag was tied around the wound, trying and failing to stem the blood. Devar held his expressionless look on his face as Dextri walked in, barely looking up from his trance at the interruption, a tear still clung unashamedly to his cheek. He cuffed it off and sniffed, shaking his head slightly without jostling his brother.

"Don't try to sweeten it, Dex. We both know a death wound when we see one," he said, tight lipped at holding in his grief.

Ingvar twitched at the sound of his brother's voice, but his eyes remained closed. "I've sent the lad to go and get the Seeress, but we need to stop the bleeding," Dextri murmured, falling to one knee next to them and examining the wound.

136

Right on time, Olsten limped through the back door with more clean rags, floating in a bowl of steaming water. Hobbling as fast as he could without his improvised crutch, he passed the rag to Dextri who nodded his thanks, then sank into the nearest stool with a sigh and began unlacing his boot. Devar made to remove the bandage, but Dextri firmly grabbed his wrist and shook his head.

"You just keep him still, Devar. This won't be pleasant." Devar's expression tightened but he took his brother's hands and held them in an iron grip. Gingerly, Dextri untied the knot that kept the makeshift bandage in place and with tender hands that belied their size, he began to remove it whilst using his other hand to clean the crusty blood from around the wound with the new cloth. Ingvar groaned in his delirium but didn't wake. A feeling of uselessness came over him as he caught the smell oozing out of his gut, his friend wouldn't survive without the Seeress' help. They only had one option to slow it down and give Ingvar a slight chance. Dextri looked up from the wound into the grief stricken but pleading eyes of Devar, who made the connection at around the same time as their eyes locked.

"Do it," he almost begged Dextri who wasted no time. He rose fluidly and rushed to the cooling fires of the forge, pulling on the thick leather gloves used to re- move the blacksmith's work from the heat. He saw the white-hot metal of an unfinished scythe head poking out of the flames, already cooling without the help of the bellows but still fit for purpose. It sang as he brought it out of the coals, which spat sparks out in displeasure at having their work interrupted, then he was back at Ingvar's side and putting his entire weight onto his legs.

"Keep him held, brother" Dextri warned Devar, but the man didn't need tell- ing; wounds had been cauterized by them all in the past.

"Wait!" called Olsten, who threw a small axe handle over at the trio. Under- standing instantly, Devar caught the handle and placed it into the slack mouth of Ingvar, forcing his mouth shut before resuming his vice grip on his brother's arms and taking a deep breath.

"Do it, Dex," he said resolutely.

Dextri took a deep breath, steeled himself, then pressed down with the blade. Sizzling flesh bubbled, doing its cruel but necessary work of melting the flesh back to- gether and sealing the wound. Ingvar's eyes shot open as he tried in vain to flinch away from the searing heat; his initial ragged intake of breath increased to a low animal moan, then escalated as the agony intensified. Ingvar arched his back despite his restrictions then screamed.

✶✶✶✶✶

"I think that's enough room lads. Keep some of the young 'uns waiting with buckets just in case a gust of wind decides to play its tricks, but the rest go home to your families, we'll finish up here!" Livius shouted above the roaring of the flames.

The upper floor of the inn had long since crashed down, picking it's time to cover Ingvar's screams, for which Livius was grateful. He'd had a feeling what would need doing, but the already spooked villagers glanced towards the wretched sound with unease. The two men Balzor rendered helpless sat moaning across the square; Livius had personally dragged them into view to avoid any chance of escape, but the lad had done them good and proper.

Fire prevention achieved, Livius turned his attention to the drowsy pair, barely conscious due to blood loss. He'd probably have to ask the Seeress to heal them before they bled out - although they didn't need to know that. He put on his best sinister smile and stalked over, aiming a kick at one of the men who had just enough awareness to flinch before the jolt of pain woke him fully. To his credit he didn't cry out.

"So, your lad back there didn't really divulge your purpose here... now he's dead. Your chance at living rests solely on what you tell me in these next few minutes," Livius said as casually as he could, keeping that smile on his face and knowing the contrast was unnerving to the best of men.

The man mumbled something, but whatever was said was muffled by the mask both men still wore.

"It'd help if you took those off," Livius suggested, but the man flinched again, knocking into the other man and dislodging him out of his trance.

Livius cackled "You can't be that fucking ugly, surely mate?"

The man's eyes hardened and he reached up to his face slowly, then ripped the mask off like a scab. Livius' sinister smile was wiped off his face as all decorum fled and he lunged like a viper, punching the man in the teeth and rocking his head back.

"How many of you went over Mika, you bastard?!" he raged.

Because the man in front of him was another man he knew and had thought of as a brother, Mika smiled as blood dripped from his cracked, dry lips.

138

"Hey, Livvy," he taunted. "Went over where? To being sick of being taken for granted? Working for a pittance to fight against our own kind to protect people who don't even realise what we do for them? Brother, I've always been here. Just took me a while to come out into the open."

Livius snarled and moved forward, grabbing fistfuls of the dark robes and wrenching his 'friend' into the air until they were nose to nose, his useless legs supporting limp toes as they trailed the ground.

"Kerazar!" Livius growled furiously.

Mika laughed again, albeit sounding more forced this time. "Kerazar? Brother, all of us are just Kerazar that lost our way. Why should we give everything for people who give nothing back? The kingdom gets taxes, we get wages, but what do we *really* get?" Mika retorted, flecks of blood spitting from his mouth onto Livius' face. "Merchants sneer at us as they wear their gaudy robes, richer than we'll ever be for zero risk. Peasants have the audacity to claim equality as they clamour for scraps of bread to survive. And don't even get me started on the General. That prick is so high and mighty he – ",

An outburst of breath as Livius punched him hard in his stomach cut off the last of his reasoning and he was dropped unceremoniously to the floor. A slight cry escaped his bravado as his body finally succumbed to its pain. Peripheral vision alerted Livius to Alkor approaching, rubbing soot off his face with his already sweat stained shirt.

"He looks familiar, guessing he's another turncoat?" he said, seemingly unconcerned that his father's men had betrayed him as he ruffled his hair to dislodge the rogue bits of ash that had nested there.

Only his eyes betrayed the fury that lurked inside. *If there was ever any doubt that he's a Sain, those eyes would dispel it,* Livius thought with unease. He could see the same unease reflected in the eyes of Mika and the second unknown attacker, but Mika began to rise and spit some insult or other. A flicker of movement was all that announced the savage kick that rendered the traitor unconscious, eyes rolled up into his head as he crumpled back to the dirt.

"Now..." Alkor began calmly. "Whilst your mate there has a nap, you can answer our questions."

As Alkor was speaking, he stalked slowly towards the remaining man, crouching lower to speak to him eye to eye. Whatever he saw in those eyes spooked him as much as any torture could have done. He tore off his own mask, surprising Livius at the fact that he wasn't one of the Sain guards and began to babble.

"They move from village to village, killing and burning, leaving no-one alive but the records forget about us. The ones that are missing. The ones that they leave *alive*! They take the ripe ones. The ones that are the perfect age for fighting or some sort of trade. If we don't comply, we die. There's only so many times you can say no after being in a cell for days without a pot to piss in or water to quench your thirst. For fuck's sake they have my *sister*!"

The shrill screaming voice bit through the intense, forced calm that the young Sain exuded with his presence alone. Surprise flickered across the ruthless façade that Alkor had adopted, his prejudiced assumption dashed with the clear emotion ripping through the captive's voice.

"Let me get this straight... you're not here willingly?" Alkor said, unable to keep the disbelief and contempt from his voice at the insinuation.

A flash of anger crossed the man's face, and he bared his teeth at the young Sain.

"Look at what's in front of you! Men have died tonight on both sides. The difference between us, is that your men believe they're fighting for justice. Half of ours fight for ideals they don't understand, forced into service by threatened slavery of their family; the others are that radical they think the prince is a God, sent by Ezimat to right the world and place the chosen ones in to power," he said, rage boiling over his attempt at keeping calm, spitting and wrenching despite the pain of his lacerated legs. "They take our families as insurance – a way to ensure we're loyal, regardless of whether we want to be."

Despite himself, Alkor felt a slight pity for the man. If what he said was true, half the Kerazar army was made up of men who were practically slaves, family ties made into chains to hold them against disobedience. Despite himself, he could see the niches that such a system would leave for infiltration, for destruction. Then he was dragged back to reality as his tired brain registered the last part of the man's tirade.

"The prince? Prince Krinar?" Alkor exclaimed.

The man's face changed from outrage to confusion within seconds and someone Alkor thought to be much older than himself, revealed his age to be much closer to allow comfort in killing him. His harsh face suddenly became mellow, strong cheeks changing to fleshy and dark eyes glinting tears above what was a hard exterior. His sneer seemed like a boyish smirk and his posture sagged as he realised the revelation he'd let slip. He sighed.

"Who else but royalty would have the power and the means to plan something this big? The Hounds have been his puppies from the start. Half his troops have his same twisted mind, and the other half are bribed to turn a blind eye to the atrocities then a whole contingent is blackmailed into serving his twisted ideals. The prince is following in his uncle's footsteps. Strength. Will. Rule." Resignation lined his voice as he explained what he thought was the inevitable.

Alkor sighed and the hardness left his eyes. Livius let out a breath he didn't know he was holding as the Sain ferocity winked out, replaced by a look of pity and righteous vengeance.

"If this is true Livius..." he began, rising from his crouch to look at the man whose crooked smile was for once absent. "We need to warn him. If the prince is in on it, the King might be too. My father is with them both right now and would be the greatest obstacle in their plans."

"I know lad, I know," said Livius. "One thing I also know about the King is that he'd sooner die than go over to that way of thinking, I can promise you that. I'll saddle up a horse and be on the road at first light which judging by the tweeting from the trees, can't be too far away".

Livius rubbed his eyes and yawned at the prospect. Alkor however, perked up.

"There aren't many horses left, but if we're quick we can -" Alkor started but was silenced with an abrupt hand from Livius.

"Not a chance lad, you're needed here. Your father would have my hide if I brought any untrained man into the field against the unknown, let alone his own son. I'll travel quicker alone, much quicker than looking after your lordly arse," he said, a ghost of the crooked grin returning to his face. "No buts!" he added as Alkor opened his mouth to protest, instead subsiding into a sulky silence.

The authority that the situation had lent him had quite clearly run its course, and he was once again the untrained youth being forbidden his adventure.

"Fine," he said glumly.

Livius turned and began to make his way in the direction of the stables, coughing slightly as the embers let out a burst of smoke.

"But Livius?" Alkor shouted at the man's retreating back. Livius stopped and half turned back.

"When you get back, we'll revisit that lordly arse remark." Livius' shoulders shook with silent laughter, and he gave Alkor the finger then broke into a jog. The seriousness of his task warranted speed.

Smiling to himself to try and unknot the sudden ball of anxiety that had wedged itself deep within him at the revelation, Alkor turned back to the conscious prisoner. He was muttering slightly under his breath, tears streaming down his cheeks as he berated himself and whispered his sister's name.

"Josee, oh God Josee," he repeated, grabbing fistfuls of his hair and slapping his head in penance.

Alkor felt the same pity that he'd felt earlier at hearing his words, trying and failing to harden his heart against the man's whimpers.

"Josee is your sister? How would you like to break the chains of her life and ensure nobody will hurt her again?" Alkor probed, letting no doubt enter his words, making his voice iron. The man looked up with wet eyes that were full of disbelief and a little scorn at the offer.

"They'll kill her before we even reach the nobles house…" he said, all belief and hope draining from his voice as he persuaded himself it wasn't possible.

Alkor shook his head and put his hand on the man's shoulder, gripping it tightly to convey as much strength as he could through that action.

"So, some nobles are in on it too? We can save her, that I promise you. But you need to tell me everything you know about the Hounds…"

✶✶✶✶✶

Ragged breaths came from the Seeress' throat as she walked with a speed that belied her age. One night! That was all she'd hoped for. How typical of the Gods to make the one night she needed to watch over her heir to be the night the village needed her most in years. When the boy had turned up at her door, sweat gleaming off his face and practically begging her to save his friend, she just couldn't help herself. *Always did have a soft spot for the young warriors,* she thought grudgingly.

Not even giving her time to don her cowl, the lad rushed through an explanation, focusing on the combat as the young ones usually did, but she got the information she needed - one man on the brink of death from a gut wound; two with slices in their legs which he seemed very proud to tell her that he himself had inflicted, and many minor injuries for the others. A small price considering the odds, but that opinion wouldn't have got her many cheers with the village. So here she was, rushing to the aid of another stubborn sword wielding imbecile who just *had* to play with pointy things. Although one thing the lad had told her tonight was true. The trees did look sinister.

She took a deep breath, absorbing the earthy smells tinged with acrid smoke, and increased her pace. Superstition didn't hold her the same way it did the younger ones, but you could never be too careful with nature. Her lamps that she usually kept burning to light Aria's path had long since fizzled out - the last on her list of chores that night.

As she trudged down the path, she thought about her decision to leave the boy to watch over her granddaughter and shrugged. There really wasn't anything wrong with her tonight, but first contact with that kind of power always left a person disorientated, not to mention unstable emotionally, though she already was when it came to him.

Two bloody weeks and she was star struck; good job the boy was just as infatuated with her or she'd have to box his ears for breaking her heart. The energy she could feel bouncing between them had the feel of fate around it, but her dreams had been strangely silent concerning Aria recently and that worried her. For decades she'd been able to focus her dreams on things she cared about, the sleeping visions were her close friends and had never let her down. Until now.

The worry she felt over barely seeing her granddaughter's future cut her more than she cared to admit; despite being able to heal, to fight, even to see most things, the one thing she *needed* was to make sure Aria was safe. Not being certain of the path forward for her as she always had been troubled her deeply, but she knew somehow that although being close to the boy left her closer to danger than ever before, she was also much safer than she would ever be without him. How she knew this, she was unsure, but she knew.

A shaft of light peeked through the trees and the first of the birds began to tweet, nature oblivious to the night's terrors and carrying on regardless. Rabbits darted across the path, chasing each other playfully as they stretched out their cramped muscles from their slumber. But with the light came an equal amount of darkness. It illuminated two men who she'd always thought too sweet for soldiering, but who craved to be a part of it nonetheless; that craving had eventually killed them, and they lay next to each other in the undergrowth, tree roots caressing them and forgetting their animosity in favour of honouring the dead.

"Oh, you two," she said sadly to the corpses, black blood crusted around the folds of their fleshy necks. "You should've followed your father into hunting, you deserved better than this."

She reached down to touch each of their cheeks, brushing her fingers lightly over their shocked eyes, closing them and sniffing slightly. No time for emotion yet, not with other lives left in the balance.

Stalking free of the wooded path, the smell of burning became much stronger, and smoke permeated the air above the houses, ash flaking from the sky like snowflakes and resting softly on the ground. She heard men shouting, orders being relayed and the hissing of quenched fire as water was thrown on to the flames to battle the inferno. She heard the ghost of a hideous scream underneath the rest of the cacophony and her steps quickened involuntarily. She knew the sound of a dying man, and she also knew the sound of other men doing stupid things trying to save them.

Luckily this one was the latter, but it meant there wasn't much time. She began to rush towards the forge, plunging into the dimmer and smaller alleyways around the cottages to avoid the carnage happening around the inn. She preferred to walk alone anyway, and speed was sure to be hindered if she walked past the villagers at breakneck speed – a superstitious lot, those villagers.

At the end of the alleyway, dead men lay strewn across the road in a strangely organised line, despite laying obviously where they fell. Some had their heads so drastically pulverised that no man, woman or child would ever identify them whereas others still had cloth coverings over most of their faces and could have passed off as sleeping, despite the odd angle of their legs as their bodies had crumpled.

She recognised one instantly and growled, knowing this was the one the boy had told her about - the traitor. A low whimper, carried on a gust of wind from the end of the road, brought her back to her task and she strode past the grisly graveyard, then entered the forge.

The expected heat that came with a blacksmith's house of trade was a lukewarm welcome, but the welcome she received from the men inside was hotter than if the bellows were working all day.

"Thank the Gods you came," the man she knew to be Devar said, which made the other man with his head in his lap his brother, Ingvar.

She already knew Dextri. He smiled weakly as she entered, head in his hands and elbows resting on his knees as he sat next to the embers, a discarded scythe blade on the floor next to him. The fact that the blade was still glowing slightly, and the sweet smell that only flesh could procure hung on the air, explained the rest to her without having to ask.

"Gut wound. Lost too much blood, cauterised?" she said systematically, cutting straight to the point.

Devar nodded grimly, tears racing down his cheeks, clinging to his jawline, clear tracks down his otherwise dirty face. His brother was shaking visibly, sweat coating his forehead and his breath coming in staggered gasps. Devar held his arms strongly despite his clear distress.

"Dextri, over here. Hold his legs as tightly as you can, if he kicks me halfway through this, I swear to Ezimat that cane Olsten's leaning on from his hiding place out the back will be so far up your arse, you'll be spitting wood," she commanded, causing Dextri to jump out of his skin and leap up to help.

Nobody disobeyed a Seeress, not even Dextri. Olsten, caught out from his attempt to avoid the proceedings, shuffled in guiltily. His own injury left him struggling to stand, so he sat down gingerly on an anvil with a heavy sigh.

"Right gents, this won't be pretty. A wound that has already been sealed is a much harder enterprise than me sealing it myself. My power works from the inside, out. So, working from the inside will involve this power feeling like it is forcing its way through the wound, though visibly we will see nothing. It will be excruciatingly painful for your brother - he will writhe, he will kick, and he will struggle. Do *not* release him. He might already be too weak to withstand this kind of healing, but it's this or his wound poisoning him slowly to a painful death. Olsten, make yourself useful and get some more clean rags and I may consider healing that tiny sprain you're making seem so dramatic. Go!"

The methodical way she gave the orders soothed Devar's nerves slightly, but the urgency that hid underneath her tone of voice also revealed how close they were to the tipping point of his brother's mortality. He took a deep, shuddering breath, then honed his warrior's focus to the task; he saw Dextri had been ready within seconds, pinning his legs in a grip that even Sarnat would struggle to break. Both nodded their readiness to the Seeress, who lowered herself to her knees with a care that only comes from age and began to remove the bandage.

Ingvar instantly gasped as the crusty material peeled off the layer of skin that had fused to it, revealing a nasty, puckered burn that wept yellow tears at being disturbed from its uneasy home. She tutted and threw a glare at the two men holding him, who looked sheepishly away. Though it was that or bleed to death, the men knew they'd done a shoddy job in their haste.

Discarding the congealed bandage, she held her hands above the injury, feeling the heat conducting through the air from his body, and opened her mind to the Gods. No matter how many times she felt her senses broaden, she still felt a thrill as the healing began to take effect. It seemed not only to do wondrous things, like stitching up an otherwise mortal wound, but also raised her own mood, as though something inside her was being healed too. That was, of course, until the screaming began.

As predicted, Ingvar began his escape within seconds, weakly at first but gaining strength as more of his wound knitted together. Devar grunted at the strain of holding his brother but held firm. Dextri on the other hand barely flinched - Ingvar's legs tethered to the ground despite his attempts to buck the huge warrior off. Though he grimaced in sympathy, it wasn't his first time seeing a healing, just not on this scale.

Most Seers or Seeress' stayed in cities or towns acting as midwives, doctors - even advisors in some noble houses - though those were mostly corrupt and enjoyed the money from fake predictions they delivered to feed egos. Any healing was usually conducted in those conditions, very rarely on battlefield wounds. Plus, the energy it took to undergo healings on this scale was huge; you'd need an army of seers alone to heal all the minor wounds of war.

The Seeress could feel the worms of power rummaging around Ingvar's organs, soaking up everything that could poison his body and repairing damage already made. She felt a single bead of sweat break out just above her eyebrow, the only indication of the pressure she exerted as she directed the flows further and further towards the entry wound, raising her hands up as though dragging it out on a line.

As she reached the first layer of outer flesh, Ingvar's eyes flew open and he stopped screaming, instead taking a horrible, drawn-out intake of breath and arching his back at an impossible angle, despite the efforts of the two men. Luckily, the Seress was experienced and much too wise to rely on external help, so instinctively rose with the man, keeping her distance exact as the power began to breach the cauterisation, shafts of light beaming through half-formed clots, his skin moving like a nest of ants as it warped and healed in ways beyond the realms of men.

With a whoosh, Ingvar released the breath which had been ripping into his lungs and collapsed to the ground, the power releasing as his body relaxed on the stones. The Seeress sagged back to her knees, breathing heavily, whilst Ingvar seemed in a deep slumber, the contrast massive compared to mere minutes before.

"Is it... done?" Devar asked uncertainly, unwilling to break into the Seeress' moment of peace as she recovered.

Both men were still gripping their comrade tightly, not yet given the command to relax themselves.

"It's done," she said wearily. Both men sighed in evident relief, tentative smiles breaking out onto their faces as the realisation hit that their brother was alive. "Clean the wound area with the bandages when Olsten returns, and make sure he gets plenty of rest. Strictly no training, lots of food and lots of sleep!" she added, tiredness taking out the sting of command from her voice. Not that either men would dare disobey. "Now, where are these other two that the boy injured?" the Seress asked.

"They should be in the square, near the inn. Should've known he'd brag about that the swine. I'll come with you, those two have a lot of explaining to do," Dextri said, rising and cracking his knuckles. "And Dextri doesn't have a lot of patience for bullshit tonight."

*****

"Hold up, so your sister is in the service of the Munat's in Torizo? I find it hard to believe they're traitors; my father grew up with half their household!" Alkor exclaimed.

The man shook his head slowly, shrugging at Alkor's comment. "They might be completely unaware of the situation. Like I said, she's just a maid, employed through what to them is an external service. She stays on the grounds, does their work and runs their errands, but technically is in the employ of another company who is paid by that household. A sub-contract of sorts," he explained, becoming more exasperated by the second. "A lot of noble houses do it from less than reputable sources, most likely the black-market slave trade. They can feign ignorance that way if it ever comes out in the open. This is no different. She works for my life, I work for hers; some of the 'maids' in the company *aren't* forced into service, but they dispatch the others if a traitor's in their midst. So, you see, if I choose your side, I'm well and truly fucked."

Alkor drummed his fingers on his chin thoughtfully, pondering over what the man had told him. Outside of the local area, he knew almost nothing. He'd been transported to Torizo by wagon, blindfolded the entire way and told only enough to ensure his loyalty - where his sister was, what would happen if he didn't comply, those sorts of things.

It was only recently that he'd realised it was the prince in charge when he'd hidden in a merchant's wagon for two days as it served the royal party and the General, awaiting orders from a man called Varnan; it was there he'd heard the same voice that had given him orders before, usually from behind the standard hood and mask of the Hounds. Peeking through the wagons curtain had revealed the prince, and the depth that the roots of betrayal had reached.

"Thank Ezimat for that! If his madness had really spread that far we would be totally screwed. So, the Hounds are just out there in plain sight? Living regular lives until ordered otherwise, then returning as though nothing has happened? That's cold," Alkor said distastefully. "Have you seriously never thought that people like that will just kill your sister to avoid a mouth to feed, once you don't return?"

Clearly what happened after his death hadn't even crossed the lad's mind and Alkor let out a sigh at his stupidity.

"What's your name?" he asked gently, which threw the man off at the sudden contrast in moods.

"Joseph," he replied warily. Before Alkor could respond, the arrival of Dextri and the Seeress interrupted the conversation. He rose from his crouch quickly, turning eagerly towards Dextri to ask the question that had been in his mind most of the night. Before the question left his lips, the laugh that came from Dextri answered it for him.

"He's alright lad. Completely wiped out, but alright," he said, prompting an elated cry from Alkor as he moved to embrace the Seeress before remembering himself and stopped halfway, hands raised like the village idiot. Dropping them quickly and stepping back, he bowed very low to her and muttered a heartfelt thanks. The Seeress looked exhausted but waved away his thanks with a trace of a smirk on her face.

"Let's get on with this before I change my mind or collapse on my face," she said impatiently, gesturing at the men on the floor.

"Alkor, what have you learned?" Dextri asked.

Alkor ran through a summarised version and let him know that he'd knocked Mika out within minutes of him talking. Dextri's eyes bulged as he took in the unconscious man on the floor, his face red as he struggled to contain his anger. His hand moved to his stolen sword hilt, and he took a half step forward before controlling himself.

"Traitorous cunt," he hissed at Mika, and right on time his eyes flicked open.

He sat up and groaned, then held his head delicately, giving it a slight shake before taking in the fact he had company. When he saw his former officer seething in front of him, he attempted a sneer and tried to rise but was slammed back to the ground by Alkor's fist connecting solidly with his chin. This time, he remained conscious, but his sneer stopped before it started.

"You're a big man, eh little Sain? Hitting a man whilst he's down," Mika laughed, a cough breaking through his words, giving a broken retort.

"You're lucky I don't make sure you never get back up, you worm. As it is, Joseph has told us everything we need, so as of now... you're disposable," Alkor said.

The grin on Mika's face flickered to worry before cementing back in as though nothing had changed. The furious glare that he threw at Joseph wasn't missed by anybody there, and Joseph cringed as it rested on him for the tiny second.

"So, what did you promise him? His sister would go free? Ha! I can tell by the look on his face that you did. She'll be dead before you even reach Torizo. Unless one of us reaches one of the senior officers to report our triumph here, she dies. If you try to rescue her, she dies. If he dies or betrays us, she dies!" he bellowed, attempting to terrify Joseph into keeping his mouth shut.

What he did, however, was confirm Alkor's hunch that his sister was dead regardless. Joseph muttered something under his breath, his face showing a hint of defiance despite being obviously terrified.

"What's that, pup?" Mika taunted, the sneer returning to his face.

"I said, ENOUGH!" Joseph roared, kneeling up seemingly without pain and squaring up to Mika, who flinched back an inch before regaining his posture. "If whatever happens, my sister dies, I'll spend my last days ensuring every last one of you follows her into the mud, whatever the cost."

Mika cackled. "You couldn't even plant a seed in the mud you maggot, let alone a warrior."

But Joseph had finished with him. He turned best he could to face Alkor, fury radiating from him in waves that Alkor could feel kissing his skin.

"Lord, if you can give me your word you will fight this tyranny and free my sister from her chains, my sword is yours, such as it is," Joseph said quietly. Though he sounded sincere, the menace in his voice was unnerving.

"How do I know this isn't just a ruse? An attempt to gain my trust to survive the night, then kill me in my sleep?" Alkor replied.

Joseph looked hurt at having his word doubted, sagging back to the floor and deflating. Suddenly, he rose, his eyes gleaming feverishly. "Alkor Sain, I pledge my loyalty completely to you and your line. I vow to protect, obey and die for you, until Ezimat's hall burns, and the Underworld consumes all. My life, my soul, my blade is yours," he said, his face so serene and sure that even Mika's face registered shock.

A broken oath on Ezimat's hall was as good as condemning yourself to the Underworld without committing any other sin – nobody broke an oath like that. Alkor stood open mouthed, gaping at the others around him with similar dumbfounded expressions.

"Boy... you realise the oath you just gave binds you tighter than any other you could give a King?!" the Seeress said, even her weariness extinguished as icy shock rippled through her.

Joseph turned to meet her eyes, and she saw a steadfast determination in his gaze and knew he wouldn't break his word - not that any sane person would. He nodded, looking back at Alkor who still had the same astounded look that he'd had since the oath was uttered.

"My lord, all my life I've been searching for purpose. First with my parents, then when they were killed, with the Hounds who killed them. Until this day, I had never found it. But I see a goodness in you, and I would give myself entirely to you and hope that it will lead me and my sister to salvation," he said earnestly, and Alkor finally clamped his mouth shut.

Alkor moved slowly towards Joseph, the weight of the moment not lost on him and his steps placed delicately to not upset the tension that had sprung from it. He could practically feel the hostility emanating from Mika.

"Not to say you don't sound sincere, Joseph, but less than an hour ago you tried to kill us," Alkor said.

Joseph squared his shoulders.
"Nevertheless, I will prove my oath to you before all this is over."

The seeress stepped forward and placed her hands just above Joseph's legs and opened her mind once more. These wounds were not life threatening, but they would have ensured Joseph would never walk again, and with the oath just given even she felt honour bound to give him a fighting chance at keeping it. Dextri, knowing what to expect, rushed to her side and pinned him to the ground, ignoring his confused cry at the rough treatment.

Alkor locked eyes with Dextri and saw a torrent of emotions threatening to consume him. He opened his mouth to say something, but no sound came out. Dextri just smiled and shook his head in a sad but enthusiastic way at the same time.

"To gain such loyalty so quickly... you truly are your father's son, boy," he said gruffly, tensing as the power began to rip through. The young man screamed as his flesh put itself back together and the muscle reformed. As feeling came back into his legs, his scream faded to be replaced with utter amazement.

"But... I don't... how?" he said, before his eyes rolled back into his head and he collapsed.

The Seeress almost joined him on the ground until Dextri reacted and caught her with his strong arms, his gentleness in contrast to his warriors' facade.

"I think that's enough for one night, even for one as powerful as you my lady," Dextri said, supporting her entire weight on his arm effortlessly. She snorted and shook her head before forcing her legs to take the strain off her helper.

"I might be old, but I'm not dead. You will not carry me home!" she said sternly, secretly glad of the man's strength as the effects of the night began to make her legs shake. Alkor stood rooted to the spot, still looking at his new potential liegeman unconscious on the ground, as though confused about what to do with him.

"He'll be okay, he just needs rest. Put him with Ingvar. Devar knows what to do. What about this one?" she added, gesturing weakly towards Mika, who's predator eyes scanned the situation to see what could be gained.

Seeing the need in his eyes as he saw his former comrade's wounds be healed ignited something in Alkor; he snapped out of his trance and snarled at the prone man. To his credit, Mika didn't even flinch, staring defiantly at the blue eyes that had suddenly turned hard and merciless.

"My father's son you say, Dextri? What would my father do to traitors?" Dextri looked at Mika, then smiled.

*****

Soft heat stroked her skin as her weary eyes forced themselves open, seeing the fireplace cheerily throwing warmth her way as she lay on soft cushions. She jolted upright, suddenly aware of the reason she'd been unconscious in the first place; torrents of power searing her nerves and forcing its way through her veins, rendering her unable to breathe or move. What she saw through her blurry eyes was a similar vision to that she saw every morning. Her bedroom, the pot of flowers to the side, the rainbow wool rug untidily strewn across the floor. What her vision struggled to comprehend was a crouched form with long red hair sat directly beside her bed, its strong arms clutched around her hand, refusing to let go.

The jolt upright dislodged her hand from the figure's grip, but it didn't try to attack her. If anything, it moved away, a worried look on its face as it raised its hands defensively. *Balzor,* she thought. Her body relaxed instantly, a deep sigh escaping her lips as she allowed his hands to take hers again and eased back down.

She felt so tired, her body aching as though she'd worked a day tilling the fields, her brain shutting down like a day solving riddles. Being here, lying in bed with Balzor beside her lessened the blow slightly, allowed her to – She shot upright again, tearing her hand away from his and dragging the blankets up to her chin as it hit home that Balzor was sat next to her whilst she was in bed. His eyes widened in shock, and he rose, stepping back slightly and holding out his hands trying to reassure her.

"Your grandmother told me to watch you, but you looked uncomfortable on the floor. I brought you in here and settled you in bed, sitting with you whilst you slept," he stammered, crimson face emitting a sheen of sweat which sparkled in the light.

His heart was pounding, he hadn't even considered what she would think as he'd lifted her off the floor and carried her into her bedroom but seeing it from her perspective, he realised how it looked. He took a couple of steps back, half turning to-wards the doorway and lowering his gaze. Aria's eyes softened, and she smiled.

"No, stay," she said, lifting her hand from the blankets and reaching for Balzor. He froze, uncertain, his eyes shifting uneasily towards the front door as if worried.

"Are you sure? Your grandmother almost flattened me when I barged in the first time. Never thought the power could tie you up like that, but you live and learn," he said, stepping slowly back into the room as if waiting for permission. She beckoned, and he resumed his original position, taking her hand in his and chuckling.

"Wait, you've been here twice tonight? Tell me everything, it seems I've missed a lot," she prompted as he settled back into position.

His eyes lit up at the question, but there was a shade behind the eagerness. He explained the entire night quickly, slowing as he described the fight outside the inn then speeding back up again. He was clearly bragging as he told her about his pivotal moment in the fight, downing two enemies from the shadows before revealing himself to draw their attention which helped sway the fight in favour of the Annarites. But throughout the whole thing he never mentioned being 'flattened' by her grandmother.

"Okay, okay, I get you're a fearsome warrior," she teased. "But what did you mean about being flattened by a frail old Seeress?"

"Well... what I said. I barged through the door after finding the bodies, terrified they'd come this way and hurt you too. When I came through the door, she sent me flying across the room with only a look, then wrapped me up in some sort of spell," he said, sounding slightly awed but with an edge of fear in his voice.

Aria froze. She knew that Balzor didn't know the gem of information that he'd just disclosed was one of her greatest secrets, one her family had kept close to home for many years. The stricken look on her face caused Balzor to stop talking, concern etched on his face as he took in her expression.

"What's wrong?" he said.

Aria opened her mouth, but no sound came out. She coughed forcibly and cleared her throat, then tried again. "What you have just told me cannot leave this room. Seeress' are known for healing, for predictions, for *life*. What you are describing is the complete opposite of those notions," she said, eyes imploring Balzor to see what he'd clearly not considered before. He looked confused, he hadn't put two and two together and made four; he'd just gathered the information and not used it.

"What are you saying?" he asked, face scrunched as he began to comprehend her intention but unable to make the connection - until he remembered the bonds and the force knocking him to the ground, the fire in the Seeress' eyes at the possible danger he presented.

Aria saw the revelation dawn in his eyes as he understood, his mouth popping open in a perfectly round shape.

"I can see you understand... our family is different. We have an extra branch to our power," she said in an almost desperate way, starting to clutch his hand in case he tried to run. She could see him connecting the dots, understanding what had happened.

Instead of a fear, a look of excitement appeared on his face.

"You can fight with the power?!" he exclaimed, a huge smile on his face and at a volume where the rest of the village could hear. Her mortified look quietened his tone as his face changed to an apologetic grin. She subsided slightly as his question echoed around the room, the terrifying quote silenced. But it had still been voiced.

"I can't... not yet... but yes, my line has the capability. Grandmother has explored all aspects of the power, to her it's second nature; my mother ignores the fact that it resides within her, instead using her predictions to see flaws in the market to sell her wares. I can feel it there, especially now, waiting to be tapped into. Most lines are lucky to get a prediction whilst they sleep, some can predict futures years ahead. Some heal near death wounds; some can barely cure a sniffle. But barely any can use their power offensively, and none that can broadcast it. As far as I know, our family is the one of the only lines that can - hence the importance of keeping it secret," she said, frantically trying to justify it.

Balzor did nothing but smile at the admittance. "Aria, I would never do anything to endanger you. I would never spread your secrets, do anything to belittle you, or hurt you in any way. I'd literally *die* for you," he said, pure truth shining through his voice that clogged Aria's throat with emotion.

She took her hand from his and cupped his cheek in her palm as she drew him close to her, nerves on fire. His eyes switched from an earnest look to one of hunger, and she felt a stirring in her breast. Her breath quickened, pulse racing as his hand grabbed the back of her head, pulling her towards him with a gentle savagery that only excited her more.

Their lips touched and she moaned quietly as his tongue traced hers, electricity piercing through them at the contact. The door opened behind them with a bang. They broke apart instantly, Balzor lunging for the sword that lounged on the floor, Aria leaping back with a guilty look on her face. Balzor spun around with his sword bared, only to shrink back in embarrassment and fear.

"Now then!" rasped the Seeress' voice. "What do we have here?" "Grandmother... we were just... I mean to say that..." Aria stuttered, hands flapping wildly in her useless attempt to come up with an excuse.

"I carried her in here after you left, Seeress. Seemed better than the floor. Then er... she woke up," he finished lamely. Balzor averted his eyes from the Seeress, finding a stern looking Dextri behind her, trying and failing to keep a knowing smirk off his face. As always at the wrong moment, Balzor felt a bubble of mirth creeping its way through his body. All the pent-up excitement, then getting caught by Dextri, it was all he could bear. He could feel heat suffusing his face as he clenched his jaw against the laughter that strained to be free. Thankfully, Dextri came to the rescue.

"Since his tongue seems tied, Seeress, I'll get him out of your hair and apologise on his behalf. I'll spar with him tomorrow and won't go easy on him," he said, stepping forward and clasping his hand on the shamed lad's shoulder. The Seeress only had eyes for Aria. She waved her hand dismissively, and Dextri took his leave, Balzor following close behind, eager to escape the most awkward situation of his life.

Balzor closed the door behind him, took one look at Dextri, and snorted. The snorts burst into full laughter, well within range of the Seeress and Aria. It didn't help when Dextri joined in, and they hurried away like scolded children to avoid the tongue lashing they'd get if they lingered. Balzor's laughter was short lived though, as alarm shot through his body at the unasked question.

"Ingvar?!" he gasped, furious with himself that that hadn't been his first thought. Dextri continued to chuckle at the situation, dissolving his fury slightly.

"It's okay lad, she got there in time. He's gunna feel like shit for a few days but he'll live," Dextri said, still chuckling. "Besides, you've got much bigger problems now. I'd love to be a fly on the wall when you next see the Seeress." Balzor groaned.

*****

Back inside, the Seeress sighed and rubbed her bony fingers on her temples. Aria prayed that she hadn't heard the laughter from outside.

"Men" she cursed, making Aria flinch and rise from her bed, bare feet feeling cold despite the fireplace roaring.

"Grandmother, it wasn't what you think," she pleaded, embarrassment still pumping through her. Her grandmother chuckling was the last thing she expected.

"Girl, by your age, I had men chasing me just for a glimpse of my ankles. Kissing me in a bed was something they only dreamed of. It was *exactly* what it looked like!"

156

she chortled, glee on her face at the mortified look on Aria's. "Next time close your bedroom door; it'll buy you some time. But that's not why I'm close to skinning you alive," she added.

Aria's embarrassment quickly changed to confusion, brows knitting together as she struggled to understand where the problem lay. "Well, if that's not what the sour look on your face is for, please enlighten me," Aria retorted, a hint of anger entering her voice as her defences were thrown up at the accusation.

"*Our family is one of the only ones that can, hence the importance of keeping it a secret,*" the Seress quoted, a lack of anger in her voice deflating Aria's before it even started to burn.

Aria's eyes widened. "How could you hear that?!" she whispered in shock.

"A small trick to enhance senses. Figured if we didn't get back in time, you'd be having your fun, so I would've made more noise coming in. Getting caught smooching is one thing, being literally caught with your pants down is another. But back to the subject at hand, why did you tell him?!" she said accentuating the final five words and making Aria cower slightly, only to rise up again with her newly flared anger.

"Tell him? You literally put him on his arse and tied him up, how could I not? Even the dullest button in the box would put the pieces together. At least this way he found out properly rather than blabbing his mouth with all the other warriors in the inn one night!" she shouted, eyes blazing.

Herb pots on the windowsills began to shake, rattling together with a high-pitched clinking, some even fell and smashed. The furniture began to bounce off the floor, its dull knocking in contrast with the herb pots, the house now an orchestra of sounds. Aria's eyes lost their blaze and widened in shock, as she felt the stirrings of power come to her unbidden.

"Rein in your temper, girl. Your emotions are heightened tonight, and power is linked to emotion. Be calm," the Seeress ordered, unfazed by the outburst that had begun to shake her home.

Aria, however, was petrified. She'd lost all her anger as soon as the surprise sank in, but she still couldn't release it. It was nothing like the waterfall that crushed her earlier; instead, this felt more like a stream that she could direct, but still without any start or ending point no matter how hard she searched.

"Grandmother... I can't," she said, beginning to hyperventilate.

"I said *calm!*" barked the Seress.

The flow of power was cut off instantly, whipping back into her brain like a lash and losing the mixed feeling of euphoria and terror. Aria collapsed to her knees and began to shake, sobs wracking her body as she tried to apologise through the tears. The Seeress kneeled beside her and wrapped her arms around Aria's slender shoulders, holding her tightly and shushing her. The shaking subsided and the sobs eventually worked their way to a sniffle. Aria looked up through wet eyes at her grandmother, wordless thanks conveyed. The Seeress kissed her forehead and gave her shoulder one last rub before rising.

"It seems we'll have to start training you quicker than I anticipated. The power is a wondrous thing, but as you can see, it has a mind of its own that needs moulding. Since you'll not be working anymore anyway, we'll start first thing tomorrow," she said softly, offering Aria her hand to help her rise, which she took gratefully.

"I just couldn't let go," Aria stuttered, taking deep breaths. "I knew what I was doing and how it was happening, but stopping it was beyond me. I couldn't see the beginning or end of – hang on, what do you mean I won't be working anymore?" The Seeress sighed, hands going to her temples again.

"Make a pot of tea girl and sit down. Your boy left things out, it seems I've got a lot to explain."

✶✶✶✶✶

A gentle breeze glided through the air, nudging the trees playfully as it went by, carrying pieces of ash through the air and making them dance to the tune of a woman's wailing. The sun hadn't yet opened its eyes from its slumber, but the light had begun to break through the glum morning regardless, unaware of the tragedy that had changed the lives of Saternac yet again.

The two Dick's, now moved from their embrace near the roots, had been formally arranged on the path. The culprits who'd rescued the bodies from the under-growth were also with the source of the woman's wailing - their father, Rindu, their mother, Annel, and their older sister, Mariak. Mariak stood with tears streaking down her face, no sound coming from her mouth and shaking as she leant into her father for

158

comfort who, in contrast, stood still as stone, face unmoving and dry eyed. The grief was evident if you looked closer, the tightening lips that loosened ever so slightly as he almost lost control, the darting of his eyes between the bodies of his sons and the remaining woman with them.

Annel was inconsolable. Her hands tore through her hair as she knelt beside her boys, red rims surrounding wild eyes that summoned an unending waterfall of tears; mouth wide open and emitting screams that could only leave a person's throat at discovering how cruel the world actually is.

Stood to the side, hands clasped across his front and head bowed so as not to intrude on a private grief, stood Alkor. As if synchronized, Rindu and Alkor both looked up at the approaching footsteps. Rindu nodded, dead eyes returning straight to the scene of mourning. Alkor beckoned to them both, indicating to step off the path and away from the grieving family to give them privacy in their moment of despair.

As Dextri and Balzor approached, stepping into the bracken with a rustle of grass and snapping of twigs, Mariak turned and locked eyes with Balzor. Those eyes, in comparison to her father's, were more alive than ever. They blazed with unmasked fury at the sight of the trio attempting to converge behind them and she shrugged free of her father's embrace, storming towards them.

"You were supposed to keep us safe! We aren't warriors! My brothers weren't warriors despite carrying weapons and playing at it! Instead, you drink every night in the inn and play with swords during the day to keep up pretences, whilst my brothers pay the price for your incompetence. Explain yourselves!" she shrieked, ignoring her father's muted pleas behind her to cease her tirade.

Annel's wails had finally stopped, eerily silent on the pathway, the trees that were sinister earlier pausing in the wind, as if cocking their heads to listen. Balzor opened his mouth to reply, but nothing came out. Dextri moved forward, hands out in front of him in what he thought was a consoling stance.

"Now see here, we can't be…" he began.

"Dextri! Don't," Alkor said sharply. "Just don't."

The big man froze in disbelief, unsure whether to reprimand the young Sain or obey. But before he could decide, Alkor moved past him and took the girl's hands. By some miracle, she didn't pull away, but her eyes remained hard.

"There's nothing I can say to ease your pain, nothing I can do to cover your loss. Your brothers died guarding a gate that hadn't been attacked in years, they probably thought themselves safe. My father rode out with the men, hunting the rebels who destroyed our town all that time ago, but we were betrayed. Half of the men from one of our patrols are the same as those who attacked tonight. We were hit by people sworn to protect this town, this region. We were hit by betrayal. None of this changes the dreadful truth, and none of it will bring your brothers back, but I swear to you on Sain honour, they will be avenged," he said.

Mariak wrenched her hands from his and walked stiffly back to her father, burying her head into his chest as the sobs finally came, erasing the silent tears for the full grief her mother had displayed.

Rindu looked at Alkor and just shook his head, no life returning to his eyes. Annel however, rose and turned. Those eyes were the worst of the three, they glinted murderously at Alkor. Annel stooped to pick up one of her son's spears, pausing a moment to rest her hand on his cheek before rising again.

"Annel..." her husband said warily, poising himself to leap at her should she try to do what the spear implied. Alkor was shocked, hand going to his sword hilt before he realised that she was his responsibility, despite the threat. He dropped his hand from the hilt and knelt on the floor, bowing his head as he did so.

"I swear to you on my honour as a Sain, I will stand against this betrayal with everything I have," he said calmly, despite her evident hostility.

She gave a dry laugh. "Get up fool boy! A lord doesn't bow to his subjects. The man you left alive - Mika. This is a blood feud, and it can only end one way," she hissed icily. Her husband's eyes finally came alive at the comment, and he unlaced Mariak's arms from around him, reaching to pick up the remaining spear. Suddenly, Alkor was facing two armed villagers and their daughter, all with the same undeniable look on their face – murder.

*****

The screams lasted an age. Three usually innocent villagers had sated their bloodlust and grief on the only man they could blame. Rindu was a hunter, knew how to skin a boar expertly; his daughter had followed in his footsteps after the two Dicks decided to become militia. Her technique wasn't as precise but was even more brutal because of

160

it. They didn't make it quick, and bit by bit the horrified village had come to view the spectacle, drawn by the agonised shrieking in the square.

Alkor stood transfixed, wanting to look away but aware that everybody was watching. This was his town now. To look a coward or weak skinned in front of them was unthinkable. He watched, fighting the bile rising in his throat as flesh was stripped piece by piece from the once proud Mika.

Dextri had left the instant it had started, muttering about honourable deaths and a warrior's way. As far as Alkor was concerned, any traitor left his honour the moment he turned his back on his friends. Balzor shared the same sentiment, standing at his brother's shoulder and watched unflinching as the family tore the warrior apart. No man could endure that sort of torment for long, his screams becoming ragged breaths as his body slipped into delirium to avoid its torture. His eyes rolled up into his head and he began to convulse, red froth bubbling from his mouth as he shook uncontrollably in his final moments. He took one last, rattling breath, and was still.

The family stepped back from the mess before them, fury spent with the gore that caked their forearms and faces. Annel threw up noisily. The spell that had entranced her broken, and the realisation that her sons were still dead still very much there. She began to sob again and collapsed to her knees. Her hands cupped her face, smearing blood on her cheeks that the tears forged a path through on their way down.

Mariak and Rindu stood rooted to the spot, not moving to comfort Annel, their chests heaving. None of the villagers dared move towards them, terrified eyes absorbing the scene before them, seeing the Praker family in new light, a much darker one. Alkor stepped forward in the silence that permeated the village.

"Tonight, has been a night as terrible and gruesome as all those years ago, orchestrated by the same beasts we've all shivered to hear the name of: The Hounds. Two brave men died in their attack from the shadows, died defending the gate to buy us time. Tonight, because of their sacrifice, the Hounds were defeated and proven not to be wraiths, but mere men! The result is in pieces on the floor before you. But a new revelation has come to light which shocks the entire foundations that our kingdom is built upon. The so-called Hounds are in fact traitors to everything we stand for; they are Annar soldiers corrupted to Kerazar ideals, or men captured from villages with hostages to force their loyalty. The fact that they are here now, just after my father has left to eradicate what we thought were the same rebels, shows the corruption has reached much higher than we anticipated. To a height that threatens even my father and the King on their quest!"

The village erupted into shock, muttering at the words and disrupting the announcement. Alkor waited impatiently for it to subside. Seeing the young man had more to say, neighbours nudged their friends to an uneasy silence, eyes flickering to the blood-spattered family still in the centre of the square, transfixed with Alkor, hungry glares fixated on him. Alkor took a deep breath and began again.

"We've sent a man to warn them, but in the meantime, we need to prepare for the worst. Farmers, gather what harvest you can and bring it within the walls, fill up the cisterns from the stream. Anyone able to draw a bow and shoot needs to take shifts on the walls, with horns to alert others to any danger. But most of all we need information."

His eyes shifted to the crazed Praker family, his own gaze now hard and icy, the genetic Sain authority lancing from them. "I know I have no right to ask, but I must. You know the woods better than anyone, how to stay hidden, how to track. We need to find our patrols, if they're still breathing bring them back here. You will be our eyes and ears until we know more," he said, tone indicating that it was more an order than a question, despite their loss.

Annel looked at Rindu, and Rindu at Annel. They weren't warriors, but the loss of their sons had hardened their hearts to stone. She nodded curtly at him, and he moved to answer. Mariak took the situation out of their hands before he could.

"First, we bury my brothers. Then, we hunt. This time, for much better prey and to sate a much different hunger," she said, teeth bared in a feral snarl.

Silence greeted the words, and Alkor only nodded. Behind him, the sun began to awaken, its rays bathing the village in light and warmth. But the world had never seemed so cold.

Chapter 9

Aldred Sain rode at the front of the snaking column, silently seething. Arrogant was one of the many words that rattled around his head to describe the prince along with stupid, pampered and buffoon. The lightning-fast stealth mission to destroy the Hounds had become nothing more than a leisurely crawl pausing at each village, announcing exactly who they were and having nothing short of feasts at each - all paid for by the prince, of course.

He ground his teeth again. *Idiot!* What was worse, his own son had fallen in with that crowd. Aldred had struggled at the start to rein him in, bring him back to duty and the Sain guard, but it was futile. Ever since the night of cocky defiance underneath the walls of Torizo, his son had stopped listening to him. The worst of it was he wasn't actually doing anything wrong. His actions mimicked the prince's perfectly, with just enough respect for all the disrespect to sneak beneath, unnoticed, though it irked their fathers constantly.

King Malker was in the same frame of mind as the General, riding at the front next to his old friend, tight lipped and stiff backed as he weathered another chorus of laughter from behind him. When Aldred had confronted him and questioned why he allowed such a lapse in judgement, the King just shrugged helplessly.

"I promised him this would be his mission alone. If it's a royal fuck-up, it might finally get through to him that this is not just a game," he explained, though he looked sheepish as he did so.

He knew as well as Aldred that if they didn't get the Hounds now, they'd be in the wind. Funny thing to allow lives to be risked on a son being an idiot, but still they followed the prince's lead. Even the change in weather hadn't raised the mood of the older men in front. The slight showers barely even wet them, but they'd finally got rid of the infernal dust brought by the summer heat.

As the hills levelled out around them and the shrubs became full trees, then the trees became lush farmland. The raid they were anticipating became more like a stroll through the countryside. Tonight, he decided, he would confront the prince. Three days in that second week they'd only broke camp just before noon, this current day being the fourth. Well-wishers from the villages or hangovers from the nights kept them there most of the morning. Only the King's core and the Sain guard stayed sober enough to keep vigilant. They were in friendly territory now, but the closer to the dunes they got... Aldred dreaded to think what would happen if it continued.

One thing that had stayed constant was that his son still sparred at nights, though never with somebody who had any chance of beating him. He was an excellent swordsman, and he knew it, but his attention was always diverted by trying to keep one eye on the prince and one eye on his opponent. His need to impress the prince had lost him more than one bout in the first few days, and Terva relished taking advantage of his obvious lack of concentration. After those losses, he'd only sparred against people he was sure to beat with his eyes closed.

Thankfully, nobody watched Alnor enough to realise his fawning, except maybe the prince himself, but any attention was good attention in his eyes. He cheered every win Alnor got, laughed at every unfunny joke that Alnor made and brought him further and further into his own circles and out of the realm of his father.

Aldred worried that he'd never get him back after this, his whole notion of bonding during this escapade dashed by a need to impress royalty. His eyes furrowed again, but his train of thought was interrupted by the King.

"You'll make your head explode, thinking too much about your son's idiocy my friend," the King said softly.

Aldred sighed. "That obvious?" King Malker laughed.

"I've seen the same face in the mirror twenty times before. The more you try to change it, the more they rebel. It's easier just to let them find their own way rather than force them to adopt yours."

"How did the world get so different, sire? The Kerazar are getting stronger, pressing the mountain forts more and more in their attempts to breach our kingdom, but our sons and their generation seem oblivious to the threat. We've spent our lives trying to right the wrongs of one of our own. Is it fate that it's undone when we pass?" Aldred said.

The King laughed again, this time sadness tinging the joy. "Deep thoughts for this early General. All we can do is trust that we've done our part, and we've raised them right to do theirs. The fact that they're both idiots doesn't make them evil," he replied with a weak chuckle.

Aldred's eyes widened in shock before he let out a guffaw that made Moon-light nicker and turn his head. "I was unsure if calling the heir to the throne an idiot outside my own thoughts would be tolerated sire, but you voiced it for me. He and my son seem similar. They yearn to be liked, even loved by everyone. Sometimes, it's neces-sary for someone to think you're a bastard to get a job done," he said, shaking his head with a wry smile.

"Not in anybody else's hearing mind, he will be King one day. Having someone tell him his father and the General think he's a tosser might serve to breed animosity."

Aldred and Malker roared with laughter drawing surprised looks from the sons and the party behind them. Constantly serious, the sudden change to merriment was a shock to the younger core.

Bayar and Neve shifted from their position in the middle of the column to join their older peers at the front; the Sain guards who hadn't followed Alnor into their awe of the prince doing the same.

Around the fires at night, subtly but unstoppably, rifts had begun to form. The Sain guards were hugely outnumbered due to their remaining patrols not arriving, and the younger had started to defect to the prince's group around the same time they'd seen Alnor do so. Ten of the General's group, and a mere thirty of the royal group of the same mind as the King and General were left. Simple mathematics put the ratio at around three to one, giving the group a lopsided appearance at night.

Though no insult had been issued or argument had, Aldred could feel some-thing simmering as the old were pushed out by the new, discipline eroding. The upside of having so many young pups was that they all volunteered to take the watches at night, in an effort to respect to their older peers. They'd all done their fair share of that in the past. To see the same thing happening during the day made Aldred shift uneas-ily. He didn't think anybody felt the chasm opening between the group, so he kept his counsel. There would be nothing gained in causing trouble where there wasn't any, all because his aging mind played tricks on him due to the rift with his son. Keeping the smile on his face as his friends came alongside him and the King, he laughed and joked with all the rest, his thoughts boiling.

*****

Alnor looked suspiciously as the group around his father brayed with laughter yet again. He knew that wasn't how his father was, so the act irked him immensely, but he hid his displeasure by having his own fun, in his own circle of importance. They were past their time and that was displayed in the size of the factions. He liked to think of them as factions, despite being on the same side. The old and the young, the spent and the fresh, the serious and the fun.

It helped that so many of the men he now counted as friends shared his views, didn't discredit them but only encouraged. They knew they were the strongest, and they knew they deserved more from it. It had started out as little jokes about the commoners around the campfires, which had gotten worse as the ale addled their thoughts until they became insults directed at the common man in general. After a few nights, it became more. Men grumbling that they'd the strength to get more out of life or turning their ire on to the rich that sat in their homes whilst they bled for their safety. These men were silenced to start with, scathing comments quieting their thoughts before they'd even began.

But again, after a few nights, those men became louder. More began to agree and add their own thoughts to the mix, subtle thoughts that conveyed the same disgruntled feelings, sparks of anger in their bellies igniting into infernos until they consumed most of the group. Surprisingly, the Prince seemed to revel in it, using his influence to nudge people into saying things they wouldn't normally say then brushing over the treasonous remarks with jovial laughter. If it was anyone except the prince acting this way, Alnor would've assumed he *wanted* the men to become resentful towards the regime, but Krinar *was* the regime so that didn't add up. The men were drawn to him like flies around shit, he was clearly doing something right.

He felt a slight twinge in his gut which he brushed away. He'd wanted this raid to bring him closer to his father and all he'd been doing was spending time with the prince and his new entourage, but his father knew the score, didn't he? He couldn't live in the great General Sain's shadow forever. He needed to carve his own path, and being with the prince gave him that opportunity.

He decided he'd speak to his father later – not to apologise to him but to explain his reasoning. Alnor knew he'd done nothing wrong, but he still felt he owed his father an apology for something. He wouldn't return with his tail between his legs begging for forgiveness, but he also couldn't walk in with arrogance. In the end, the choice was taken from him in a way Alnor never expected. They'd stopped for the night, the setting sun winking at them on the horizon as it gave its last embrace to the crops before its hibernation. Farmers watched warily as the soldiers dismounted and began the routine of setting up tents, on edge despite seeing the red cloaks. Fires were lit and pots were hung with rations boiling for stews; some men made off towards the farmhouses with silver intending to eat fresh meat that night. The wary looks were replaced with greedy eyes when silver crossed palms, sheep and cows crossing the pastures with new owners to be slaughtered for their flesh.

As usual, Alnor downed his gear and rubbed down his horse, then proceeded to move towards the Sain's area, where the nightly training took place. Despite his misgivings with his father, he still sparred each night. He needed to keep fit after all. Maybe tonight he'd take Terva on again, as he'd been slacking in recent nights, telling himself it was the hangover or the day's ride; when, in truth, he was too busy checking he had the prince's attention than concentrating on fighting. Which sickened him. When had he become someone that needed approval from others to thrive? He gritted his teeth. Yes, Terva tonight.

As he passed the tents to reach the open space designated for training, he caught a glimpse of his father executing perfect forms, shirt off and sweat gleaming off his muscled chest in the orange sunset. His father was there every night without fail, but he never once sparred with the men; always making a joke about being past his prime and refusing good naturedly. Anyone watching him now knew those jokes were to save the men from humiliation. Each move was precise, body poised to react to anything that came near, lethality lacing his forms.

To Alnor's eyes, it was flawless, and Alnor considered himself a good swordsman, even amongst his current company. It made him want to improve, to reach that level of skill and surpass it. He ripped his eyes away from his father and began his own stretches, determination honing his thoughts as he saw Terva enter the field. His usual bull headedness was in full force as he grinned at everyone around him, shoving them boisterously and making ribald jokes. Alnor snorted, the man was a complete idiot.

"Fancy it, sir?" Terva shouted across the field to the General, who paused his current riposte and relaxed, turning a smile to the big man.

"I'm for the easy life these days Terva, leave me to my forms in peace," he pleaded, laughing and returning instantly to his forms leaving Terva shaking his head in mock disgust.

"Anyone else want a scrap?" he taunted, most men shrinking back slightly at the challenge. They'd all been on the receiving end of a sparring round with Terva, knowing any mistake would be rewarded with a large bruise in the morning.

"C'mon then big man, I'll give you a bout," Alnor called across the clearing, swishing his corded sticks in the air. Terva gave his most aggravating grin, bowed with an exaggerated flourish, opening his arms wide. "I'm only a big man to little men, young Sain," he said, waggling his eyebrows as the men around him chuckled at the implication.

Alnor rolled his eyes. Half of Terva's battle was unnerving men, either with his sheer size or taunts meant to make anger cloud your judgement. He wouldn't fall for it. Not tonight, not with his father watching. His only reaction was to step forward into a space and assume position.

As if responding to his mood, a cloud suddenly obscured the setting sun, the earlier warmth turning into a cooler evening. A brisk wind that carried small droplets of rain on its wings accompanied the clouds, leaving dark dots on the otherwise parched ground. Some men looked up in disgust, turning on their heels and running to get fires started before the downpour got too heavy, others cheered, wanting nothing more than the dust to dampen.

Alnor never took his eyes off Terva, whose own eyes narrowed at the lack of irritation from the usually irritable Sain. The General cut his own forms short and stepped back, pulling on his shirt against the changing weather but remaining on the field, hands clasped behind his back and piercing eyes ready to judge the fight, and the men in it. This wasn't missed by Alnor, whose pulse quickened as Terva stepped up to the mark. True to form, the maddening grin had returned to the huge man along with his cocky assurance. He left his guard wide open, inviting Alnor to start.

"Let's be having you, little Sain. I'll give you a chance whilst daddy's watching." Alnor didn't reply, choosing that moment to take the open invitation and leap forwards with a cry. Terva instantly closed the opening, parrying the attack with a resounding thwack that sent a jarring feeling from the tips of Alnor's fingers to the crook of his elbow. Ezi's balls, the man was strong!

Alnor danced away from a swing that was intended to knock him flat instantly. Knowing his advantage was to use his speed to dodge rather than parry, he darted around three swift, consecutive attacks of similar savagery. He laughed as the third

168

whistled past him and Terva stumbled, but the laugh was short lived. Terva had feigned a stumble to get closer, then he rammed his shoulder hard into Alnor's chest, dropping him to the floor and driving the breath right out of him. The fight had barely lasted a minute.

Terva's booming laughter rang in Alnor's ears and fed him the fury to rise to his feet, trying his utmost to keep his emotions from his face. His face twitched slightly as men around him sniggered at Terva's mocking laugh, but he reined it in.

"Are we performing here or sparring Terva? Maybe we should get you a costume," Alnor shouted above the infuriating laughter, cutting it short.

The men sniggering at Alnor's loss suddenly chuckled at the mockery of Terva, and the big man turned around, eyes narrowing. "Have it your way little Sain; that was your chance, let us show your old man a real fight this time, eh?"

Terva bolted forward. For such a big man, his speed was astounding, but Alnor had fought him many times before, and began his own defence of slipping around the attacks, parrying only when necessary and trying to deflect rather than absorb the attacks. The hits that did slip through his tactics numbed his arm, though there weren't many. This time, overconfidence didn't break through the concentration etched onto Alnor's face and he kept focus as the big man began to tire.

When the stumble came, the obviousness of the move was apparent. Leaping back, Alnor let the would-be stumble evolve into the clear attack that he'd anticipated. Falling into the instant shoulder drop which Alnor knew, courtesy of the last duel, he overstepped his mark as he barrelled in and dropped his stance, at which point Alnor danced behind Terva and cracked the back of Terva's head with minimal strength in the blow - more to antagonise than hurt. The dull thud was complimented by a chorus of 'oohs' from the growing crowd, most of which had stopped their own training to watch. Within seconds Terva had turned, red faced and furious. He began stomping back towards Alnor, growling and tensing in rage.

"Stop!" barked a voice across the clearing, causing Terva to halt immediately, though he turned towards the source with a confused irritation on his face. The small gathering of men parted slightly to reveal the General walking towards them without haste. Raindrops still pattered onto the ground, now damp with precipitation, drinking in the liquid with its parched throat. The tapping of water on the ground was all that could be heard in the uneasy silence that rested there, punctured very slightly by foot-fall. The General had never interrupted a duel before, not even when it signalled his own son being obliterated.

"Maybe the last fight, the final best of three, should be something my son should *really* work for. No offence to you of course, big man," Aldred Sain said casually, gesturing each word with his own corded practice sword. "Maybe the last fight... should be against me."

Silence continued to persevere; the statement met with none of the usual surprised gasps. It was a rare occurrence that the General was caught training in front of prying eyes, let alone aired his skills to the world. Terva's mouth dropped open, but he recovered quickly, bending his knees and spreading his arms in a gesture of welcome, tinged with a slight mockery, that let Aldred move towards his son. The General regarded Alnor coolly, never one to show favouritism of any kind. His stare could be felt cutting through the light rain directly into his son's own eyes, not betraying a hint of fear.

His father raised his own practice sword, maintaining the eye contact constantly, before saying one word. "Begin."

Alnor didn't move for a few seconds, mouth agape as he struggled to understand whether his father truly meant to fight him. The notion was in the wind as Aldred tutted, then exploded into action. He threw a few basic forms at his son, presented at a speed and precision not seen amongst regular warriors, and Alnor barely got his own sword up in time to deflect the attacks and stagger away. Though his father wasn't Terva's equal in strength, he surpassed him in every other way. A few more attacks convinced Alnor that this was no joke and suddenly his eyebrows met.

He launched his own series of blows back onto his father and could have sworn he saw a glint of satisfaction enter his eyes before it was whisked away. As they disconnected, regarding their movements carefully, Alnor saw Krinar enter the group in his peripheral vision, Varnan forever on his heels. Aldred's eyes hardened and he flew back into the fray at the sudden distraction of his son. Alnor parried the hits desperately, his feet almost becoming entangled as the speed of his retreat outran his mind's capacity to defend.

Then out of the blue, the attacks lessened, and his father offered an opening

Alnor couldn't refuse. He lunged, stretching well out of his usual range but deeming the risk viable. To his astonishment, his father did a very basic step to the left, brought his own blade to parry, then stepped away lightly. A momentary lapse was the result in which Alnor realised that his father could have won the fight there and then but had stepped away from the win.

Looking at his father's face, he could see the trace of a smirk forming as Aldred saw his son had realised the situation. *He's fucking testing me,* Alnor thought, a spike of fury interrupting his calm facade. He gritted his teeth and squared his shoulders, placing his feet delicately as he began to pace towards his father, knowing now that Aldred wanted to display his full skills to the men. Well, he'd show them if it was the last thing he did. He roared his challenge into his father's amused face, then attacked.

*****

Roaring echoing in his ears, Aldred prepared himself for the onslaught. He thought he'd lost him when the prince appeared, but he seemed to have won his attention with his quick attack, remedying the situation. Alnor had focused fully on the fight, and the instant attack after the roar alerted the General to one thing: his son had been holding back with Terva. He struggled to defend the initial hits until he got into rhythm again. It'd been a long time since anybody had defeated him in any sort of fight, so the fury of his son was a welcome challenge, even if it was a minor one. He barely threw any attacks, just enough to keep Alnor interested so that he'd keep coming. He deflected hit after hit, keeping his footwork fast to entice his son to follow. On the occasions where Alnor left an opening, he stepped in with lightning-fast attacks, pulling most of the force from them but hitting his son, nonetheless. After a few of these exchanges, his son seemed to realise the intent – to show him his faults and help him learn from them.

Alnor began to use the same forms, practising and reacting to his father's counter attacks, never making the same mistake twice. Aldred felt a savage pride in his son each time he stopped a blow that had earlier connected, and a satisfaction kindled in his breast as he realised Alnor hadn't glanced once at the prince since his first arrival. One such exchange left Alnor flagging, his strength beginning to wane. He stumbled towards Aldred, who saw the gleam in his son's eye as he thought his father had fallen into the same trap that he had in the fight with Terva, but Aldred leapt back out of the intended shove, planning to use the same trick his son had with the momentum.

Surprise flickered on the General's face, however, when his son dug his foot into the floor and pushed sideways, adapting Terva's attack into a swing powered with his entire body, aiming towards his father's legs. Aldred did the only thing he could at the notice provided and jumped into the air. Alnor's corded sticks whistled a hair's width from the base of the General's boots, and this time the momentum carried him off balance. Aldred landed lithely, flexing his knees to absorb the impact and then sprung after his son, bringing his own sticks down onto the back of his head, dropping him to the ground with a grunt.

Silence greeted the end of the fight, broken only by Alnor's muffled groans as he scrubbed the back of his head viciously in an attempt to take away the sting. When his son rolled onto his back, a smile graced his face, and he held out his hand to his father who broke into laughter, grasping the offered limb, dragging his son to his feet.

"You've been holding back," Aldred accused as his son dusted himself off, exhaling in disgust as he realised the rain had turned the dust to mush and fused it to his clothing.

"You can talk! You played with me the entire fight! Although I thought I'd get you with that last one," Alnor retorted, snorting as his father tutted and shook his head, still smiling.

"Like I told you on the road, there's life in your old dad yet!"

Father and son laughed together, meeting each other's eyes for the first time in days and the bond rekindled once again. The surrounding men joined in on the laughter, discussing the fight and beginning to look at Alnor with a greater respect than that very morning, but the laughing stopped as a high-pitched whistle and clapping cut through it, severing the moment. A flash of irritation crossed the General's face as he saw the culprit, quickly hidden but noticed by his son.

"Well, General, it seems you have been keeping a great deal to yourself. I haven't seen fighting like that in years, at least since my father used to train me. I think I could learn a great deal from you, if you're willing?" Prince Krinar said, accepting his own sticks from a smirking Varnan and shrugging off his coat.

So, the dog has his petty revenge, Aldred thought, letting nothing of his mind show on his face, keeping a steady smile throughout.

"Oh, I doubt that sire. We both know your speed alone would test my old bones to the limit, despite my earlier bravado feigning the life in them," he said, thanking Ezimat his voice didn't waver. "Maybe another time?"

"Nonsense General! Your name is spoken through the lands in awe. General Sain, saviour of the people, Bane of the Kerazar!" Krinar flattered, though his tone sounded more like mockery, and Varnan's snort reinforced the assumption. "Please, one bout couldn't hurt?"

Men around them looked on eagerly, knowing their General had held back against his son, but against a true Annarite he'd be stretched to his limits. He turned to Alnor, who was just as eager to see the prince fight his father. That, more than anything, made the decision for him. He rolled his eyes, keeping a nonchalant air as he stretched out his arms and groaned, making a show of a decision.

"I suppose these creaky joints could take one more fight, sire. If you insist," Aldred puffed, acting like he didn't want the fight but would do it for the prince's sake.

Krinar's eyes hardened, but the earnest smile was still on his face when he bowed slightly. The men cheered at the challenge as some rushed off to tell others. It wasn't every day you saw two of the best swordsmen in the kingdom spar, and it wasn't to be missed. Aldred sighed inwardly, secretly angered at the situation but knowing he'd been led like a lamb to slaughter into it. Usually, it was the bane of the young to rush headlong into a fight they probably wouldn't win, but the look in his son's eyes as he took his place in the growing crowd urged him on. He knew the prince had been taught by his father, who'd had the same tutor as Aldred. The difference was the tutor wasn't a true breed Annarite; Malker would have taught his son every trick in the book to utilise his extra speed, his extra strength - things Aldred knew he couldn't match.

He looked at the prince, stood still with his arms drooping at his sides and a slight slouch in his bearing, not ready for a fight at all. When Aldred took his stance, the prince straightened, his dog behind him leering at the General, excitement oozing off him as its master began to stalk towards the focus of his ire. Flashing a smile at Varnan's smug face, whose teeth were bared and hatred burning in his eyes, he began his own advance to the prince.

"Ready, sire?" Aldred asked innocently.

"Ready, General."

The field exploded into movement. The rain began to pour heavily from the skies, wind mimicking its sister and starting to howl its encouragement to the fight below. Men stood transfixed, ignoring the weather as they stood with open mouths, watching the spectacle. They'd never seen men move so fast. The fight between the General and his son suddenly took its place next to the latrines, as the fight between the General and the Prince took its place with the Gods.

Prince Krinar hadn't wasted a second, diving into attacks and forms unseen to most men, some new even to the General. But he hadn't survived the battles he had and gained his reputation by losing. He adapted to the excess speed that the prince exerted, changing his defence to use it against him rather than match it, instead flowing with it and doing the unexpected himself.

Huge cracks echoed across the field as hit after hit was deflected on both sides, men wondering if it was thunder rather than man-made. The fighters only concentrated on their immediate surroundings and the sticks in their hands. Chests heaving and droplets of rain mingling intimately with the sweat on their faces, they battled it out, all thoughts of this being a matter of training fled their minds. Aldred fought to show his son that the prince wasn't infallible. Krinar fought... Aldred still wasn't sure why Krinar fought; possibly to undermine the authority of his men and lead more over to the side across the fissure that was surely forming day by day, or possibly just to show off. The sparring quickly became a war, escalating quickly, the weather tailing the fighters and matching them for speed.

Forks of lightning began to lance across the sky through the heavy sheets of rain, followed closely by their bellows of thunder. Men drew the circles on their foreheads, knowing that a storm this early into Autumn could only be the will of the Gods. Aldred and Krinar didn't even react, completely engrossed. But all could see, the General was beginning to flag. Youth alone didn't beat experience. Usually the brashness ended a fight and swayed it into the older man's favour, but Krinar didn't just have youth - he had the full force of Ezimat behind him, against the force of his son, Sarnat; A true Annarite against Annarite born, there could be only one result.

One slight misstep from the General and an elated cry from the prince was the only indication that an opening had been found. As Aldred brought his sticks up to parry, he threw a desperate counter-riposte, hoping to catch Krinar off guard but the extra step cost him; the prince diving to the side, leg muscles bunching as they took his weight. He leapt back in and stabbed with perfect speed and precision, stopping an inch from the General's jugular.

Both men stood statue still; Aldred's eyes wide, keeping his breath as shallow as possible so his throat wouldn't expand further than it had to. Krinar stood there for a moment, and Aldred saw a crazed gleam in the prince's eyes that was quickly masked.

The storm sensed the mood as both men locked eyes and knew this was more than had been portrayed to their spectators. The sudden exclamation of his son broke the spell over the field, though the storm didn't abate.

"And you said I was holding back! By the Gods, I've never seen anything like it! Truly this is a fight for the ages."

The men began shouting similar things over each other, some clapping loudly and whistling at the spectacle. Aldred and Krinar stood for a moment longer surveying each other, before Krinar lowered his sword and laughed, clapping the General on the shoulder.

"My friend, I knew you were good, but I didn't realise *how* good. You almost had me there!" Krinar shouted happily, though that happiness never quite met his eyes. Alnor had trudged halfway over to the pair before Aldred replied.

"Nonsense sire, you were fully controlled through the whole fight. You've done your father proud."

A flicker of annoyance crossed Krinar's features before the fake mirth re-appeared and he inclined his head in thanks. *Annoyance at praise? Over what I wonder?* Aldred mused, but let it go as his son reached them and instantly started babbling. Aldred smiled and nodded in all the right places, but it was clear Alnor only included him in the fawning for appearance; the prince laughed and bandied words, absorbing the attention as others began to add to it.

After a few seconds, Aldred felt sickened. When did men become like women?

Complimenting and fawning, basking in attention like wives when they got a new pearl necklace. He felt a pang as he thought of his own wife, long gone. She'd never been one of those peacocks who paraded in silk dresses, clamouring for the males to see. More likely to tell somebody to fuck off rather than flutter her eyelashes. Where Alnor had gotten his personality from was a mystery to his father, he was nothing like either of them. Aldred sighed at the thought, suddenly resigned at his efforts.

"These old bones need to rest now, sire. Two bouts in one night will do that at my age, I will take my leave," Aldred shouted over the cacophony, barely heard.

He made his exit swiftly, getting claps on the back as he did. Anyone would think he'd won a battle rather than lost a training bout. He sighed again, knowing the new generations would put image before honour, money before respect, and fame before duty. Shaking his head, he crossed the field, being battered by rain and wind the whole way. Who was he to change the way of the world?

✶✶✶✶✶

Using the crowd as a distraction, Krinar studied the retreating back of General Sain. He knew the General had seen something on his face after the bout and could feel the exposure like an open wound. How could he have been so stupid! The game was already afoot, to ruin it now would be folly on his part. He jerked his head briskly to Varnan, knowing without words that Aldred would be followed, his words and movements reported.

All the while he entertained the younger, completely useless Sain. If he didn't need the boy so much, he would've slit his throat weeks ago but he stood and laughed, taking the play by play of the fight with good grace, as though he hadn't just fought it himself. Wariness crept into his thoughts as he heard the fight replayed. He hadn't been joking when he'd said the General almost had him; it was closer than he'd like to admit. He'd have to be careful when that part of the plan came to fruition, lest it go awry. To come so far and fail this close would be unthinkable, he thought as Varnan slinked away from the group casually, whistling. Now *there* was a good asset. Did what he was told, didn't ask questions, killed on command. Krinar just wished everyone was like him, obedient and loyal. Having to persuade, threaten and flatter people beneath him grated, but it was the only way. So, for now, he laughed, joked and he flattered. More and more of the guard flocked to him each day. Soon it wouldn't be like this, soon he would have the world. Krinar smiled, an evil glint in his eyes that faltered Alnor's speech slightly. Overhead, the sky roared.

*****

Alnor swayed back to the tent he shared with his father, oblivious to the hammering rain, the effects of wine coursing through him. He whistled a tune he'd heard some-where that day as his boots squelched and sucked at the sodden ground beneath him. The lightening hadn't abated, and his walk was interrupted by flinching each time a colossal crack wracked the skies.

Most men were huddled in their tents, miserable and cold without their fires. Those who'd complained notoriously about the dust the day before found themselves wishing it was back. But the Gods are fickle, and care nothing for the needs of men. The storm raged on.

As he reached the circle of tents that housed his own, he frowned at the dim light that flickered through the thin canvas walls - another reprimand for his drunken-ness from the oh-so-perfect General, then. Alnor sighed and rolled his eyes, untying the laces that held the tent shut and entering tentatively. The tent practically breathed with the wind, getting dangerously close to the candle his father had lit but Aldred made no move to reposition it. He sat on the edge of his bedroll, a full cup of wine in each hand with a surprisingly inviting expression. Alnor's suspicion mounted further when his father rose with a broad smile, handing him one of them.

"Drink, lad? All those nights with the prince must have made you immune to wine, so one more won't hurt!" he said as Alnor accepted the cup with an uncertain smile, taking a sip.

Aldred burst in to laughter. "What? You think just because I disapprove most nights that I don't drink on occasion? A cold night like this after so long in the heat does no good for my old bones, wine warms them up."

"Your bones can't be that old with how you moved today! If Krinar wasn't as fast as he was, you'd have finished him multiple times," Alnor replied, sitting down on his own bedroll with a huff, his father following suit.

"First name terms with royalty, eh? Someone's moving up in the world," Aldred said slyly, smirking at his son.

Alnor rolled his eyes, letting the comment pass though it needled. He couldn't just be happy for him, could he? The small talk lasted all of five minutes then talking about the sparring that day took up another five. When his father reached for the wineskin to refill the cups an awkward silence began. Alnor could almost see his father's thoughts as he struggled to bridge the gap that had opened suddenly, and he snorted softly before diving in headfirst.

"Have you noticed the rift between the men?"

His father jolted, his eyes going hard and expression morphing into one Alnor was much more familiar with: distrust. The atmosphere changed instantly, the jovial mood of his father switching in moments.

"Noticed it? How could I have not? Most of the men have been sucked into the vortex the prince has created. This stealth mission turned into a leisurely stroll through the countryside, filled with parties and carousing. We'll be lucky if the Hounds don't ambush us, let alone let us ambush them!" Aldred said, throwing the remaining wine down his neck like it was water. "If this is how he conducts a raid, Ezimat knows he'd never win a war!"

Alnor rose to his feet, rage burning in his breast warming his bones more than the wine ever could. How dare his father complain like a sour woman when the prince did nothing but treat the elders with respect. Upon his rise, he saw his father's rage in those ice blue eyes, controlled rather than fighting to get loose; his own was straining against its bonds, and he couldn't help but free it ever so slightly.

"In case you hadn't noticed, he's the one in charge here, not you. Just because it's not done your way, doesn't mean it isn't right," he said coolly, keeping his feet and moving slightly to the edge of the tent.

His father went quiet, sipping more of his wine thoughtfully. "He is in charge, that I cannot argue with. Even the pace I wouldn't argue with if it was for the right reasons. But to keep it this slow because you're too hungover to travel, or because a village has decent ale? Men die over less where the Kerazar are involved."

"The prince has done more for the men than you have ever done! He treats them like friends rather than his subjects, greeting every man the same and making him feel welcome. Not just like they're a soldier who obeys, but a friend who does what he does out of love rather than duty. Is that not better?" Alnor retorted furiously, face turning a deeper shade of red as his father snorted and rose with him.

"Out of love? More like out of arse licking! Even you look at the prince like a lost puppy begging for attention, and you're a Sain! If he wasn't a prince, you wouldn't look twice, and you know it," Aldred snarled, wondering how this attempt at bonding with his son had gone so horribly wrong.

"Maybe if my father had spent more time with his children rather than being obsessed with his duty, I wouldn't *need* to find attention elsewhere!" Alnor roared as thunder clapped, masking the roar from the other tents but Alnor wasn't for stopping there. "Even when you were home, all you cared about was those stupid reports and maps. Then when you weren't poring over them you were staring at the painting of mother, instead of focusing on what you still have! Taking in a peasant to try to fill the chasm left by her loss. Pfft, our family died when she did."

Aldred couldn't stop himself; his fist crashed into Alnor's chin, his son's feet leaving the ground as he flew horizontal into the tent wall, knocking over the candle and extinguishing it, dropping to the floor in a heap. The pattering of rain is all that broke the silence of the next minute, even the storm held its breath, waiting for the response.

Aldred stood transfixed and in shock as he regarded himself with disgust and surprise, eyes wide and all the anger gone from his gaze.

"Son, I..." Aldred pleaded but couldn't get any more words out.

Alnor lay in silence, propped up on one elbow and nursing his jaw. He rose, no rage on his face, just a shocked expression and dead eyes.

"I think I'll find somewhere else to lay my head tonight. We're done," he said. He turned away and strode out of the tent, flaps left open to the elements and laughing in the wind.

"Alnor!" Aldred shouted desperately, knowing that this time, it was his fault. Only the storm responded, bellowing its wrath and streaking the skies with fire. Aldred sat down with his head in his hands, not bothering to seal the tent. "What have I done?" he whispered to himself in dismay.

Outside, a shadow detached itself from the canvas and scuttled out of the small

179

camp, before looping back into the tent line. Varnan's eyes glinted as he followed the younger Sain, knowing his destination. *Tonight's turned out much better than expected, despite being piss-wet through,* he thought smugly. *Tonight, the hierarchy is broken. Tonight, is the beginning of the end.*

Chapter 10

Sheeting rain flew horizontally across the face of the Bunta mountains, avoiding the sheer edges and being pushed onto the canopy of the trees, nestling into the foliage before dropping to the floor as the leaves bent and wept their payload. The wind howled, doing its best to tear the trees from the ground, but they remained steadfast. Singular birds appeared, thinking themselves brave, before being blown aside and having to battle for every inch to return to their flock. Most animals, though, hid and shivered, praying for the storm to end. It had raged for three days, never lessening, forks of lightning preceding loud rumbles of thunder, usually bringing a heavier barrage of rain. Two creatures, however, hadn't stopped moving for the three days.

Rindu and Mariak Praker were soaked to their bones but the heat of fury in their chests kept them warm as they hunted the woods for any remainder of the Hounds. The weather was both a help and a hindrance as the wet ground eliminated any chance of dry leaves giving them away but also destroyed any evidence for them to track.

Not knowing where to begin, they obtained the patrol routes from the young Sain, and followed the paths the Annarites would have taken. They'd seen plenty of camp sites, remains of fires and small shelters; clearly spots that the men had camped at and left some comforts there in anticipation.

It was at one of these spots that they found them; men in their bedrolls under makeshift shelters, their throats slit. Some had savage holes puncturing their bodies, unceremoniously left on the ground, propped up at strange angles as though they'd dropped to the floor rather than murdered in their sleep.

"Da, what happened here?" Mariak said.

The insatiable anger over her brothers hadn't died in the slightest but the scene still turned her stomach. Cutting that prick in the village was easy - he'd deserved it - but half of these men here had been killed in their beds, potentially dreaming of their families. All that meant shit now, though.

"Looks like they were ambushed. Half murdered as they slumbered, the others tried to fight but died all the same. I'd bet my life that further into those trees there are dead men chosen for the watch that night. No doubt killed by their mates," Rindu said, no emotion in his voice whatsoever.

Mariak looked wide-eyed at her father, and what she saw terrified her. There was no recognition, no swift smile she was used to; just a cold, calculating, menace. She shuddered, wrenching her gaze away from him, preferring the bodies to that dead look.

"How can you tell?" she said, trying to keep the wavering from her voice. Her father sighed, his shoulders slumping.

"This is not something I ever imagined teaching to my daughter" he muttered, a slight bit of life back into his eyes. "The way they are arranged, most of them killed in their sleep, the others barely risen to defend themselves. They weren't warned, and nothing alerted them. A breaking of a twig or even the noise of an animal rushing away from intruders would've woken at least one of them. No... the killers were already in the camp, probably pretending to be asleep, killing their comrades before they were even aware there was a threat. I wouldn't be surprised to find out the watchman was killed afterwards, rather than before."

Mariak was shocked at how much of an insight into the situation her father had. Clearly his tendency for hunting animals stretched much further than she'd anticipated. She suppressed a shudder at the thought, but even her attempt at hiding didn't have her father fooled. He chuckled darkly.

"Humans are no different to animals, Mariak. Our perspective on them is, sure, but when it comes down to it, we all bleed, we all die. We leave a story behind for people like us to follow. We react too strongly to the death of our own, but butcher animals flippantly for meat, or in some cases for sport. Get past that reaction, and you'll see everything I said about this scene is true," he tried to explain. His daughter's eyes stayed wary, contradicting her body language that portrayed strength.

He knew the eyes never lied. He knew his daughter saw the haunted look in his own as his mind cruelly hosted the picture of his sons dead on the ground. He knew he worried her. She took a deep breath and broke eye contact, trying her best to see the area in a different light, to ignore the peaceful massacre in front of her and see the signs that came to her naturally whilst hunting.

Feeling nauseous within seconds, she tore her gaze from the face of a younger soldier, face pristine and still tucked in, throat sliced precisely, blackened blood in a small trickle down the side of his neck. Moving her line of sight to the empty bedrolls, she saw they were carefully folded back, shallow indentations of bare feet on the dirt. The image of a man lightly lifting his blankets off him, doing his utmost to make as little noise as possible flooded her mind.

"The bedrolls, folded back so carefully, done slowly to make no noise; there are only light footprints too, which makes that seem more likely?" she ventured, struggling to contain the bile creeping up as her eyes locked onto the boy again.

Such a nice incision. So perfect. So controlled. She didn't see her father's eyes light up as saliva pooled in her mouth.

"Yes, you do see it! Getting past the grisly scene is the hard part, if you can do – "he chattered excitedly, but was cut off by Mariak finally succumbing to the situation.

She fell to her knees and threw up noisily over the wet ground, retching and heaving until nothing but a string of yellow spit clung to her bottom lip. The shuddering she'd been holding in broke free in agonised sobbing, not unlike what she'd heard from her mother a few days before. Once it began, she couldn't stop. Her tears merged with the rainwater and her eyes were wide as she screamed her despair to the skies. They answered with their own roars as thunder echoed back. Her father knelt beside her, uncaring of the stinking pile of vomit and held her tightly.

It went on for an eternity inside her head, but the world was still bright when she lifted her head from her father's chest. She felt empty after her outburst, a shell of meat without function. Glancing up at her father, she realised the look in his eyes wasn't a dead husk, it was barely controlled grief and rage, behind a wall of nothing. She could see it, straining to break through the wall as he did his best to crush it. He was a bulwark to her against her own emotions, yet his own were destroying him just as much. He knew she saw what he felt, the eyes didn't lie; with a last squeeze of her shoulder he rose, gripping her hand tightly so she rose with him.

"Father, you..." she began, but realised she didn't know what to say.

"I'm fine, kiddo."

"Clearly."

He stood there for a moment surveying her, before snorting and shaking his head. Releasing her hand, he stepped away, taking a breath of the sweet stench of death; face unchanged, none of the war inside his head projecting outward. He offered her his water which she took gratefully and had a swig, swilling her mouth out before spitting it onto the floor.

After a couple of swallows, she began to feel slightly like herself again. She handed it back with muttered thanks, and her father nodded and stored it away. She felt the grief clawing beneath the surface, but held it at bay, taking strength from her bulwark.

"How do you do it?" she whispered miserably.

When he glanced at her with a questioning look on his face, she gestured around.

"All this. I'm fine with the blood, even the slaughter, but this was just so *systematic.* More like a painter who thinks battle is all glory and flag waving, rather than gore and men shitting themselves. How do you keep such a level head in what can only be described as cold-hearted murder of your own friends?"

Only the soft pitter patter of the rain on the canopy and the odd defiant roll of thunder broke the silence that stretched after the comment. He looked vacantly into the close-knit trees for a while until she was sure he'd just ignore the question and walk away, intending her to follow. When he spoke, she jumped in shock.

"To be honest, I wouldn't have a week ago. I would've thrown my guts up just like you, not noticed the obvious and ran away screaming. But seeing my two sons lying dead, discarded like dirt by some bastards who didn't even know who they were killing... that changes anyone. It's hard to explain. I know you lost your brothers, saw the same things I did and held your mother just like I did, but losing a child breaks most people. Ezimat knows if I didn't have you or your mother, I'd have climbed to a peak of the Bunta's and leapt from it. I do it because to me, nothing could be worse than seeing my sons dead on the ground, and doing this gives us a damn good chance of ensuring it's not you or your mother next. I do it so the peaks of them Bunta's don't start feeling like friends."

His gaze hadn't moved from the spot he'd been staring at since the silence began and continued after he'd finished. The break in his voice and the red rims around his eyes were the only things that betrayed him; the wall had been broken and allowed his burden to fall. Mariak's own grief took a back seat as her father shattered and she moved towards him, putting her hand on his shoulder.

Together, they spent a long while standing there, her hand on his shoulder and his arms hanging limply by his side. She never took her unwavering gaze off the nothingness, never let the sickly smell turn her stomach again, never let her hand fall. When the deep breath announced the end of the mourning, she finally let it drop.

Rindu turned to face his daughter, nodding his thanks. No more was needed. He had his walls back up; the turmoil on a leash again. She understood that all this was for her and her mother, to leave them with a father and a husband. She returned the nod, seeing the dead look return. There was no other option, no other way forward. He was doing it for them, she would do it for him. She hardened her own eyes and locked up her grief. She would become stone.

*****

"Again," Balzor huffed as he dragged himself up from the sodden ground.

Dextri flashed a taunting smile, rain racing over his face as yet another peal of thunder announced its mirth at Balzor's fifth meeting with the dirt that day.

"Not that I don't enjoy thrashing you repeatedly, little lord, but why the sudden masochism?" he said casually, barely out of breath. Balzor was winded from hitting the ground flat on his back. "For once in your life, just shut up Dextri."

Infuriating smile still on his face, Dextri made a show of stretching and throwing in a yawn for good measure. He beckoned to the sopping boy in front of him who snarled and leapt forward without hesitation. Balzor had barely gotten past the minute mark in previous fights, and this one was no different; as he had in the last bout, he over-extended and fell into an easy position for Dextri to disarm him and deliver a boot to his arse. The latter was more to annoy Balzor than to end the fight, which it did to Dextri's great pleasure. He barked laughter in Balzor's face as he whipped furiously around, long hair throwing droplets to the side as it swished to follow his head. Dextri put up his hands, still laughing at his expression.

"Balzor, take a minute. What's wrong with you? It's like you've forgotten everything you've learned in these past few weeks; plus, you look like a walking corpse. You not sleeping lad?"

Balzor's face fell, and he retrieved his sticks with a sigh, walking over to the armoury. He began unstrapping his leathers before he even got there, grunting at the extra weight from the soaked-up water. Dextri, concerned, followed just as the lad entered through the doorway. The other guards were in the town, co-ordinating the watch and helping clear the wreckage best they could, so it fell to him to babysit and train the two youths. Luckily, Alkor was currently in his allotted afternoon with Yuri, so it was only one of them he'd sent to the armoury sulking. The fact he'd slowly retreated in sullen silence triggered warnings and so Dextri followed warily.

Easing the door open, he peeked into the room first, seeing Balzor sat with his head in his hands, discarded leathers on the floor beside him. He knew it was futile the moment Balzor didn't react to the door banging, but he had to try. He wasn't exactly the hugging type, but something needed to be done.

"Right lad, what's up?" he said, sitting down on his own spot and unstrapping his own leathers. It took the full time of his undressing before Balzor finally answered, so suddenly that Dextri almost jumped.

"I would've died, Dextri," he began, then stopped.

Dextri raised a questioning eyebrow but didn't prod further; he knew when to speak and when not to. Balzor took his head out of his hands, powered up to his feet and began pacing.

"In the town, before I got to you lot. The man I fought outside the inn. I was outclassed and I knew it. If he was younger, or the fire hadn't cracked when it did, I'd have died. I felt a fear that I'd never felt when I was on the floor, just waiting for his sword to fall. The swing that ended up cutting his throat was the luckiest thing that's ever happened to me, it wasn't skill. I saw the whole thing, his disbelief, his realisation, the moment he died. His eyes Dextri. His fucking *eyes!*"

Dextri, rather than his spirits sinking, felt a compassion he didn't expect. He smiled at the lad, knowing exactly how he felt, the horror of the first kill. He shook his head and stood up, putting his hand on Balzor's shoulder sympathetically. Balzor had the same haunted look in his eyes that Dextri had seen twenty times before.

"You see him in your dreams?" he asked quietly, getting a muted nod from a tight lipped Balzor. He was shaking, Dextri realised, so he clapped his other hand on the lad's other shoulder and gripped tightly, steadying him.

"Now lad, I'm not a man of many words so I'm only gonna say this once - any man who doesn't feel fear during a fight is either a psychopath or moon addled. It's human nature to want to piss yourself in a shield wall or for your bowels to loosen when you see blood on the ground. You can't have courage without fear and that's a fact. You'd be surprised at how much of a fight like that comes down to luck too lad, so don't worry too much. You beat a man with much more experience and probably much more skill than you at the time, how you did it is irrelevant; he's dead, you're not."

Dextri could feel Balzor's shoulders steady as he spoke, the strength of the words firming his resolve but the haunted look on his face remained, despite getting a measure of pride back. Dextri tried again.

"So all this extra sparring is because one man almost beat you after a few weeks of you training? You didn't expect to become Aldred Sain overnight, did you?" he joked, shoving Balzor and releasing his hold on him. Balzor chuckled half-heartedly and shrugged, bending down to pick up the leathers and hanging them on the wall. Dextri sighed.

"As to seeing him when you sleep, this I can't help you with. I saw the first man I killed for three nights afterwards. Accusing, pleading, dying. It was easier for me since he was about to gut a child no older than five. I got mad, he got stabbed. I knew the evil that was in his mind but it still haunted me. Ask Livius about this, he was worse than most - much worse. I saw the same look you've got in your eyes now, in his too. I signed him up to the guard, set him and his mam up in a small cottage and trained him so hard during the day that he was too tired for anything but eating and sleeping, but that clearly isn't working for you."

Balzor stood still, mouth open and the look ever so slightly gone from his eyes in favour of shock. He'd only known the basic histories of the men he now called friends and brothers. Hearing something so intimate as a first kill made him feel more included than he ever felt. He'd always wanted to be a Sain, to truly be brothers with Alkor like he always said he was, but Dextri opening up was a huge step to being part of the brotherhood, part of the family.

"You didn't have to tell me that," Balzor muttered, slightly embarrassed that his own problems had prompted it.

Dextri waved his hand dismissively. "I'm over it, kid. Have been since that third morning. The way I see it, it's us, or them. We don't walk into a home, looting and pillaging and killing for sport, we do it for survival. To protect our homes and our families. Being a killer and being a murderer are two very different things, remember that if nothing else."

Light was creeping back in to Balzor's eyes at every word. It was like a balm for

his soul, hearing his worries and fears dismissed too casually; knowing that even someone like Dextri had been here before and powered through. He'd been broken since
seeing the life leave the man, seeing a life he'd stolen away evaporate in front of him.
Worry had given him sleepless nights, and when he did finally sleep, all he could see was
the deathly pale masked apparition, with those dying eyes.

"So... the dreams, when did they stop?" he ventured.

Dextri laughed, but it was an empty one. "Stop? They never stop, lad. The
initial ones do over time, but then you kill again. Even after you've killed men in battle,
there'll always be some kill or other replaying in your dreams. Some fight or skirmish
waking you up, coated in sweat. That's the bane we bear my friend so that others don't
have to. So, tomorrow, if you don't hit me at least once with those sticks, it's gonna
cost you ten laps until you do. We've all got nightmares in our head's lad - if you know
what you did was for good reason, you learn to deal with it."

"But I've never even gotten close to hitting you yet!" Balzor protested, dreams
forgotten for a second. This time, Dextri's laugh had true feeling behind it. There was
nothing he loved more than winding people up, after all.

"Well, you'd best hope you improve overnight," he replied. Balzor groaned and
sat back down, his head in his hands for an entirely different reason now. Dextri cackled
at the lad's dismay and began to head through to the baths.

"Dextri..." Balzor called, prompting him to turn at the entrance and look questioningly back. "Thank you."

Knowing there was nothing more to be said, he nodded and carried on through,
whistling a merry tune as though nothing was amiss. *Well, he did say he wasn't a man
of many words,* Balzor thought, smiling. He stood up with a chuckle and stretched his
weary muscles, before following his friend to the baths, spirits much higher than they
had been in days.

*****

Alkor threw the pen onto his father's table and grasped his wrist with his other
hand, twisting it around and massaging it to work out the cramps from the afternoon.
Yuri didn't have him nearly as much as he'd like to, but when he did, boy did he make

sure he worked. *It was almost as if Yuri employs me and not the other way around,* Alkor thought grumpily, as Yuri's disapproving look at the mistreatment of a pen washed over him.

He'd signed everything put in front of him, barely checking half of it in his haste. He'd replied to Ezimat knows how many letters, read through all sorts of figures and reports and approved passage to the mountain clans through his estate for a merchant. The only input he'd had was to suggest the purchasing of sufficient materials to help rebuild the inn, which Yuri conceded to with bad grace. He didn't see the point of any sort of substance that addled the brain, despite Alkor's attempts to persuade him otherwise. The man was never entirely satisfied unless his numbers tallied up and his papers were neat. Insufferable.

"Taking out your temper on such a lovely pen is just bad grace Master Sain," Yuri droned in his robotic voice, sweeping the pen up along with the many sheets of paper Alkor had etched his name on to.

"I think we'll stop there for the day." Alkor groaned and leaned back into the huge chair, hearing his back crack as each vertebra straightened in relief. Yuri sniffed at the groan and banged the bottom of the papers on the desk to make them in line then made them disappear into a hardwood briefcase that he carried everywhere with him.

"How my father did this every day is beyond me," Alkor grumbled, standing and stretching with euphoric results. Yuri's sniff became a snort as he turned on his heel and opened the door, somehow making that action hold a perfect amount of sass.

"With a great deal more attention and respect than you, *Master* Sain. Manners cost nothing. Good. Day." He stalked through the door and slammed it behind him, instant regret and guilt flooding through Alkor. The man was just doing his job after all. Turning his back on the quivering doorframe, lightening flashed, illuminating his mother eying him with displeasure. He sighed and shook his head.

"I know, I know. I'll get him a new briefcase or something to apologise," he said to the painting, then laughed at the stupid feeling in his gut as he realised, he'd been speaking to himself. He shrugged. It gave him comfort to speak with his mother and nobody was around. Her dimpled smile never failed to cheer him up, even with the dismal weather being visible through the window to her side. What he'd recently noticed was a flower in her hair he'd never noticed before. He'd have to ask his father about that when he got home.

Taking a deep breath, he wrenched his gaze away from the friendly face and looked outside. Water cascaded down the pane of glass, a steady flow of the cloud's tears fleeing from the thunder's wrath. The whole house seemed to shake with the storm's fury and Alkor cringed at the thought of his father out there. He even felt a slight twinge for Alnor, but he squashed that within seconds. His brother never had a protective bone in his body for him, so he wouldn't have a protective thought about his brother.

Balzor, however, he chuckled at - for once slightly glad that he'd been stuck inside with Yuri. His friend must be completely soaked with whichever sorry soul had been put on training duty today.

Alkor stood looking thoughtfully into the raging weather, vowing to speak to Balzor tonight; he'd been very quiet since the night of the attack, when you could never usually shut him up otherwise. On that night, Balzor had been full of life and energy, but each day since he'd been sinking into a quagmire of depression. He hadn't even reacted when Alkor told him of Joseph's oath, not even the slightest prodding about it. *Tonight, I'll speak to him,* Alkor promised himself, before his thoughts turned to Joseph – his sworn man, currently helping clear the wreckage.

Just thinking that made him shudder slightly, even his father didn't have the oaths of men. Oaths were for Kings, or men aspiring to be Kings. Just another thing to add to the list of things he'd pass onto his father. Alkor wouldn't want the King to think he'd gotten ideas above his station; that never ended well for anybody, even if his father was the King's closest friend.

A rumble he thought was another peal of thunder reached his ears, until he realised its source. He was starving. His roiling thoughts brightened as he anticipated Nerva's cooking; he hadn't seen her for a while, and he knew that Balzor owed her a favour since the food from his hangover. It would only be right to repay the favour himself, he supposed. Mind made up, he took one last look at his mother's portrait before turning his back on it, picking up speed as his stomach protested once again.

He was busy thinking up excuses to Nerva so she would let him eat early, when he walked straight into the hard, rotund belly of Olsten. He came to his senses quickly, though he almost lost his footing. "Olsten! Not that I'm not happy to see you, but what the hell are you doing here?" he exclaimed.

Olsten had taken a bewildered step back at their collision after which he stood looking very sheepish, looking down at his feet like a child caught in the act of misbehaving.

"Er... nothing lad. I'm staying in the barracks since, y'know... said I'd help in the kitchens to pay my way," he stuttered. Alkor had never seen Olsten look lost for words before and began to feel a sliver of suspicion, probably undeserved.

"I best be off," Olsten added, scuttling through the ajar front door without a backwards glance. Utterly bemused, Alkor shook his head after the retreating man and returned his focus to his now cramping stomach. He couldn't remember his last meal - probably breakfast, knowing Yuri. The man really was a slave driver. His mouth was practically dripping like a dog's maw as he rounded the corner to the kitchens, smelling the irresistible scent of baking bread. His footsteps quickened, intent on filling the void. His boots made loud echoes in the corridor; usually he tried to mask his steps, sneak in, get food and sneak out before Nerva could say no. This time he realised too late, wincing as he heard her voice ring out.

"Back so soon? People will start to talk..." she called as he came into the kitchen.

She turned at the sound of him walking into the room, her cheeks bright red and a twinkle in her eye. This soon turned to a mortified look as she registered Alkor stood there, and she spun back just as fast, chopping vegetables with a speed that promised a lost finger.

"No food until it's time, you know this little Sain". Suddenly the pieces came together with a resounding click, his face cracking into a smile at the revelation.

"None at all Nerva? Not even for Olsten?" Nerva froze, Alkor all too aware at the vegetable coated knife in her hand. Turning, she accented her words with a stab of the knife in his direction.

"You little swine! I bloody told him somebody would talk. I don't know what you *think* you saw, but Olsten is just helping in the kitchen. Anyway, what goes on in my life is none of your bloody business!" she shouted, taking a few steps forward. Her face now red with anger had no loving look in it, Alkor assumed a slight embarrassment. Try as he might, Alkor couldn't take his grin off his face, backing up with his hands raised in feigned surrender.

"Okay, okay! My lips are sealed, I get it" Alkor chuckled, raising his hands higher as Nerva opened her mouth and took a breath for her next tirade. "I mean he's just helping, none of my business. Roger that Nerva ma'am" he added. She was far from mollified, but she lowered the knife and resigned herself to grumbling under her breath instead. Alkor could've sworn he saw the hint of a smile around her lips as she turned back round but he decided not to push his luck, forcing the next sly comment back down his throat before his mouth could betray him.

His hungry eyes found the loaves of bread, perfectly raised and by the looks of it, still warm. His stomach roared in triumph at seeing its prey. He stalked towards the bread, cursing himself at not putting on some proper footwear for the occasion. Nerva really was his stomach's best friend and its worst enemy, as she snapped out her knife arm again, pointing directly at him. Surely the woman had a sixth sense for finding him taking food without permission.

"Two more minutes and you'll have some nice beef stew to go with it. Not a moment before will you touch my bread boy," she snapped. Alkor was sure there was humour behind it this time. He groaned in mock resignation but settled back to wait. There was something oddly comforting about watching Nerva work, humming a tune happily, the earlier rant already forgotten. Putting on some thick gloves, she took the lid off a pot simmering contentedly on the stove, getting a huge ladle and spooning out some delicious looking stew, onions and potatoes swimming alongside pieces of beef, coated in gravy. It was all Alkor could do to not leap across the room and dunk his head into the pot, but he waited very impatiently for her to replace the lid and get a large hunk of bread.

"Ok, fetch boy" she laughed, grinning as Alkor rushed to pick up the bowl, burning his mouth in his haste to take his first swallow. "Good doggy."

Alkor scowled at Nerva, hand over his mouth to make stupid breathing noises in his attempt to cool the scalding. He took his bowl and dropped the bread into it, splashes of gravy dotting his shirt, causing Nerva to tut disapprovingly. Alkor shrugged and smirked, raising his bowl at her in thanks as he was at the door.

"Oh, and Nerva?"

"Mmm?"

"I'm happy for you."

Nerva glanced up, eyes narrowed as she looked for any trace of mockery. Genuine innocence coated Alkor's face, his smile showing nothing but truth. She sighed.

"Thanks kiddo."

✶✶✶✶✶

Stepping outside of the armoury, Balzor was hit by the thought that it really was a waste of time getting dry from the baths. The downpour soaked him to the bone the instant he stepped out of the door, his momentous warmth dissipating in the icy rain. Dextri stepped out right behind him, letting out an exhilarating whoop, opening his arms wide to embrace the elements.

"This'll put hair on your chest lad! Drink in Ezimat's fury!" Dextri shouted into the wind, words being whisked away. Balzor looked at Dextri quizzically, thinking the man insane to enjoy this.

"Ezimat's fury can wait till I'm inside thanks!" he called over his shoulder, beginning to walk back to the house.

"Whatever. Forgot you had tiny balls. Make sure you get some sleep; you're on the midnight watch. You and the other lord are replacing me and Lortmund. NOT two men you wanna piss off. Got it?"

Balzor shivered, more at the implied threat than the freezing rain, but nodded his acceptance before turning back to the doors, slightly ajar and promising a dry haven. He heard Dextri cackle behind him, then heavy footfalls off in the direction of the town. Seems he didn't like the weather as much as he was letting on.

He tried his best to keep a measured pace, making it a contest of wills between him and the storm. The storm won. Ten strides from the door he broke into a run, getting into the threshold and slamming it shut. As the echoes of the slam stopped ringing in his ears, Balzor heard somebody trying their best to stifle laughter. He turned slowly to see Alkor sat on one of the side benches, a mouthful of bread and some sort of stew; he wasn't trying to stifle laughter, he was trying to keep the food in his mouth – and failing. Bits of bread sprayed out of his mouth, making wet slaps on the floor and spattering the pristine tiling with splashes of brown stew. Coughing a few times to clear his throat, and still chuckling, he dumped the remaining bread in his bowl.

"Forget to dry off, did we?" he said, smirking as he raised the bowl to Balzor. "Here, you seem like you need a warm meal." Balzor narrowed his eyes but didn't say no to the steaming stew, not that there was much left. He sat down beside his friend and ate noisily, Alkor looking on in disgust.

"You're supposed to chew it, not bloody inhale it!" he exclaimed. Balzor grunted but didn't reply, too intent on his empty stomach for his brain to process speech as well. He'd heard it somewhere that if you wanted more than one task completing simultaneously, don't ask a hungry warrior. Well, he was more than proving that now, mopping up every last morsel before glancing up from the bowl at Alkor. His friend had lost his look of disgust, being replaced with a slightly impressed look.

"You probably won't even have to wash that you know?" he said. Balzor flashed a wolfish grin as the last of the bread slid down his gullet. Shrugging unapologetically, he rose to return the bowl to Nerva, knowing to leave it on the bench would be to invite his destruction – not to mention no more of her cooking for a week.

"Oh, Balzor?" Alkor asked.

"Hm?"

"Nerva asked me to remind her about Olsten, but I'm gonna get some sleep. You mind reminding her for me?"

Balzor glanced at his friend but saw he was already halfway up the stairs, so shrugged and called his acceptance. He didn't see the smirk on Alkor's face that was quickly branching out into full scale laughter, taking the slow shaking of his shoulders as a shiver from the brisk air. Wondering what she needed reminding of, Balzor hurried to the kitchens. He left the kitchens narrowly avoiding a well-aimed wooden spoon and more than a few choice words, thrown by a very irate Nerva. Utterly bemused but realising he'd been duped; he took the stairs two at a time with a feeling of humour tinged with annoyance in his belly.

Alkor's door was half open when he reached it, but he still gave it a boot in the hope of startling his friend. His hope was dashed when he saw Alkor casually lounging on the bed, a lopsided smirk on his face and poised ready to leap up to escape his friend's wrath. Balzor's laugh dismissed Alkor's worries, and he rolled out of his position and sat up to join in with the mirth.

"You knew what would happen, didn't you?" Balzor accused in mock outrage.

"If it's any consolation, I caught it happening and got the full force of Nerva too," Alkor replied.

Balzor chuckled. "That does kind of help. Go on then, why did the mention of Olsten make her mad?" Balzor stood and listened, his mouth opening wider and wider as the story unfolded. "Hang on... Nerva and *Olsten?* How can you be sure?!" he exclaimed.

"C'mon mate, would she really fly off the handle like that if it wasn't something more than Olsten helping her with the cooking? Do the math." Balzor snorted and took a deep breath, running his hands through his still damp hair as he contemplated the situation.

Suddenly, he jumped like a shocked animal and pointed at his friend as an idea bloomed in his head. Alkor raised his eyebrows questioningly but said nothing. "Alkor, you know how we have a multitude of favours we owe Nerva...?" he asked, trailing off at the end.

Alkor's eyebrows went further towards his hairline, his look changing to one of confusion. "Go on..." Balzor was now hopping around in excitement, moving his hands around stupidly as though putting the pieces of a jigsaw together. "I think I've thought of a way we can pay them all back, whilst apologising for treading on her toes with the situation, though it'll mean no sleep for us tonight. Here's what we're gonna do..."

✶✶✶✶✶

An hour later they were both dressed for the watch, heading into the village much earlier than their intended time. When Alkor heard the plan, he had to admit it had merit, though it meant an extra tired watch for them both that night. Falling asleep on watch would likely hold a lesser penalty here than out in the field, but a lashing would be the least they could expect for a secret slumber. They'd both clued Olsten in on their plan - he'd denied profusely that anything was going on before relenting and admitted there might be. He was on board. It was a fairly simple idea, but one they knew Nerva would appreciate more than a bauble or trinket, though abandoning her kitchen even for a morning would have her with nervous jitters before long.

As the gates on the manor's side of town came into view, they hailed to capture the guard's attention, hearing a shrill voice doing his best to be heard above the parapet. Stood shivering in the downpour, they waited impatiently. A scraping was heard next, then a small head appeared to the side of the gate, face flushed and embarrassed at the delay.

"Couldn't find the blasted box, who goes th... Oh it's you two, hang on," the young boy said, jumping down from his podium and rushing to lift the locking bar from the gate. Grunting and muted swearing was all they heard for almost a minute before a deeper, questioning voice cut the struggle short and the gates were thrown open, revealing the sullen looking lad and just the man they were looking for: Traf.

"We really *are* scraping the barrel if this one's on the gate, eh Traf?" Balzor joked, tousling the boy's hair who furiously slapped the hand away.

"I would've got it off on my own eventually," the lad grumbled, Traf guffawing and clapping a hand on his shoulder.

"Course you would, Oli, course you would!" Traf chuckled to his youngest son, who softened slightly at his father's touch but still glared at the other two.

"What brings you in so early, lads? Your watch isn't for another few hours yet if I'm not mistaken."

"To see you, actually. We're thinking of giving Nerva a morning off, doing a breakfast for her and Olsten," Balzor began, until Alkor nudged him hard in the ribs, making him jump and look at friend in outrage.

Traf just chuckled again. "Nerva and Olsten eh? At least something good came of that night. I won't say a word!"

Huffing like a wounded animal, Balzor carried on with the plan. "Problem is, to give Nerva a morning off, we have to find breakfast and dinner for Dextri, Ingvar, Devar, Yuri and us two. It's only a problem because me and Alkor haven't even cooked an egg before, let alone food for that many. So..."

"So, you need me to produce the food, whilst you take the credit for a job well done?" Traf interrupted with a sly smile. Balzor shrugged, unperturbed.

"Pretty much!" he grinned, then Alkor took over.

"Second problem though, we won't have the funds for this lovely food without accessing them through Yuri. So, we need a proper invoice, which I'll sign before it even reaches Yuri, then hand it to him personally. He can huff and puff all he wants, but the top and bottom of it is that whilst my father is away, I'm the only Sain signature, which in the end is all that matters since it's Sain money," he said.

Traf's smile only grew wider until he started to laugh. "That sounds fair, but I want to come with you to see Yuri's face when you hand it to him. Deal?" he said, offering out his hand.

Alkor smiled and grasped the baker's hand. "Deal."

Traf took the lead at a hurried pace, wincing as the huge raindrops battered his shoulders consistently. Rounding the corner to the bakery, they saw the blackened husk that used to be the inn in front of them, defeated beams hunching over, trying to be the last ones standing. Villagers who had volunteered for clearing the wreckage were finishing up for the night, the last of the light now fading. Too many had had close calls working in the darkness; after a couple of broken fingers, Dextri stopped work after sunset. Better to be rebuilt slowly than not at all.

The smell of damp ash lingered in the air, tinged with the mouth-watering smell of Traf's bakery, ovens off but still emitting the glorious scent. Alkor was pleasantly surprised at how fast the inn was being cleared. Most of the second floor had now fully collapsed and been moved, piles of roof slate stacked at the side for re-use. His thoughts didn't linger long though, as the savoury smell assaulted his nostrils again.

"On second thoughts Traf, I think we'll have a few cakes for tonight too," he said, Balzor nodding in agreement.

Traf snorted. "On your head be it. Yuri will kill you," he replied.

"Worth it" Balzor grunted, and Traf snorted again.

It wasn't long before they had the promised parcel of food, filled with sandwiches, cakes and other sugary treats. They had one large basket to feed them, a smaller basket for Olsten and Nerva, then a lumpy wrapped piece of cloth that Balzor stashed under his coat for later. After a heartfelt thanks, which Traf waved away, they left the bakery with the surprisingly heavy prizes.

"Carry this back to the house? It weighs a bloody tonne!" Balzor complained as he heaved it along, Alkor glancing innocently back at his friend with his much smaller basket.

"Mine isn't too bad, mate" he taunted, but Balzor didn't bite. As if on cue,

Devar walked round the corner, Ingvar close on his tail.

"Ingvar!" Alkor exclaimed. "How are you feeling? Fully recovered?" Looking anything but, Ingvar gave a tired smile and shrugged. "Not too bad young'un, no holes in me so nothing a good night's sleep won't fix! What's in the baskets?"

"Well, this large one is what's feeding you tonight, and in the morning," Balzor said, stepping forward eagerly and dumping it next to Devar who grimaced at its size.

"Let me guess, you expect me to carry that back whilst you sit atop the wall on your merry arses?" Devar deduced, scowling at Balzor's happy nod of the head.

"Lovely. What's it for anyway? Where's Nerva?" Alkor spent a few tedious minutes explaining yet again about their plan only to gain an interrupting cough from Ingvar which sounded suspiciously like the words 'arse kisser'. Rolling his eyes, they passed the burdens of food to the two men, giving the smaller one to the recovering Ingvar. "That one, give straight to Olsten. Do NOT eat it, I know what you two are like," Alkor warned, causing Ingvar's eyes to widen innocently as he spluttered in indignation.

"We would *never,* my lord!" he mocked.

Balzor snorted and shoved the man. "For once, don't be a dick," Balzor said, and Ingvar laughed, assuring them just this once he'd refrain.

As the two brothers walked back in the direction of the house, Alkor looked at his friend. "Suppose we'd better relieve Dextri and Lortmund then?" he said, struggling to keep the dismay out of his voice at the prospect of another dull night on the wall, tiredness seeping into him at the thought.

Balzor sighed dramatically but began to slope towards the gate they'd entered through, Alkor just ahead of him. As they reached the base of the ladder, Dextri had finished his round of the wall and gave them both a broad smile, despite his sodden appearance.

"Well pups, you're not late, I'll give you that. Early actually unless my timing is off?" Dextri boomed, whistling loudly to attract Lortmund's attention who waved gratefully and began to descend a ladder close to his current position. Dextri braced his feet and slid down the outer rungs, absorbing the impact with a bend of his knees and turning to them both questioningly. For the third time that night Alkor related their plan, this time the words 'arse kisser' weren't even masked by a cough. Dextri never did mince his words.

Alkor rolled his eyes at the comment, shoving past the big man and placing his foot on the bottom rung.

"Just save some food for us, eh? I know how fat bastards like you can eat," he called over his shoulder. Dextri's eyes flashed, and he spun, lashing out to try and grab Alkor's ankle, but he was already well out of reach, looking down with taunting eyes like a cat in a tree against a dog on the ground.

"We'll see who the fat bastard is when we're training tomorrow," Dextri grumbled, turning back and giving Balzor a clip round the ear for good measure, before striding away. Balzor looked up to Alkor in outrage at the unfair assault, but got no sympathy from his friend, who was chortling at the bad luck. Balzor began his own ascent of the ladder, each step upwards sending his mood spiralling downwards, even with the sweet treats in his pocket. He reached the top and rummaged for the treats, passing some over to Alkor in bad grace before cramming a whole apple tart into his mouth without dignity. For a few seconds his jaw worked furiously to chew the food into a manageable size, whilst Alkor looked on in disgust.

"I think my brother has the right of it, you really are bloody disgusting. See you in a bit," Alkor said, setting off in one direction whilst Balzor went in the other; they'd traverse the wall in opposite directions, reaching the other gate and crossing paths. Dextri always said it was better to do the full wall rather than a side each. Men tended to miss things if they watched the same area repeatedly for hours. The weather continued to roar as the last of the tart slid down his gullet, and he drew his coat tightly around him. After an hour, he knew that the apparently waterproof jacket would be sodden and offer no warmth at all, but for now, it served.

He grimaced as he passed the empty torches atop the walls that usually danced with friendly flames to warm your hands, long since extinguished by the storm. Knowing the only respite from the wind would be near to the Seeress' house, he began to hurry, mentally chiding himself for barely watching outside but wanting a warmer place to finish his desserts.

The corner of the wall where the Seeress and Aria lived was the only area with trees on both sides, though some on the outer side had been cleared to reduce access to the parapet. Double sets of trees served as a slight buffer to the wind so it was a favourite for any sentries; plus, it gave him a chance to see Aria, it had been a couple of days. Aria hadn't said anything about the power or her family since the night of the attack, only that the Seeress was keeping her training to stop her abilities getting out of control before she knew how to use them.

In response, Balzor had thrown himself into his own training, hard. His chat with Dextri had slightly loosened the knot in his chest but the truth was he was terrified. Adrenaline had coursed through him during the fight, and he'd still felt the fear hitting him at his core. Since then, his dreams had woken him in the night shaking, sheets damp with sticky sweat that his nightmares tore from his skin. Usually, it was the dead man's eyes haunting him, but a close second was his terror of his own death. He'd done his best to explain to Dextri earlier, who had done his best to help, but the only real easing of the fear was around Aria. The warm feelings she brought to his life was the best cure he'd found, and all this training on both sides had limited that contact. It was with more than a little anticipation that he entered the shadows of the trees near the small cottage, eyes straining in the gloom to pick out the pinpricks of light that would announce its location.

When he found the house in the trees, he realised the stupidity of it all; she'd hardly be out getting soaked by the rain without reason. He snorted to himself and tore his eyes away from their quarry, this time doing his job and looking outside rather than in, though he still paused to stuff some lemon cake whole into his mouth. A short whistle almost made him inhale the entire cake at once, and he began a coughing fit as he turned towards it. What he saw lifted his spirits tremendously, though brought blood flooding to his cheeks in embarrassment as crumbs sprayed out of his mouth.

Aria had stepped out of the cottage and started to wave, though now her hands were on her knees in an attempt to control her laughter at his sorry state. Knowing it was futile to hide his shame, he raised his hands in a 'What can you do?' kind of way then performed an exaggerated bow before waving back enthusiastically. He wished he could hear her laughter, but the storm had other ideas, whisking it away before it got close.

She waved back once more, pulling her collar up on her shirt up before hurrying back inside, a slight backward glance the last he saw of her before the door slammed shut. Shaking his head at his own gluttony, he spent the next stretch of wall finishing the lemon cake, the warm feeling he'd been missing back in his belly, keeping the demons away.

He crossed Alkor at the opposite gate, Oli glaring at them both from beneath this makeshift shelter he'd erected at the base of the wall. He was constantly asked why he stayed near the gate all day and his response was always that he wanted to help somehow, though it didn't stop him sulking as if he was being forced.

He clocked a suspicious look from Alkor as they passed each other, wondering at his friend's jovial mood, but he just threw a wink his way before carrying on, swallowing the final mouthful of cake, slightly disgruntled that there wasn't another one. Keeping watch in weather like this was harder than any other so he had to strain his senses much more. Every sound was muted on the damp undergrowth, every tree blurred in the rain to look like a man. The lack of light would stop a glint on any armour an attacker would be wearing, so they could be at the wood's edge before Balzor even caught a glimpse. But he did his round, keeping watch the best he could, his newfound mood helping pass the time.

As the gate where they'd climbed the ladders came into view, his stretched hearing found a faint rumbling in the air. At first, he mistook it for thunder, casually strolling as though nothing was amiss. But the closer he got to the road, the heavier it became until it was the unmistakable sound of hooves. At the other side of the wall, he just about made out Alkor's frantic arms waving and pointing towards the gate and he knew he'd heard it too.

He sprinted along the top of the wall, wind and rain whipping at him but paying it no heed as he cursed himself for forgetting to put the sentry horn into his belt. *Too intent on the bastard cakes,* he thought as his feet pounded along the wooden parapet. Alkor beat him there by a few paces, ripped his own horn from the hanger above the gate and blew as hard as he could.

A slight squeak was produced, not the blaring that usually sent the birds fleeing from their nests. Alkor grimaced at the poor attempt, spat to clear his mouth, then took a deep breath. This time the notes rang true. Three short blasts, followed by a fourth long, mournful one. He waited five seconds then repeated the same notes before dropping the horn back on its hanger, looking at Balzor nervously. Balzor returned the same look but nodded at his friend; they knew what they'd heard, what they could still hear.

First to arrive was Lortmund, with Svein at his heel and a few of the local lads that Alkor recognised but didn't know personally. They carried longbows, strung ready. They'd all volunteered for this and, although they weren't military trained, all could take a dove on the wing at a hundred paces. Most village boys were adequate with bows, especially Saternac boys; their parents still remembered the initial attack of the Hounds, so ensured their children weren't defenceless. Lortmund and Svein took position at either side of the gate, and the other lads nocked an arrow, then waited.

Within moments, the first rider was spotted on the road, followed closely by what seemed like a full patrol returning – twenty armoured riders, armed to the teeth and trained better than most in the kingdom. The nervous look on Alkor's face changed to a tinge of fear which Balzor knew was mirrored on his own. He hoped the storm would work in their favour and hide what would look like weakness.

The patrol slowed at the sight of the closed gate, spreading out on the road, five riders abreast, four ranks deep. There was no chance they hadn't heard the horn, and they knew what it meant. What they didn't understand was why it was directed at what was so clearly an Annarite patrol without an enemy in sight. One of the riders advanced cautiously, taking off his helmet and eyeing the wall with the two young lads atop it. He squinted into the gloom and raised his hand in uncertain greeting.

"'Lo friend! Alkor, is that you, young 'un? And Balzor? Let us in, it's pissing down out here!" the rider shouted above the storm. Confusion spread through Balzor at his name being uttered, having no clue who this man was. He glanced at Alkor, who had a slight relief etched onto his face at the man, which calmed Balzor slightly.

"Lo Herman! We've had a slight change of authority around here since father went away, orders are orders. We must wait for our officer to arrive before we allow entry, I'm sure you understand?" Alkor called back, trying his best to look sheepish, as though he knew it was nonsense.

Either the storm disguised his terrible acting, or Herman had no reason to distrust. He rolled his eyes and growled his assent, falling back to the riders who released an audible groan at the delay. Military to the core. They did nothing but groan and settled down to wait. Alkor turned to Balzor, locking eyes for a moment and nodding slightly - so far so good.

After a few minutes, the familiar tramping of men came behind them, and they turned to see Dextri in full armour, followed closely by Devar and Ingvar. Alkor made quick hand signals, out of view of the soldiers below, to enlighten Dextri to exactly how many were out there. Dextri nodded swiftly, no trace of concern on his face. He unbuckled his sword from his belt, turning to the fourth figure who accompanied them, the key to the entire plan working: Joseph.

They were unsure and definitely didn't trust the young man, but Alkor had put his faith fully in him, the oath he'd sworn was more binding than anything else. The Seeress had backed up this claim and nobody argued with a Seeress. So, although Joseph hadn't been allowed weapons since the attack, Dextri released his own weapon into his care, keeping his grip tightly on it as Joseph's hand closed around the scabbard. He stared hard into the lad's eyes, baring his teeth.

"If you betray us here, you'll be the first with an arrow through your neck. The young 'un might trust you but I don't. This'll go a long way to earning that trust. Don't let us down!" Dextri growled, his threat doing nothing to the younger man's composure. He nodded, expression steadfast, and Dextri released his weapon.

Joseph buckled it on to his belt and began to climb the ladder, hands grasping the rungs with sure, quick leaps. As he reached the top, Alkor clapped him on the shoulder and nodded, no trace of fear at betrayal in his eyes as he stepped aside to let Joseph take the lead. Herman motioned to the patrol, who took a further twenty paces then stopped again, so they could all hear this new face speak. Joseph took a deep breath, then began.

"None of you know me, so you must be wondering how I come to command a Sain. The answer lays at the prince's feet. Prince Krinar's plans have come into fruition, may Ezimat bless his name. Those who were loyal to His Highness and not to the false regime, step forward now to claim your reward!"

Most of the patrol had furrowed eyebrows and confused looks on their faces, murmuring uneasily to each other but some started eagerly and urged their horses forward, breaking free of the ranks and ignoring the questioning calls from their comrades. *Only five, thank Ezimat it's not more,* Balzor thought, face impassive as his stomach lurched.

"You five are chosen to serve, loyal to the core as we knew you would be. Come friends, enter and reap what you sow. Open the gates!" Joseph bellowed, as Alkor frantically signalled behind his back as his oath man spoke. At Joseph's order, Svein and Lortmund wrenched up the locking bar and ripped the gates open, knowing this part of the plan depended on speed. Only the strength of the two giant blacksmiths could have opened them as quickly as they did and, as the five men came into view on the street, the lads with bows drew back their strings, straining with the effort of reaching their ears. The five elated men started to trot forwards leaving the flabbergasted patrol behind them, before they reined in at the sight of the drawn weapons in front of them. They glanced between each other nervously then looked to the top of the gate at Joseph, who stared back without emotion. This time, it was Alkor who spoke.

"You betrayed your oaths, you betrayed my father, and you betrayed your comrades. Here is your reward. LOOSE!" he said, not attempting to conceal the fury in his voice anymore.

The men blanched and attempted to turn but, the instant the command was spoken, the lads sent their shafts flying, and at that distance even a child couldn't miss. They rocked back from their saddles, shafts hitting to send them gurgling to the ground in an explosion of gore. Only one of the men survived the initial volley, choosing to drop out of the saddle behind his horse as soon as he realised the danger and began to canter into the undergrowth as the arrow intended for him sailed above his head, narrowly missing the patrol behind, who flinched instinctively and raised his shield.

Most of the patrol had locked their horses together at the volley, unhooking their shields and looking coldly towards the town they all thought was home. They drew swords as they saw the archers loping out of the town but, before they could decide to charge, the lads had nocked and sent another volley, arching towards the fleeing man, falling down and hitting the mark.

The horse whinnied as two of the shafts missed the rider and plunged into its back, rearing as the second one hit, unseating the man who'd taken an arrow in the shoulder blade and one miraculous hit to the side of his neck. He crashed to the floor and the horse bolted, half mad with pain and distress.

The lads whooped as the traitor fell but soon realised the angry muttering from the patrol was directed at them. Fear entered their eyes as some of the men shouted and charged, despite their comrades trying to hold them back. None of them understood what had happened - only that some village lads had shot their friends.

The lads cast their bows to the side and ran, all decorum gone in their haste to escape the wall of horseflesh coming towards them, promising death. Alkor's voice was lost to the wind as he bellowed for the men to halt, desperately waving his arms as he saw his plan going awry. Killing loyal men was never part of it, but the dismay spread through his body when it hit home that more men could die today. As the lads passed through the gate, yelping to get it closed and trying for the haven of nearby buildings, Dextri, Ingvar and Devar leapt into view, each carrying huge shields, their weapons sheathed.

"HOLD!" Dextri roared, and finally the charging men slowed, they'd heard that voice before and knew it was to be obeyed. Horses ground to a halt in front of the shield wall, dirt and stones rattling against the wood and cutting into the shins of the men holding it, making them wince slightly but stand firm. One of the men tore off his helmet, practically frothing at the mouth.

"Dex? What the FUCK just happened?!" he snarled; sword still bared.

"Sebastian, calm yourself. Trust me when I say this was necessary. Those men were traitors to their oaths. We were attacked by the Hounds whilst you were gone. Half of them were our own – Mika and Petra were two we knew. Let us explain," Dextri said calmly, lowering his shield slightly.

The men gasped at hearing Mika's name, though didn't seem totally concerned about Petra. Mika had been a friend for years; Petra was relatively new. Sebastian's eyes widened at the revelation, and he lowered his blade limply to the side of his horse, which was pawing at the ground uncertainly after the random charge. "Mika, a traitor? I can hardly believe it," he mumbled; all the fight gone out of him.

"Believe it, mate. It was hard to stomach for us all, Livius especially. He's gone to warn the General of a deeper conspiracy, but we'll explain all that later. For now, put away your swords and take the horses to the stables. There'll be no more bloodshed tonight."

As Dextri was talking, the rest of the patrol tentatively rode into Saternac, glancing left and right as they entered in fear of an ambush. Hearing Dextri's final words, they sheathed their weapons and dismounted, most looking with a curious anger at their bleeding comrades in the road.

"You heard the man, horses to the stables! We're not some noble woman's gossiping circle here. Get to it!" Herman shouted, and the men jerked into action. A life-time of training and taking orders was hard to ignore and, aside from the General, Dextri was the highest authority to them. They shuffled off with their nickering mounts, one of them taking the reins of Herman's horse, who strode towards Dextri with a grim expression.

"Not to sound like a parrot, Dex, but what the fuck just happened?" Herman said quietly as the men rounded the corner to the stables. He 'd hung his helmet on his horse's saddle, wet hair plastered to his head. Dextri took in his old friend's features, and saw no betrayal lurking in his eyes, no tensing of cheek muscles in his round face. He propped his shield up against the nearest building just as the lads who'd done the shooting crept back into view, cringing and retreating as they spied Herman still there in full armour. Dextri sighed.

"Get the men back to the manor, I'll address them there. No use explaining everything individually. Suffice to know that we were attacked by traitors, and this was Alkor's plan to reveal them from any returning patrols. Worked a charm to be fair - not that I'll ever tell him that - his head's big enough. You lot!" he said, barking the last two words at the hiding lads. "You did some good shooting there, let's see if you can dig just as well. Five graves, the men were once one of us, they lost their way. Then you can take these shields back to the forge whilst we fill our comrades in on the situation."

The lads walked sullenly from their hiding places but didn't dare argue with the wall of muscle. Surprisingly, none of them seemed to care that they'd killed a man that day.

"And you two!" he added at Balzor and Alkor, both of whom were making their way towards the ladder. "You've still got hours left yet; don't go thinking we can relax now."

They jumped slightly at the order but had the good sense to look sheepish before saluting and beginning their rounds again. Joseph climbed down the ladder, arms out and head bowed as he returned the sword to Dextri. Dextri's distrust hadn't abated, but the lad had made a start to gaining his approval. He nodded and the lads mouth twitched into a small smile before he walked back toward the manor. Dextri sighed again, turning to Ingvar and Devar. They shrugged as if to say, 'He did what he said he'd do' before leaning their own shields against Dextri's and following Joseph back to the blessed warm and dry.

"Come on then mate, seems we've got a lot to catch up on," he said to Herman, who wholeheartedly agreed.

They marched off in their friend's wake, leaving the two soaked youths patrolling the wall, heads held high as they felt pride seep into their bones thanks to their part in the plan. It had run like clockwork, and they had their loyal men back around them. Now they had a fighting chance.

✱✱✱✱✱

Chatter erupted around the dinner hall as men tried their best to voice opinions above the babbling of the rest. Dextri had told them his version of events, leaving nothing out, not even the fact that Joseph was one of the attackers. This earned him a few dark glares from the soldiers which subsided slightly when Dextri added that he was forced into service and had since sworn an unbreakable oath to Alkor.

When he reached the part of not being able to save the inn, it seemed as though the men were even more distraught than he could've imagined. Betrayal and murder were fine, but take away a soldier's ale after a day's work? Unforgivable! Thankfully, the men accepted his story without a great deal of questioning though it left a bad taste in their mouths that they'd travelled with men who had long since been traitors.

The biggest shock, which wasn't surprising, was that the main perpetrator was none other than Prince Krinar himself. Most men there had fought alongside the prince and though they thought him a pompous prat, traitor seemed a harsh word to add to his name. It took Joseph's full tale from start to finish to cement the idea into their heads but finally they seemed to settle themselves and look towards Dextri once more.

"I hardly need to stress the severity of the situation at hand, lads. For now, we sit tight, and hope Livius reaches the General in time. We keep watch night and day and no drinking until we know what we're up against." He raised his hand at the mutters

207

that broke out. "That's an order I'm afraid. We need to be ready at a moment's notice, not sat with our heads up our arses with a hangover! Right lads, get some sleep. Sebastian and Axel, relieve the young 'uns from the wall at first light. Dismissed!"

Sebastian rose with a salute almost a head shorter than Dextri but with an equally bald head. Axel, the other chosen sentry, did the same. He was slightly taller than Dextri, which was a feat unto itself, but had long dark hair that tickled his shoulders greasily. He dropped his salute and both men strode out, the short, stocky and bald Sebastian in direct contrast with the tall, lanky, long-haired Axel as they walked through the door. The men filed out after them, the loud hubbub of mutters making the air heavy with concern as the truth began to sink in. In the end, only Herman remained behind, sitting down next to Dextri with a huff, head sinking into his hands.

"The world's gone mad, Dex," he said running his hands through his hair lightly. How the man had found time to comb and wax it was beyond Dextri.

"Tell me about it, mate," Dextri replied. "One minute we were having a drink in the inn, taking the piss out of Balzor since he's love drunk on none less than the Seeress' granddaughter, the next we're running for our lives and the inn's ablaze."

"Hang on, you kept that quiet! The young 'uns involved with the Seeress' granddaughter?!" Herman said incredulously. "Now I know earlier I said we weren't some noble woman's gossiping circle, but this I've *got* to hear." Dextri laughed for the first time that night and launched into the tale, even adding the bit about the Seeress catching them both almost in bed together. Herman's eyes widened and he whistled slowly. "The lads got bigger balls than me, that's for sure. Fair play to him there," he chuckled, rising from his seat. "Ah I needed a good laugh like that after tonight, that's for sure. I'm gonna rest my weary bones now, though. Night mate."

He clapped a hand on Dextri's oversized shoulder then made his exit, leaving his friend alone with his thoughts. Dextri stayed sat on the bench, resting his elbows on the table behind him and hanging his head back with an exasperated sigh. He hadn't expected the men to take the news so well, especially after they'd culled five of their own mere moments before. But the trust of their brotherhood was sacred, and they'd all scorned the dead men, cut out the rot without regret and moved on swiftly.

His thoughts turned now to his General, worry settled on his stomach at the precarious situation he was in, though he wouldn't yet know it himself. He mentally urge his friend on, willing speed to his mission and sending a thought to Ezimat for his safe return.

"Get there Livius, for all our sakes," he whispered under his breath. What would happen if he didn't, Ezimat only knew.

✳ ✳ ✳ ✳ ✳

Livius was miserable. He had sacrificed much comfort for speed, and this storm had sprung up out of nowhere. He'd used a sizeable portion of his coin to purchase warmer clothing at a passing merchant caravan, but refrained from wearing it during the day, preferring to wait until night-time to avoid water inevitably soaking the garments. He'd felt lucky the first few nights - renting a room in a village or giving a few coppers to a farmer who let him use the hayloft – but tonight was the first night he was regretting the light skinned tent he'd brought with him. Sure, it was much easier to carry, but with the wind howling and the rain battering the thin canvas, the fleece lined clothes he'd counted on barely kept the chill away. There hadn't been a storm of this magnitude at the start of Autumn for as long as he could remember; it was just his luck that one would strike up now. Either that or the Gods were truly angry, which didn't bear thinking about.

Water did wonders for covering up tracks, too. Two hundred men were fairly easy to follow, and he knew which direction they were going, but the last day he'd struggled to find old campfires, relying on sopping horse dung to confirm he was still on their trail. His gelding was just as tired as he was, and she was just as irritable. He had to leave her saddled to save precious time, but she didn't understand that; he'd already promised her a week's rest and all the hay she could eat when they returned. He earned a reproachful glance in return, but she carried him and that's what mattered.

He'd woken from his fitful sleep feeling barely more rested than when he'd shut his eyes but forced himself to rise and fold up his tent regardless. He'd decided to leave the warmer clothing on today, praying to Ezimat that he'd find somewhere to dry them later or that this damn storm would let up. He couldn't be more than a couple of days behind now at the speed he'd been going, the last farm he'd passed had excitedly told him that the royal Prince had passed on the night the storm began, buying every bit of food they could spare for well over the asking price.

As he folded the tent, grimacing distastefully as freezing water eagerly ran down his forearms, he pondered over the last bit of information he'd gleaned before leaving. The General duelling the prince? That didn't sit right with Livius. Everything he knew about the General indicated discretion, hiding the extent of his skill so he'd always have an edge; even Livius had only seen him let loose once, and that was in the heat of battle, but duelling a true Annarite and holding his own for so long? That was a feat that would test even the General.

Knowing what Livius knew now gave the duel a much more sinister feel to it, despite the farmer's awe at seeing such a spectacle. Was Krinar testing his opponent out, to be sure he would win when it came to the real thing? The thought was running through his tired brain as he mounted the disgruntled gelding patting her neck to ease her jittering.

"Not long now girl, a couple more days at most. We'll get there in time, won't we?" She nickered as he dragged himself up into the saddle, and he took that for her way of agreement. He dug his heels in softly as his own words reverberated around his head. He just wished he knew.

Chapter 11

Blades of grass danced to the wind's song, tickling Aldred's ankles in a pleasant way. The meadow somehow always held its dazzling beauty, even when the winter came and the flowers died, but in spring it was so vibrant, so alive, he could almost feel its personality filling him with love.

It was either that making Aldred feel happy and content, or the image of perfection that walked alongside him, a radiant smile gracing her features, dimples on her rosy cheeks and a small button nose sitting between the lot. Her eyes were closed against the sun's caress as she twirled around between the poppies and marigolds, sweet laugh tinkling alongside the orchestra of birds.

He knew she kept her eyes closed to imagine the field they were in whilst sampling the orange hues of warm light that the sun gave her eyelids. Watching her for a moment, entranced, he began to thank Ezimat that he'd put her in this world and fated him to meet her. His wife. His Lorelai. Right on cue, her eyes burst open. He knew then that it wasn't the meadow he could feel the love from, it was that gaze. Fiery and playful, her chocolate eyes locked with his own piercing blue, and sparks flew. He took her hands, and they spun in the grass, laughing at the stupidity of the scene.

Though he loved her dearly, more than anything he could possibly imagine, they never had been the lovesick couple - especially not the couple who spin in the meadow like the love stories in the plays that the masses begged to see. So, though he wanted to clasp those hands forever, he leant back slightly and released her, letting the speed and her atrocious balance do the rest of the work for him. She careered off into the poppies, falling flat on her back, though lightly. He would never forgive himself if he caused her any pain, intended or otherwise. No hesitation, he leapt onto his own back at the side of her in an explosion of dandelion seeds, instantly emitting a sneeze as they attacked his airways. Lorelai was scowling at him good naturedly as he landed but couldn't keep a straight face at his sneezing fit and descended into laughter once more.

"Next time you could at least pretend to care if I was dying," he accused as his puffy red eyes stopped watering. Hay fever in the spring was the bane of their relationship. Lorelai loved the meadows and forests; he hated them, so naturally they spent a lot of time in them.

"Oh, don't be so dramatic my love. You're the one that dove into them, not the other way around," she replied airily, swatting another dandelion in his face playfully. He blew the seeds straight back at her, and they settled in her hair. Rolling her eyes, she settled back into the grass without swatting them off, sighing in contentment as her head nestled amongst the petals. They lay there for a while, fingers intertwined watching the birds toiling to build their nests. Aldred was acutely aware of her other hand tracing circles on his forearm, rising higher until it eventually cupped his face. He turned, almost too willingly, and looked once again into her eyes, this time seeing a fierce hunger in them as she used that other hand to drag his lips to hers, crushing herself against him. Dandelions forgotten, they tore of each other's clothes in savage abandonment, no words needed as his hand traced over her body, caressing between her thighs. She bit his lip and moaned, then the rest was a blur. After, she lay with her head against his chest as the breeze kissed the sweat off their bodies.

He'd thought the steady rhythm of his breathing had sent her to sleep but, after a while, she sighed and propping her elbows under her chin, watched him. Since they still hadn't dressed, he was just as content to watch her. He began to think there was a chance for another round of passion, knowing himself more than ready, when she spoke.

"You'll have to make amends with Alnor, you know," she said, eyes losing their playfulness and a grave look upon her face. Aldred's stomach lurched as he heard his son's name. It seemed out of place coming from her mouth. Alnor? His son? He could see Lorelai getting angry and did his best to take the quizzical look off his face, racking his brain to think of what he had to make amends for with a two-year-old boy.

The sky darkened, the sun darting to its hiding place behind an unnatural black cloud with startling speed. He felt a small drop of rain land on his forehead as he glanced to the skies, just as they opened and engulfed the meadow in a torrent of rain. Rolling over, he tried to reach the pile of clothes and cover them both in a futile attempt to get dry, but the clothes were gone. He brushed his hands through the grass, frantically trying to find them but knowing somehow that they weren't there.

Lorelai's voice interrupted his search, the now pleading tone causing him to spin around in alarm, looking for danger. His wife was now a few paces away, soaked to the bone and shivering in the harsh wind, reaching for him in desperation as the once beautiful meadow expanded, empty grassland placing itself between him and the love of his life.

"Lorelai!" he screamed, knowing his heart couldn't take this, not again.

"Make amends my love. Makes amends" she called back in a surprisingly soft voice that carried on the wind despite the crash of thunder overhead. He watched helplessly as his wife drifted slowly away, a sad smile adorning her face like he'd seen a thousand times before; knowing it was useless but still doing his best to reach her, battling against the hurricane and roaring his defiance.

"Amends."

A colossal thunderclap hit the sky, wrenching Aldred Sain from his para-dise-turned-nightmare back into the land of the waking. Rain battered the tent above him and the half open door leapt around in the gale, clapping against the mud loudly. He could hear men muttering in the tents beside him, though outside it was still pitch black, barely past midnight. It took him a while to register why the flap was open, but when he did, the dream came crashing back and his stomach dropped to the floor.

Alnor. They'd argued badly, he'd struck him. Things hadn't been the best between them since the start of the raid and when Alnor crossed that line, when he'd mentioned Lorelai, he'd snapped. Standing from his bedroll, dejected and stooped, he tied the tent with practiced hands. The memory had haunted his dreams for almost two decades, ever since he'd taken the post as the General of the Annarites, but never had it been so vivid, so real. It always ended happily, as the true memory had. This was the first time she'd been ripped away from him, and the wound was savage. It was like she had been taken all over again, such was the pain. He could tell from the concerned murmurs around him that he'd screamed her name in his sleep; the men had known Lorelai, loved her as they'd loved a sister as they did their General. But he couldn't bring himself to care. Body shaking with sobs, he collapsed back onto his bedroll, fingernails biting into his palms as he tried to take away the pain by inflicting more.

The storm continued to bellow its fury whilst Aldred Sain wept at what he had lost. When he awoke, he felt hollow. Red rimmed eyes forced themselves open and he grabbed his waterskin to clear the gritty taste from his mouth, throat scratchy from the prolonged sobbing of the night before. Embarrassment flooded him, and he found himself fervently hoping the surrounding men had heard nothing more than the one exclamation of his wife's name. General of the Annar weeping in his tent like some child after too much ale.

Aldred sighed, dragging himself out of his bedroll and splashed his face, dragging on his thicker, waterproof clothes as the hard pattering of the rain was broken by an interfering peal of thunder, making him jump slightly. He snorted. Crying all night and being scared by the weather? Ezimat's balls, he was going soft. Shaking his head and clenching his jaw, he unlaced the hastily knotted tent flap and stepped out into the tempest. The wind did its best to wrench the flap from his grasp as he re-tied the knot properly, whilst harsh rain battered his broad back from black clouds that engulfed the sun's light, leaving the morning a very dull grey.

Men did their best to shelter meagre fires as they miserably tried to boil their porridge, with water dripping off their noses as they stood abruptly to salute the General. "At ease, lads. None of that out here" Aldred said, waving his hand to stand them down.

A chorus of 'No sir' greeted his words as they fell easily back into their morning routines, all creatures of habit. Spying Terva on the outskirts of the furthest fire, Aldred moved over to him. "Morning big man. Any spare going for me?" Aldred enquired, gesturing at the pot above the fire.

Terva had cleverly arranged his tent flaps to cover the fragile flames, using the makeshift roof to mostly shelter the fire and himself. He lifted his chin towards the pot and spare bowls, raising his own spoon from his bowl to take a mouthful.

"Help yourself sir," Terva replied, dripping porridge from his mouth down his shirt as he did, shrugging apologetically and continuing with his gorging. Aldred laughed dryly, taking one of the bowls and ladling out a generous portion before digging in without further comment. As they sat with only the sound of their slurping and the storm puncturing the comfortable silence, Aldred did his best to draw his thoughts away from his late wife, instead thinking of how best to fix what seemed an unbridgeable ravine between him and his son. He was sure a few days riding would mellow him, but he also felt as though he needed to make amends rather than let it fester. He'd never hit his son before and didn't abide by it when others did the same to their children; a clip round the ear to teach respect of your elders, of course, but never actually assaulting them. He would have to go to Alnor today, swallow his pride and apologise. *Make amends,* he thought with a pang of sadness.

"Something on your mind, General?" Terva asked, placing his now empty bowl on the ground.

"That obvious?" Aldred replied.

"Well, aside from having a face like a smacked arse, I heard you and the little Sain getting a bit heated last night, then saw him stomping off. Guessing you had a bit of an argument?"

Aldred paused before answering, furious that he'd let his temper get the better of him and allowed the men to hear it. "Something like that. He'll come round," he replied dismissively, shoving the last of the porridge into his mouth and swallowing quickly. "Thanks for the porridge," he added, passing the bowl to Terva's waiting hands and making to walk away.

"General?" Terva called questioningly.

Aldred froze in his half turn and raised a questioning eyebrow. "Mmm?"

"Nobody will mention it, but I gotta ask. You okay? Heard you shout Lorie's name last night," he said, avoiding his eyes as Aldred looked at him sharply. Not many could hold that gaze, and Terva knew he was on thin ice mentioning Lorelai so casually. Seeing the big man suddenly look so timid soothed Aldred's initial flare of anger, and he resorted to chuckling softly.

"I'm fine Terva, truly. Just wine-addled dreams mixing with an argument with my son is all," he said, clapping a hand on the huge man's shoulders. "It's nice to know you care though, under that tough exterior," he joked, giving him a shove.

"Pardon the disrespect sir, but piss off," Terva grumbled, and Aldred laughed as Terva swilled the bowls with water before slinging it out on to the already sodden floor. "This slow pace is grating on me, sir. Aren't we menna be killing rebels?"

"If it helps, I voiced my concerns to the King. He told me he put the mission into his son's hands and will let him make his own mistakes. How else will he learn, I suppose," Aldred said.

"Seems shoddy, if you don't mind me saying General. Possibly letting the most notorious rebels in the history of Annar take flight just to teach your son a lesson?"

My thoughts exactly Terva. My thoughts exactly, Aldred thought. He was alarmed that the discontent he'd been feeling had clearly begun to spread amongst the men and vowed to speak to the prince himself today.

"Sir!" a voice called from across the clearing. Aldred turned to see a man in a red cloak gingerly walking across the ground, doing his best to avoid stepping in any puddles or mud. He saw Terva roll his eyes and mutter something under his breath but paid him no heed.

"Report, soldier" he said, straightening his back and resuming the role as General.

"Prince Krinar asked me to tell you we'll be riding out within the hour, sir. He says the rebels will expect us to slow during the storm and will assume they have more time; we're increasing speed to surprise them," he said, clearly reciting the words as he heard them.

Terva paused in his muttering and looked at the General, eyes wide. "It seems he heard your prayers, Terva," Aldred whispered. "Tell the Prince we'll be ready to move," he said, louder now for the messenger to hear. The man saluted, then back-tracked around the sloppy ground, holding his cloak up like a dress.

"Like a lady in a bloody ballroom court," Terva spat, and Aldred couldn't disagree.

Finally, a feeling of purpose returned to Aldred, and he took a deep breath. "Right lads, out of your bedrolls! Quick breakfast and we're on the move. What do you think this is, a holiday?" he bellowed, startling a few of the drowsy men around their fires and causing more than a few exclamations from the tents of men sleeping off their wine.

Within seconds, the small camp was buzzing with a rushed intensity, barely anybody grumbling at the sharp wake up call. The discontent went further than just Terva being bored, it seemed. The pace quickened considerably, much to the joy of the older men. The King rode with renewed vigour, glances of pride towards his son at finally stepping up were hard to miss for the men around him.

In contrast to the ambling speed and the casual conversations, the next few days passed in companionable silence, eating up the miles at the steady canter, only stopping for minutes at a time to water their horses and quickly relieving themselves before continuing. The stops at night were still conveniently next to farms, so the men were still well fed, but they were much later than before and leaving much earlier in the mornings. The storm raged above, but that only served to put fire in the warriors' bellies, knowing their prey would be hunkered down and weathering the onslaught, all the while waiting on their doom.

Throughout those days, Alnor kept well away from his father, only the odd glare during the day breaking through the wall that had been thrown up between them. Aldred tried to go over to his son, but each time his son saw him coming and moved away, forcing Aldred to ask an awkward question of the prince or one of his men. They looked amused at the General's feeble attempts to make amends with his son. After the fifth attempt, Aldred's temper broke and he refused to try again. He had overreacted, yes, but his son had his own fair share of wrongdoings. An uneasy tension had settled over them both as they kept their distance and focused on the task at hand.

Aldred noticed a sudden increase in sentries at night, showing that though the prince played the darling with the men, he still knew his work. He offered to take a watch himself every other night but was politely rebuffed by Krinar. "General, you've spent years performing exemplary service to the kingdom. It's time to let others do the work," Krinar had said, a perfect smile on his face as he did so.

Time to let others do the menial work sounded far too much like let others take over to Aldred's ears, but the infuriating politeness left no room – or reason – for an angry retort. Aldred inclined his head, accepting what he was convinced was a barbed compliment and kept his head down. The word retirement always seemed absurd to Aldred, but it was becoming a pleasant thought as this expedition continued.

Almost a week after the storm started, the heavy downpour and the roaring thunder finally began to dissipate, replaced by a weak sunlight without warmth, as if the sun had taken as much of a battering as the men. Men sighed in relief that night, though still looked grim as they dragged half damp clothes over their heads, shivering in the chilled air as they did their best to dry garments next to their roaring fires, unencumbered by makeshift covers and stray raindrops.

Aldred, never one to set himself apart, sat around the fire alongside Terva. They sat gratefully in the grace of the flames, watching their clothes steam in the heat as their teeth chattered, the cold of the day still not quite gone from their bones. Tramping boots broke the reverie and they turned to see the King striding across the clearing towards them, the twins in tow looking eager as they saw the inferno.

"Ah, General! Thought I'd find you here. Room for an old monarch around the fire? Oh, and his pets I suppose," he said, gesturing at the twins who scowled at him good naturedly.

"Of course, sire, if you can ignore the fact we've both sacrificed our clothes to get them dry," Aldred replied.

"If you can't beat em…" the King said, throwing his own coat over his head and hanging it next to the fire. "Join em! Halfway, at least."

They laughed as they sat, exchanging pleasantries whilst rubbing their hands together near the fire to regain feeling. Terva had thrown what remained of their spices into a pot, adding their rationed meat and some potatoes, and it boiled happily over the flames, giving a mouth-watering aroma that kept assaulting their nostrils at regular intervals. Neve had brought a small flute and played softly as Bayar kept chiding him to play a more upbeat tune.

"We're at a bloody campfire, not a funeral!" he whined at his brother, but Neve took no notice.

It soon became apparent that King Malker hadn't just come by the fire to idle the night away, though, as his eyes kept glancing towards the General, his mouth slightly opening as if to say something, before thinking better of it.

"Sire, as much as I love your company, that gormless look on your face has me almost begging you to leave. Cat got your tongue?" Aldred eventually said exasperatedly.

Malker laughed softly. "You know me too well my friend. Right to it then! Krinar's scouts have sighted the beginning of the dunes that mark where we think the Hound's lair is situated. We should be there this time tomorrow. I've suggested we leave the road around midday and wait for nightfall before advancing, using the cover of darkness to hide our attack. Thankfully, he's agreed without argument. I think he knew his old dad would've pulled rank this time. It's one thing letting him lead this raid, but it's another to let men die for nothing," Malker said.

As he was speaking, Terva was leaning further forward until he risked singeing his eyebrows over the fire, such was his excitement. If the big man loved anything more than his food, it was a good fight.

"About bloody time, if you pardon the language sire. I've been spoiling for a good fight for days now!" Terva exclaimed, clenching his fists and baring his teeth.

"With a face like that big man, they'll run before you draw your blade," Neve said sarcastically, taking a break from the flute to throw the barb. Poised for the moment, Bayar snatched the flute of his hands and instantly began a bouncier tune, much to Neve's chagrin. Terva, though, roared happily at the change and began singing boisterously about a farmer's daughter, the words making Aldred cringe but Neve barked with laughter. The King shuffled closer, dropping his voice lower for his ears only.

"My son wants to see you privately later, to discuss the plan of attack. He means to split his un-blooded men in amongst our veterans I think, to steel their nerve when we clash with the rebels," he murmured. Aldred nodding firmly, surprised at Krinar's insight - that's exactly what he would've done in this situation, and he was finding a grudging respect for the King's son. As if reading his friend's thoughts, Malker snorted.

"He's actually a bloody good soldier when he gets round to it," Malker said. Aldred's shocked look of innocence made the King laugh.

"Hey, you know when I'm holding out on you. Fair's fair. This time tomorrow we'll be round a roaring fire again, drinking looted wine and finally being rid of the bastards who pillaged your home all those years ago."

The thought seemed to pull part of the fire in front of them into Aldred's belly, as he clasped hands strongly with his oldest friend.

"Finally, sire. They'll be punished and the kingdom will be safe once more," Aldred replied, baring his teeth as Terva began to dish out the stew.

But the hunger for food had been replaced by the hunger of something far more satisfying: Revenge.

★ ★ ★ ★ ★

Alnor stood absentmindedly brushing his horse down, pondering over the offer the prince had so casually thrown his way. Already, the thought had taken root within him; to be free of his father's yolk and to ride in Krinar's own warband, hopefully as his right-hand man. He'd have to be out of his mind to refuse.

Yet the thought of abandoning his family to forge his own path was a daunting one. Ever since he could hold a practice sword, he'd been training to take over his

219

father's legacy, to hopefully one day become General of the Annar and lead armies in the King's name. Forever with his father's shadow hanging over him, promoted to rank out of favouritism or sense of honour, what Krinar had offered him would still leave that prospect open, but nobody could then refute that it was done by anything but his own skill or initiative. He'd be his own man, just like he'd always wanted.

Right on cue, Krinar walked into the clearing, a welcoming smile on his face as his eyes found Alnor. "My friend! I was hoping to find you here. Our fathers are meeting us at my tent soon, to discuss the plan for tomorrow night," Krinar began, moving towards him slowly. When he got close enough, he continued in a muted voice. "We need to talk, before that time."

Alnor's brow furrowed, having never known Krinar to have to hide his intentions. "Why sire? Something wrong?"

"You know already what the camp's mood is. They're tired of their restrictions, low wages and little reward. They're worried that after the battle, the threat will be gone, and they'll be out of work. No threat, no soldiers. The common people won't need protecting. Therein lies our problem; common people who do nothing to deserve the protection they get, profiting from it, whilst the men who do the protecting being on the streets, out of a job and penniless," Krinar said, voice still low and covered by the walls of horseflesh.

"I despise that as much as the next man sire, but what can we do?" Alnor said uneasily, not liking where this train of conversation was going; especially not liking that it resonated deep within him, easing itches that he didn't know were there.

"The time for change is coming my friend. The old ways are dead, it's time to make way for the new. Can I count on you Alnor? To do what you know is right and save the kingdom from disarray, when the time comes?"

Alnor's instant reaction was to nod and agree, but though the words connected with him, he hesitated. What the Prince was suggesting was almost close to treason. Alnor shook his head, knowing the prince would never suggest something so drastic, but knowing that the ideology Krinar was suggesting was in line with his own. He thought his father meddled too much, was too righteous in his ways. Maybe the Prince felt the same? The shackles of their fathers could be broken in one sweep, freeing them both and creating a stronger kingdom, a better land for the free.

"Of course, my Prince. You can count on me for anything," Alnor replied.

Krinar smiled and clapped a hand on his shoulder. "Okay my friend, here's what we will do."

Around an hour later, they were both washed and sat around a fire in front of Krinar's tent, where Alnor had been staying since his fight with his father. Varnan was with them at first but made his excuses and slipped away from the fire, knowing the company they'd soon have. There was a chill wind in the air, barely compensated by the sun's weak rays as it dropped below the skyline. Both Alnor and Krinar rubbed their hands together around the flames, doing their best to bring circulation back to frozen fingers. Alnor knew that Krinar had already passed the plans by his father, who surprisingly approved without argument.

The problem was, Alnor could also sense that Krinar needed Aldred's approval to move forward with the perfectly sound strategy so, when the King and Alnor's father stepped around the corner, their arrival heralded by the squelching of military boots in the sopping mud, Alnor saw Krinar take a deep breath and steel himself before he rose from his position by the fire.

"Father, General. Thank you for coming. Hopefully, by now my father will have briefed you on the plan?" Krinar said.

Aldred nodded and smiled. "Everything I've been told is satisfactory, my Prince," Aldred replied, gaining a sense of satisfaction as he saw Krinar wince at the higher ground taken by the General. Krinar took a deep breath and smiled back at Aldred.

"I'm glad you find it so. Merging the un-blooded warriors with your own veterans will ensure that nobody will rout when the fighting inevitably gets nasty. My scouts have found a woodland around three miles from the start of the dunes, it is here that we will leave our horses. We will then split into three groups - one continuing West as we are, the others looping North and South in a pincer movement and coming around behind the rebels and catching them in our net so none will escape. My father and I will be in the main group coming at them head on; seeing the Prince and the King in the frontline of the attacking force will reinforce the assumption that we're the main attack rather than a diversion. Meanwhile, you will loop around in the South party, whilst Varnan loops round with the North party. By this time tomorrow, General, we'll have the

221

Hounds in our grasp!" Krinar said seeming to deflate slightly as the plan left his body.

Alnor couldn't help but seem wounded at the slight to his command. He opened his mouth to retort to the prince, but his father beat him to it. "What about Alnor? Would he not be better leading the North party?" Aldred said, breathing a sigh of relief that the plan wasn't completely stupid.

"Forgive the slight, General, but I want Alnor next to me in this attack. It's not an insult to his character but a compliment. I'm sure he'll speak to you about this soon. As of yet, it is not my place," Krinar said tentatively, the timid act seeming odd on him.

Aldred turned sharply to Alnor, who did his best to keep a straight back and ignore the sudden scrutiny. The eye contact heralded a look that demanded answers before the night was over. It was more to Alnor's pity that Krinar seemed to have finished his speeches prematurely, stepping towards the King.

"Father," Krinar said in a low voice. "Come, we should speak about other matters." He glanced obviously towards Alnor and Aldred, who feigned ignorance. Malker snorted at the awkward situation before rolling his eyes and moving off into his son's tent. Both Alnor and his father knew this was a ruse to leave them alone, but they kept the look of indifference as their friends left the area. Aldred, having days of pent-up arguments inside his head, went first.

"Son, I'm sorry, I didn't – "

"Father, whatever you're about to say, don't. Families fight, then it gets forgotten," Alnor broke in, sharing a sense of weightlessness he saw replicated in his father.

Aldred let out an explosion of breath. "Thank Ezimat, son. I thought that we'd never get past the rut we'd sank into. When we finish this raid and get home, all of us Sains can spend some real time together, we can – "

Alnor leapt in before his father could finish. "Father, I won't be coming home." The revelation echoed in the small clearing of tents. Aldred took a few moments before reacting, staring into the flames of the fire before Krinar's tent before turning to his son and responding.

"Why?" he questioned. Alnor froze for a small moment, before firming the resolve that had built over the past few days.

"Father, I must forge my own path. I cannot stay beneath your shadow any longer. The prince has given me an invitation to move into his war band. I need to move away from you, to find the man I mean to be," he said seriously, breathing an inaudible sigh. "I'm struggling to differentiate between being a son who looks up to his father, and a soldier. And I need more than just sitting in Saternac, waiting with only my *brothers* for company."

Standing up to his father was a different game in person, he didn't realise how hard it would actually be. But now the words were out there – despite the disdain at his use of the word brothers - he felt a small relief that he wouldn't have to say them again. Hearing the gears grinding in his father's brain was a small price to pay. Silence ensued once again, but this time it was more companionable; Alnor saw the different emotions flicker over his father's face. A flash of anger, followed closely by hurt, then an impassive expression, before acceptance settled over harsh blue eyes that had sent many-a-men reeling.

Aldred sighed. "I suppose congratulations are in order then. Beginning a war band with the prince is exactly how I started my career and look where I am now! But, my son, you were never in my shadow; you and your brother were always the light that kept me going in the darkness. Promise to visit in between your mighty escapades," Aldred said, a whisper of a mocking smile on his face.

"Hmm... maybe if I'm not too busy saving the world and such I'll pop down for a night or two," Alnor said airily.

His father barked a laugh and dragged him into a rough embrace, rocking to and fro. He released him quickly, clapping both of his hands to Alnor's face and staring right into his eyes. "Know that I am proud of you always, my son" he said.

Tears sprung to Alnor's eyes which he fought back with everything he had. "Thank you," he managed to croak back. Anything else would've broken him and had him running back to Saternac instead of the life he wanted. Seeing the turmoil in Alnor's eyes, Aldred ruffled his son's hair. Alnor recoiled, good naturedly slapping away his father's hand, using it as an excuse to step away.

"Thank you for understanding," he finished, his voice steadier this time.

"Believe it or not, I remember being young once myself. Though keep your own honour son, despite being with a crown prince. Krinar doesn't seem the type to make friends as easily as he seems to have with you."

Alnor felt heat creeping up his neck but forced himself to hold his tongue as his father nodded sharply to his son before turning to leave the clearing. As he reached the edge he paused, as though he wanted to say something, before steeling himself and leaving without a backwards glance.

Alnor released a breath he hadn't realised he'd been holding. Half of him had been yearning for his father to rage and shout, telling him he couldn't just leave and forcing him to stay, but that was the boy who needed to be reassured and told everything was okay. Alnor was a man now and needed to make his own path. His father would see his views on Krinar were wrong. He was half free of the yolk he imagined himself under. Krinar's plan would see them both break their chains.

*****

Walking away from the clearing was one of the hardest things Aldred had ever done. He'd kept his emotions in check and given an appearance of a supporting father, when all he'd really wanted to do was scream that his son was an idiot to follow such a man. He'd known something like this was coming, Alnor was too much like his father to want to stay – too stubborn and headstrong. Aldred chuckled without mirth. Who would he be to deny his son a chance to live his life? He himself had started his own life the same way, though technically he'd kissed a Princess before fighting a Prince to earn his place. If anything - Alnor's way was much more legitimate, but it still didn't stop the feeling of betrayal Aldred felt as he left his son.

He couldn't quite shake the feeling of distrust he had over Krinar. He'd seen something in the prince's eyes on the night of the duel, something that he'd only ever seen on the battlefield. The man wanted him dead and barely tried to hide it. Aldred wracked his brain to come up with a feasible reason as to why the Prince of the Annar would want his loyal General dead but came up with nothing. He shook his head. A storm had started mid fight, it must have been a trick of the light, he berated himself. Alnor trusted him enough to give him his oath, so Aldred would be supportive too. It helped that Krinar had finally started to act like a real leader. His plan of attack was sound, and Aldred wouldn't have changed a thing if he'd planned it himself, but it didn't stop him picking it apart in his head as he lay down for the night, dropping into a fitful sleep filled with battle cries and darkness. Thankfully Lorelai didn't get ripped away from him that night, so he awoke without any awkward questions or looks of sympathy.

As he opened his tent, weak sunlight greeted him, sending its small warmth into the air, breaking through the earlier storm's menace. He ate his breakfast in silence, watching the men around him murmur quietly, anticipation thick in the air as the orders came through that they'd reach the woodland within hours, poised to make the attack that night. Even Terva didn't fool around or throw his usual ribald comments, choosing instead to keep quiet and strap on his armour, checking it twice before mounting up with the rest.

None of the usual faction distancing appeared in that morning ride either; instead, the younger men blended in with the veterans they'd be standing next to during the fight, striking up conversations and acting as though the past couple of weeks were a dream. Aldred, content at seeing the invisible rifts begin to heal, encouraged the mixing of the groups, even finding time to mend his own fracture with Varnan.

"So General, it seems we're to lead the flanking parties?" the ugly Varnan asked him.

Aldred had no reason to dislike the man but couldn't help the emotion seeping through. "Seems that way," Aldred said tightly, instantly regretting his tone. "We'll meet at the back and then move to finally crush the rebels; I couldn't think of a better man to have by my side," he added in an attempt to cover the blatant slight. He ignored the chill in his spine as he said the words, preferring to accept the smug satisfaction from the man as they sank in.

"So, we will, General," Varnan replied, hardly keeping the disdain from his voice. "Do your best to not be late, eh?"

Aldred seethed at the words, his temper doing its best to break through his control. It wouldn't do to lose his composure in front of the men, so he managed a grim smile at Varnan. "I assure you, my disgusting friend, that I won't be."

Varnan snarled, wrenching his reins away from Aldred and making the men around them hide their mirth. Aldred straightened his back, attempting to hide his glee but instead clearly displaying it for all to see. The men around him broke into sniggers at their General's obvious happiness, enjoying Varnan's discomfort as he dragged himself away.

After that, the journey became monotonous. The final fields ended in scraggly fences, giving way to the dusty ground again, shrubs doing their best to grow in the environment, tired sunlight bathing the sodden ground in its slow attempt to dry it out. The haze of sunlight illuminated the beginning of the desert in front of them, dunes rising in the distance, the odd wispy copse of trees gracing their eyes amongst the expanse of grainy ground. Woodland to the South encompassed their view, earlier scouts sent there to secure the area and hold it for their arrival. They broke off the obvious road angling over the final stretch of grassland to take the woods out of view of the dunes and dismounted in their shade. Krinar dismounted with them, walking along the men and saying his piece.

"Rest for now, my friends. When the sun hides its glare, we'll move under the cover of darkness."

The warriors took this to heart, rubbing down the horses and using the valuable time to run whetstones over their weapons, or bring out the dice. Veterans lay and shut their eyes, knowing that on campaign sleep is the most valuable of currencies, not the winning of coin on a gamble. But with the sun recovering its strength, beaming the boiling light down onto the meagre canopy, not many men slept.

Aldred stood at the tree line, watching the dunes for any sign that they'd been seen, preferring his own company than the warmth of friendship. A sense of unease travelled through Aldred as no scout appeared on the dunes. The Hounds had escaped capture for many years, and they hadn't done it through a lack of secrecy. It seemed too good to be true that they'd caught them unawares after all this time. But still the Annarites sat, biding their time for nightfall, gathering their wits for the attack. A brisk nod was all Aldred received from his son as he watched him walk across the camp, getting ready for the events that night. Aldred forced himself to leave him to his own devices, allowing him the free will he so clearly wanted.

The night came quicker than expected though, when the moon surfaced, it retained much of the sun's warmth, giving the night a sickly and sticky feel, to the chagrin of the men. It was supposed to bring cooler temperatures, and those who wished for warmer nights during the storm, suddenly wished for the cooler days to tease the sweat off their skin.

It wasn't long before men were congregating without order amongst the trees, waiting for the prince to give the command to advance. Aldred sat on a stump waiting for the order to form up. He had to appear nonchalant or else he'd make the men nervous. Inside he was reeling, but to let his doubt seep out into the men was a thing he'd never let happen before and wouldn't now.

As the moon's welcoming light bathed the harsh dunes, Krinar took a final walk amongst the men, muttering reassurances and keeping spirits up. Just as a good leader should, Aldred grudgingly admitted to himself, whilst roughly chewing on the dried beef rations they'd gorged on without a fire being lit.

Terva rose from his own perch, fully armoured and wearing an excited grin as the time to form up for the battle approached. No orders had been given to rise, but Terva's infectious personality had caused the men in the area to stand and begin to gather their weapons. The motion had kickstarted the camps to jump into action, spreading through the woods as the sense of anticipation lanced through the trees. Lines formed early, Aldred joining them as the throng became insatiable, itching and waiting for the order to move. It didn't take long before the hubbub brought the prince from his tent, bringing with him Aldred's son and the King, finally bringing silence to the encampment.

Krinar scanned the warriors, nodding to himself as though what he saw was satisfactory. "Men of Annar, tonight the bane of our existence will be eradicated. Take heart as your blades are wetted, finally freeing our kingdom! Annar!" he shouted hoarsely, barely above a whisper.

"Annar!" the men hissed back.

The whisper of the troop's response landed on Krinar's ears, and the prince smiled. Aldred saw his son next to the royal heir, back straight and looking his best commanding self. Alnor didn't even glance in his father's direction, choosing to keep his adoring gaze on Krinar as he delivered his speech. He saw the small smirk on Krinar's face as he turned, adding to the unfounded suspicion Aldred couldn't help but feel. He brushed it off, passing it as a biased emotion based on Alnor's infatuation. He formed up next to his wing, ready to move out in the Southern group, catching Varnan's eye in the group opposite and nodding reluctantly.

Terva, forever unshakeable, nudged Aldred out of his reverie. "Cheer up, General! A few more hours and we'll be chilling around the fire with ale, toasting our victory," he said.

Aldred flashed what he hoped was a reassuring smile, Terva grinning easily and turning to pump up the men around him. It seemed like mere minutes later that Krinar gave the orders to move out, words washing over Aldred like dirt over a horse's rump. But he firmed his resolve and shouldered his way to the front of the men, glancing left and seeing Terva at his flank, feeling strong with the huge warrior there, but still wishing Dextri held the honour.

"Alright men, silence from here on out. Muffle your armour with rags and watch your steps. The next noise we make will be our swords sinking into flesh. Move out!" Aldred murmured, attempting to keep his voice quiet despite the need for urgency.

It worked, as men brought their shields overheard and drew their weapons. The moon kissed their blades as the unforgiving mud did its best to suck at their feet as they marched away. It had begun.

★★★★★

Alnor's mouth was dry as he advanced on the deadly dunes, making as much noise as possible and ensuring the torches were held overhead. He knew the flanking parties were hidden in the shadows at either side, looping around the back. His group were to draw as much attention as possible to allow the others to get into position and hit the enemy from the rear. Emboldened by the roars of the men around him, he drew his sword and bellowed his defiance to the moon and quickened his pace.

Collectively they sped up, the line becoming haggard and disjointed. Mismatched shouts to reform came from the veterans laced through the ranks, causing most of the hot-headed younger men to slow down sheepishly, some with sulky glares at the restraint. They all knew the strength of a single line, so fell in with only a slight grumble.

"Steady men! We won't lose our own to rashness tonight," Malker ordered, voice strong over the cacophony.

Alnor could have sworn he saw a slight twitch on Krinar's face as his father issued the order and he smiled grimly. It seems both their fathers interfered at the

228

worst times, at least his own father had finally decided to let him make his own choices. Hopefully, after tonight, things would be better for them both. The thought warmed his bones as they began their ascent, boots fighting for purchase and sinking into the still damp sand.

The wind was much hotter this close to the desert, blowing in their faces and carrying irritating specks of grit that spattered their faces, drying out their mouths and causing men to cough amidst their yelling. It was a sullen line that finally crested the dune. If the Hounds had decided to rush them at that moment, they might have had half a chance. As it was, the whole line halted and took a moment to reform as figures rushed frantically below them, doing their best to throw on armour and form a meagre line to defend.

Alnor's eyes narrowed in confusion as he realised the large force they were expecting was absent. Only a skeleton crew existed, scurrying between the bedraggled tents. But a plan was a plan. Krinar gave the order, and the signal to advance was given.

Alnor's eyes strained against the harsh light into the gloom beyond, trying to catch a glimpse of his father. He was rewarded within moments by seeing Terva's great form, typical infuriating grin on his face, his father at his shoulder. Feeling a slight pang at the earlier conversation, he vowed to make more time to fix their relationship before they parted, rather than the uneasy friendship that had formed.

Looking out of place next to the glory of his father, he saw Varnan at Aldred's other shoulder, looking decidedly gleeful, his usual sneer enhanced at the thought of the coming fight. Ripping his eyes from the opposite line, he studied the camp before him. There was no order amongst the tents, fires randomly dotted between them - everything Alnor assumed a rebel camp to be. Almost *too* perfect.

A lack of scouts had niggled at his father's mind for days, and for the first time Alnor felt it too. He'd dismissed it as an older man's doubts, trying his best to hinder his son's fun; but seeing the men below, barely looking scared and - if anything - looking arrogant, he began to reiterate his opinion. The veterans laced between the redcloaks seemed to pause as they took in the situation, taking the same train of thought as Alnor had finally come around to. Krinar held up his hand as the ambush closed on the rebels and the encircling army came to a grinding halt.

"Are you the rebels they call the *Hounds?*" Krinar called sarcastically, getting a round of cackles from the sycophants around him. The man at the bottom of the dune just smirked.

Cackles sounded around him. They usually included Alnor, but this time they made him feel sick as he realised something was off. Krinar's plan had gone wrong. But the Prince exuded confidence, so Alnor tried to firm his back and smile with the rest. It wouldn't do to let his doubt show. One of the few men in the camp stepped forward from the tiny shield wall they'd created, flashing a cocky smile. Suddenly, it sank in what Krinar had meant when he'd told Alnor the plan. *The old ways are dead, it's time to make way for the new,* that's what he'd said. *The old ways are dead*.

As the thought vibrated through Alnor's mind, the lines dissolved around the circle. The red cloaks all took a step back, getting confused glances from the men around them. In that moment it all clicked, and there was nothing he could do to stop it.

$$\star\star\star\star\star$$

Aldred and his wing blundered around in the darkness, their attempt at secrecy laughable as men cursed quietly and slid around on the sand. The rags they'd stuffed between their armour was their safeguard, and it paid its dues ten times over as they advanced. That, and the uproar the main attack was causing on the opposite side of the dunes.

It had been suspiciously easy to loop around the back, his men keeping a trained eye on the ridgeline for watching eyes. There were none and this more than anything played on Aldred's mind as they advanced, but they were much too deep into the plan for him to start complaining now, so he shut off his thoughts and narrowed his focus to the task.

They reached where he judged to be behind the rebel camp and carefully began to ascend towards the crest. A snaking wall of darkness began to loop around to their flank, warnings sounding in his head before he realised it was Varnan and his ilk. Mentally berating himself for such skittish nerves, he took a deep breath to calm himself, raising a hand to halt his men and letting Varnan join up with him. It rankled to see the man sneering as he approached, but it cut him further to know that he'd have him at his shoulder, where a man of honour should be. But he firmed his resolve and nodded to the arrogant man, turning to face the ridge again and moving together as one, anticipation lacing the air and making their steps sure but rushed.

Aldred's heart was beating faster and faster as they got closer to the top. His palms began to sweat, and he had the sudden urge to empty his bladder. Why did the same things always happen before a battle? You could fight one every day of your life and fear would still rear its unwelcome head and try its best to render him useless. He clamped his teeth together hard, stopping the growl building up in his throat before it began. The uncomfortably hot wind did nothing to dry the sweat that was beading on the back of his neck, which he could feel trickling down his already damp back. He pushed all these things behind; the fear, his discomfort, even his anger, finding an unmovable ball of calm before the chaos began.

Reaching the top, they came above the ridge as one solid line, making Aldred give a begrudging nod to Varnan at his steady control. He'd half expected the oaf to go charging over the hill alone. Across from them, he saw the main force dressing a messy line. It seems Malker had let his son run the show again. His friend had too much patience for Krinar. Nevertheless, they reformed quickly and began a swift advance down the dunes, sending the men below them into disarray as they attempted to don armour, too late. *Much too easy* Aldred thought grimly.

Krinar held up his hand to halt the group, bringing the entire circle to a halt. "Are you the rebels they call the Hounds?" Krinar called down to the men. Aldred could've sworn he heard a jest behind the words. He reached for his axe just as the reply made his blood run cold.

"Well, you could say the Hounds are everywhere sire! Almost as if they're right... next to you." In unison, the men between his veterans stepped back, arms poised toward men they'd sworn to fight alongside. It was at that moment that Krinar darted forward like a viper... and stabbed King Malker through the heart.

Chapter 12

Little more than a second passed, but it felt like an eternity. Malker's eyes registered shock before sinking into a bottomless pit of hurt and betrayal. The world froze in that moment, giving the Prince and the King their final moments to say goodbye. Krinar's face was impassive as he looked upon the dying face of his father, then quick as a lash he withdrew the sword, letting him crumple to the ground unceremoniously. Then, that second ended.

An eruption of action seemed to rinse through the clearing, as the red cloaks followed suit, plunging their swords into the backs of their would-be-comrades before they had time to defend themselves.

True to form, Terva and Alnor's father span instantly, batting the blades away from their intended targets and preceding to carve their way through the traitors' ranks. Alnor watched aghast as Varnan stepped out of the General's bloody path, allowing others to do the dirty work of tiring him out. Terva's roars could be heard throughout the clearing as he battled in his warrior's fury, but in the end it was futile. The huge form suddenly sprouted the tip of a spear as he turned too slow to deflect the lethal shaft which pierced his midriff, the roaring mouth suddenly spitting red in anger whilst he dropped to the floor, his bellows cut off as he choked on his own blood.

In comparison, his father was almost Ezimat reborn. He tore through the shields around him with his great axe, creating three new widows and was ready to create a fourth when the slimy Varnan stepped back atop the red dune and seized the General, placing his dagger firmly around his neck so that a small red droplet slid down its hungry edge.

"Drop it, *General,*" Varnan hissed, the high-pitched voice carrying across the clearing.

Aldred Sain snarled and struggled, but in the end had no other choice. He let the axe hit the floor with a muted thud, then was forced to look at Krinar, who sneered in contempt at his beaten adversary. But he said nothing and turned to Alnor, raising an eyebrow.

"Out with the old and in with the new don't you think?" he asked innocently to the flabbergasted face of the younger Sain.

"To make change sire, not to massacre everyone we hold dear! Have you lost your mind?!" Alnor stuttered.

Krinar's face grew hard and he slammed his gory sword back into its sheath.

"Hold dear? You forget your place, Alnor! Haven't we spent this whole journey complaining about our fathers' control? How do you expect to escape it without being rid of them? The King and the General of the Annar don't just disappear, they need to be *made* to disappear."

Krinar's fury cowed Alnor as he took in the King's limp form on the floor, surrounded by Bayar and Neve - ever loyal and ever close - a whisper of shock painted on their faces. Alnor had to stop the same thing happening to his own father, if it was the last thing he did.

"I understand, my Prince. May I speak to my father?" he murmured. Krinar searched Alnor's face for any sign of deception or pity. He found none, nodding his acceptance and let Alnor descend the dune, sand cascading down the slope as he came close to the fake camp and its betrayers.

His mind whirred as he thought of ways in which he could convince his father he'd had no part in this, that he didn't know. But every argument or phrase he turned around in his brain sounded cheap even to him. He'd spent every night of the journey with Krinar, agreed with every point of view and sided with him in every way. In his soul, he'd finally felt like he was accepted, that he was where he belonged. This though, this might be too much for him to bear; he'd known things needed to change, but never once did he think that something this drastic would be the answer. He passed the smirking men around their fires, their sickening faces making Alnor's own expression hard as he swept by them, a figure of haughtiness in a sea of contempt.

Raising his eyes, he saw Varnan doing his best to make his father kneel and his father refusing to even stoop. A wave of pride hit him, knowing that a Sain would never kneel, even in the face of death. He started his second climb of the night, this one much more foreboding. He had to drag his legs up the sandy bank, a big contrast to his earlier excited lope before what he'd thought was a battle. His spirit couldn't have dropped further, his heart now throbbing in his throat, making him want to retch at the savage events of the night.

He reached the top, and his eyes met a piercing intensity that he'd only ever found in his father's eyes. He became acutely aware that he still held a naked sword coupled with his shield, but refused to put either of them down, feeling like he was in a crowd of enemies rather than friends. The General's voice cut through the intense air.

"Did you know?" Aldred said flatly.

"No father, I swear," Alnor pleaded. "The plan was always to put Krinar in charge, but never would I have dreamed it meant something on this scale. Please, you've got to believe me."

His father snorted. "You've planned this haven't you? Get rid of both of your fathers in one night, take their places and reap the rewards. The great King Krinar and his *General.* You both make me - "

His father's voice was cut short as Varnan pressed his sword harder to his throat. "That's enough of that my lord," Varnan said casually, hardly keeping the glee from his voice. "You don't want to upset your little son now, do you?" His father snarled but was held fast by the promise of instant death if he resisted. Alnor's temper bubbled to the surface.

"Release him," Alnor ordered, unable to keep a quiver of anger from his tone.

Varnan glanced behind Alnor's back like a dog seeking approval from its master. The command must have been barked because he lifted his sword and stepped away, though he kept it levelled at the General's back, who stood firm. Always regal, always proud. Alnor could feel the menace emanating from his father and knew he had to say something.

"Father, please. I didn't know. I knew the regime needed to change - all the men knew it - but I'd never have moved forward knowing my comrades were to be slaughtered like this. But with their deaths comes a new era. An era where we can stand side by side as lords of the Annar, father and son."

Any hope of a redeeming response from his father was dashed by the look on his face as Alnor's speech ceased. A multitude of emotions crossed his face in a miniscule amount of time, but it was enough to make out the two emotions warring for dominance: disgust and disappointment. Alnor's heart dropped.

"*All* of the men? What about the ones that are actually loyal, the ones that lie dead at your feet? Don't disguise your words Alnor. What you've done is treason," his father said coldly, refusing to take that impenetrable gaze off Alnor. He reflected on years of shame for letting his father down, doing everything for his approval but always seeming to fall short; all the excitement of the last few weeks building a relationship with him, ground down to nothing in a moment. Suddenly, a surge of anger reared its head, and Alnor found himself on the offensive.

"Is it treason to want a King on the throne who cares about the men around him? Treason to want to throw off the yolk of oppression strapped onto us by the weak who think they're strong? No, father. What you and the King have led the kingdom to is treason," Alnor screamed into his father's face. Aldred didn't give his son the benefit of a flinch. Aldred Sain, true to his name, did nothing but snort.

"Think what you want, Alnor. The victors usually write history to look favourably on themselves, in this case I'm sure it will be no different," he said wearily, the look of disgust leaving his face.

Disappointment finally won out, and the child in Alnor did its best to escape. "Father, please... just *attempt* to understand me for once," he pleaded, dropping his shield and reaching out with his hand but Aldred batted it away savagely.

"You. Are. Not. My. Son." Aldred hissed the final word. It seemed louder than any of the chaos that night, cutting right through the glimmer of hope Alnor still had, exposing raw, hard pain. With utter fury, Alnor's rage won out as a scream tore the skin from his throat, and he used the fury-born strength to bring his sword up like a whip, hacking into his father's neck. The blade sank halfway through before wedging itself. Time froze as the whole clearing held its breath, waiting for the colossus to fall. General Sain sank to his knees, shock coated his face and mirrored Alnor's who released his sword, allowing it to fall with his father.

Alnor's mouth opened and closed like a fish, his mind unable to comprehend what had just happened, what he'd done. A peace came over Aldred in seconds. The worries of the world were his no longer as his mortal soul released them. A spike of panic for his younger son's safety interrupted the harmony, but it was swiftly carried away, replaced by the face of his love, beckoning to him in the meadow. The moment ended, and Aldred Sain crashed to the ground, never to rise again.

*****

Krinar had to admit, even he hadn't expected it when Alnor screamed, and half hacked off his own father's head. He'd had to force himself to keep his face straight at the comical sight of the mighty General dropping to the ground, head flopping and his son's sword stuck into his neck. A terse response had broken out of Krinar's calm demeanour earlier, causing him to rant slightly at Alnor, which he'd regretted instantly - not that he needed the whelp's approval, but he did need him. To lose him now, even slightly, would slow his plans down and leave them open to the Sains joining forces against him later.

Krinar snorted softly. Fat chance of that now, due to Alnor's unforeseen reaction to a comment nobody else had heard. Although he wanted to clap sarcastically at the display, he firmed his jaw and moved quickly across the clearing, past the flabbergasted 'rebels', to the younger Sain's side. He clapped him on the shoulder, satisfying his need to applaud slightly, and sighed audibly.

"It doesn't feel like it now Alnor, but this was for the greater good. It will allow our kingdom to finally heal. The men here are loyal, none will know what transpired here tonight; only that the King and the General were slain in a valiant attempt to rid the Annar of rebels that have plagued them for years. We'll return as heroes of the people; our fathers will stay revered and all will be well," Krinar murmured in what he hoped was a comforting voice.

Across from him, Varnan could barely keep the smirk off his face and Krinar shot him a venomous glare out of view of the stricken Alnor. Taking a deep, shuddering breath, Alnor knelt next to his father, eyes glistening with what Krinar could have only imagined was hurt. Maybe regret, he wasn't sure; his slaying of his own father had only brought relief.

The wedged sword had come loose as the General hit the floor, giving Krinar a reason to stoop down next to the grieving Alnor. He wiped the blade through the sand to clear the blood, then handed it to him hilt first. Alnor recoiled like he'd been passed a live snake, a look of horror on his face as though he hadn't been the one to wield it.

"Not that blade... never that one again," Alnor rasped.

Restraining an eye roll, Krinar instantly took his own blade out of its sheath and switched them around.

"This way, we each carry a portion of our sins between us. It is our burden to bear but bear it we will" he said solemnly. Alnor ripped his gaze from his father's corpse and looked directly into Krinar's eyes. He took a huge stuttering breath, then grasped Krinar's sword. They rose together, Krinar doing his best to look serene at what he was sure Alnor thought was pivotal moment in his life, clasping arms firmly. Their gazes still locked, Alnor sheathed the traded blade and took one last look down at his father.

"The greater good," he whispered.

"The greater good," Krinar agreed.

*****

Leaping down from his snorting gelding's back, Livius stumbled slightly as his cramped legs groaned at the impact. He hadn't slowed his pace since he'd left Saternac, he and his grumpy mount were at the end of their endurance. As he righted himself, he turned to put his head against her frothing snout, causing her to nicker in delight amidst her laboured breathing.

"We made it girl, we made it," he murmured, taking her reins and tying her alongside the multitude of horses around her, taking another's feed bag as reward, ignoring the angry growl from its original owner. Glancing around, he saw many horses he recognised, Moonlight amongst them. He gave her a pat as he walked by and called out for any guards or scouts that could help deliver his news.

Silence greeted his request. He started to feel uncomfortable at the situation, knowing that neither the General nor the King would have left so many horses unattended, even during an attack. Something was wrong, he could sense it.

Just as the thought entered his head, he began to hear the crashing of swords on shields, accompanied by loud shouts and war cries. His blood ran cold, that noise signalled only one thing: the start of a fight. He dashed through the walls of horseflesh, his fatigue forgotten. *Please don't be too late,* he begged Ezimat as he sprinted towards the sound, seeing a bulk of men cresting the dunes around a mile in front.

As they reached the top, the first ranks stopped solid before they began their descent. Whatever made him pause there probably saved his life, as he saw a lot of the red-cloaked men step back behind their comrades, raising their blades. Livius felt a deep pit in his stomach; he opened his mouth to try and shout a warning but was much too late. Shield brother executed shield brother right in front of his eyes. He clamped his hand to his mouth to stop the cry of anguish escaping and alerting them to his presence.

Standing in the open, shock rooting him to the spot, he watched helplessly as the traitors casually withdrew their swords from their "friends'" before moving forward down the dunes. Just like another day to them, killing comrades and not even blinking.

237

He felt a rage begin to form within, his sword arm itching to taste the blood of the men who'd killed those who'd trusted them so easily. Something held him back from the charge, a niggling voice in the back of his mind screaming two words: *Warn Alkor*.

He stopped short of drawing his blade - there's nothing like the sound of a sword being drawn to alert seasoned warriors to a man at their backs, even in the cacophony. So, he crept. First sprinting - trusting the sand to muffle his footfalls - then, on all fours like a dog. He felt the sand trickling beneath his fingers, warm wind whipping the cold sweat that had broken out on his face.

As he saw the last red cloak disappear behind the hill he slowed his own ascent, not wanting to charge headlong into the men. He came near to the top, hearing the echo of voices behind the crest of the dune, tiptoeing the last few paces before finally peering over the crest. A sharp intake of breath was his response to the scene, as mere paces in front of him were dead men and the face of King Malker staring lifelessly into oblivion.

The heart of the treachery was exposed in that moment, Livius knowing for sure that Joseph had told them the truth – the prince was the leader. It wasn't the dead King's eyes that held Livius' gaze, it was the image at the opposite end of the dunes. He could see his General, stood proudly with a sword poised at his back by an ugly bastard, Alnor stood before him, pleading. He watched the younger Sain tense at a comment he didn't hear, then a heartwrenching scream pierced the air, ending as Alnor sent his sword cleaving into his father's neck.

As much as he willed it, Livius couldn't wrench his eyes from the picture. He watched the entire thing; the shock on Alnor's face as he realised his folly, the masked amusement on Krinar's face as he went to comfort his friend. He saw the swapping of swords before Alnor and Krinar clasp arms. He turned and ran.

Warning Alkor of this betrayal was more important than the futile revenge his furious heart wanted to exact, though it took a great effort to keep bounding down the dune to the horses rather than begin killing. He reached his gelding contentedly munching on the stolen bag of oats, realising instantly that she wouldn't be able to outrun a chase if it came to it. He needed a remount to take with him, each horse sharing his weight and keeping a near constant journey back home.

Barely hesitating, he turned to Moonlight. One of the only named horses in the entire herd, owned by Aldred since the day he was born. It seemed wrong to leave him to traitors. He nickered in pleasure at the familiar face, giving no resistance to Livius as he leapt onto his already saddled back, digging his heels in to lead him to his own gelding.

Livius galloped from the herd, his gelding snorting indignantly at its interruption, whilst Moonlight neighed in pleasure at being allowed to ride free. Livius noticed none of this, his head whirring with what he'd seen, one thought resounding prominently over the rest: *Warn Alkor.*

★★★★★

Sweat sheened Balzor's face as his sleeping cry dragged him from his fitful sleep, almost falling off the couch in the roasting lounge of the Seeress' house. He flailed as the shock of the dream almost dropped him off his makeshift bed, then again as he saw the Seeress' hard eyes boring into him, accusing with a hint of amusement.

"Would you like to tell me why you are staining my couch with your nightmares, young warrior?" she said sternly.

Balzor's eyes darted frantically for Aria, but she was nowhere to be seen. "I just... y'know..." he floundered, trying his best to find an excuse for him sleeping on that particular couch with Aria missing from the equation. They'd been sneaking lunchtime rendezvous every day since the patrol had returned, relishing the time together whilst the Seeress spent the morning gathering herbs. He never once imagined that he'd get caught passed out alone in the heart of her house without Aria present. As though reading his thoughts, the Seeress snorted.

"Don't worry, young'un. I've known about these secret meetings since they began, the girl can keep nothing from her grandmother. The worry is a granddaughter of mine courting a boy who clearly has troubles. Tell me lad, the nightmares... What are they?" she said, voice changing from comical to serious within moments.

Balzor froze up, unsure how much to admit about what kept him awake at night. Looking into those severe eyes, he decided the complete truth was the easiest option. Nobody lied to a Seeress after all. He let out a huff of breath.

"It's his eyes, Seeress" he began. "The man I killed outside the inn; his vision haunts me every night. His last rattling breath, the blood spurting from his throat... the thought that he has a wife and children at home that will miss him walking through the door. But his eyes tear into me and blame me for what happened, as if it wasn't me or him. He would've killed me, and it was a mixture of luck and instinct that allowed me to kill him first."

The Seeress sighed, all irritation at finding the lad on her couch evaporating at his revelation. Despite catching him and her granddaughter in a heated position that night, she knew that he was good for her. Not only had her studies improved, but she was more excited than she'd ever been since she'd met him. It could just be young love, but something in her gut told her it was something more fated than that; what that fate could be was unknown to her yet, but the Gods sang to her that this had to happen. She sighed again.

"Lad, you'll probably see his eyes for the rest of your life. Killing a man should never be easy; if it is, you're either evil or have no emotions. All you must tell yourself is that the killing was just, and the nightmares will be easier to bear," she said, doing her best to alleviate the lad's worries.

She soon changed her tack as the pitying look on his face didn't change; she had no time for boys feeling sorry for themselves. "Right, enough of that. Off my couch and back to work, this town doesn't protect itself!"

Her barking orders resulted in Balzor launching himself to his feet, glancing around for any indication where Aria had gone. Finding nothing, he sheepishly muttered his goodbyes to the Seeress before rushing towards the door. As he reached it, turning the handle with his clammy hands, he discovered a newfound courage.

"Seeress, thank you. It occurs to me that I don't know your name..." he said, leaving the question hanging, door half open and his feet ready to leap out if this interaction went wrong.

He sighed mentally as she chuckled dryly. "Osri, young'un. Though Seeress is fine," she said.

Balzor gave a half smile, unsure whether knowing her name was a blessing when she'd added the order to keep addressing her as Seeress. Stepping out of the door and closing it lightly, he breathed in the lukewarm afternoon air, the oxygen a balm to his hammering heart; one on one conversations with the Seeress, Osri, were never easy since he knew about her powers. He'd kept that to himself as Aria had begged, but it still hid in the corner of his mind. Nobody wanted to piss a Seeress off, and that was without the knowledge that she could attack with the power. With that thought, he jogged off towards the trees, mentally cursing Aria for her part in leaving him to the wolf.

As he reached the treeline, out of view of the cottage, he slowed and exhaled, enjoying the smell of the now friendly woods as he inhaled. It was then that something crashed into his back, sending him sprawling to the floor. Rolling over to react to the attack instinctively, he recognized the beautiful, chocolate coloured eyes gazing at him.

"I'm sorry! I'm sorry! You looked so peaceful, I figured I'd go into town and get us something to eat for when you awoke. I saw my grandmother cross the square and hid like a coward. Did she find you?" Aria spluttered. Seeing her face so distraught and inches away from his own caused him to refuse a response. He brought her lips towards his, crushing them together in an unexpected display of passion amongst the undergrowth. Her savage intake of breath was all the reward he needed as she melded herself to him, grass tickling his ears as her hands caressed his face, forgetting her earlier apology. They broke apart moments later, breathless and more than a little aroused, laughing embarrassedly.

"I guess that means I'm forgiven?" Aria teased, breathing lightly into his neck.

"Suppose I could let you off this once," Balzor replied, shrugging and making her laugh. "But you realise there was no reason to hide? She knows about our little meetings." Aria's mouth dropped open, attempting to form words but instead closing and her shoulders slumping. Balzor laughed, knocking her elbows out from underneath her and catching her head on his chest. She surged back up, and he saw a flash of anger in her eyes as she clambered to her feet.

"How can you laugh?! You realise the trouble we'll be in, and how much harder it will be to see each other in between training?" she scolded. When Balzor chuckled again she huffed and threw her hands into the air. "Men... everything's always a bloody joke," she grumbled, starting to turn away in her irritation.

Balzor reached and grabbed her shoulder, turning her back towards him and putting on a consoling face. "I've already spoken to her. It was hard not to – with me asleep on her couch and all? She seemed fine with it. She even asked more about my dreams than the fact I was unattended in her home," he said.

"Your dreams?" Aria probed.

"You know, the ones from the night of the attack." Aria sighed in relief. This time Balzor burst into laughter.

"Well, I'd hardly tell her about dreams involving you now, would I?" he teased back.

She swatted him in mock indignation, smirking but mollified, though slight red circles had appeared on her cheeks at the comment. "Maybe one day you can explain these dreams about me in further detail," she said casually, stepping towards him and placing her hand delicately on his chest. His pulse quickened, and he wondered how he could be so breathless without exerting himself at all. Maybe this required a different type of training than fitness? He moved into her, slowly now, and saw her eyes registering excitement that matched his own.

"GIRL!" came the interrupting shout that instantly sent his blood running cold. Aria disengaged from him within seconds, eyes darting guiltily though the foliage to scout for the culprit. Seeing nothing, she sighed and pecked Balzor on the cheek.

"Another time" she promised with a wink, before stepping away and quickly walking away. "Coming Gran!"

Balzor stood watching her retreating form, a longing in his body at the missed chance. He'd never felt that way since the night of the attack, but he'd snapped out of it pretty quickly when they'd been caught. It took a while for him to calm down, thoughts running through his head telling him he couldn't go back to training like this, it would only get in the way. Shaking his head, he chuckled. "I'd never hear the end of it from any of them if I returned with a hard on," he muttered as it finally went down.

Finally happy he was calm, he broke into a steady jog back towards the manor, offering his thanks to Ezimat that they'd been released from watch duty to train for longer hours. There were enough men to cover the shifts since the patrol returned, and he'd hated the boring long hours of contemplation atop that wall. As he broke through the treeline, he saw Traf and raised his hand. He waved back amidst carrying a tray of baked goods. They'd all relished the meeting between Alkor and Yuri as they gave him Traf's bill for Nerva's morning off. It was worth the man's reaction to see Nerva happy, albeit sheepish that everybody had so clearly seen the relationship blooming between her and Olsten. He laughed aloud at the thought, gaining some odd glances from merchants selling their wares. Uncaring, he swept past the village centre, marvelling how he could still have his breath now, when Aria had taken it away in moments.

✶✶✶✶✶

Mariak trudged dejectedly through the undergrowth, fatigue forcing her to not care about the noise she was making. They'd looked for miles around the dead patrol, trying to gather more information to bring back to the village, before admitting defeat and turning back. Even now, her father stepped lightly, barely a branch breaking on his path despite him being as worn down as she was. He glanced back disapprovingly as her heavy footfalls sent another cracking sound firing around the trees, she just rolled her eyes.

"We're literally less than a mile from Saternac, father. Who do you expect will still be around here?" she found herself saying, sounding whiney even to her ears. Her father didn't answer, giving her a chance to show she wasn't just a child. She snorted but began to step carefully; seeing her father's mouth twitch slightly was enough to show his amusement.

"No matter where you are, you should move quietly until it's ingrained into your bones to do so. It only takes one mistake and your prey gets away; days or weeks wasted because your body was unruly. It's a tool, use it," he said flatly.

Mariak knew he wasn't annoyed; he just liked to teach her everything - more so since they'd found the patrol. She had a niggling feeling that he used to be much more than a regular hunter, but she hadn't had the courage to enquire. Taking his advice though was an obvious reaction; he clearly knew his trade, no matter what that trade was.

Seeing the trees beginning to thin, she sighed in relief as the wooden walls of her hometown became visible. It was amazing how much you took being dry for granted, her feet constantly damp as the canopy stopped the sun drying the ground. Not for the first time, she cursed the earlier storm, knowing it not only kept her cold and shivering, but also erased any tracks they might have found. As they came close to the town, they saw the gates stood open, armoured men questioning everyone who left and entered. More men were patrolling atop the walls, and she felt a twinge of unease at seeing the sunlight glint off their weapons.

"Da... how do we know they're ours?" she asked, knowing he'd know what she meant. He spent a moment chewing his lip before replying.

"Truth is - we don't. But they don't know why we're out here, we just tell them the truth: that we were hunting in the forest but didn't find any prey," he said.

Mariak laughed at the brazenness of the comment but saw its merit. They strode up to the gate like they had every right to be there, stopping when the two warriors stepped to bar their path. Rindu stepped back slightly, hands raised, just like a timid village man would do.

"Whoa, friend. What's the extra security about?" he said, smiling uncertainly.

"Routine. There was an attack here a few nights ago. Dextri has ordered the walls to be manned. What's your purpose here?" one of the guards said robotically as though he'd said it twenty times that day.

"Hey, that's Rindu and his girl! Let 'em through," a voice beyond the gate said. Rindu nodded his thanks and smiled to the guard who shrugged and stepped aside.

"Whatever you say, boss." Walking through the gate they saw the voice's owner, and Rindu broke into his first real smile in days.

"Herman you old dog, how are you?" the hunter boomed, clasping arms with the warrior and dragging him close.

"Less of the old, hunter," Herman replied sternly, unable to stop the smirk on his face. "Come. Dextri will want to know what you found," he added softly so nobody could overhear. Rindu nodded his assent to the command, turning to Mariak and putting his hands on her shoulders.

"Go back to your mother, she's been too long alone. I'll meet you there," he said to her, ignoring her gritted teeth at her dismissal, then turned on his heel following Herman towards the manor.

Mariak bunched up her fists and growled under her breath before stomping away towards their home. She wanted more than anything to help her father's report, but knew he was right, her mother needed her home - plus, she could finally get out of her damp shoes. Relaxing at the thought, she picked up her pace to almost sprinting speed but kept her footfalls light, her father's words resounding in her even then.

✶✶✶✶✶

Laughter boomed across the practice yard as Dextri fought off Alkor and Balzor simultaneously, though not without effort. They'd drastically improved over the past few days, having Dextri's full attention for most of the daylight hours finally bearing fruit. The lads worked as a good team, Dextri mused, as one sought to widen his defences whilst the other utilised the opening. Years of training on his part allowed him to dance away from them, their youthful energy keeping them on his tail and making a full disengage impossible. Dextri was fitter than most warriors he knew, but even he was hard pressed to keep his wind at the unending barrage of attacks from them both; not that he'd ever tell them that.

"Is that all you've got, little lords?" he taunted, narrowly stepping out of a blade swing whilst parrying another with his shield. Alkor barely reacted to the barb, continuing his attack without so much as a glance. Balzor on the other hand, bared his teeth and leapt forward in anger, only realising his folly as Dextri's practice sword swept Balzor's own out of the way, using the backswing to hit him hard across the face, knocking him to the ground.

Ready for Alkor, Dextri leapt backwards and was rewarded by the whistling of Alkor's blade over his shoulder. *The lad sees an opening, that's for sure*, he thought as he pivoted, cracking his sword on to the young Sain's wrist, causing him to yelp and drop the weighted wood.

"So close!" he seethed whilst massaging his wrist, as Dextri dragged Balzor up off the floor, an angry welt rising on his cheek.

"Yet so far..." Dextri chuckled. He sized both the boys up before continuing. "So, why did you lose?"

Both began to babble several excuses, from attacking too early to leaving too many openings. Dextri held up a hand to halt the tirade.

"Yes, to a number of those things. But there was a point you could have had me beaten, if Balzor didn't lose his head at the taunt," he said, Balzor hanging his head in shame. "You've got heart lad, but you can't let emotions rule you. The minute you let anger cloud your judgement, you'll lose your head, literally. Emotions are great things, will give you energy beyond what you would usually muster, but you must control them. Use anger to give your arms strength, not to attack in haste to hurt the man you're angry at. Think!" he said. As he finished his speech, he saw Herman break

245

through the trees on the road to the village, Rindu Praker directly on his heels. "We'll end it there for today, we've got company."

Both lads turned to trace their teacher's view, eyes widening as they saw the hunter striding purposefully towards them.

"Since you were the one to send him out, it seems fitting you hear his report first" Dextri said casually to Alkor, who nodded in thanks. Although Dextri had seen the leader Alkor would become that night, he hadn't let him lead in the General's absence. He wasn't ready yet, but he was close, Dextri thought. Alkor raised his hand in greeting, Herman and Rindu angling towards them on the practice field before halting a few paces away.

"Welcome home" Alkor began, clasping hands with Rindu and stepping back. "Did you find anything?" Rindu took a deep breath and launched into his report, telling them where they'd found the dead patrol and his conclusions. He also told them they'd found no other tracks in the area, so couldn't deduce if they'd had any other help apart from Petra, but he thought not.

"Those men were betrayed by their own. My guess is the traitors in the patrol were the ones that attacked here that night," Rindu finished, looking into the young Sain's eyes, seeing the serene blue pool turning to ice as he did. He wasn't the only one furious, the other men around him were tight lipped and clenching their fists at his findings.

"Thank you for everything. Please, get some food from Nerva and warm your bones by the fire before you go," Alkor offered, gesturing to the manor.

"If it's all the same Lord, I'd like to see my wife," he replied. Alkor nodded in understanding. He made his farewells and left much quicker than he'd arrived. Herman whistled with raised brows as the hunter receded, breaking the tension that had settled on the group.

"Well at least we know the only other men are with the General. Anyone else who tries to come into Saternac wearing armour won't be one of ours," he said.

Dextri nodded thoughtfully. "Nevertheless, we'll keep the wall manned. It only takes one lapse in concentration and men die; I won't have that on my conscience," Dextri said, getting a salute from Herman as he too returned to the village to finish his watch.

"Right lads, show's over. Put your gear away, but I want another twenty laps out of your sorry arses before you hit the baths!"

They sagged at the command but knew by now to not complain lest the laps increase to thirty. Dextri smiled manically.

"Good boys, you're learning."

Just over an hour later, Balzor was floating contentedly in the large bathhouse, humming a tune as Alkor sat with his arms on the side, head tilted back and half asleep. Seeing an opportunity, Balzor continued humming the tune to alleviate suspicion, before sending a tidal wave of bath water over his friend's face, leaving him spluttering and coughing.

"If I weren't tired from today..." Alkor grumbled, wiping cascading water off his face as Balzor moved away laughing. "What's put you in such a good mood any-way?"

"Brother, we almost had Dextri today. If I didn't lose my head, we would have. Barely any man in the guard can beat him, and half of them couldn't beat him with help. For us to last so long shows we're getting better, almost as good as the rest of them!" Balzor said gleefully, his recent foreboding evaporated. He felt free that night, the threat of the dead man's eyes seeming inconsequential next to the fact that his feeling of invalidity of skill was finally passing. They were *good.*

"If you keep your head, maybe next time..." Alkor taunted, cascading water over Balzor's smiling face in revenge.

"Maybe next time we can win, you idiot!" Balzor laughed, his mood not easily dismissed despite Alkor's insult.

For the first time since the attack, he didn't feel the bottomless pit of fear that had haunted him; confidence had finally settled into his bones, and it felt good. He wiped the dripping water out of his eyes and leant back onto the bath edge, ignoring his smirking friend as he let the day's aches fade in the settled warmth of the water. A moment of quiet companionship ensued; the silence comfortable between them both after so long as brothers. Alkor snapped Balzor out of it with a question in a smug tone.

"So... heard you got caught on the Seeress' sofa?" Balzor's head slipped off the bath side in shock and he was submerged, coming out coughing from his instant inhaling of fluid. Alkor roared with laughter as his friend struggled to breathe, until he finally gained enough air to ask the counter-question.

"How do you hear that?!" he gasped.

"Well, Svein found out about your little meetings, then asked Aria why she was alone; doesn't take a genius to put two and two together when Aria practically buries herself in the ground as her grandmother walks by. How badly did she surprise you?"

"She literally woke me up then gave me the third degree on my evident nightmares. Didn't seem too bothered about the fact I was there actually... anyway she sent me away and then I bumped into Aria in the woods, frantic and assuming the Seeress had ripped me a new one. One thing led to another..." Balzor said slyly.

Alkor's eyes widened in shock. "You did NOT make your first time with Aria against a fucking tree?" Balzor snorted, shaking his head as his mind wandered to the afternoon.

"Of course not! Although I think if her grandmother didn't call it may have happened in the undergrowth. I've never known a feeling like this, brother. It's like every time I'm near her my veins are on fire. I'm more breathless in moments with her than in a whole day's training with Dextri!"

"Well, maybe if you put more effort in against Dextri we can win tomorrow..."

"You know what you can do brother?" Balzor said.

"Mmm?"

"Just fuck off!"

Alkor guffawed and pulled himself out from the bath, Balzor mimicking his friend and doing the same, scrubbing vigorously with the towel to get dry before dragging a shirt over his head. They left the bath house in good moods, not even dampened by seeing Dextri catching them as they were exiting, a glum expression on his face to match the dim setting sun behind him. The thing is with good moods, they never last.

"What's up Dex?" Balzor said cheerfully as the huge man approached.

"Meeting in the food hall, now," he ordered, then stalked away towards the house where most of the guard were already filing in. Jogging to pull alongside their mentor, Balzor prodded again.

"Dextri, what's this about?" A glance from Dextri at Alkor, something deep and hidden in his eyes, caused Balzor's stomach to plummet. Nothing phased Dextri, so it must be bad.

"Livius is back lad, and it's not good." Balzor's first reaction was relief at their friend returning home, and he could tell Alkor felt the same as they shared an excited look between them, tempered only slightly by the latter end of Dextri's response. This time, Alkor tried.

"Is he okay? Did he find them?" Dextri stopped without warning, both lads moving forward a full step before being caught and spun around to face him with a quick jerk of his arms. They made to protest, but the look on Dextri's face quelled any rebellion they had at being dragged around. It was a look that Balzor had never seen on Dextri's face before, and that scared him more than anything. Anguish was barely held at bay as Dextri's eyes found Alkor's and relieved their burden.

"He found them... Your dad's gone lad. Alnor killed him."

✹✹✹✹✹

Roars of anger and denial reverberated around the feast hall of the manor. Livius stood at the head of the table, raising his hands for quiet. No-one could quite believe what they'd been told. The King and the General were dead, killed by their own sons? Preposterous.

Beside Livius, Alkor sat staring into nothingness, usually fierce blue eyes glazed with a vacant look. Nerva had melted at the news, sitting in the corner of the room crying softly on to the stained shoulder of Olsten. Most of the men were arguing amongst themselves about what to do; some said they should alert Torizo, force them to close their gates against the traitors; others said they should defend the town and wait for the dust to settle rather than kick an already seething hornets' nest for the sake of revenge, however just. Politics wasn't something they got involved in, despite the fact that their beloved General had been caught in the crossfire. Surprisingly, Dextri gave no input whatsoever, instead sitting beside Alkor in complete silence with tears leaking from his eyes, having given up trying to keep a hold on his despair.

"Alright, alright. Let's not bicker like untrained youths; what are the options?"

Livius tried to shout over the cacophony, to no avail. The men kept up their tirade, directing their arguing at nobody in particular until somebody decided to bite back. Livius threw his hands up in exasperation and sat heavily back down, taking a huge gulp of wine as he did. Herman clapped his hand on to his shoulder, rolling his eyes in a way that said, *you tried*.

Balzor, however, spent the whole meeting listening intently, then when the debates erupted his temper began to fray. The two most important men in the kingdom had been murdered by their own kin, and some of their best warriors were trying to serve their own interests, already thinking to the immediate future. He took one look at his friend, who stayed sat as a husk, shocked to the core by the news, and his rage bubbled over. He stood abruptly, letting his chair fall back with a clatter.

"ENOUGH!" he bellowed.

Dextri looked sharply at him, noticing as he did that Alkor had stayed in his distraught reverie. The men, however, fell silent, looking at the young warrior in differing ways; some, amusement; others, anger that a whelp thought he could order warriors around. But Dextri, Ingvar, Devar and Livius looked on in interest. Even Joseph stepped out of the shadows, startling some who hadn't even known he'd been there. He'd shadowed Alkor ever since his oath, always protecting him.

"The entire kingdom has been thrown into turmoil and you sit here squabbling like bairns. Let's not mince our words and try to find ways around this fact; two great men have been killed by their sons in a bid for power. We have no idea how deep the treachery runs, so we can't just expect the city guard to consist of loyal men, or men that would disobey a Prince of the realm, which rules out alerting Torizo to the plight until we know more. That leaves two options - bow down... or fight."

The conversations exploded again, some returning to earlier debates, but most choosing to direct their ire at the boy who'd rose at their head, the no named orphan with no rank. Within seconds, the table had quietened again, causing Balzor to look around in confusion until he found the reason - Alkor had risen from his own chair, a blazing conflict of emotion raging across his face. Only his eyes betrayed the full depth of fury and ice-cold despair that lurked inside, and they were terrible to behold. The warriors subsided, then Alkor spoke.

"There will be no choices. Every man in this room knows in their heart what has happened, and every man in this room knows what the retribution must be. I will not allow treason to go unpunished. The Hounds being revealed as the Kerazar is one thing, but for them to have infested the entire realm and led to my father's death? This is unforgivable. Men we considered loyal, turned over time; *good* men killed to satisfy the Kerazar's desire for power. Here and now, I name Prince Krinar as a traitor, an enemy of the realm. If anybody has any grievances, air them now."

Deathly silence followed, contrasting with the earlier tirade. Men shot furtive looks between each other, before locking their eyes back to the insatiable Sain eyes that had commanded men in this room for a lifetime. As one, the men of the guard nodded their assent.

"Right then."

Just like that, Alkor sat down and resumed his earlier stance, all anger evaporated. Resolute men became slightly nervous, Alkor's statement seeming empty with his lack of a follow up. Seeing his friend like this tore Balzor apart, but he also couldn't allow the men to continue bickering so soon after they'd put their faith in Alkor. He nudged him, and when Alkor looked up at him he knew that his friend was out of energy, the death of his father wiping him out; usually fierce eyes holding nothing but a dead look. *Time for me to try again,* Balzor thought.

"We know this town better than anyone, but to hold them at the walls would surely invite our destruction with so little numbers. Even a quarter of their force would number around double what we have; so, we need to think smart. The one thing Alnor will want is Alkor to be in his custody. There'll be no attack to his command if the only other Sain is in his hands." He paused, taking in the warrior's receptiveness. The hard eyes from earlier had thawed slightly, a tinge of respect taking its place. A quick, imperceptible nod from Dextri gave him the confidence to continue. He took a breath and went on.

"Also, the bastard absolutely *hates* me."

Smirks and chuckles around the room eased the remaining tension he was feeling. He grinned. "So, let's say the idea would be to use us as bait, get the men to follow us into a ground of our choosing, somewhere they won't expect?" Much more civilised voices spoke this time, they went through all the pros and cons of the simple yet effective plan he'd put to them.

"We could use the woods, the trees will hamper their progress and split them up. If we know the paths, we can lead them on a merry chase," Dextri said, a loud chorus of 'ayes' greeting his proposal.

"There's the warrior's glade, where Alkor and I used to steal the practice swords and hide... we could find that even in darkness!" Balzor said, flipping the finger to the group as they laughed in mockery at their childish name. Upon hearing the debate, Alkor's glazed eyes got a miniscule spark back into them. Although he added nothing to the cause, Balzor could tell his friend was listening and taking it all in. After almost an hour of planning, they settled on something most agreed on.

"Fucking hate digging..." Ingvar grumbled.

"You hate any sort of manual work, you're a lazy turd," Devar replied. Jeers from the rest of the guard caused Ingvar to scowl and resume grumbling. Even Alkor cracked a faint smile, tinged with sadness at the jibe between brothers. Balzor could see the grief still warring beneath the surface, but he knew his brother had harnessed it, used it for his own gain. As if hearing Balzor's thoughts, Alkor rose once again at the table. Jeering and laughter fell silent yet again, as all stopped to hear the youngest Sain speak.

"The plan is set. We show no mercy, leave *no-one* alive; these men are traitors and murderers who don't deserve trial. Howls will become cries as they meet the Sain guard, and we rip them limb from limb. They call themselves Hounds. We will show them there's more than just one predator in the woods. There are *wolves*."

Balzor howled, and to his surprise Livius, Devar and Ingvar leapt up and followed suit. Soon the rest of the table joined in, fully caught up in the moment. Dextri warred with the urge to keep his composure in front of the men, but his grief and rage won out and he howled to the heavens. His earlier thoughts about the lad not being ready to lead were dismissed. A Sain was back in charge, and he was out for blood.

Chapter 13

"Ach, I just can't keep the concentration!" Aria raged as the spoon she was attempting to levitate clattered back to the table after mere seconds of it being in the air. Her grandmother tutted and stood up from the table, that infuriating look of calmness on her face.

"It's not concentration that's needed. It's holding onto your power and directing it how you need to" she said. As she was talking, a block of firewood floated into the fire and she lit the flame with a snap of her fingers, all whilst she stirred her tea with the same spoon Aria had just dropped. Her hands were clasped in front of her as all this was happening, the calm look replaced with a smug one. Aria groaned and put her own hands on her head, massaging her temples with her fingers.

"You've been at this for four times longer than I've been alive! You can't expect me to just master it in a matter of weeks" Aria complained.

"Less of the whining girl and try again. You've come remarkably far in a short period of time. Your concentration isn't the problem, it's your emotions. You're scared that your power will get out of control again. Am I right?" Aria sighed. As usual her grandmother had gotten straight to the heart of the problem without beating around the bush. In truth, she was terrified. Not only was the first use of her power excruciatingly painful, the second had almost caused a minor earthquake. Every time she was connected to the power it felt both joyous and petrifying. It made her feel like she could do anything, which was what scared her. One slip and she could lose her meagre control, bringing the walls down around them or burning down the woods. She took her hands off her temples, then looked into her grandmother's eyes.

"Every time I get to grips with it, my memories flicker back to losing control. If you weren't there with me that night..."

"Strike that from your mind. I was there, and you're new to this. I will *always* be there until you know you have control. Now, try again."

Gritting her teeth, Aria forced herself to open her mind for what felt like the hundredth time that morning, the feeling of elation spreading through her as her veins electrified. Fear coursed closely behind, which she did her best to dampen as she focused on the spoon. As she saw it begin to quiver, the panic set in and she almost lost her connection. With a great effort of will she shoved the panic back down, smiling triumphantly as the spoon floated out of the cup, dripping scalding tea over the table. Instantly worried about her grandmother's reaction to the spillage, she lowered the spoon back into the cup and stirred the tea, before letting it drop back down with a clink. Her grandmother smiled.

"Well done girl. The fear will vanish in time, once you realise there's nothing to be scared of. We'll leave it there for today. Any moment now.... Come in Balzor!" she said.

Aria jerked her head to the door as it was pushed tentatively open, then back to her grandmother with wide eyes. "You *need* to show me how to do that," she murmured as Balzor closed the door. Her grandmother cackled. She turned to Balzor as he was closing the door.

"I didn't know you were coming today?" One look at his face when he turned around was all it took for her to rise and move quickly over to him, putting her hands on his shoulders as she saw glistening in his eyes, shoulders slumped dejectedly.

"What is it?" she asked urgently. She could feel the tension in his body as he struggled to stop the shaking. He took a deep breath.

"Aldred, the King, all the men. They've been betrayed; the Hounds got to them." Stunned silence greeted his words, only the crackling of the flames puncturing it. Her grandmother recovered first.

"Sit down boy, tell me everything."

He made a few shaky steps towards a chair before sinking into it heavily. He then began the tale, and Aria could see it was hard for him to relate. She could only begin to imagine what expression was on her face as he was talking; judging by her grandmother's wide eyes and furrowed brows it can't have been much different to hers.

"The plan must have been years in the making, Hounds spreading like a disease throughout the kingdom until they had enough support to come out. What I can't grasp, is why the prince would lead a rebel group against his father, when the Crown would've been his eventually anyway?" he concluded, leaning back on the chair.

Aria noticed red rims around his eyes as he knuckled the tiredness away. "I wanted to tell you before you heard it from anybody else..."

Sitting in silence for a moment as the news sank in, she startled as Balzor spoke up abruptly. "I've got to go. We don't have a lot of time, and we've got a huge work-load if we're going to beat whatever comes at us. I'll take my leave, Seeress," he said, bowing to her grandmother before turning quickly and giving her another kiss, this time lingering on her lips; almost more than was proper in front of company.

He broke free from her and squeezed her hand. "Just in case," he added, mischievous grin on his face.

"Yeah..." she replied, suddenly short of breath.

He chuckled and moved towards the door, seeming much steadier this time, nodding to her grandmother and stepping outside. As the door closed, her grandmother called out, "Oh, Balzor?"

He came back in, looking nervous now; like a naughty child being scolded by his mother. "Yes, Seeress?"

"It's Osri, to you." Aria watched as Balzor's mouth dropped open in surprise, echoing her own reaction. She struggled not to laugh as he opened and closed his mouth for a moment, before clamping it shut and smiling tentatively.

"Thank you... Osri" he said, then practically ran out of the house. Aria released the laugh, and her grandmother followed suit, shrugging her shoulders at Aria's questioning look.

"What can I say, I like the lad," she said. "Okay, head back in the zone. Try again, and this time don't drop it!"

"Like it's that easy," Aria complained as she took her position and opened her mind. It was going to be a long day.

*****

Sweat sheened Balzor's face, dripping off the side off his chin and nose in tandem. His shoulder muscles were screaming in protest as he and Svein swung a pick yet again at the solid ground, Alkor beside them spading the loose ground out of the hole. They'd drawn the short straws of digging the pit traps, whilst the lads from the village carted the excess soil away for other use; mainly to avoid the pits being obvious, though.

Svein had stripped off early to avoid the heat, but it only ended with his huge bulk glistening with sweat, the dirt sticking to him and causing him to scratch every two minutes. Balzor had left his shirt on after that; avoiding the body shame next to his monster of a friend had nothing to do with it, of course. Through the canopy, the last weak rays of sunlight were retreating to their slumber, leaving the foliage looking glum in its absence. With the falling sun came the blessed coolness of evening, though the work kept them sweltering.

They'd dug three identical pits at the three entrances to the clearing; the trees allowed a single man to walk through elsewhere, but the natural choice would be to follow one of those paths. The soil that they'd dug out was positioned further back, beyond the vision of any entering. The lads from the village who could use a bow were to hide behind that, then use the heightened ground to pour arrows over the Annarites' heads into the enemy. Essentially creating a killing ground to whittle down the Hounds' numbers before engaging them physically.

A warm feeling was kindling in Balzor's chest as he dug, and it took him a while to realise that it wasn't just revenge building there, it was excitement. Gone were the fears and the nightmares that plagued him, the training he'd put his body through to make it a machine of war burning them out of him. He finally felt like himself again, and Aria had been no small part of that. Without her and his friends around him, he probably wouldn't have left his bed for weeks, in his own cocoon of misery. It was with high spirits that he dug the back breaking hole, before discarding the pick and hammering sharpened stakes into its base.

As if waiting for that moment, Dextri's voiced boomed across the clearing to down tools for the night.

"Don't want any of you dozy bastards to break a finger or impale yourselves on the stakes. Plus, I know Alkor's scared of the dark," he said. The group laughed as Alkor clambered out of the hole and gave Dextri the finger. "Good work today lads! If the two little lords can run quick enough, we'll have a good fight on our hands."

Balzor rolled his eyes good naturedly as Alkor helped him out of the pit to the jeers of the rest, then helped him dragged the bulk of Svein out after. The village lads began throwing a cover of sticks and leaves to ensure the ground didn't look obvious, covering the lot with some of the spare dirt then more leaves for good measure. Dextri came and stood beside them, tutting appreciatively.

"They're not gonna be so cocky when a stake goes up their arse, eh young'uns?"

"Some people tend to like things like that, sir," Svein said innocently.

"Each to their own lad, each to their own. We'll cut their throats after, don't think they'll like that, eh?" Svein chuckled.

"Right, I'm getting back to my da. Mam will cut *my* throat if I let stew go cold!"

"Aye lad, day's over with now anyway. Back to the manor lads! Tomorrow, we make sure we know these woods like the back of our hands. Balzor and Alkor are used to playing around in trees like children, so they know the area. We, on the other hand, don't. We do NOT want any surprises, we dig up any unruly roots, make sure we can't trip over stones; if I lose my head because of a stone, I'll haunt you bastards for the rest of your sorry lives!"

The lads cheered and laughed, though the words were mainly for the few of the Sain guard that had joined them that day. Most were on sentry duty at one point of another, so the work had been done by those the village could spare. Most trudged off instantly at the command, relieved that the day's work was done, but Balzor and Alkor stood side by side surveying their work. Dextri walked behind them, clapping a meaty hand on each of their shoulders.

"This is our best chance lads," Dextri murmured. "Whatever happens in the next few days, just know that I've never been as proud watching you two grow up. I know your dad felt the same, whether he said the words or not." Balzor was assaulted by a wave of emotion, one glance at Alkor showed his reaction to be a stage further, as a single teardrop rolled down his dirt-stained cheek, leaving a track of cleanliness in the dust. He saw his friend clench his fist tightly.

"I can't believe that Alnor went this far. He's always been a dick, but to murder our father... He wouldn't even have the balls to try it, let alone go through with it. Someone's been dripping poison into his ear," he said, kicking a stray rock in his temper. "In one stroke I found out my father was dead, and that I'd have to kill my brother. All my family, gone!"

Feeling like he'd been kicked in the gut by the last comment, Balzor forced himself not to take it to heart. He'd always known he'd never be a Sain, Alkor always being the one to tell him otherwise; hearing Alkor disregard him in that notion cut him deeper than he'd ever let anyone know. He swallowed past the lump in his throat and clapped Alkor on the back.

"You've still got me, brother."

"And me, young'un" Dextri added.

As if realising what he'd just said, Alkor blanched and smiled sadly and apologetically. "Well, not *all* my family. I'm sorry lads, my head's not in the right place tonight. I think I'll grab an early night, unless you need me, Dex?"

Dextri shook his head, and Alkor walked away quickly, fading into the gloomy treeline at the edge of the clearing. Balzor suddenly realised how dark it'd gotten in the short space of time since they'd stopped work; it seemed Dextri made a good call ensuring they stopped when they did.

A trickle of water could be heard from the nearby stream passing the village, the only thing to break the companionable silence that had fallen between Dextri and Balzor. Balzor felt Dextri's hand slip off his shoulder, then heard him clear his throat loudly.

"We best be off too lad, before Nerva has our balls for letting her food go stale."

"She might be too busy with Olsten's balls to bother with ours," Balzor replied.

Dextri snorted. "Don't let her hear you say that, or you won't get fed for a week!"

"I think I'll have a wash in the stream and make a detour on the way back, if it's all the same to you, Dex?"

"Let me guess, a brown eyed detour?" Balzor laughed and they turned to walk out of the clearing.

He knew he was being obvious in his attempts to see Aria, but he couldn't care less. She'd been a vital part in him getting through the past few weeks, he wasn't sure whether he could have done it without her.

When the walls came into view, Dextri said his goodbyes and set off towards the village, and Balzor veered off toward the stream. He heard Dextri chatting in the distance, his voice a low hum as he got further away, then his huge, booming laugh. *You could hear that laugh from Torizo, the bloody idiot,* Balzor thought with a smile, reaching the stream and stripping off, leaving his clothes hanging over the branch of a thin tree nearby.

Steeling himself for the bite of the water, he took a deep breath and jumped straight in, submerging himself completely in the chest-deep water and scrubbing his hair vigorously. He surfaced, blowing water from his nostrils and exhaling harshly, feeling the water sap away any heat his body contained; after the day of toil, it felt wonderful. Washing the sweat and dust from his skin, he leant back in the water and closed his eyes, enjoying the feeling of contentment blossoming in his belly. What he hadn't accounted for though, was a visitor.

A low whistle jerked him from his relaxed state and set alarm bells ringing as he struggled to right himself in the water in his panic. The joyous laugh that followed instantly put him at ease.

"Dextri told me I'd find you here, though he failed to mention the state you'd be in," Aria giggled, leaning against the thin tree that had held his clothes. They were now dangling from her outstretched finger, amusement on her face. He didn't know whether to be mortified or to laugh, so he settled for both, trying to cover himself with his hands and failing.

"Aria I... er..." he stammered, having no clue how to get out of the situation.

"Well, I was going to come and see you in the forest... figured you'd worked later than expected. Couldn't have you forgetting about me now, could we?" she teased, letting his clothes fall unceremoniously to the ground, conveniently much too far away for him to reach from the edge of the stream.

"How could I forget about you?!" he asked, feigning outrage.

She laughed again, this time with a slightly intense look in her eyes. "Could you pass me those?" he added, gesturing to his fallen trousers.

"I could..." she started, reaching up to the shoulder on her dress, sliding it to the side and letting it fall down her arm. Any awkwardness he'd had fled within seconds as she stepped into the water and crushed her lips to his.

✶✶✶✶✶

The jolting gait of his cantering horse did nothing to help Alnor's dark thoughts, as the relentless sun beamed down on the back of his neck with harsh rays.

That morning, they'd passed the farmstead where his father had duelled Krinar and lost. He'd envisioned the memory from that point on, the duel taking on a whole different perspective now that Krinar's intentions had been revealed. The rest of the warband was jubilant, drunk on the fact they'd brought around a new age for the kingdom, forever the prince's sycophants.

A few days earlier, Alnor would've felt the same, but the image of his father's face constantly imposed on his thoughts, bringing him guilt and immeasurable grief. He'd loved his father despite everything, but in a fit of rage he'd become the man's death. Telling himself it was for the greater good, a sentiment backed by Krinar, he powered through the guilt and kept going.

They'd made much better time than on the way back, which felt more like a leisurely ride amongst friends than the attacking force they were meant to be. Krinar was pushing them hard, wanting to spread the word of his father's heroic death against the Hounds, and cement his rein with the nobles. Hints at a larger plan were thrown around the campfire at night, only a select few let in on the full scope.

Alnor wasn't yet amongst those set few. He knew Krinar didn't trust him, his objections to the prince's methods putting a boulder in the way of what he'd thought was a friendship. They spoke often, Krinar reassuring him and consoling him in his grief, attempting to be the father figure he'd dispatched, but the connection they'd had before evaporated, leaving Alnor realising he'd been used. He sighed, knowing that he'd have to live with the consequences; he might as well reap the rewards that came from his black deeds. It grated on him that Moonlight had seemed to escape the horses they had left, vanishing into thin air as its rider had died. He had only the great battle-axe that he now carried to remember his father by. It was much too heavy for him to wield, but much too sacred to leave behind.

Digging his heels into his horse, he increased his speed to ride alongside Krinar, gaining a disdainful look from Varnan as he did. The man had constantly thrown jibes at him since the night of the attack, accusing him of weakness and being too soft to do what must be done; always out of earshot of Krinar of course, though Alnor was sure Krinar knew. He threw his own scathing look back at the worm of a man, then cleared his throat to get Krinar's attention. The prince turned, an easy smile on his face in contrast to Varnan's scowl.

"Alnor! Just the man I wanted to see." he exclaimed.

"Oh? How so, sire?"

"Nothing major, I just wanted to see how you were doing; I know the past few days have been challenging for you. How've you been sleeping?"

Alnor considered lying in to hide any weakness in front of Varnan but knew that the dark bags under his eyes were impossible to conceal.

"Not great," he admitted. "I'll get over it, sire. Nothing that time won't heal, and we've got enough of that until the capital."

"Ah, yes. That's one thing I've been meaning to tell you... We won't be going to Grea."

Alnor's heart sank. He'd know that he had fallen from the prince's good graces, but he never once thought that Krinar would abandon him, leaving him to return to Saternac in disgrace.

"Sire, I know that I've disappointed you but please, don't send me away," he pleaded. Krinar looked at him quizzically, sharing a glance with Varnan who smirked at Alnor's discomfort, then looked back and locked eyes with him.

"I won't be sending you away, Alnor. I have some business at the Buccai Pass before I return to Grea. I'll be taking twenty men and leaving in the morning, leaving you in charge of the rest," he said. This confused Alnor greatly since they'd just spent the last few days riding hard in the opposite direction to the pass. Before he could voice his question, Krinar continued. "I know what you're thinking, but the timeline must be brought forward. You'll take fifty of my red cloaks back to Saternac to spread the news of our victory – and of our loss. Use the men to maintain order. Send the rest on to Torizo to tell the Munat family to announce my reign. The men will know what to do from there."

Alnor couldn't help but breathe a sigh of relief on hearing that he wouldn't be left behind. So many questions burned in his throat and, after nodding his assent, he felt like he was squirming in his saddle with the effort of containing them. Fortunately, Krinar noticed his discomfort. He chuckled without humour.

"Whatever it is that's tickling your balls, Alnor, ask it."

Alnor smiled sheepishly. "Just two things sire. The Munats... were they a part

261

of this? I find it hard to believe they would be anything but steadfast to both our fathers, since they trained with them as boys."

"No, they weren't, thank Ezimat! They'd have blabbed the entire thing years ago and had me in a cell. That family is much too honour bound for treachery, even if it's for the greater good!" Krinar exclaimed, this time laughing with humour behind his voice. "Not many noble families were involved, the less that know the better. Much easier for the transition if the kingdom doesn't suspect a thing, just a brave King fallen in battle and his son taking over, as it should be."

Alnor laughed along with him, though he had to force the mirth from his mouth. Even to him, it sounded hollow as it left his throat, so to Krinar it must have sounded completely empty. He either didn't notice, or feigned indifference.

"And the second question?" Krinar prompted.

Alnor let the tension drain from his body as the humour went back into Krinar and he began to feel at ease, like he had in the past. "The Buccai Pass? Are you planning to venture into the Kerazar's tribe lands with such a small number of men?"

This time, Krinar's laugh was full throated, genuine pleasure in the sound. What Alnor didn't like, however, was Varnan's cruel laugh accompanying it; the man's voice made his skin crawl, but his laugh was so alien it almost knocked him sick.

"What's funny, sire?"

"I thought you might have put the pieces together, Alnor, if somewhat disjointed. The way we've been talking for weeks, this entire group's views. Don't you realise we're more alike to the Kerazar than you think?" he said.

Alnor felt a sense of dread settle in him, eliminating the tiny portion of ease he'd only just acquired. "What are you saying sire?" Alnor said, horrified.

"What he's saying, pup" Varnan drawled. "Is that he's not going to the Buccai pass to harass the Kerazar... he's going to let them in."

Alnor rode in stunned silence as the two men laughed, warriors around them catching on and realising who the joke was directed against. Shame-faced and shocked to the bone, he let his horse slip back slowly without comment, the taunting laughs echoing in his ears. One last thought that raced through his mind as the jeering faded,

What have I done?

Krinar watched Alnor retreat and wondered if he'd gone too far. He needed to keep him on side - preferably on a friendly basis to avoid any future friction. The fact that the boy had cut his own father's head off put them in the same boat, so for Alnor to betray him would be putting his own head on a spike. Betrayal wasn't an option for Alnor, he'd deal with his sulking later, he had more important things to deal with now. He'd take a minor precaution to ease his mind, pass the whelp on to somebody else.

"Varnan," he called quietly. His faithful hound reacted instantly to his command.

"Sire?" responded Varnan.

"I want you to be one of the fifty that accompanies Alnor. We need to make sure his conscience doesn't give up the game before we're fully secure."

Varnan pulled his face, the smile vanishing at the unwanted burden. *Ha! He thought he'd be coming with me,* Krinar thought with glee. "Why so glum? Look on the bright side - if he does think to come clean, you get to kill him. And his brother too if you wish."

Krinar knew the hatred Varnan had for the Sains, though he'd never probed why. The loathing had passed to his son, who'd eagerly volunteered to infiltrate the guard at Saternac, beginning Alnor's conversion years earlier. Their family would be rewarded when all this was over - let nobody say that King Krinar of the Annar wasn't a gold-giver. A look of cruel intent flashed across Varnan's face at the thought of killing the Sains, and Krinar applauded his own brilliance. You have to let the dog off the lead at some point.

"I assume you're keen for the task?"

Varnan smiled hideously.

Osri hummed to herself as she stirred her tea, allowing the peaceful process to calm her mind after the most vivid dream of her lifetime. She'd known as soon as her eyes wrenched open what it had meant, as all her kind do. To remember a prophecy was unheard of - hence the constant need for an apprentice to be by your side, lest they remain undiscovered. But there was one that all Seers - man or woman - remembered: the sight of their own death. The circumstances and results of her death were an unforeseen perk for her.

Some seers did their best to thwart their demise, given the prewarning. They would prevail for a time, but Ezimat's reapers came for all in the end. To cheat death was to cheat the life you're living; nobody could live forever. Most, however, chose to say their goodbyes and enjoy their last moments, taking the gift they'd been given; not everybody had chance to kiss their loved ones before they died.

Seeing what the dream entailed not only led her towards the peaceful route, but also actively ensured that she passed in that specific manner. This was something she'd never expected, but something she knew must happen for the good of the kingdom, maybe for the good of the world.

She clinked the spoon against the side of her cup – having a premonition of her death was no reason to stain her table with tea. Sitting down lightly at a chair, she stared out of the open window as the first tendrils of dawn crept their way into her home. Shivering slightly, she flicked her fingers towards the fire and ignited it with a thought, smiling slightly at the thought of Aria's attempt to do the same thing the night before. The log had floated perfectly, she'd even ignited it with a degree of skill; the problem was she ignited the rest of the logs in her storage box. *Can still smell the bloody smoke, idiot girl,* Osri thought with a dry chuckle.

Her thoughts of Aria inevitably led her down the route of her dream again, to the face of the red-haired boy she'd fallen for. Osri had always felt a twinge of fate surrounding the boy, and since he'd been besotted with Aria, she'd known that their fates were intertwined, neither reaching their full potential without the other. But she finally knew why that twinge had included Aria in its scope. She sighed, not for the first time wishing that her granddaughter wasn't a part of Ezimat's plan.

Standing and taking a sip of her tea, wincing as it burned the roof of her mouth, she walked over to her desk and grabbed some parchment that was strewn untidily over it. Walking back to the table, she floated an envelope, a pot of ink and a quill over to her. *No use having these powers if I've got to use my old legs to fetch everything,* she thought gruffly. Sitting back down, she unstopped the ink bottle and dipped the quill into it, pausing to allow the excess ink to drip back into the pot. Ezimat be damned if she was going to stain this bloody table when she was so close to deaths door. Drawing the circle on her head to avoid bad luck against her curse, she lifted the quill and began to write.

For a short while, only the crackle of the flames and the scratching of her quill broke the pleasant silence of the morning. As she finished, the birds began their morning song. Osri heard shuffling in the next room, alerting her to Aria's surfacing. She signed the bottom of the letter hastily before putting it in the envelope, sealing it with a flick of her wrist before scribbling Aria's name on its front and stuffing it into her robe, just as Aria walked through her bedroom door.

"Morning Gran," she muttered sleepily, stifling a yawn as she shuffled over to the teapot and poured herself a cup. "How long have you been up?"

"Oh, just a little while. Had a bad dream and it was almost morning, figured I'd get up to see the sun rise."

Aria looked at her quizzically and Osri shrugged; her granddaughter knew she hated early mornings, but her sleepy state hadn't allowed her to get suspicious. She'd have to be careful over the next few days, lest Aria figure out something was amiss and attempt to change her mind. *Always did have a knack for making me spill secrets I shouldn't be spillin'* she thought, frowning at the back of Aria's head. Maybe she'd get up early for the next few mornings, spend as much time with the girl whilst she could. She itched to tell her what she'd seen in the dream but knew it would lead to more questions than she could answer without revealing her intentions. No. The letter would suffice, she wouldn't have long to wait until she got it. She'd just enjoy the dawn with her granddaughter for one of the last times of her life.

Chapter 14

Heat roared from the forge, accompanied by the familiar hammering and the odd grunt from Svein as his arms yanked the hammer up for yet another strike on the glowing iron. He was so engrossed in his work that he almost leapt out of his skin when a cold, slender hand rested on his bare shoulder. Jerking violently, he knocked the unfinished horseshoe to the ground in a tornado of sparks. He spun, raising the giant smith's hammer, then froze in shock as he took in the small form in front of him. He lowered the hammer as she smirked at him.

"Mariak, why'd you sneak up on me like that?! I could've taken your head off" he said.

She only smiled broader before poking him in the chest as he lowered the hammer. "You'd have to be quicker than that big man, a bairn could get away from you at that speed," she teased, brushing a stray lock of scruffy hair out of her face.

To Svein's eyes, she looked as though she'd just come out of the forest; small twigs broken off in her hair, a smudge of mud on her cheek and breeches with holes in the knees, and a lurking sadness beneath her eyes that Svein could only imagine the depth of. He bit off his retort as he saw her eyes, not wanting to add anything more to their grief.

"Aye, if you say so. What d'ya need?"

"Straight to the point. I like that in a man. I need some knives, weighted more on the tip than the handle, made for throwing."

"I know how to make throwing knives," he grumbled, and she laughed.

"Well, aren't you a clever giant! Just three will be good enough for now, I can use my bow for most things, but when things get up close and personal..."

She stepped forward and stroked his arm. "Knives are much better." Stunned by her brazenness, Svein didn't pull away until she'd stepped back, smirking again and leant against the doorway.

"And the hilts?" he called as she turned to leave.

"I'll sort those, you just sort the blades my giant friend." Then she was gone.

His father came in through the same door moments later, looking bemused as he looked over his shoulder. "What was she after?" he asked suspiciously.

"Throwing knives," Svein grunted, picking up the tempered tongs and retrieving the scalding horseshoe off the ground. His father nodded his assent, but queried no more, though a smile appeared on his face.

"She said she'd sort the hilts herself."

"I'd imagine she'd fashion them out of bone or wood for throwing knives, our kind of hilts wouldn't work, especially for someone as small as her. Mariak, isn't it?"

"Aye." said Svein.

"Poor family, to lose so much so quickly. Still, it was a dark night when they sated their bloodlust on Mika, however much he deserved it. I'd wager she could use those knives."

Svein didn't know what to say so just nodded and placed the horseshoe into the coals and moved to pump the bellows again. Blasted girl had made him lose the heat; he'd have to start all over again now. He knew what his dad was about, trying to make him open up a bit more about women, find someone to settle down with; his mam had put him up to it, Svein was sure. *If I was going to find a wife, it wouldn't be Mariak bloody Praker,* he thought as he began to pump.

*****

"The pits are dug and covered; everyone knows the plan. All we have left to do is wait," Balzor stated to Dextri.

Alkor was leaning back on his chair, absentmindedly picking a rogue piece of meat from his teeth as he surveyed the room. Men were at ease again, content with their lot, eating and laughing around the table with their comrades. But there'd been a pit in Alkor's stomach since he'd heard the news of his father's demise, falling into a depression he couldn't seem to get himself out of.

After that first night, he'd pulled himself together on the surface, but beneath was a torrent of emotions fighting to break through his façade. He thought he'd had everybody fooled, but Balzor and Dextri kept shooting questioning looks his way as he was brooding. Knowing he'd have input more to keep up his ruse, he spat the meat on to his plate and spoke.

"We need to get somebody out on the road to give us some kind of warning. Let Rindu and Mariak take a horse each and get on the highest hill they can find; as soon as a dust cloud is spotted, they race back and let us prepare ahead of time."

"Aye young'un that's a given, not sure if those two are the best choice for horseback, though. Herman, Sebastian… up for it?"

"You know me Dex, always up for a ride," Sebastian replied, getting hoots from the men. Herman just nodded his assent as he quaffed yet another cup of wine.

"Woah, slow down on the berries Herman; can't be hungover if you need to race back," Dextri complained.

Herman didn't even grace that with an answer; instead, he finished his drink and smacked his lips appreciatively. "When have you EVER known me to get a hangover Dex? Still drunk maybe, but never hungover!"

Alkor watched as Dextri mulled over the comment, then raised his eyebrows and nodded with a purse of his lips. "Aye, you are one of those arseholes who can weather the storm pretty well," he admitted. "But peace of mind, eh? One night off won't kill you."

"It bloody might," Herman grumbled, but didn't pick up the pitcher again. The guards began to slope off slowly back to their quarters, leaving Balzor, Dextri, Livius, Ingvar, Devar and himself – the core as Alkor liked to think. Herman was close becoming one of those intimate friends, but the bond that was forged by standing shoulder to shoulder in battle was stronger than anything. They sat in companionable silence for a while, until true to form, Balzor opened his mouth.

"Do you think we can actually win? Like, *really* win. Not just this upcoming battle, but the one after that, and after that until the kingdom is cleansed?"

Silence greeted his words at first, as they contemplated an answer. Surprisingly, it was Ingvar that came up with one first. "We can, but we need to be smart. Root out the problem, town by town, city by city, starting with Torizo. We've no idea who's turned and who's loyal, so we'll have to tread careful. Taking out those makeshift slave traders Joseph told us about would be a start. We'll also need allies, the mountain clans maybe? Possibly those weird Eastern kingdom rejects too, if they'll fight. But that's in the future. Let's keep our heads on our shoulders first, eh?"

Devar snorted at his brother's more than adequate answer. "Brother, that was the most I've heard you speak in ten years, and I hate to admit it, but it makes good fucking sense!" Laughter spread through the room and Ingvar scowled at his brother, returning to silence.

The ice was broken now though, and some of what Ingvar said had confused Alkor. "I'm unsure if this is me being an idiot but... Eastern kingdom rejects?" Livius' eyes widened in surprise.

"Don't tell me you've never heard of them?"

Alkor shook his head. He could see Balzor perk up his interest at this topic too; it felt good to know it wasn't just him. "They're called the Aahn. How much do you know about the Eastern kingdom?"

"Nothing much, except that they do great spices and only fight in defence of their land, never offensively," Balzor replied.

Livius nodded thoughtfully. "That's pretty much the essence of it to be fair. They defend against any incursions on their land but will never expand due to their belief Ezimat is a peaceful God who doesn't condone war. It's a good thing for us because it means they'll never invade our lands, and trade makes both our kingdoms wealthier. But, in the early days of the Kerazar, King Elart secured a foothold in their kingdom, knowing they wouldn't attack him, and tried to use it to get through the mountains to us. Obviously, Malker and your father couldn't abide that, so they made a deal with the Eastern kingdom. We'd root them out, our kingdoms would become allies and trade; but they added one more demand to that. There were factions within the Eastern kingdoms that wanted nothing more than to use their martial prowess offensively, which was against their religious law. So, we gave them a corner of land in the south of Kroidort forest if they promised to fight the Kerazar if they ever invaded... bringing us to the present."

Balzor's eyes were almost popping out of his head at the story, and Alkor could only imagine his were doing the same. How had they never heard about that? Balzor asked that very question just as the thought came into Alkor's head.

"Because it's a bit of a sore subject, giving up land so close to Grea in return for a pledge to fight that Malker knew would never be needed," Dextri said.

"Well, hopefully it never will be. They only pledged to fight against the Kerazar, not in a civil war between traitorous nobles and loyal ones – the Kerazar invading would be *much* worse than that," Livius said, taking a swig of wine and looking at his cup in disgust when he realised it was empty. "And on that note lads, I'm going to bed. Unlike Herman, I *do* get hangovers, and I can already feel one coming on. G'night."

"Aye, us too" Ingvar and Devar said in unison, rising together.

"And then there were three," Balzor said with a thin smile. "So, these Aahn will only fight the Kerazar... what about the mountain clans?"

"Probably the same if you can ever get them to leave the mountains. They war with each other more often than not and keep themselves to themselves. That's why Lortmund left originally - he was sick of fighting over petty grievances or perceived insults against honour," Dextri said.

Alkor was positive his eyes nearly fell out of his head this time.

"*Lortmund* comes from the mountain clans?" he said incredulously.

Dextri looked at him oddly. "You didn't know? I thought Svein would've told you."

"It's not something you think to ask a friend. Oh, mate, any chance you're from the savage mountain clans?" he said, raising his arms up and pulling a face like a fool.

"Did his size not give you a clue?" Dextri scoffed. "The man and his son are fucking monstrous, even by my standards."

The more Alkor thought of it, the more obvious it became. Only one thing struck him as strange, though. "I thought the mountain clans took their clan's name as their surname?" he asked.

"Aye lad, they do. When Lortmund met Martha, he took her family name rather than his clan's. Saternac is a welcoming place, but back then people were mistrustful of outsiders. You need to remember; the clans are forever fighting each other. Until Lortmund, we never traded with them, the risk was too great. Lortmund changed a lot of people's perspectives and set up a good relationship with his clan, who just so happen to be the first you encounter in the mountains." Dextri explained.

Balzor whistled slowly. Alkor could see that his friend was as amazed by this revelation as he was.

"I've never known him to leave and visit his family. It must have been lonely for him at the start?" Balzor asked.

Dextri's eyes suddenly took on a nervous look, piquing Alkor's interest in Balzor's question. "What? What's the look for?" Alkor said. He and Balzor exchanged a confused look, then Dextri sighed.

"It's not my story to tell young 'un, but also something that you shouldn't go and ask him outright. I know you two are a pair of nosey bastards though, so I'll tell you the basics, so you don't put your foot in it. Lortmund didn't just leave because of the clan feuds or the skirmishes. He left to avoid being put in a position that he'd spent his life trying to avoid."

Livius chose that point to step back into the hall; judging by his face he'd heard the initial conversation and decided to intervene.

"Dex..." Livius warned, but Dextri waved him off.

It seemed despite his warnings to Herman, Dextri had consumed more than his fair share of wine that night. *He always was a talker after a drink,* Alkor thought amusedly.

"You see, Lortmund wasn't just any old mountain clan warrior. He was a contender for chief of his clan, which is only possible with certain bloodlines, according to their code."

"Bloodlines? As in only certain families?" Alkor said.

"Sort of, but that's the part I *won't* get in to. Basics only, remember? Suffice to say he had the blood, and if more than one contender has support at the time of the chief's death, they fight for the spot; the only other option is to leave, which Lortmund did."

"He gave up on being chief to avoid a fight? Doesn't sound like the Lortmund I know," Balzor retorted.

It seems he'd had more than he could handle tonight, too. Dextri reached over and clipped him around the ear, making Balzor yelp in surprise and look angrily at him.

"Don't interrupt little lord, I've not finished yet. The only other contender was somebody who he held dear above all others; someone he wouldn't fight for the sake of a title he never wanted."

"Who?!" Balzor urged. Livius took over, the curve of his mouth alerting them that it was unwillingly.

"You know Lortmund - he cherishes family above all else. It can't be hard to deduce, surely?"

Dextri slammed his cup on to the table, belched loudly and wiped his chin with the back of his arm. "His brother, young'uns. Lortmund's brother is chief of the Yurak clan - hence why he can't go back. It'd be seen as a challenge to his brother's authority and force him to fight. So, Lortmund can't help us regarding them."

After that, the talking faded to a comfortable silence again. After finishing their drinks they sloped off to bed with a nod and murmured goodbyes. Leaving together, Balzor and Alkor walked up the staircase noisily, yawning into the back of their hands. Alkor's mind was reeling at what he'd heard that night, thoughts of the coming conflict for once at the back of his thoughts. Judging by the small smile on Balzor's face, it seemed his mind wasn't on either of those things.

"What do you think about Svein, eh?" Alkor asked, breaking into his friend's daydream. Balzor jumped and looked at him guiltily before replying.

"Wha - oh... yeah that. It's a shock, that's for sure! If you think about it, Svein could've been a clan chief," he replied, somewhat sheepishly.

"Alright, spit it out. I'm guessing with that stupid expression on your face that your thoughts were on a certain Seeress' apprentice."

Balzor's face went red, then he laughed. "That obvious, huh?"

"Not kidding! You've not been with it all night. Everything okay?"

"More than okay brother, more than okay." Alkor's eyes widened as he came to the only possible conclusion for his friend's smug expression, and he grabbed Balzor's arm to force him to stop.

"You and Aria, and you never said anything?!"
A full-blown grin erupted on his face as he struggled to contain his glee.

"Brother, it was unbelievable! We've heard stories about Torizo's pleasure houses, but this felt so different to what they described. I just kinda froze. I didn't have any idea what to do when I saw her, then suddenly it just seemed so *right*. Although the fact she caught me bathing in the stream didn't help things, it was fucking freezing!"

"She caught you in the river?!" Alkor laughed as they reached Balzor's room. They stood gossiping like a couple of noble ladies for what felt like the longest time before tiredness forced them both to bed. They parted company with Balzor still smiling stupidly, and Alkor walked to his own room with his own grin on his face, happy for him.

Alkor's mood evaporated as he stepped into his room. The candles had burnt low, leaving it dark and uninviting. Shivering, he closed the door and began to strip down, dreading the dreams to come. They'd been more vivid of late, his tired brain conjuring up visions of Alnor murdering his father. Hopefully tonight would be different, the wine dulling his senses and muffling his head. Licking his fingers, he pressed his index and his thumb to the drained candle, extinguishing it and plunging the room into darkness. He threw the sheets over his body and attempted to settle down. His last thoughts, which should've been about Balzor's happiness, were invaded with questions about his Alnor's intent. The wine only served to inflame his rage at the thoughts, hardening his grief into a white-hot ball of fury. That night, sleep came slowly, his mind focusing on only one thing: Vengeance.

✶✶✶✶✶

Joseph awoke as the thin light of dawn landed on his eyelids, alerting his structured mind that it was time to rise from slumber. He'd always been an early riser but usually preferred his mornings to be laid back or doing trivial things. Since he'd sworn his oath to Alkor, he'd rose each morning and dressed instantly, making his way to the practice field where he knew his liege lord would begin his morning training. He kept himself to himself at nights, preferring his own company more than the distrustful stares that the guard continued to give him, despite his earlier actions. The day at the wall was a test for him, he'd known that; one that most except Alkor didn't expect him to pass. But to him, an oath was stronger than anything, and he meant to keep it. Nowhere in his oath, though, did it say he had to eat with his lord and endure the awkward atmosphere that seemed to constantly follow him.

So, a quick call to the kitchens after food had been served in the hall, the plump woman - Nerva he'd heard her called - taking pity on the young outsider and giving him something to take away with him. He liked her, she reminded him of his own mother before the Hounds had killed her. Thinking about her always ensured anger would rear its unwelcome head, so he steered his thoughts away. Anger was a warrior's weakness; one he intended to stop before it even began. He was decidedly less skilled than the warriors here, getting only very basic training before being sent out to do his former master's bidding.

Walking out on to the field, he cursed himself as he saw Alkor and Balzor already running laps. They were dedicated to becoming the best they could be, and Joseph resolved there and then to strive for the same thing. He'd finally found a purpose that night, the oath revitalising him and giving him hope; not just for him but for his sister too. If anybody could help him free her, it was the young Sain.

After he heard most of the men come back the night before, he'd lain awake for a while until their murmuring voices began to silence. Slightly later, the two brothers appeared - Devar and Ingvar. The fact that they were half drunk made it easy to overhear their conversation, and what he'd heard was a balm to his tortured soul. Dissolving the establishments that shackled his sister, rooting out the Kerazar, giving all a safe place to live, weak or not. Although he already thought he was in the right place, hearing all this had cemented it further.

Quickly stretching, he began his own morning run around the field, not bothering to keep up with the two brothers - he'd tried that at the start, but the pace they'd set left him gasping for air before the end of the second lap. Keeping his own pace made sure he could keep going for the same amount of time, albeit not as many laps. After the laps, the three of them stood panting together, catching their breath in silence as they waited for Dextri. Before long, Alkor and Balzor began giving each other amused looks, before Alkor snorted.

"So much for not drinking too much wine! Looks like we're doing the sequence without his critical eye this morning, thank Ezimat! Do you think you've got it yet, Joseph?"

"Yes lord!" he replied.

Balzor laughed at the response, and Joseph felt his cheeks heating up. "What's so funny?"

As Balzor's laugh faded, Alkor replied. "You don't have to call me lord, Joseph. I'm barely a bloody warrior yet, let alone a leader! C'mon, let's get our practice swords and start, no point wasting the day because Dextri has a fuzzy head."

They chuckled in unison and moved to the armoury, each picking a weapon and returning to the field. Soon they were lathered in sweat. The crisp morning air transformed as the sun began to crest above the treeline, bathing them in a sudden wash of heat and light. It was around this point that Dextri came across the field, shading his eyes from the glare and looking slightly worse for wear. Balzor paused in his sequence to cackle at his mentor, who growled back at him.

"Didn't take your own advice, eh Dex?" he called, resuming his sequence a few steps behind Joseph. Alkor smiled but didn't cease his movements.

"Nothing some of Nerva's bacon won't sort out," he grumbled. "Carry on, and when I get back I'll make sure I flatten you harder than ever for that remark."

He strode towards the manor, Balzor cringing at his stupidity. Alkor burst into laughter at his friend's discomfort. "One day, Balzor, you'll learn to keep that big mouth shut," he grinned.

Balzor rolled his eyes and continued his sequence, but Joseph swore he could see a trace of anxiety in his movements now. Nobody wanted to anger the best swordsman in the Sain guard when he had to spar with him moments later. Joseph was immensely happy about the fact that nobody would spar with him until he'd got the sword sequence correct and was confident in it. Seeing the way some looked at him, he was glad; more than a few of the men would take sparring as a chance to hammer some humility in to the new kid, especially when they happened to be a Hound in the not-too-distant past.

More men filtered out of the housing block, which was used as a barracks, some going to switch with the wall's patrols, the others retracing Dextri's footsteps for breakfast. They all raised hands to the trio, though scowls were on some of the faces as their eyes found Joseph, and he struggled not to squirm. Balzor and Alkor didn't notice however, so he pretended not to; no use creating problems where there weren't any, though it didn't stop the uncomfortable feeling blossoming in his chest at every foul glance he received. It didn't take long for Dextri to wolf down his hangover cure and get back to the field, Balzor looking nervously at him, whilst Alkor threw his friend a knowing smirk.

"This is gonna be *fun*," Dextri said evilly as he reached the two lads.

Joseph restarted his sequence, despite his body warning him of its discomfort, but adjusted his position so his view included the sparring trio. They faced off and wasting no time Balzor darted in on the offensive, Alkor a close second as he swiped at the opposite side of Dextri.

It always shocked Joseph to see such a bulky man move as quickly as he did, but watching him sidestep one blow whilst blocking another, he appreciated the skill of him.

Even against two opponents, he was finding openings to their counterattack.

Balzor and Alkor were also impossibly fast, only the weight of experience keeping Dextri from being floored in the first minute. Joseph paused mid sequence as Alkor dropped to the ground, clubbed in the face by Dextri's meaty hands. He put Alkor in between him and Balzor, touching his practice sword lightly to the dazed Sain's throat.

"Dead," was all he said, then he stepped back to the side of the prone figure, still reeling from the hit. Balzor moved away from his friend, acknowledging that he was now alone, and held his sword, ready. Unencumbered by the dual attacks, Dextri exploded into motion and launched a savage attack on Balzor. Although prepared, he was knocked back three paces by the first hit he blocked, then dodged the next two with speed that came from youth.

After the first direct hit, he tried to step away, using Dextri's strength to his disadvantage and tapping the mighty swings to the side rather than meeting them head on. Joseph saw Dextri's face change from the anticipating smile to a narrowing of concentration, and a slight surprise that Balzor was weathering the storm so well. The relentless tirade continued, neither of them tiring as they impossibly picked up the tempo of the fight.

It became clear after another minute of the battering, that Dextri was beginning to turn the tide. Balzor just couldn't get near him, whereas he was dodging with a hair's width each time. Joseph saw him begin to tire, though he'd developed a respect for the young warrior that he didn't have before. In the end, Dextri couldn't be denied. He knocked Balzor's defence wide and swept his sword toward Balzor, who span away with a valiant effort to recover swinging wildly at him, before stopping as he realised Dextri's sword was at his throat.

"Dead!" Dextri barked, and Balzor chuckled.

Alkor, who hadn't even bothered to rise from the floor and was propped up on his elbow, lay there looking flabbergasted. "Where the *fuck* did that come from?!" he exclaimed to his friend, who shrugged, attempting to be nonchalant but failed miserably as he grinned.

"I guess the angry Balzor took a back seat today," he said, still smiling like a proud child. Even Dextri nodded to him with an opponent's respect.

"The way you turned my attacks rather than meeting them head on. THAT'S how you beat a stronger adversary which, at your age, is almost anybody older and with actual pubic hair," he said mockingly, but ruffled Balzor's hair after it, who moved away disgustedly. "Well done lad, keep it up!"

Balzor seemed to swell from the praise, especially when Alkor clapped him on the back with a grin. "Look at his head! I never thought it could get any bigger but fuck me!" Alkor taunted, earning himself a swipe from Balzor which he ducked. "You pulled that out of your arse anyway, it's hard enough with both of us let alone just you!"

Joseph laughed at the obvious display of affection between them and instantly regretted it. Dextri turned to face him and saw him stood motionless, Joseph becoming the focus of the huge warrior's attention.

"And what are you gawping at?! Nobody said you could stop. If you wanna protect your new lord you need to be able to fight, so get your arse in to gear. Ten laps for being fucking bone idle!" Dextri bellowed.

He flinched but instantly dropped his practice sword and began to run; he'd seen what defiance got from complaining about an order, and he didn't want to do twenty. Balzor and Alkor roared with laughter at his reprimand, and Joseph heard Balzor say "At least it isn't us for once."

"What was that young'un? You think I've missed you out? You're best off giving me twenty laps then for good measure. Twenty laps then a fight with me, whilst I relax on this lovely, sunny morning and watch you work."

Balzor and Alkor groaned but set off all the same.

"For that, add another five. That'll stop you complaining like fucking children every time I give you a command! Take a leaf from our Joseph's book and listen, eh?"

✶✶✶✶✶

Galloping hooves were all Herman could hear on this fine Autumn morning. They'd left Saternac just over an hour previously and they'd ridden hard to reach the first hills, having formulated a plan as to not be taken unawares. Herman would crest the first hill to give them vision, poised with the hunting horn to warn Sebastian if they were coming. Sebastian would then move forward to the next hill and do the same, allowing him to move forward. If Alnor or any of the prince's retinue were seen, the horn would be blown, and they'd ride back at breakneck speed to warn the others.

The plan seemed sound, but it didn't stop his nerves jangling. Any man who said the prospect of a fight didn't excite and terrify him in equal measure was either insane or a total liar; at the speed Livius was convinced he'd got back in, they should see Alnor and his ilk within the next day at the most. Anticipation completely erased the fear at the thought of the older Sain brother; Herman had always disliked the lad, but knowing his betrayal turned the dislike into outright hatred. To betray family is one thing, but cold-hearted murder to usurp their position reeked of both desperation and evil. Herman didn't associate Alnor with evil. Desperate for attention and arrogant, yes. It seemed his judge of character had been wrong.

He forced the thoughts out of his mind and focused on the task at hand as he steered his horse off the road, tied him to a thin, straggly tree and began his climb up the hill. The previous hills they'd climbed didn't even deserve the name, but this one was a mountain amongst molehills. He decided halfway up that this was the one they'd watch from, knowing even if they found another, it might be too far along the road. Their job was to scout and report back, not to get caught and executed.

He crested the hill, glancing back towards Sebastian and seeing his figure in the distance. Taking a square piece out of his pack, he buffed it with his shirt and flashed the sun towards the other warrior – the signal for it being clear and to join him - then settled down to wait, facing the road towards Torizo and boring holes into it with his eyes.

It wasn't long before he heard the crunching of feet behind him, then Sebastian's call to confirm it was him. Earlier, it had seemed prudent to take this many precautions, but sitting there atop the hill it all seemed peaceful without a whiff of danger on the wind. Almost enjoyable, if he didn't have just dried beef and leftover bread to eat whilst they waited.

"Thought you'd appreciate something a bit more filling," Sebastian said casually as he sat down next to him, holding out a wrapped package that had a mouth-watering aroma.

Herman took it eagerly, before pausing suspiciously. "Where'd you get this?"

"Don't worry, I didn't pilfer Nerva's stock; I picked them up from Traf first thing whilst you went for the mounts."

"So, whilst I did all the work, you went for food?"

"Do you want it or not? I'm sure I could eat two..." Herman covered the package territorially, causing Sebastian to laugh. "Thought so. Eat up, chubby!"

Herman didn't need telling twice, swiftly unwrapping it and salivating at the sight of a perfectly cooked meat pie, juices pooled on top, waiting to be devoured. It had cooled slightly on the ride which allowed Herman to eat it quicker, licking the remnants off his fingers before Sebastian got halfway through his. Giving a content sigh, Herman settled back into his watchful stance, just wishing for more of the delicious morsel. Sebastian took his time with his own, taunting Herman by eating noisily and groaning in pleasure.

"You're making that sound almost sexual; shall I give you a moment?" Sebastian snorted but ceased the incessant noises and finished his meal with the least amount of annoyance possible.

Once he'd finished, he couldn't help but pester Herman more. "What do you think about the young'uns?" he asked, swallowing his final morsel and smacking his lips.

"Which one? There's three now. The two little lords, and the young Sain's oath man."

"Still not sure if I trust the oath man, despite the Seeress' assurances of his loyalty. But I meant the other two. Alkor's more like his father than he knows... him I can see leading men just like da'. Balzor, however, seems a force of nature. Both together maybe, could merge and become something great; hopefully we'll get the chance to see."

"Hmm," was all Herman could reply.

The two lads were young, to pass judgement so soon would usually be unfair; recently that was the least unfair thing in their lives. But Herman had felt something the other night, when he'd been inexorably dragged into the howl along with the rest of the guards. The lads were worth following - Alkor clearly becoming his father's son, and Balzor seeming a blaze that was only tempered by his friend. Either way, both were worth saving, which was why he and Sebastian were sat on a hill, waiting for the men they'd named enemy to arrive. They'd picked a side, time to let the chips fall where they may.

Sitting in thoughtful silence, Herman enjoyed the cool breeze kissing his face, so much stronger at the top of the hill than the bottom, where it was used as a buffer.

Usually, the strength of wind even at this time of year was enough to make a man shiver; but although the peak of the hill allowed the wind free rein, it also failed to stop the relentless sun that pierced the wispy clouds, which made the wind a welcome respite from the scorching heat.

He was enjoying the peaceful silence, taking in the wondrous views of the rolling land, birds tweeting their delight at the scene, until Sebastian started drumming a tune onto the sides of his pack, whistling quietly and glancing around impatiently. Herman remembered why he hated sentry duty with him, the man gets far too bored, far too quickly.

"Will you bloody stop that!" he snapped, spinning around to his friend.

"Stop what?" Sebastian asked innocently.

Herman growled and turned away, causing Sebastian to laugh mockingly, though he stopped for the moment. Less than a minute passed before he began drumming again; Herman snorted and threw his hands up in exasperation, standing and stepping away from him. Not even the pie could make him tolerate the aggravating man for a moment longer. Sebastian didn't cease his efforts, but at least the distance between them muted it. True to form, Sebastian began hitting it louder.

"You're taking the piss now, mate. Knock it off!"

"That's not me." Herman jumped out of his skin as the reply came from directly behind him, turning to face his friend, who was looking wide eyed at the road. Quiet for once, he raised his hand and pointed, Herman following the direction and realising the drumming was made by hooves and not by Sebastian. A dust cloud hovered in the air beyond the next batch of hills, confirming the fact despite them not having a visual.

"It has to be them," Sebastian murmured.

Herman nodded his agreement. "Time to go, I think."

Not needing further encouragement, Herman careened back down the hill, the peaceful morning shattered. His horse looked up expectantly, neighing in annoyance as he leapt up into the saddle and cut the rope rather than wasting time untying it. Sebastian did the same. They dug their heels in simultaneously, both horses diving forward in excitement at being given their head.

Herman leaned down flat to his horses back, whispering in its ear. "Faster,

faster." Understanding the urgency if not the words, the horse's muscles bunched tighter as it exerted itself. Herman heard Sebastian whoop at the side of him, the sound being snatched by the wind as they flew back to Saternac. *The man just can't be serious for one moment,* Herman thought, though he smiled at his friend's excitement at the tension of the chase.

After a while, he twisted in the saddle, breathing a sigh of relief when the earlier dust cloud wasn't visible from their lower vantage point, knowing Saternac wasn't further than a mile ahead. The weight in his chest lifted as he realised, they'd make it back with more than enough time to warn their friends. After that, the real work would begin.

Chapter 15

Cantering at the head of fifty of Krinar's redcloaks, Alnor did his best to look impassive as the familiar hills rolled by, not letting any of the sycophants see emotion, hidden behind the cold face of a warrior. Whispering had started behind hands when the prince had left, then elevated into sniggering as he attempted to give orders to the war band. He gritted his teeth at first, telling himself that they didn't know him, didn't yet believe in him. Two days that had lasted; after that he began remembering their faces. His order to spar every night wasn't well received, but aside from a few grumbles, it was abided by. Varnan helped in that regard; the man had clearly been sent by Krinar to ensure his loyalty, and the men double checked every order Alnor gave with furtive glances at the ugly man, proving that Varnan was really in charge, despite appearances.

For sparring however, Varnan seemed to agree wholeheartedly. Alnor was thankful to the man, a small glimmer of light breaking through his initial loathing. Maybe they could make it work, in time. But the order wasn't given to test Varnan, it was given to wipe the smirks off the faces of those who thought him a lesser man. In one session, he'd flattened three of the main culprits in quick succession, allowing their lackeys to see how easy it was to do so. The sly comments soon stopped after that, at least to his face. Sometimes, respect was only given by a show of strength, and the heir of the Sain line had more than enough strength to pass around. Even Varnan had nodded to him that morning, no trace of mockery on his face for once as he saddled his horse and mounted.

As they neared his home, he rode with his head held high, doing his best to exude the same confidence he had on his departure from Saternac. It seemed like forever ago that he and his father were laughing on this very same road where Alnor had felt like the previously absent bond was forming between them.

Blinking tears out of his eyes and hoping the men around him assumed it was due to the wind, he spurred his horse on past the memories. Totally ignoring the questioning look thrown his way by Varnan at the increase in speed, he dug his heels in, forcing the rest of the party to follow or be left behind. He couldn't seem to shake the homesick feeling that had solidified within him, leaving him wanting nothing more than to see his brother and the manor. Knowing he had to keep his brother detained soured the image of their reunion slightly, but the anticipation of banishing that peasant Balzor eliminated most of the bad thoughts, replacing them with relish.

In an ideal world, if the attack that he had recently found out Krinar had instigated on Saternac had succeeded, his brother would be in chains and Balzor, Dextri and that ilk would be dead, leaving Alnor to come in to save the day and be seen as the hero. Krinar's methods were drastic but, Alnor had to admit, they worked. It was with his head held high, blatantly ignoring the turmoil in his breast, that he rode towards his home, the liberating Sain returning as the hero.

The walls of his town came into view and a horn blown from Varnan's mouth announced their arrival, lest they be taken as enemies and the gates closed. No answering horn ensued, which wasn't surprising. *Saternac rely entirely on patrols, and their patrols are dead,* he thought with a grim smile.

They rounded the corner, the thick trees finally shifting to reveal the open gates and a sight Alnor didn't expect to see ever again: a flash of red hair dashing into the trees, followed closely by a tall figure who paused, looking at the approaching party with what Alnor could only describe as a Sain's defiance. He stifled a smile as his brother raised his arm towards them, drawing his sword with the same gesture and pointing it in a clear challenge in their direction - a challenge he didn't want. Losing any more family was *not* an option, but he'd come much too far to lose everything to his brother and his common pet.

Snarling, Alnor barked his orders. "Back forty men, dismount! Arm up and follow them into the woodlands, at the very most they could have mustered untrained villagers. Bring my brother back to me alive! The rest... enjoy yourselves."

Some of the men cackled as they dismounted, but all looked towards Varnan for confirmation after the order was given. Alnor growled at the obvious threat to his command but seeing Varnan nod allowed him to save face.

"Go!" he roared, feigning ignorance. Satisfaction flooded through him as they jerked to his order and broke into a run. "The rest of you, keep moving. I would be in my father's manor within the hour!"

He knew he sounded pompous, giving orders for others to do the dirty work whilst he relaxed at home, but he didn't care. Neither, it seemed, did the men, as they cheered at the thought and began the leisurely ride towards the town, one of the first times they hadn't questioned his orders instantly.

Spirits raised, he rode through the town gates with his reduced retinue, slowing as he reached the centre, dismounting and staring in dismay at the burnt husk that was his favourite pastime. Villagers paused in their clearing of the inn then resumed with barely a glance, stable boys appearing and taking their horses without delay. He surveyed the area, irritated at the lack of attention, before seeing a small boy he recognised, stood with a common beauty he did not. Looking the girl up and down, he shouted to the boy as he remembered his name: Oli, the baker's younger son.

"Oli, lad! What happened?"

"Alnor, is that you?" the boy replied, eyes narrowing in distaste.

Alnor curbed the annoyance that lanced through him, choosing the friendly route instead. "Aye lad, I'm back home. Where is my brother?"

Oli snorted, looking more angry than friendly. Alnor felt his stomach squirm in an almost furious response, struggling to keep his fake smile on his face as the boy replied.

"He knows what you've done, Alnor. He knows, and he's vengeful." Alnor's blood ran cold, but still the plastic smile stuck.

"Boy, I've done nothing but serve the realm and killed rebels. And you, pretty girl... I think I'd have remembered you around here before. What's your name?" The girl looked shyly away, not responding to the question as the young lad snorted again at his attempt at flirting.

"What, Oli?" Alnor snapped, losing his patience. Oli laughed in evident pleasure.

"Barking up the wrong tree, Alnor. Balzor will cut your throat if you try." Wide-eyed, the girl frantically kicked Oli in the calf, causing the boy to furiously turn, ready for a retort until he saw the expression on her face. Making the connection, Alnor smiled darkly.

"So, you're dear to the peasant boy, are you? I think you'd better come with us..." The girl began to dart away between the houses. To Alnor's great pleasure, Varnan anticipated the escape, clubbing her down heavily and dragging her back to her feet, dazed.

"Excellent" Alnor stated happily. "This way the family reunion will be inevitable." Men around him laughed, delighted at the display of cruelty Alnor had given them. The sound resonated within him as an acceptance. He took the girl's arm from Varnan and half dragged her towards the manor. Balzor would come to him if he survived, or his girl would suffer the consequences; nothing would stop his rise.

*****

Branches whipped his bare face as he darted around the massive trunks that support-ed them. Keeping his eyes half closed to avoid those grasping tendrils of wood, Balzor risked a glance over his shoulder. Aside from Alkor being close behind, he could see figures doing their best to follow them through the undergrowth. He smiled ferally. Let them come, they were ready.

They passed the first tree with a chunk of bark scraped away, the marker they had to follow, as though they needed directions. The brothers had grown up in these woods, knew every tree like family; they'd boasted it for years, but the confidence with which they dashed between the trees confirmed that it wasn't just bluster. Balzor passed the second marker and slowed, knowing they'd easily outpaced the traitors. It wouldn't do to lose them in the trees, all their hard work undone because they'd been *too* good at fleeing. Alkor almost barrelled into him, stopping just in time and looking in alarm.

"Move, brother!" he hissed, trying to shove him back into action.

"Wait! Let them get closer, we're going too fast."

Alkor paused, seeing the wisdom in the comment but also looking over his shoulder at the advancing figures. "Maybe not stand still and make it obvious though, eh?" he said, breaking into a leisurely jog and pulling ahead of Balzor.

Sighing, he set off after his friend, surprised that he didn't feel any fear at being pursued. Every day he'd thought of his cowardly feelings, worried they'd surface at the wrong time and render him useless. But the ceasing of his horrific nightmares had seemingly eliminated his fear, bringing him a weightlessness he'd never had before. He laughed aloud as he danced over the roots, getting a quizzical glance from Alkor to which he returned a grin. Alkor shook his head at him whilst rolling his eyes, passing the final marker and breaking through into the clearing they'd designated as their battle-field.

Finally, Balzor's heart began to thump, sweat erupting on his brow as he saw the line of shields, the huge form of Dextri in the centre, bulwark of the Annarites. They reached the line, men parting to let them through before closing again with an audible clack. Though they were adequate fighters, both lads hadn't trained enough in the shield wall to be trusted, didn't yet have the strength of the fully grown men in front of them.

Svein and Lortmund, despite having the strength to rival Dextri, stayed behind the wall with their huge hammers, imitating the tactic from the night of the attack, poised and ready to crush heads from their slightly higher vantage point. Balzor knew the village lads were behind them, hidden by the mound of dirt made from the pits; he felt happier knowing they were at his back, a surprise for the men chasing them.

Seconds passed, though it felt like an eternity. Men stamped and shifted impatiently, the only indication of the nerves that riddled the warriors. Feeling a nudge in his back, Balzor was gently pushed forward . As he turned in confusion, he saw a small, hooded figure walk up to Svein, pulling her hood down to reveal a surprisingly gentle face for the situation.

"Stay safe, big man. It'd be a shame if you died before we could... get to know each other," she said, standing on her tiptoes to kiss Svein on the cheek, who blushed furiously as she walked away.

"Was that..." Balzor began.

"Mariak, aye lad," Lortmund said with a smirk. "Seems her and my boy fancy each other."

The men around them chuckled softly, the tension seeming to leak from them as the mirth took over. Svein growled at his father, but said nothing, standing in silence with his face a disturbing red that Balzor rarely saw on his friend outside of the forge. The laughter was cut short, however, when the chasing men finally penetrated the treeline, stopping at the wall of shields in front of them. Unlike the Kerazar, these men were men of Annar, knowing the shield wall just as well as the guards did. They waited until enough of their number joined them and locked their own shields together, looking formidable with almost twice the numbers of the Sain guard. Dextri didn't even flinch at the challenge, lowering his shield and stepping forward from the wall.

"Which one of you wants to die first?" he called, throwing his arms wide and leaving an inviting target. The men in front of him were too well trained to respond to such an obvious bait, instead walking forward cautiously, their wall impenetrable.

"Worth a try," he mumbled, backing towards the Annarites again before re-joining the wall. He then began to bang his sword on to the rim of his shield, Livius immediately following suit and the others joining moments after, raising the clearing in a cacophony that sent animals scurrying from their hideaways and birds erupting from the trees. Balzor felt a spark ignite in his blood, his pulse quickening in anticipation as he saw the men that had come to kill him advance unflinchingly. Then as a small crack burst through the sound of the bangs, he smiled.

Advancing men suddenly disappeared beneath the ground, blood curdling screams emitted from the previously dug pits, as the stakes pierced flesh and ended lives. Shock registered on their comrades' faces, turning quickly to fury at the deception as they passed between the pits in the thin paths that Balzor and Alkor had recently traversed in their escape. Shields hung loosely on their arms as they stepped tentatively now, testing the ground beneath each step for any more hidden traps, not realising they were inviting more pain.

"NOW!" Dextri bellowed.

Balzor heard the crunch of dirt behind him, the thrumming of arrows instantly following. If they'd had more archers, the fight would've been over right there. Two men dropped, their heads rocking back in an explosion of gore as arrows found their marks. Another got his shield up just in time, the arrow ricocheting off its rim and careening into the bicep of the man behind, causing him to howl in pain but put up his own shield in response, grim eyes peeking over the top, promising murder. Three more harmlessly skittered across the shields of men who were now prepared, then the barrage stopped. A broken line of men was left, silence enveloped the area as both groups surveyed the ground in front of them, assessing the threat. That silence was broken by a single word uttered by Dextri.

"Advance!"

Already formed up, the guard stepped in unison towards the disarrayed traitors, panic in their eyes as they tried their best to create a wall quickly. They knew if the guards hit them now, they were finished. Knowing this, the guards increased their pace, slowing just short of a jog to ensure their line remained firm - frantic movements being the reaction of the men in front, clicking shields together with the utmost haste.

With seconds to spare, a respectable wall formed in front of them, which they crashed into with a mighty crack. Desperate heaving ensued, neither side giving or gaining an inch from their efforts. Though the traitors had more men, the wall was hastily formed, the pits behind stopping the extra men from adding their weight to it.

"Lortmund!" Livius roared strain evident in his voice.

Balzor felt a hand on his shoulder and stepped back from his position, where he'd been stood ready to fill a gap if one appeared. Silver streaks were appearing between the opposite shields, giving reason to Livius' panic as a red line appeared on his arm.

"Seax's" Lortmund growled angrily, as he and Svein stepped into the gap made by Balzor and Alkor.

Balzor's blood ran cold at the word, knowing the guards were outclassed in the wall without a seax of their own. "Fucking hate those oversized knives."

Though the guards had their swords, the sheer length of them made for awkward stabbing in the shield wall — hence the seax, a short, thick blade made for quick stabs and puncturing through armour - something the guard had anticipated and prepared for.

Lortmund and Svein raised their huge hammers above their heads and bellowed an incoherent war cry, bringing them down with strength only borne from the forge. *And the mountain clan heritage,* Balzor thought wryly. His stray thought was banished as the two giants smashed their hammers onto shoulders of men who could do nothing but stare, terrified, at their retribution bearing down upon them. Two men were pulverised in seconds, Svein and Lortmund stepping back as those silver serpents licked out, attempting to pierce arms that had presented themselves. Free of men in front of him, Livius stepped into the gap and stabbed to his right, trusting his shield and Dextri on his left side to protect him there. Balzor saw Livius' blade come up red, then he was back into the wall.

"Three down, only another thirty or so to go!" Livius cackled manically.

"You enjoy this too much" Ingvar spat good naturedly at his friend. The fact that banter was thrown around at a time like this bemused Balzor. It was better to make light of a life and death situation, it seemed. Wary now of the hammers, the attackers renewed their assault, using their numbers to start to envelop the guards rather than push through them.

"If they get round our flanks, we're finished," Balzor muttered under his breath. Upon hearing this, Alkor leapt into action, dragging Balzor towards the right flank and drawing his sword.

"Svein, Lortmund, take the left!"

Without questioning the young Sain's order, the two blacksmiths rushed to the opposite flank, swinging their hammers madly at the men who were eagerly beginning to wrap around. Balzor and Alkor, however, had no way to keep them at bay. Keeping their shields up, men advanced on the two younger warriors, seeing their youth as an easy way to get their kills.

"Balzor, remember Dextri," Alkor whispered, barely audible over the clamour going on around them. Balzor nodded imperceptibly and drew his blade, wishing he had a shield. The fact he probably would have been run down before he even reached the clearing with the extra weight barely crossed his mind. He began to feint to the left, swinging his blade madly to look inexperienced to the warrior and yelling wildly. The men grinned above his shield, taking the blow easily on its boss and stepping forward for a killing blow on the unsteady Balzor. Just before the man's blade pierced his belly, Balzor used his momentum to twist off his left foot, the lunge missing him narrowly and causing the man to overextend. His grin vanished, replaced by a snarl as he tried to counter Balzor's swing, just catching it with his blade before it chopped into his neck. Moments later, his snarl turned into a cry of agony as Alkor drove his sword through his back into his heart, twisting and ripping the blade out, letting him fall disdainfully to the ground.

"Traitor!" he spat, kicking the man and pillaging his shield, turning to join the wall to help.

"Alkor!" Balzor shouted, but he was too late.

A man crashed his shield into Alkor, sending him sprawling to the floor. Balzor leapt to his friend's aid, but he didn't realise that Alkor wasn't the man's target. Free from opposition, he sliced his sword into the leg of the outside man of the wall, dropping him to his knees. The man in front roared in triumph and smashed his seax through the fallen guard's teeth, stepping into the gap made and turning inwards towards the next man in: Herman.

Seeing the threat, Herman barked an order loudly, and the guards began to fold in amongst themselves. *Bending rather than breaking,* Balzor realised as he dragged Alkor to his feet before charging to bolster Herman, who was now facing two opponents. He saw a flicker in the treeline to his right and felt a small glimmer of hope in his breast as he traded blows furiously with the man in front, Alkor doing his best to use his stolen shield to defend. This mode of fighting couldn't last forever, he knew. Gritting his teeth, he fought on.

*****

Muscles burned in Svein's arms as he sent his hammer crashing in to the shield of a gaunt-faced man trying his luck. He'd lost count of how many times he'd lifted it that day, but it felt like more than he ever had done in the forge - although in the forge he'd never had the satisfaction of seeing smaller men fly back six feet each time it connected. Glancing at his father, he saw an expression that he'd never thought to see amid so much death and carnage: an expression of joy. Dancing back from the punch of a shield, his father barked a laugh into the man's face before rapidly bringing his hammer down to crunch into his overextended arm, making him scream and scatter back with shattered bones.

"Gods I've missed this! Takes me back to the good old days with your uncle Torval. Granted that was with an axe not a hammer, but still," he said wistfully, seeming to completely ignore the situation in front of him as he reminisced.

"I thought you said the good days were after you met mam," Svein grunted, sending yet another strike at a shield. He knew if he fought like his father, the other man would win; he'd had no warrior training at all, just relying on his brute strength to keep them at bay. His father seemed to thrive on it, revealing a side to him that Svein had never seen before, a much more lethal side.

"Aye lad, the good times did. Doesn't mean to say I didn't love the times before, aside from the rage."

Time for talking ceased as more men stepping forward stopping Svein enquiring further. He'd heard about his father's warrior rages from his mam, something about mountain clan blood and heritage. He knew it was why his father had left, but that was all he'd been told. Every probe got rebuffed curtly by both his parents, not for the lack of trying. Looking at him now, Svein couldn't see any of the famed fury, his father's booming laughter echoing around the clearing as he kept the men at bay with ease.

He saw two men edging around the side of his father, laughter faltering as it dawned on Lortmund he was being overwhelmed. With a roar, Svein dove at the men, choosing this time to punch the hammer towards them instead of swinging like a madman. A sickening crunch was his reward as his face caved in on itself before the man could react, dropping like a puppet with its strings cut. Shock rooted him to the spot as he realised that he'd seen the light leave the man's eyes before he died. His comrade screamed and dove at him, bulling him to the ground with his shield and pulling back his blade. Svein looked defiantly into the man's eyes, determined to show he wasn't afraid, when a knife sank into the very eyes he was looking into.

Taking a moment to savour the fact he wasn't dead, he turned and scanned behind him, seeing a small outline leaning against a tree. He nodded his thanks, Mariak waving as sarcastically as she could manage before disappearing back into the foliage. God's the woman infuriated him!

Alarm lanced through him as he heard the bellow of a wounded animal, spinning quickly and seeing one of those seax's rip from his father's bicep, leaving his arm limp. He burst into motion, rushing to his father's aid as two men converged on him; he was struggling to lift the hammer properly with just one arm. Everything seemed to slow, Svein watching horrified as his father's guard was knocked aside before being stabbed in the gut savagely, the man ripping out his blade and kicking his father down.

A mist descended over Svein's vision as he charged with an agonised cry, the man looking up in time to see the massive hammer smash into his face, lifting him off his feet and knocking down two others beside him. Unable to control his fury, he waded into the press of men, using every part of his body to kick and headbutt the attackers, fracturing the outside wing and sending a ripple along their line. With a roar from the Sain guards, they forced the attackers back a step, the first real movement since the walls met. Svein didn't see what was happening around him, didn't care. All he could see was red.

*****

Balzor desperately parried a blow aimed at Alkor's neck, being forced back a step by the strength of the blow and struggled to regain his feet. His arms felt like lead, but none had died around him; just the brutal forcing of shields with the odd attempt at flanking was the main action happening.

Hearing a mighty bellow from the opposite wing, he took a vital second to glance over his shoulder, seeing nothing but almost *feeling* a change in the fight. The wings that were inevitably wrapping around their wall began to crunch in, Balzor beginning to go on the offensive, seeing fear in his opponent's eyes. One of them darted forward attempting to throw him back, but he leapt backwards and deflected the blow easily, exchanging a flurry of hits before he fell back behind his shield and into the wall.

Balzor flinched as blood suddenly flecked his face, confused until he saw the feather protruding from his opponent's neck. Coupled with whatever caused the shudder in the attackers, the fight began to turn as the traitors were surrounded; no man could fight with arrows pouring into their back.

Stepping over the body of the shot man, Balzor wrenched the shield from his cold arms and heaved it onto his own, joining the end of the wall and forcing the enemies back. Terrified of the archers behind and unable to bring their shields to bear, the men began to break, Sain guards yelling in triumph and stepping forward another step before the rout began.

The first men to run clearly forgot about the pits behind them, falling to a gruesome death of impalement. Most kept their heads, a testament to their mettle as they formed a square of shields and retreated step by step, warily dodging the vicious pits and the biting of the arrows with quick ducks behind the shields.

Suddenly, one corner of the wall fractured, a monolithic being smashing into it with a savage abandon, knocking the careful retreat into turmoil. With that one corner, the rest seemed to lose the control that they'd held, breaking from the square and turning to face the newer, more dangerous threat.

Blinking in surprise, Balzor realised that it was his friend with his hammer ripping his way into the attackers, barely flinching when blades pierced his flesh or hits connected with his face. Decorum vanishing, Balzor yelled and charged at the men, thoughts of tactics vanishing in the moment as it dawned on him that his friend would die without help. He knew without looking that the men behind would follow, with the certainty that was borne from a deep-rooted connection with them.

First, he heard Dextri and Alkor roar, and their feet begin to pound, Livius, Devar and Ingvar a breath behind; Herman bellowed wordlessly and followed, which prompted the avalanche of guards to throw caution to the wind and let their souls expunge the pent-up tension that the shield wall had contained.

Wind rushing past his ears, Balzor focused on the man in front who'd glanced fearfully behind, and half turned to defend himself. Barely pausing, he dipped his shoulder behind his own shield and rammed the man, throwing him off balance. Slashing right, he narrowly missed slicing a chunk out of a face, pushing left with his shield and opening a very small gap, which he deftly stepped into. Before they could react and force him out, Dextri collided with them and threw them further back, his more precise strikes connecting, cutting down two men in quick succession in a fountain of blood. From there it was a massacre.

The attackers broke completely, attempting to flee in all directions and discarding weapons along the way. Arrows hammered the now open bodies of the men, the second arrow already in the air before the first release had sunk into flesh. Every village lad knew how to hunt, shooting two arrows in a short time was the difference between felling a deer in the moment, or tracking it for miles as it eventually bleeds out. None of them had shot at a man before, but the practice wasn't much different.

Like chickens free of their cage, the men bounced from danger to danger, their numbers whittling from either sword thrusts or arrow points. Balzor found himself with a free moment in the carnage after the man in front was gutted by Herman and looked for Svein, finding his friend on one knee panting furiously. As he approached, Svein rose with a wild look in his eyes, hefting his hammer towards him until registering the enemy wasn't there, most of them lying dead or wounded by the giant, pulverised by his hammer. Losing that wild look, Svein became the friend that Balzor had known; with its loss, came a look of pain.

"Da," was all he said, dropping his hammer and rushing back to where the wall had broken. Balzor's stomach lurched as he saw his meaning, Svein dropping to his knees and cradling Lortmund's head on his lap, sobbing softly. Balzor approached slowly, wanting to be there for his friend but not wanting to intrude on the privacy of the moment. He stood at a respectful distance; eyes alert for any rogue attackers that fancied trying their luck.

A few seconds passed and loud cheering erupted behind him, making him jump and turn to look. Sain guards were howling in triumph, the sound hollow in the face of his friend's sorrow. Not wanting Svein to be alone any longer, Balzor clapped his hand on his shoulder; one look at Lortmund's wound and shallow breath gave him all the information he needed to understand the situation. Choking on his own misery, Svein's tears unashamedly cascaded on to his father's forehead which he wiped away with a tenderness that belied his size. Lortmund lay there with open eyes, looking at his son with a small smile on his blood-flecked lips.

"Son..." he whispered before breaking into a savage round of coughing.

"Save your breath, da. We'll get you to the Seeress, she can sort this. Won't we Balzor?"

Balzor opened his mouth to agree with his friend, hope blossoming in his chest at the thought of the huge blacksmith surviving the mortal wound. One look from Lortmund persuaded him otherwise.

"Balzor?" Svein said, turning with confusion in his eyes.

"It's too late, lad. I'll take my final breath before the woman even gets out of Saternac. There's something you need to do after - "

"No! Da - you're going to survive this. Tell him Balzor! Fucking tell him!" Svein's screaming alerted the nearby guards, who judging by Balzor's quick head count, had only lost one of their number so far.

Dextri was there first, Livius nearly as fast. The rest piled up quickly, Alkor being the last to arrive with a questioning look on his face.

"What's all the... oh," he said, the final word more of a squeak as his breath caught in his throat. He fell to his knees next to Svein. "No, it can't be." One look was all it took for anyone, even a child, to know that Alkor's denial was futile. Svein turned angrily to him.

"He isn't going to die! Why is everybody so sure he is?!" he screamed again but was cut short by his father's gentle hand turning his furious face back to look in to his eyes. His voice subsided as he wept uncontrollably. Balzor looked away from the scene, his own vision blurry as tears clouded his eyes. He blinked them away rather than be shamed in front of the guard but saw most of them with their own sorrow clear on their faces, Dextri most of all. Tracks ran through his dirt-stained cheeks, Livius' arm around Dextri's shoulders as he cried. Barely a sound permeated the battleground, even the groans of the wounded fell silent, dropping into the clutching hands of death.

"There's something... you need to do," Lortmund forced out of his unwilling throat. Svein shook his head, his eyelashes parting with their payload once more at the movement.

"Go... to my brother. If you don't... it will consume you."

"Consume? Da, conserve your strength, you're not making any sense."

"Go to him... before... it's too late," Lortmund rasped, his eyes beginning to flutter as his body began to succumb to its wounds.

"Da, stay with me please!" Svein begged, but begging never worked with Ezimat's reapers.

A rattling sigh was the last noise he heard from his father, and Svein roared his agony to the skies. Men around him grimaced at the raw pain lacing the sound. Balzor had never felt grief from the death of his own parents, having never known any different; he'd felt a twinge of pain as he heard of Aldred's demise, which still hurt now. But this, this was pain of the sort that Balzor had never seen before, even including the night of the original attack. It resonated within him, including him in it whilst also keeping him separate simultaneously.

As the roar faded into the depths of the woodland, the enveloping silence resumed. Even the birdsong seemed muffled somehow, as though the canopy was doing its best to give them the privacy; they deserved to mourn the passing of a great man. Alkor remained on his knees next to Svein, staying within his peripheral vision, so his friend knew he was there.

Svein, however, was in his own world of grief. His massive frame was shaking, though no sound emitted from him; he still clasped his father's hand as though strength alone could bring him back from the brink. Dextri's eyes had ceased their streaming, though they remained red-rimmed and glistening, boring into the lifeless eyes of one of his oldest friends.

Gritting his teeth, Balzor cleared his throat, shattering the moment and causing many of the men to start slightly. As if on cue, the sound took on a new volume, the birds piercing the leaves with their singing once again, sounding strange with the current mood.

"We should get to the village. Livius, Sebastian, use the traitor's weapons to hack a couple of saplings down and lash your cloaks to it, we'll stretcher Lortmund home with the honour guard of a king," Dextri said, voice sounding weak even to Balzor.

"I'll carry him alone," Svein said.

"Lad, even I'd struggle with..."

"I'll CARRY him!" Svein growled, and that was that.

Svein stood, grunting with the effort as he heaved his father into his arms, carrying the huge man like a babe. If the situation was different, Balzor could have laughed at the sight; all he felt at that moment was a wave of pity mixed with pride in his friend. Sebastian and Livius still felled two saplings, using the makeshift stretcher to carry the body of the guard who'd died, covering his destroyed image with a red cloak stolen from the attackers. Mariak stepped close to Svein, touching his arm and murmuring something the rest couldn't hear. Svein didn't respond, and she walked away with a sigh.

"What of the enemy dead?" Alkor asked as he rose from the ground.

"Leave them to rot," Dextri snarled, which the men were more than happy to do.

Marching back, there was no talk. Every few minutes, Dextri offered to share the load with Svein, but was promptly rebuffed. Every man there looked on in awe as the young blacksmith performed a feat of strength that none of them could half match, without seeming to notice he was doing so.

The crackle of twigs and laboured breathing were the loudest sounds that accompanied the party as Saternac came into view. No guards were on the walls. They shambled through the open gates, no welcome or parade to herald their victory. The archers murmured a goodbye before slipping off to see their families, most of the guard asking leave to do the same, which Dextri granted, albeit with restrictions.

"Ten minutes, let them know you're safe. Alnor wasn't amongst the dead, which means he's still here, probably at the manor. Until we know how many he has with him; we stay as one. Ten minutes!"

A chorus of "Ayes," and "Yes sir," greeted the words, the men rushing to find their loved ones to make sure they were safe. No-one knew if the attackers had hit the village first, despite Alkor's assurances that they'd been followed instantly, and worry had been a constant companion for them all on the way back. Suddenly, a sound Balzor had been dreading hit his eardrums: the wailing of a widow. Martha waddled towards her son, screaming hysterically at the sight of Lortmund's lifeless form, her pregnancy forcing her to slow her speed, though it certainly didn't lower her volume. As she got close, Svein fell to his knees, his arms somehow not giving out as he placed his father reverently on the ground; his mother beat her fists against her dead husband's chest in defiance.

"You promised you'd come back, Lortmund. You promised, you promised!" she kept shouting repeatedly, until finally Svein grabbed her hands gently. She fell into her son's embrace and they cried and hugged each other tightly. Balzor's breath caught in his throat yet again, and before the tears came, he turned and walked away. He had no direction in mind, but instinctively his feet began to carry him towards the wooded path that led to the one person who he knew could make him feel better. A small pattering of feet came from the street in front, Oli skidding around the corner and calling Balzor's name repeatedly.

"Not now Oli, I'm really not in the mood," Balzor sighed.

"He has her!" Oli yelped, grabbing Balzor's hand and forcing him to stop.

"Who has who, Oli? Seriously I can't be bothered with your games right now."

"Alnor! He has her!"

"Oli, what are you..." Then he knew.

His stomach sank, an ice-cold rock dropping from his chest and sending shivers through his whole body. *Aria.* Without any hesitation, he turned away from the woodland path and began sprinting faster than ever before towards the manor, his heart pounding and ears ringing, either anticipation or fear building in his belly, filling him with a huge amount of energy that he didn't think he possessed.

Just as he was about to run into the square, a figure stepped out before him. At that speed he couldn't even dodge, let alone stop; he crashed into him full pelt and fell bodily to the floor.

"For fuck's sake, Balzor, what's gotten into you?!" Alkor yelled as he struggled to his feet, massaging his leg where he'd fallen. Leaping up, Balzor tried to resume his run, but Alkor caught his arm in a grip. He growled, trying to rip his arm away and keep running.

"What is it?"

"He's fucking taken her, Alkor. Your brother has Aria!"

Balzor saw the colour drain from Alkor's faced as he released him, allowing him to run again. Hearing the heavier footfalls behind him, he glanced behind and saw Alkor keeping pace. He'd known Alkor wouldn't let him go alone, and a small pinprick of gratitude broke through his fear at the loyalty he felt he didn't deserve.

"Oli, tell Dextri!" he heard Alkor call behind him followed by the lad's shrill assent. Help would arrive eventually. *The question is,* Balzor thought worriedly, *Will it come too late?*

✶✶✶✶✶

Closing the door to her cottage, Osri let out an explosive breath of anger. She'd wanted so hard to rip that Alnor's intestines from his throat when she'd seen him take her granddaughter but had forced herself to stop. Once her mind was set on a course, she'd been damned if she'd let some idiot Sain change it by being rougher than expected.

Clicking her fingers, she lit the fire, using her other hand to float over the kettle to heat it above the flames, grumbling as she did so. She sat down heavily on one of her chairs, grimacing as the wood hurt the bones at the base of her back.

"If I could go back again, I'd invest in some bloody better chairs," she muttered sullenly, before barking a laugh. *Talking to oneself, a sign of madness even at the end,* she thought.

A whistle alerted her that the water was boiled, a comforting sound she'd heard a million times in her lifetime, all the sweeter now that it would be the last. Choosing to not use her power, she poured herself a cup, dropping a sugar cube into the boiling tea and stirring contentedly, before placing the pot to the side. She looked at the unopened letter on the table, knowing Aria would find it and know why it had to be this way. It wasn't just her granddaughter she was saving.

Scowling at the uncomfortable chairs, she walked slowly over to the window, breathing in the scents of her herbs that sat proudly on the windowsill, lording over their brethren flowers in the garden. She stroked the leaves, disturbing a bumblebee which flew into action at her touch and directed itself towards the flowers instead. Watching it work, she sighed at the beauty of nature, knowing it was the simple things that made the world go round. The bee wouldn't care when she passed, aside from the fact that the idiot girl would probably forget to water the flowers for a while. Osri smiled, a warm feeling sat nicely on her chest, part tea, part love. If there was anything that she'd give it all up for, it was Aria. She knew this was the only way the fate Aria was destined for would come to fruition. Osri couldn't intervene.

She rested her arms against the windowsill, sipping at her drink and watching the bee work, and waited for it all to end.

Chapter 16

Alnor sat at the head of the table in the Sain manor, feet up as he picked at his teeth with the remainder of a chicken bone. *My manor now,* he thought, a pang of sadness and shame interrupting his feeling of euphoria. He still hadn't shaken the burden of guilt from his shoulders, and was beginning to feel like he never would; with his new-found power came a heavy heart, it seemed. But it was as though it kept rolling like a snowball, gaining momentum and size until there was nothing he could do but go along with it. The unconscious girl by the door was testament to that. One bad choice led to another, at least this one would bring him within arm's reach of the peasant boy – if he lived, that is.

Varnan had taken too much pleasure in hitting the girl though, Alnor thought with disgust. Gods but he hated that ugly man. Cruelty seemed to be the currency of Varnan and the others, anything less would make him seem weak; he could make his apologies later, do what was necessary now. Didn't mean he had to like it. As if hearing his thoughts, the girl groaned and her eyes flickered open, switching from confusion to alarm in moments. She rocketed up, breaking for the door without a moment's pause. Alnor had to admit, he was impressed with her speed considering she most definitely had a concussion. Varnan, however, was quicker. Grabbing her arm, he threw her bodily to the floor, turning to face her as she rose, eyes blazing. He tutted, wagging his finger at her like somebody would to a child.

"Now, now lass. Let's not add a blackened eye to that lump on your head, eh?" Varnan taunted, getting a snarl from her as she looked for an alternate exit, frantic movements making the rest of the men laugh.

"Leave her be, Varnan," Alnor called, the man backing down with a grin, hands in the air in surrender. "Girl, sit and eat. We may be here a while."

She frowned at him, a stubborn set to her face as she shook her head with a thinning of her lips. Alnor shrugged.

"Suit yourself, then."

She scowled at the response, before dragging a spare chair away from the table, sitting separate from the rest of them. Men cackled again, hooting and jeering at her. This time, she smiled back, though without humour.

"Keep laughing you fools. You've just kidnapped an apprentice to the Seeress. Do you think you'll still be laughing when she finds out?"

Laughter stopped instantly, the men looking uneasily between each other and shifting in their seats. Even Alnor felt a superstitious shiver crawl down his spine, despite having spoken to the Seeress on many occasions. People who were chosen by the Gods weren't to be trifled with, a notion most agreed with, even Kerazar. Her smile became a full grin now, seeing the discomfort she'd caused with just a single comment. Knowing he had to salvage the situation, Alnor put on his best disarming smile.

"There's no need for that, Aria. I can call you Aria, can't I?" She remained stony faced, which irritated Alnor no end, though he kept it hidden, continuing as though she'd responded. "Excellent! You're just here to ensure your boyfriend doesn't do anything stupid, when the time comes. My men have orders to keep them both alive; it's only the men who have led them astray that have to die, the traitors."

Well, Balzor I only want alive so I can kill him myself, but she doesn't have to know that, Alnor thought with a grim smile. The girl's eyes narrowed, seeing a change in the flattering look as the thought flickered through his head.

"Everyone here knows the truth, Alnor. You half-severed the General's head in a fit of childish rage, now you've come back to assume his mantle on your unworthy shoulders. The town knows of your betrayal, the guard knows, but most of all... Alkor knows. The only stupid thing him and Balzor could do, is leave you alive!" she hissed.

Alnor felt his smile slip from his face, heat diffusing across his cheeks as he struggled to keep his rearing anger in check. He failed.

"Now listen here, you little witch. My brother will fall into line without your peasant boy to whisper his poison in his ear. As for that runt, he'll be dead before the sun rises on the morrow; you'd do well to cut your losses and act like he never existed."

As the last word left his mouth, glasses around the table shattered, including the one in his hand. Shards of the cups stuck into the hands of the men holding them, almost everyone at the table leaping to their feet with exclamations of surprise and more than a little fear on their faces. Circles were drawn on foreheads to avoid the ire of Exat at the mistreatment of one of his chosen, but Alnor's eyes barely left Aria, despite the blood dripping from his fingertips.

She'd closed her own eyes, taking long, deep breaths and grabbing fistfuls of her shirt. One final deep breath and she seemed to relax, her eyes re-opening to survey the room. He could have sworn she looked nervous, a thin sheen of sweat coating her forehead, catching all the stray, thin hairs in its grasp. When her gaze met his, she looked away quickly, the anger gone from her expression as she did her best to look nonchalant. This, more than anything, increased his curiosity more. *I wonder,* he thought.

There had always been rumours that some families of Seers had different abilities. Some could remember their prophecies, others could dive into the minds of others, eliminating the need for torture. But one rumour always seemed ridiculous to him, scoffed at by anyone he'd mentioned it to, even by his father. Without a thought to decorum, he strode across the still shocked room and grabbed the girl by her arm, wrenching her around to face him as she yelped with indignation.

"Could it be true?" he breathed as she struggled furiously. At his words she stopped and looked quizzically at him, as though he'd gone mad. He snorted. "You can't hide from me, girl. And everybody was *sure* that Seeresses couldn't use their abilities offensively."

Aria went white at the comment, trying to drag her arm free of his grip whilst attempting to laugh. "Have you any idea how *mad* you sound?"

The men sat quietly, sucking on cut fingers but watching the confrontation intently. They'd heard his words and her obvious attempt at ridicule; even Varnan – the only man to not be injured from the explosion - had lost his usual sneer as he leaned forward in his seat. The man never drank anything but water from his own waterskin.

"How does it work? Do you have to be angry? Threatened?" Alnor persisted, feeling his pulse quicken in anticipation. To be in control of his very own battle witch, the Seeress could send his name down through history; he couldn't let her slip through his fingers if he was correct. Backhanding Aria across the face, he kept his hold on her arm and roughly forced her back to face him. She cried out in shock, a red welt already visible.

"Tell me!" he yelled. Hearing a crash behind him, he spun quickly, his free hand dropping to his sword, drawing it in one fluid motion. He kept his iron grip on Aria's arm, who to Alnor's disgust was crying softly. The cause of the noise however, brought an evil grin to his face. *Finally,* he thought. Dragging Aria in front of him, he raised his sword to her throat, grinning even more at the response it elicited from the source of the door crashing open.

"Take your fucking hands off her."

★★★★★

Slowing to a jog now that the manor was in view, Balzor tried to calm his mind from the frenzy it had riled itself in to. He knew that going forward filled with rage would get him killed, though it was hard to stop it pulsing around his body.

A quick scan of the yard revealed no obvious signs of a trap, the lack of guards on the door a testament to Alnor's arrogance, or stupidity. With each booming heart-beat, it seemed his senses seemed to heighten, Alkor's footsteps behind him echoing loudly in his ears. He could've sworn he heard glass shatter from the manor, followed by muted cries of men. Frowning, he stopped suddenly, Alkor running past him for a step before halting and turning around with a questioning look.

"What?" he said.

"Did you hear that?" Balzor asked. Alkor looked at him quizzically, not even needing to speak this time to voice the question. Glass smashing? I think in the manor."

"The only glass windows are in the bedrooms, Balzor. No way you could have heard them breaking from here, even with the breeze blowing this way. You sure?"

Straining his ears, he listened attentively for a few more seconds, before shrug-ging his shoulders. "Must have been mistaken."

Alkor rolled his eyes and gestured to the trees that they'd just emerged from. "Maybe we hug the trees until we're closer, then sprint across the yard to the door. Less time to be seen that way. Alnor will have taken her to the hall, he'll want her close for leverage in case the men he sent don't capture us. Our advantage is that he has no idea they didn't succeed, or that they were defeated so spectacularly. We should use this to whittle whatever numbers he has left, wait outside the hall door then pick off whoever leaves before we make our move. All men have to piss eventually," he said, grinning sidelong at his friend, who managed a very half-hearted smile back.

Grin vanishing, Alkor clapped his hand on Balzor's shoulder. "Brother, we *will* get her back."

Taking a deep breath and steeling himself, Balzor nodded resolutely. They fad-ed back into the trees, using the trunks to hide from the enlightening grasp of the sun. In the end, they needn't have bothered; nobody even left the manor, let alone actively

303

looked for intruders. It was arrogance, Balzor decided - not stupidity - that led Alnor to decide against sentries. Here, he must consider himself the lord of the land - more men than the whittled down Sain guard, in the manor he grew up with, a hostage in hand. Balzor bared his teeth at the thought, loosening his sword in its scabbard, still sticky with blood and gore. He cursed himself for not wiping the blade down properly, totally unsheathing it and keeping it low to the ground, lest its glint attract unwanted attention.

A quick glance and a nod to Alkor sent them both sprinting across the grounds at breakneck speed, focusing only on reaching the main door before being spotted. Again, their caution wasn't needed. They reached the door, pressing their backs to the sides and catching their breath. They knew the hinges squealed; if they were going to get noticed, it would be now. Chest still heaving, Alkor looked nervously at Balzor, then wrenched the door open quickly. The expected shriek from the un-oiled metal echoed around the entrance hall, sending shivers through Balzor as the sound grated on his ears. Cringing, they waited with bated breath for the inevitable alarm. Seconds seemed like an eternity, but as it came close to a minute the lads sighed in relief at their luck, though both knew it wouldn't help them forever.

Choosing stealth over speed, they crept now through the hall, soft footfalls barely making a sound. This wasn't their first time sneaking in at the wrong time. Granted, in the past it was only to get an early meal out of Nerva, but the technique was still the same. As they passed the stairs and moved towards the feast hall doors they heard a sound, both spinning in alarm and levelling swords in the direction of the kitchen. Olsten froze, almost dropping the jugs of wine and fear registering in his eyes until he realised who it was in front of him.

"Fool boys! Almost had me shitting in my pants there. How are you here? Where are the rest?"

"Behind us, hopefully close. Olsten... he has Aria," Balzor replied, an edge of hysteria in his voice.

"I know lad, I've seen. So far, he's been civil, I've watered down their wine and keep going in on the pretence of refilling their cups. I'd have done something myself, but there's a few of 'em and only me and Nerva here. Please tell me you have a better plan than taking them on between the two of you?"

Alkor made to reply but froze as the sound of his brother's raised voice was heard from the door. "...have to be angry? Threatened?" Alnor said, voice rising with each word.

A loud slap came next, followed by the unmistakeable yelp of pain from a female throat. "TELL ME!"

Reaching for his friend, Alkor tried to stop him from what he knew Balzor would inevitably do, but it was too late. Balzor raised his leg and kicked the doors savagely, which swung open at speed, crashing into the walls with a bang.

"Take your fucking hands off her," he said coldly, his voice carrying across the now silent room.

Men unsheathed swords at the threat, then chuckled as they realised the danger was less than they'd initially thought. Red cloaks were strewn untidily over the backs of chairs that had just been knocked over from a hasty rise. Shards of glass dotted the floor, patches of wine decorating around them. A particularly ugly man even had the audacity to sit back down at the table. Something about him niggled in the back of Alkor's brain, a familiarity that brought him to instantly dislike him, for no apparent reason - aside from the invading of his family home.

His eyes were drawn back to his brother, who to Alkor's horror had a blade pressed against Aria's throat and was smiling evilly. *Something's changed with him. He was always a dick but was never inherently bad like this,* Alkor thought.

Looking at his brother, he felt an odd wave of love for him mixed with loathing. Strange that you could still love the man who killed your father. His thought process was cut short by the voice of the very man he was inspecting.

"Finally! If it isn't my brother and his pet peasant. My men didn't take too long catching you then; I expected to be waiting much longer than this."

Balzor's nostrils flared and made to move forward, not bothering to respond. The red cloaks that stood between them and Alnor brought the tips of their swords up, a bristling wall of pointed steel that stopped any passage.

"Tut tut, peasant boy. And here I was thinking you might've learned some manners in my time away. I suggest you put away your blade and kneel to your new lord."

*****

305

Snarling, Balzor stepped forward, intent on breaking his way through the spiky wall, despite the odds. The men tensed as he got closer, adopting more defensive stances in preparation. In the end, a sharp cry and the contrast of red on soft skin stopped Balzor in his tracks quicker than the steel ever could. Alnor had pressed his own blade to Aria's throat, drawing a single drop of blood that rolled down her neck like a teardrop, leaving a crimson line. But, despite the pulsing feeling in his head magnifying to an almost unbearable level, Balzor stopped. He watched the droplet until it soaked into the material of her shirt, then looked up into her eyes. Seeing her fear barely masked in them only heightened his helpless fury, but he knew he was rooted to the spot.

"That's it, peasant boy. At last, you've learnt restraint... Now... KNEEL" Alnor screamed, spittle flying from his mouth, giving him a deranged look. Balzor's eyes shifted from Aria's and met Alnor's. Doing his very best to convey the depth of his hatred, he bared his teeth and forced himself to kneel, ignoring the jeers from the red cloaks at the act.

"You too, brother," he added, much calmer but still commanding.

To his credit, Alkor just snorted and made an exaggerated flourish as he knelt; a small victory for Balzor as he saw the anger flash through Alnor.

"Disarm them, then reprimand the idiots who let two potential enemies enter with their weapons!" Alnor ordered, his men moving forward to take their swords disdainfully and throwing them to the side.

Balzor chuckled dryly and without mirth. "You really are a total idiot, aren't you Alnor? Trained men wouldn't allow us in with weapons, we killed them all before coming here to kill you." The jeers and laughter stopped at that, although some men snorted contemptuously. Alnor however stood open mouthed, his sword now drooping as he struggled to comprehend this new shock.

"You lie," the ugly man said softly from his seat, menace lacing his words. "Any guards left here were killed weeks ago, and no other patrols are around."

A sharp intake of breath behind him caused Balzor to turn his head to find the source, puzzled as he saw a realisation dawning on Alkor's face.

"I knew I recognised something about you! Tell me, who was Petra to you?" Alkor exclaimed. Turning back, Balzor admitted he could see some resemblance, but never enough to see the connection. Especially in his current state, blood pounding in his head and the tension amplifying his senses more than seemed humanly possible. The mixture of euphoria and rage was a strange concoction, not even attempting to stay separate but merging into one solid flow of energy that pulsed around his veins. The ugly man paled at the comment and stood.

"Was, boy? Why do you say was?"

The room was deathly silent now, everybody feeling the threat in the man's words as he walked slowly towards Alkor. Desperate to divert the attention, Balzor took over.

"Was usually means past tense. You know, when somebody dies in an easily thwarted attack on a town?" he said as casually as he could.

The man's head snapped round, fury bringing a red flush to his neck as his slow walk escalated and he backhanded Balzor across the face. With a grunt, Balzor fell to the floor, hearing the familiar sound of the sword leaving a scabbard and preparing to launch himself backwards. But help came from the most unlikely place.

"Varnan, calm yourself! The peasant is trying to cloud your judgement, do not fall to his deception. If what he says is true, I swear I'll let you have him, but not right now. I've got a different type of torture in mind first," Alnor said, glee in his voice at the final words.

The man – Varnan – stood with his chest heaving, sword pointed at Balzor as he rose to his feet, resisting the urge to smile mockingly at him. With a growl, he sheathed his sword and strode to Balzor nose to nose, who didn't flinch.

"Petra would've demolished you with a blade, so tell me who murdered my son, or your death with be excruciatingly painful."

Balzor stared straight back at Varnan, still doing his best to keep the smile off his face at his successful barb. Though he worried it might have been too successful, at this rate the man would kill him before Dextri arrived.

"The man who did kill Petra will be coming here in a few minutes to finish off the rest of you. Right big bastard he is, name's Dextri. Almost a score of the Sain guard is behind him too. Might be easier to run," he said, to which Varnan punched him savagely in the stomach, doubling him over coughing.

307

"Varnan..." Alnor warned. "Go out front, be my eyes. If these supposed guards appear, we can make scarce out of the back, I know a route. Reinforcements will soon disperse the rabble, but for now we seem to be outnumbered."

To Balzor, it seemed Varnan wanted to disobey Alnor and kill him there and then. He could only imagine the type of grief and anger that was bubbling beneath the ugly man's surface, but he hid it well. Barging past Balzor's still hunched form, he stormed out of the room, but the menace didn't leave with him. Attention now turned back to the situation at hand, Alnor brought his sword back up to Aria's neck. Surprisingly, she didn't recoil this time, concentration fixed on her face as if she had some sort of internal struggle going on. She looked straight at him. He saw something glint in her eyes, then she slowly closed them, breathing rhythmically. Over the top of her head, Alnor had a smug smile.

"Now then, back to the situation at hand. Bind them!" he barked at the remaining red cloaks, who barely paused in cutting strips from their cloaks and roughly grabbing Balzor's arms.

Hearing an outraged cry behind him, he knew Alkor had been given the same treatment. He barely even struggled, his face still throbbing from the previous hit. Tousling his hair mockingly and laughing, the man binding him stepped back, but stayed within range. They were taking no chances, despite thinking they were no threat - which, Balzor thought, is true. No swords, leather armour, hardly trained. The only thing he had was a strange feeling coursing through his body which kept escalating beyond his control. He squirmed slightly in his bonds, feeling like insects were crawling through his veins. Men behind him chuckled again, thinking this a poor attempt to break free, no doubt. Even Alnor's grin grew broader.

"Wriggle like the worm you are!" Alnor jeered to him. Lowering his voice, he leant towards Aria's ear like a lover. "And you, care to admit what you really are and join me?"

Her eyes flew open, ripped out of whatever trance she was in by his words. Fear, uncertainty and anger crossed her face before she whispered her response. "Never."

"Well, my darling, it seems you're less than useless to me." And he drew his sword across her throat.

The moment slowed. A crimson arc of blood jetted from the incision, her eyes registering alarm, then disbelief, then a terrible sadness. She tried to move her lips, wordlessly mouthing towards Balzor as he watched the scene in horror. Her knees buckled and Alnor dropped her with a look of relish on his face, watching Balzor's reaction.

Alkor began bellowing behind him, but Balzor couldn't take his gaze off her. He watched in silence as her life's essence drained from her. The insects in his veins skittered faster as a colossal grief joined the torrent of rage and euphoria. He kept his gaze locked with hers, doing his best to transfer his own life to her, as if sheer force of will would bring her back from Ezimat's door. Her eyes dimmed, lids beginning to close as exhaustion set in, then with a severe wrench of his heart, her light went out.

His body began an unstoppable trembling, fists clenching behind his back as he felt a rumble in his chest. An aggressive growl came from his throat. Alnor's cackle ringing in his ears, he raised his attention to the hated brother. Something in Balzor's face must have disconcerted Alnor, because he took a step back. His laugh faltered and a trace of fear fell upon his face. Pressure built in his chest, his blood feeling like it was on fire with no escape, killing everything inside him until he had no choice but let it explode. He screamed with a primal violence, a bestial roar that sent a shockwave pulsing from his body, knocking everybody off their feet. He snapped the bindings that held him with ease, grasping his gore-soaked sword from the floor.

Then he was moving.

*****

A ringing permeated his ears as Alnor groggily rose to his feet, head pounding. Some sort of concussive force had launched him from his feet, ripping his sword from his grasp and led to him cracking his head on the floor. Straightening up and trying to shake the blurred vision from his eyes, he pressed his palms to his temples and massaged rigorously, to minimal effect. A few seconds served to do what his attempts could not; what he saw made his mouth drop open.

Three of his men were already down and he watched as Balzor parried a sword with ease, lopping off the man's arm in the same movement. As he fell to the floor screaming, Balzor had already leapt to the side to avoid a swing that would have decapitated him, coming up with a kick to a leg and cutting the attacker's throat.

Alnor watched, mesmerised, as the peasant ripped through his men, moving fluidly whilst the red cloaks seem to wade through mud. Even when his father fought, Alnor had never seen anything close to this. There was only one person he'd encountered with that kind of speed and precision.

Krinar.

It cannot be, he thought. But the more he watched, the more he was sure. The shockwave, the incredible speed... the final confirmation came when Balzor drove his sword straight through the mouth of the final red cloak standing in an explosion of bone and cartilage.

Grey eyes stared mercilessly into Alnor's own – the trademark of a true Annarite. Balzor stood in front of him, a red demon with his teeth bared, and Alnor was ashamed to admit that he felt fear. Since when could the peasant boy cause that reaction from *him!* He was a Sain, not some common whelp. With a snarl he leapt forward, unleashing a flurry of blows to test Balzor's defences. He felt his spirits fall as none of the attacks got near him, some missing by mere inches as the whelp casually sidestepped and dodged.

Balzor snapped forward, suddenly. Alnor barely had time to bring his own blade up to deflect a blow that would have cut him in half. He gave a sharp intake of breath at the strength it took, numbness lancing up his arm from the effort.

For a second, Balzor was close, those granite-hard eyes boring into him, then Alnor headbutted him. Balzor staggered back, raising a hand involuntarily to his spurting nose, stumbling over the body of the man he'd recently dispatched.

With an elated cry, Alnor jumped forward, arms overhead to bring his sword down in a two-handed swing that held all his pent-up rage and bitterness. Balzor hit the ground, air whooshing from his mouth and a pained look entering his features. Fully anticipating his blade to rip Balzor's skull in half, Alnor grinned maliciously... until somehow Balzor's sword met his in a clanging that echoed around the now mostly empty hall. Only corpses and Alkor remained. Beginning to stir from his unconscious state, Alkor's groans accompanied the reverberating clang of Balzor's desperate parry.

Gritting his teeth, Alnor put all his Sain-given power into forcing the edge of his blade between Balzor's eye sockets. Unforgiving, it began to move closer and closer to the peasant's face. Alnor roared with the effort. *The whelp shouldn't be this strong,* Alnor growled internally, then blanched as he felt a sickening connection to his testicles. A slight weightlessness was all that warned him before he was flipped head first over the top of the contest of strength.

Landing heavily on his back, he exulted, realising he'd somehow remained in possession of his weapon, though the elation was short lived. As he began to rise, Balzor had once again surpassed Alnor's expectations, swinging a savage kick to his head and knocking him back down before he'd risen halfway; this time his sword fell from his fingers, mere inches to the side. Fighting the urge to vomit as his vision spun like he was drunk, he rolled onto his back, reaching for the hilt again.

"You killed her," he heard Balzor say, deathly quiet, promising violence.

Still dizzy, Alnor lunged without warning. He was deflected with ease, feeling a sharp pain in his wrist and hearing the clanging as his sword once again fell from his hand.

Frantically looking to the ground, he tried to locate his only chance at survival before the whelp cut him down. When his eyes found it, he froze, unable to register what he was seeing. A hand was still attached to the hilt, fingers twitching slightly but still clamping hold. The pain intensified in his wrist and Alnor finally looked down. Only a stump remained, blood spurting from the congealed end of what used to be a glorious arm. *My hand*, he thought.

That's when he began to scream.

★★★★★

Barely any satisfaction came when Alnor began to scream. Balzor only felt an immeasurable grief. The pulsing had finally stopped but had been replaced by an amazing strength and speed that his fury-addled mind couldn't comprehend. Somehow, the men around him had been thrown from their feet, he'd even passed Alkor unconscious from the invisible blast.

Not questioning anything except his burning desire for revenge, he'd ignored his friend groaning softly on the floor. Balzor had to admit Alnor's whimpering brought a slight satisfaction to him, to see his nemesis on the ground beneath him on his hand and knees was a very small balm to his now tortured soul.

A fresh wave of sorrow washed over him as the image of her dying face flashed through his mind; the pained look in her eyes, the way she fell limp; the sinister look of glee in Alnor's face as he registered the dismay in Balzor's own. Finishing the cycle, the agony turned to anger again, and his vision focused in on the pitiful form beneath him.

Alnor was beginning to reach for his sword again, still whimpering. Furious, Balzor kicked him in the face again, hard. Alnor fell onto his back with a gasp, remorse the bottom of the list in Balzor's mind.

"YOU KILLED HER!" Balzor shrieked, stamping hard on to Alnor's shin, which broke with a disgusting snapping sound. The answering howl echoed around the hall, cut off sharply to be followed by laboured breathing as Alnor struggled to regain his composure, sweat beading on his forehead with the effort. He rolled quickly and began to crawl on his elbows, cradling his stump as he cried softly in his worm-like state.

Disgust welled in Balzor, for an instant eclipsing the massive wall of hate that towered above all emotions. Built upon a foundation based on years of abuse, the monumental crest the grief and loss over Aria. The crying and the whimpering did nothing but topple over that infinite wall and leave the rubble staining one huge word on the ground: execution. His arm raised of its own accord, halfway up before he forced it to stop, choking down the relish to stop himself from killing in cold blood. Beating him in a fight – yes - but who was he to choose who lives and dies like a reaper of Ezimat? The other voice inside him was telling him that neither was Alnor, yet nothing had stopped him.

Seconds passed with nothing happening, even the pathetic attempt to crawl away had ceased, Alnor turned onto his back in exhaustion. His face had gone chalk white, his frame shaking from loss of blood. Hair stuck up at odd angles and a crazed look was on his face; he mustered some defiance and spat weakly in Balzor's direction. The only thing Balzor looked at was his eyes. He saw no remorse there, just wild pain and a hatred that mirrored Balzor's own.

"Brother," a voice croaked, snapping Balzor out of his trance.
He spun and saw Alkor sitting, beginning to stand slowly and holding out his hands

towards him, imploring him. "He's not worth it. Let him stand trial, bring him to justice the right way. Don't let this blacken your name; whatever he's done, he isn't worth your life."

Balzor knew Alkor's words were just - coming from a noble family, Alnor would be avenged if he was killed by the hands of someone from the common class. He knew that coming from a family like that, the trial wouldn't be fair. So, a common girl had died in a battle for Sain manor - wasn't the loss of a hand enough punishment for a rash decision? He could hear the arguments now, hear the Judge clearing Alnor's name. He gritted his teeth in anger.

"He killed her," he said for a third time, this time barely a whisper.

Hesitation gone, he whipped around his sword on a precise route to Alnor's jugular, seeing him flinch and raise his arms in futile defence. Before he struck, however, he heard a distinct voice he never thought would grace his ears again, saying one word. "Balzor..."

✦✦✦✦✦

Aria's eyes flew open, her hand going to her throat in an instinctual reaction to... something. She couldn't remember what. Sitting up in confusion, she took in the dim light of the forest, moonlight piercing the canopy. There was no birdsong, no croaking of insects or whisper of wind on the air; just a solid block of silence permeated by her own breathing. Tiny balls of mist flickered in the air, seeming to dance in the ethereal light whilst creeping slowly towards her as though blown by a breeze that didn't exist. As they got nearer, she could make out small shapes on the edge of their glowing aura, squinting to see through the blur of light they were emitting. *Wings!* Alarm coursed through her. She'd heard stories that reapers came in all sizes, dependent on which God sent them. Most people just referred to them as Ezimat's reapers, but almost any God can send them, even the minor ones.

Knowing from the feeling in the air that these were from a female deity, she let the alarm fade and a warmth spread throughout her body, accepting her time had come. Ecstatic smile on her face, she prepared to die.

"Begone!" a sharp command said, ripping through the euphoric atmosphere and sending the small reapers skittering away to hide amongst the glum tree trunks. Sounds began to return, albeit muted. She looked around feverishly, trying to find the voice that had scattered the beautiful beings that would have embraced her. When she found the source, she gasped.

"Gran?!"

Her grandmother smiled, the grey from her hair gone, replaced by long, dark locks that bounced as she walked towards her. Tell-tale wrinkles that used to squint and allow Aria to discern her grandmother's moods had vanished, smooth and flawless skin in their place. She looked *young.* Her smile, however, remained the same. Just the right amount of playfulness there to be her friend, balanced by the perfect amount of stern-ness to enable her to be a grandmother, and a mentor.

"Always pulling you out of trouble, aren't I girl?" she teased, swatting Aria's shoulder with much more strength than she was used to.

"But... How're you, y'know..."

"Young? Attractive? Excellent tits? It seems this purgatory brings you to what you still imagine yourself to be. And by Ezimat was I a looker in my time!" Aria laughed, the sound tinkling across the muted forest and seeming out of place. Cutting the laugh short, she frowned.

"Purgatory?"

"Aye girl, you heard me right."

"But that means... we're either in death, or on the brink!" Aria hissed, unable to keep the panic from entering her tone. She glanced uneasily back to the trees where the miniature reapers still hovered, now giving her a whole different feeling.

Her grandmother chuckled, waving her hand to disperse her hysteria. "Relax, relax. Don't you remember the night where you nearly caused an earthquake? What we were doing?"

Memories flashed before Aria's eyes as though she was watching somebody else's life. The image her grandmother was referencing didn't come at first. At first, she saw a fountain of blood cascade towards a young man's face, who was knelt and bound beneath her, long red hair braided over his shoulder, his body quivering as he watched... her. *Balzor!*
She screamed internally, then the image was gone, whipping back with incredible speed to her and Balzor in the lake. His admission of love, her feeling of ecstasy as she heard

the words. Skimming further, she found the memory she was looking for, her grand-mother's house shaking uncontrollably as a pain ripped through her body that demand-ed release, the bond that had been forged.

"Gran, no!" she said as the memory hit home. Her grandmother smiled sadly, reaching out and placing her hand delicately on Aria's shoulder.

"Grandmothers aren't supposed to outlive their granddaughter's girl, and Seeresses shouldn't outlive their apprentices. Teaching them would be such a waste, that way."

"Neither should you die so the other can live! I can barely harness my power at will, let alone use it. That's why we're in this mess in the first place!"

Outlines of tree trunks merged as the tears began to blur Aria's vision. They left her eyes and floated towards the treeline, the reapers emerging from their hiding places to playfully bounce them between each other. Fun felt out of place in this strange dimension, the scene almost made her laugh. Watching the reapers brought a strange tugging on her subconscious, urging her to let go of her woes and follow them to para-dise. Warmth began to seep into her tired bones yet again, and she took a step forward towards the light. A stinging slap snatched her vision from the beckoning afterlife, her grandmother's tutting bringing her back into herself.

"Focus girl, we don't have much time. Two things to know about your powers. Number one, controlling them is easy, they're linked to your emotion and can spasm accordingly. Separate your mind from your body when using your power. Deep breath-ing and clear thoughts, just like I taught you. Number two, use nature to amplify your power. The sun, the moon, the weather, they all help. Learn to control your mind, the rest will happen naturally. Ezimat knows you'll have enough time on your hands soon."

The last words brought a knowing smirk to her grandmother's face, a hint of amusement breaking through the seriousness.

"Gran, you're making no sense. I can't just *decide* to make my powers work; I've tried that and – "

"Shush, no time. These pests are tugging at me as we speak, I can't avoid them forever." By pests, Aria knew she meant the reapers. They'd stopped bouncing the tears around, playfulness abandoned as they darted around, angry now. Menace threaded through the clearing and the wind broke through whatever force was holding it back. It howled its defiance at being contained, whipping her hair into a frenzy and buffeting her away from her grandmother. Aria screamed, reaching out to grasp her hands before she was torn away forever. Intense effort was on her grandmother's face as she struggled to fight the pull of death. Shouting over the gale, she continued.

"The boy! You must guide him. He's the first outside of royalty in over three centuries. Ezimat must have great plans to choose him so young."

"The boy? What do you – "

"Balzor, fool girl! He needs you to succeed, to temper the fire inside of him. The young Sain has done an admirable job so far, but he can't hold him forever. He was born to fire, and fire will consume him without help."

"The first *what* outside of royalty? What fire? Gran, I don't understand..."

By now the reapers had reached her grandmother, swirling around her in the hurricane and beginning to lift her up, out of reach of Aria's desperate hands.

"Gran, no!" Aria screamed, leaping into the air.

She was knocked to the floor with a concussive force, then her grandmother was out of reach. The wind seemed to follow and Aria felt the echo of the glowing warmth she'd felt earlier, the reapers getting their prey as her grandmother succumbed to their embrace and began to find peace.

Aria's vision barely blurred this time as tears cascaded down her cheeks. They fell to the floor now instead of rising, giving the feeling of reality again. Her eyes met her grandmothers amidst the chaotic spinning of dazzling light, and she smiled. Aria choked down a sob as her grandmother rose, smiling weakly and falling to her knees, suddenly exhausted.

"Temper the fire," her grandmother whispered.

The sound of her voice was crystal clear as though she was right next to her, as if they were her own thoughts. Head heavy, she tried to look up once more, but it was in vain. The world began to spin as the unnatural, soundless domain began to return, and Aria knew her grandmother was gone. Sadness welled inside of her, and she toppled forward from her knees to land on the soft undergrowth of the forest in a light snapping of branches and thorns. Feeling no pain, she lay in a trance, feeling more comfortable than she'd ever felt in her life.

A tugging began once more, though this time she had no strength to fight it. The expected warmth never came. A harsh cold grip cocooned her as she stayed motionless on the floor, unable to move. Her breathing slowed as her body began to shut down, piece by piece. As her eyes began to close, she wished she'd let the warmth infuse her, and the reapers take her onto better pastures.

Icy fingers clawed their way down her throat, up into her nostrils, in her ears. She could hear swords clashing, a scream and a familiar voice filled with agony she would've done anything to ease. As the cold reached her lungs, she began to see the Sain Hall. Alkor was pleading with Balzor for something she couldn't decipher.

Knowing she had to help with Balzor's sorrow, she reached out and shouted his name. It came out as more of a croak than the intended yell. She saw him spin round, shock registering as she realised his usually brown eyes were a hard grey. He dropped his sword, and he was running. The effort of holding out her hand became too much, and she let it fall. She felt Balzor take her into his arms, cradling her face, sobbing uncontrollably and kissing her forehead. Then everything went black.

✳✳✳✳✳

Varnan staggered out of the entrance to the cursed Sain manor, blood streaming from a scalp wound he'd sustained from the shattering door. He'd heard Alnor mention the girl had powers, and after feeling the shockwave, he wasn't about to stick around to watch them unfold. His eyes took in the group of men sprinting out of the trees from Saternac. Honing in on a bear of a man in front, fury eliminated any other emotion at the thought of that man killing his son. Drawing his sword, he took a step forward. *Dead men don't get revenge,* he thought, gritting his teeth and almost letting his anger rule him. Almost. He raised his sword to point at the group, ensuring all saw and recognised the challenge he was issuing.

"DEXTRI!" he bellowed, watching the big man at the front miss a step at the sound of his name. Etching the man's face into his mind, he turned towards the trees and began to run, sword still bared. He hadn't lasted this long by acts of heroism, and he wasn't about to start now. Alnor and his men were finished, but he still had Krinar to fall back to. To plan his revenge from a place of power. One thing was certain – Dextri would die.

A quick glance over his shoulder confirmed the guard hadn't given chase, content to let one man escape in their haste to help the boys, but he didn't slow. It wouldn't take long for the red cloaks to fall; he wouldn't have been surprised if they were already dead, judging by the explosion of power that had come from that room. As soon as the dust settled, one fleeing man would come to the forefront of their attention, and the guard would give chase. Being leagues away by that time was in his best interest.

Engrossed in his thoughts, he almost missed the glint of reflecting sunlight, a tell-tale giveaway that all warriors know. Keeping his course, he readied himself. Knowing that seeming unaware would be his only advantage, he acted oblivious until he hit the treeline. He lunged toward the glint.

Against the odds, the man deflected the fatal thrust, though the ferocity of it knocked him back a step, sending him sprawling as his foot trapped behind a tree root. A satisfying crack and a scream brought Varnan little reprieve as he pivoted to deflect a blow that would have split his skull in two. The strength of the crazed looking man surprised Varnan but became his advantage. Expecting to behead with the attack, the man overstepped and stumbled, leaving him open to Varnan's backswing. Never being one to miss, Varnan's swing took the man in the side of the neck, ripping the sword from his grasp as the momentum carried him away.

"Ingvar, no!" the man with the snapped ankle screamed, but Varnan was already moving, abandoning the sword to the man's neck.

Speed would be his only friend now; a sword wouldn't help him if the Sain guard caught up. A thrill passed through his body as he anticipated the chase, knowing himself still fit despite his ageing years. But underneath the superficial feelings and the thoughts of survival lay the raging torrent of grief that housed the loss of his son. Shoving everything down and focusing on the moment, he left his emotions in a hard ball of iron that kept his body moving. The one phrase that had stopped him attacking earlier echoed around his brain. Dead men don't get revenge.

Chapter 17

Stirring from dreams of blood and chaos, Alnor's eyes flickered open. He sighed deeply, glad the nightmares had ended, that he was back in his bed awaiting another day. Fleeting glee passed his mind as the dreaded hangover that usually destroyed him was avoided, and he let his head relax on the feathered pillow. A twinge of pain in his wrist made him grimace and he made to lift his arm, grunting with the effort and causing the pain to increase. Alarm lanced through his body as he felt the coarse feeling of rope around his wrists and ankles, and he began to flail.

"It's no use, brother. Even if you could rise, that splint in your leg wouldn't let you get far," he heard a familiar voice say at his bedside.

"Alkor?" croaked Alnor, turning his head fractionally to the side and confirming his hunch.

"Wha- What happened? Why am I bound?"

As he asked the questions, he knew the answers. Memories he'd thought were savage dreams came flooding back, sickening him and forcing him to close his eyes. He prayed to Ezimat that it wasn't true. His father, the prince, the girl; even the whelp. The last thought stuck in his mind as he realised the implications of what he had done hit home.

"He's Annarite," Alnor breathed.

Alkor's eyes narrowed, and he stood over him. "What?"

"The peasant, he's Annarite. He's ascended."

"Ascended? Are you in your right mind? You have to be *born* an Annarite to be one, it doesn't just get randomly gifted!" Alkor said.

Knowing this not to be common knowledge, Alnor opened his eyes again, fixing his brother with what he hoped was an earnest stare. "The King, the Prince, they're *true* Annarites. Not chosen by Sarnat to be his warriors, or Exat to be seers... chosen by Ezimat to lead his people to better times. Chosen by the father of the Gods, to be the leaders of our race."

"The prince? The same man who led you into killing our father and betraying your people?!" Alkor said, voice raising to just below a shout, anger evident in his tone.

Alnor tried to raise his hands imploringly but screamed as the stump scraped along the rope. The sound seemed to calm Alkor down and Alnor could've sworn he saw concern on his brother's face. That, after everything, prompted him to hold nothing back.

"Brother, nothing I ever say will redeem what I've done, I won't even try. My mind was warped by promises of glory and a new age, but it was my jealousy and fury that killed our father. My thoughts always angled towards Annarites being superior to the world. All the prince did was put me amongst like-minded people and encouraged that belief. If I'd known what his ulterior motive was, I would never have listened."

A lapse appeared just after, Alkor seemed to mull over what he'd heard. Alnor had never felt uneasy around his brother before but laying there waiting for his response almost made him squirm. As he was about to try and clear the air, his brother spoke.

"Your *thoughts* brother, ring all too closely to Kerazar motto. These are *people*, not just playthings for others who have the strength to take what they desire. If what you say is true, I'm glad that someone like Balzor has been chosen over someone like you."

A spasm of rage tore through him and, judging by the look of disdain on his brother's face, he hadn't hidden it well.

"Even now, you struggle to control your hatred of him. Our father saw that in you, even distanced himself from Balzor in a hope the lesser attention would deter your pettiness. You essentially deprived Balzor of a father, because you believe yourself *better than him.*" Alkor practically spat the final three words at him, sending with them a wave of shame he never thought he possessed when it came to Balzor. Relentless, he went on. "Friendship, loyalty, love. That's what makes you a real person brother, not where your born or who your father is. If you'd realised that years ago and not been under the spell of a psychopath, or surrounded by sick men we wouldn't be where we are now. Instead, we're here, and you're crippled and awaiting trial for the murder of the Annarite General."

As Alkor was ending his tirade, he rose from the small stool he was perched upon and turned to leave, the look of his retreating back enough to make Alnor try to rise again, with the same result. At least this time it was a pained gasp rather than a scream. Alkor's eyes, however, didn't hold any remorse at the pain; though he did turn back.

"Being less of a man hasn't changed me, Alkor. I regretted killing our father within moments of it happening. I also know that at the time, I couldn't have stopped my fury overflowing if I'd tried. One minute he was trying to be the doting dad, the next he was berating me over something I'd said or done. Over so much time alone, I'll admit it wore me down, then when he said I wasn't his son, it broke me. But I swear to Ezimat, I had no clue that Krinar was going to kill the King and open the gates to the Kerazar. I want the merchants and nobles to pay us more, not for those slavers to destroy our cities."

Alnor had been staring at his stump throughout his own admission – more a plea than anything – but after the dead silence that followed, he looked at his brother. Alkor was standing open-mouthed with eyes as wide as shields, not a little fear mixed in with the shock.

"He's WHAT?!" Confusion was Alnor's first reaction to the outburst, until it continued in ever increasing volume. "You didn't think to fucking *lead* with the fact that the prince of the kingdom is going to let in the Kerazar hordes? Maybe the pain has sent you slightly senile but for *fuck's* sake Alnor!"

This time he turned quickly, not stopping before he'd wrenched the door open. Panic shot through Alnor. This could be the last time he saw his brother before his trial and inevitable hanging. Death didn't quite scare him as much as it used to, but the humiliation of a noble son being hung was something that cut him to the core.

"Alkor!" His brother turned, face full of agitation and worry. "Leave me a blade."

Distrust broke through the agitation, then a flurry of emotions Alnor couldn't place before Alkor reached for a small dagger at his waist. Walking briskly back to the stool, he stabbed it hard into the wood, leaving it quivering. Without a word, he spun on his heel and left, slamming the door behind him.

Agonising moments passed in which Alnor watched the knife dance, knowing it was a jig put there by all those he'd wronged, and by his own unbearable guilt. He imagined each shake to be a ticking of one of the clocks he'd seen in Torizo, the hands swaying to the beat that held his sanity intact. When it finally stopped, a flash of dread went through him, smothered with an even larger flash of fury. He worked to free the arm which still had fingers attached, yanking until his wrist was almost as ugly as his other arm. He breathed a sigh of relief when the cord eventually snapped. Reaching for the blade, he wrenched it free with considerable effort. Staring at the tip of the dagger, his mind betrayed him, and blurred vision announced the coming tears.

Allowing himself some time, he made his apologies to his family before Ezimat, letting the invading tears fall from his lashes, staining his silk sheets. Regret and pain were his main thoughts, but a prayer for Krinar to fail was also in there, amongst a hope that Varnan had met his end tonight. Even in his state, he couldn't bring himself to spare a prayer for the peasant boy.

Chuckling sadly to himself, he wondered whether Alkor was truly right; maybe he deserved the disdain his brother had for him. It was this stray thought that gave him the strength to lift the blade, placing the tip in just the right place before slicing neatly. He made three cuts before his body began to give up, his fading consciousness barely registering the burning pain above his woes. His grip gave way; the clattering of the knife couldn't break through the deafening silence that had blocked his ears as the blood escaped the wounds. As his eyes began to flicker and his mind began to shut down, one final plea broke through. *Survive, brother.*

★★★★★

Hardly hearing the words being spoken, Svein stood near the roaring inferno of the three pyres. Beside him, his mother was weeping openly, not even bothering to wipe the snot running onto her top lip. He'd felt numb since last night, even the sight of Devar on his knees howling at the loss of his brother didn't break his desolation. The pyre in front of him held his father, his rock for so many years, his mentor and best friend. The fact that the next pyre held Ingvar probably should have ignited further sadness, but it just bounced off. Hearing that Alnor had taken his own life that morning had only given him a moment's satisfaction before he'd become stone again. The entire village had turned out, surrounding two of the three pyres to pay their respects to men who'd died in the defence of their village; men who they'd loved and cherished as their own family, who all there had known for a lifetime.

Alnor's pyre had two stationary figures in front, one of them showing no emotion at all: Alkor. The other was Joseph, standing like a shadow; he deemed himself personally responsible for Alkor's defence since last night, shouldering the blame of letting his lord run off alone and outnumbered.

Svein hadn't spoken to Alkor since him and Balzor had ran off after Aria. He'd sat in the arms of his mother all night, weeping like a babe. They'd talked more than they'd ever talked before — about his father's past, how they'd met, what he'd been like. His mother had agreed with his father's last words, a trace of fear warping her features from sadness as she heard his explanation of the fight. It seemed she'd seen his father in a rage similar in his youth, and although it was in her defence, she'd never wanted to see it again. It was with a heavy heart that he watched his father's soul float up to Ezimat's reapers with the sparks, knowing that when the flames died down, he had to leave.

He might have been excited in different times; getting information out of his father about his mountain heritage had always been like getting blood from a stone. Funny how in his death, all the information had come, wanted or not. But now, feeling the heat and smelling the sweet incense of human flesh, he found he'd much rather have been a blacksmith who knew nothing of the clans.

A touch on his elbow startled him out of his reverie, and he glanced left to see Mariak standing there in silence. She nodded at him, then stood by his side gazing into the flames. Annoyance lanced through him at the intrusion into his private grief, but he couldn't deny the slight blossom of something beneath the sorrow, so he let it be.

Slowly, he dragged his gaze towards the Sain manor as he saw the doors open. Through the doors shuffled Balzor, Aria leaning heavily on his shoulder, showing the effects of her apparent surge back to life. Thinking about it made Svein uneasy, even though the hill of sorrow that was threatening to overflow within him. Nobody should be able to escape the Reapers; he wouldn't even wish that on his father. But it wasn't Aria that held his attention in that moment. Even stooped with his arm around her, Balzor seemed different. Lithe movements and obvious strength aside, there was his eyes — a sharp grey, an unnerving predatory look behind the usual jovial exterior.

He watched as Alkor said something to his brother but stopped with his hand half raised, letting his arm fall without saying a word. Balzor smiled grimly, clapping him on the shoulder with his unencumbered arm and continuing his shuffle. To Svein, the message was clear: Balzor loved Alkor, but would not stand with him in mourning. Grieving the man who'd bullied him his entire life before executing his girlfriend was too much for any man.

Crackling and roaring, the pyre that held his father let out a sigh of sparks and heat, causing Svein to step in front of his mother to stop the inevitable singed clothing that would result. His mother remained oblivious, staring vacantly at his chest, which bunched over as he winced at the pricks of flame on the back of his neck. As she saw him flinch, she chuckled dryly, a touch of life on her face again.

"Even in death, your father plays his tricks on us. Stop grieving you two, he's saying. He doesn't realise that's harder than it bloody looks!" she said, pulling Svein away from the fire into the cooler air. "He wouldn't want us to fall apart like this."

At those words, she placed her hand lovingly on her swelling belly, grabbing Svein's hand with the other. What surprised Svein, however, was the loving gaze she held included Mariak, who shifted uncomfortably with the attention.

"You look after him, girl," his mother said, sending a shock through Svein.

"I will," Mariak replied, as solemn as he'd ever heard her. Opening his mouth to get some sense out of the situation, he was interrupted – or saved – by Balzor coming with Aria still on his shoulder, though looking stronger after the brief walk.

"Martha, Svein... I don't know what to say. Lortmund was a great man," he mumbled, ill at ease with his attempts at comfort.

Aria stepped off her perch on his shoulder, wrapping her arms around Martha with tears in her eyes. "I'm so sorry for your loss. It's a cruel world that lets a man like Lortmund pass. I only wish that I could've gotten there in time to heal him."

His mother choked back a sob, pulling out of the embrace and gripping Aria's upper arms tightly, a sad smile on her face. "Don't you go thinking about healing and timelines, girl. You went through an ordeal that none of us could imagine; both of you did."

Her eyes moved to Balzor as she finished the sentence, who met her gaze with a pitying look in those hard, granite eyes.

"Take that look out of your eyes young 'un! I won't tolerate pity, especially from ones I brought up alongside my little Svein here."

Svein snorted. He hadn't been called 'little' since he was thirteen, but he supposed he always would be in his mother's eyes. He liked it that way. His mother arched her eyebrow at him, amusement breaking through the aura of woe that had surrounded her since news of his father's passing. Then his thoughts were brought back to the earlier comment made by her.

"What do you mean, look after me?" he said accusingly to his mother. It was her turn to chuckle now. "As *if* you could look after yourself, big man. Don't you get it yet? I'm coming with you," Mariak said simply.

Svein growled and made to retort, but Aria's laugh cut him off. "Arguing with your mother *and* a hunter seductress would be a very bad move for you here, blacksmith," Aria laughed.

Blacksmith, big man, little Svein. Why couldn't anybody just say his fucking name normally?! Seeing all three women with knowing smiles on their faces did nothing to soothe his growing annoyance, so he did what he usually did and kept quiet, albeit grudgingly.

"I'm gonna go and check on Devar, before I get in the middle of a domestic," Balzor teased lightly, looking concerningly at Aria.

"Go, Balzor. We'll look after the death cheater," Mariak said, a flash of surprise crossing Aria's face at the blatant comment. A small nudge with Mariak's elbow into Aria's ribs eased the cool atmosphere that had come with it. Bloody women, communicating without words since the dawn of time, without men understanding any of it. Balzor nodded in thanks and walked away slowly, checking over his shoulder multiple times as he did.

"The boy is besotted with you, girl," his mother said fondly. "Never thought I'd see the day that that lad would risk everything for a girl, even one as beautiful as you. It's a shame he lost his mother's eyes, though."

Svein's ears pricked up at the mention of Balzor's parents, an ever-elusive topic between anyone who'd known them. He'd known his mother had told Balzor everything she knew about his parents, but he'd kept it close to his chest. Seeing Aria's interest perked alongside his own, he decided to ask the question he knew she wouldn't, excitement obvious despite the grim setting.

"You knew Balzor's mother?"

"In a fashion. You forget, in those days we were two villages; both villages knew each other, traded, had weddings together. I used to see them when we traded in their village, but your father did most of the bartering and we all know his memory is useless.

I didn't even get their names!"

Svein barked a laugh, smirks appeared on the girls face as well. The mention of his father had brought his thoughts back to the matter at hand, however, and his laughter soon dissipated. "Fuck, I'll miss him," he sighed, the smirks changing to looks of pity in moments.

He hated that. He could deal with sadness, but pity was unbearable. His mother put her hand on his shoulder again and they stood in companionable silence, no longer feeling crushed by the grief, amongst friends. He watched as Balzor stood with the rest of the guard. They'd spread out evenly around his father's and Ingvar's fire, murmuring softly into Devar's ear as the man stood vacantly with tears streaming down his face, his leg splinted. A weak sun did its best to lighten the mood, but the sombre atmosphere seemed to reflect into the sky, where birds still sung and the bees still buzzed, oblivious to the inconsequential happenings of humans. For a moment, Svein envied them; to be so free from responsibility and emotion, not tied down by menial things. But as he saw Alkor detach himself finally from his brother's burning grave, he knew an easy life wasn't possible.

Joseph shadowed Svein's oldest friend, causing a firm feeling of distrust to form in his belly. Even after his deeds, he couldn't fully accept him. He saw Alkor nod gravely to Dextri as he passed, the big man's eyes red in his own private battle with his loss.

"Svein I..." he began, but Svein cut him off.

"Don't. I know what you're going to say, attempt to apologise for something that you couldn't have stopped; my father knew the risks, we all did. I won't judge you for mourning Alnor either - no matter what he's done, he's still your brother and deserves to be mourned by someone. Just don't ask me to mourn with you."

His mother looked at him hard but held her silence. To Alkor's credit, he smiled weakly.

"Fair enough. When do you leave for the clans?"

"As soon as my father's ashes are retrievable. Half of him will come with me to his birthplace, the other will stay with mother. Two halves of his life when he lived, it seems fitting to keep it that way in death."

Blurred vision accompanied his response, and he felt another wet line trace a line down his cheek. Alkor didn't look away, but stepped forward and clapped his shoulder, keeping his hand there whilst Svein cried softly. Other touches around him alerted him to the rest of his small group lending their support, and they stood in a small circle, mourning their dead. Alkor's face showed no impatience but knowing him for his entire life made Svein notice tell-tale signs that indicated Alkor was distressed.

"Spit it out, mate. What's on your mind?" Alkor blanched, clearly thinking he'd been subtle about the situation. He snorted softly. "Alkor, I've known you my whole life. You can try to hide it all you want, but I know when something's up."

"Well then…" he began, then launched into his final moments with his brother. Svein didn't care that his mouth fell open; the words that his friend spoke were surreal. Balzor, an Annarite? The Kerazar being let in by none other than Prince Krinar himself. As Alkor finished his revelation, they stood in shocked silence for a moment. Then Aria spoke.

"So that's what she meant!" she hissed.

A confused look from Alkor led her to elaborate. "When I, you know… died, I went to some sort of realm. I saw my grandmother there and she told me some things; one of them being that Balzor was the first outside of the royal family in centuries - that must be what she meant. The first true Annarite."

Svein finally closed his mouth with a clack of his teeth, letting an explosion of air come from his nose at the confirmation of something that seemed impossible only yesterday. Watching him now, Svein saw the strange way of moving he'd noticed earlier, and it all made sense. As though sensing eyes upon him, Balzor looked up, gesturing to Dextri and the others to follow as he made his way over to them. Puzzled looks on their faces at the interruption to their grief, they followed reluctantly.

"Tell them again," Balzor said, clearly having heard the conversation from that far away.

Skirting over that fact, Alkor sighed and started again, this time quicker. Mutters greeted the news this time, some gripping their sword hilts or drawing the circle on their heads to avert evil. Others shot Balzor incredulous looks, as if struggling to believe. Dextri shrugged.

"Well, least you're on our side, lad. Maybe you'll beat me in a duel now?"

Balzor snorted and shook his head. "Fat chance of that, you'll sulk for days if I score a hit." The guard chuckled, lifting the sombre mood slightly, that weak sun finally finding purchase on the ground and bringing a warmth to their souls, one that the fires never could.

"True enough, young 'un. Question is, how do we deal with thousands of screaming Kerazar tribesmen, who are allied to our own fucking royals?"

"That is what I want to talk to you about," Alkor said, turning back to Svein. "We need the mountain clans."

Svein stood there, stunned. Surely Alkor couldn't expect him to persuade people he'd never met to fight a war they had no part in? Sure, the clans hated the Kerazar, but the Annar weren't their friends either. Looking into Alkor's eyes, he could see that's exactly what he expected him to do.

"You're mad. How the fuck am I meant to do that? I'm not even sure if they'd welcome me, let alone fight for us. When my father left, he became outlawed by clan law, and though he maintained the love of his family, the clan would never have taken him back. He's lucky they even traded with us because of his connections!"

Alkor made to speak, but to his surprise his mother butted in first. "Svein, they'll welcome you. Your uncle will relish getting to know his brother's son, and there's no law against allowing the son of an outlaw to come home. Clan laws are more like guidelines anyway. When they know what you are, they'll let you come."

His mother's final comment caused only a few furtive looks, for which Svein was thankful. He didn't think he was ready for people to know what he was. Choosing to ignore the looks, he nodded to his mother, who smiled back.

"What say you, Svein? Will you try?" Dextri probed.

Thinking quickly wasn't Svein's strong suit. He knew the longing in his breast was more than just a longing to understand his heritage. He wanted to help his friends ensure their survival in a war they'd be hopelessly outnumbered in. Nevertheless, he held his tongue for a moment, ensuring no rash decisions were made by a promise during his grief.

"Aye, I'll try to rally the clans. Ezimat knows how, but I will."

Dextri nodded at him, respect in his eyes at the blacksmith's boy who'd been forced to grow up. Turning back to the pyre, Svein closed his eyes, imagining his father looking down on him from Ezimat's hall. Would he be proud or would he be cursing him for promising to bring his people into a war they weren't a part of? He stood watching the rogue sparks punctuate the sun's rays until the pyre began to collapse. He still didn't get his answer.

✶✶✶✶✶

Balzor shuffled down the path to the Seeress' house, the comfortable weight of Aria warm against his body, his arm wrapped protectively around her. No matter what she said, he knew she wasn't quite right. Any fading light the dying sun emitted was hampered by the canopy, so they shuffled in a dim world, finishing the day off with the same feeling it started with.

At first, he'd been ecstatic. Seeing Aria alive had filled the raw hole that Alnor had ripped open with her murder. Then, she'd woken up sobbing and inconsolable, rambling about how her grandmother was dead, of reapers and a breezeless wind. When he'd finally been able to settle her, she struggled through an explanation that he'd found ludicrous the more he heard. It fit perfectly to the last day, so he decided to just accept it and move on; he was just happy she was alive.

After, he'd left her in his room to pester Nerva for some food, ignoring the disapproving looks eating in his room had gotten him. It seemed returning from the dead barely warranted that in Nerva's book. Idle chatter, as she buttered a large plate of bread and ladled two steaming bowls of soup, informed Balzor of Ingvar's death. She'd carried on bustling around for a few moments before realising he'd stopped responding, turning suspiciously before putting the plate down with a sigh.

"Sorry, lad. I thought you already knew."

The soup went cold as Balzor stained Nerva's apron weeping, her large arms wrapped around him as she clasped him to her breast. Grief for Lortmund was there too, both men having risked their lives for him, both now dead. Even the guard he didn't know, buried in a grave outside of town. Olsten had come in at one point, muttering an excuse before taking his leave just as fast. Balzor didn't care that he'd looked like a child in the arms of his mother, losing two sword brothers deserved his tears. She lifted him softly away from her, wiping his face with the arm of her sleeve before cupping both his cheeks in her hands.

"Now, you've got it out. Best go and feed that lass of yours, eh?" she said, punching his shoulder lightly. Balzor chuckled wetly, sniffing and cuffing his nose with his own sleeve. Nerva exclaimed in disgust. "I've no clue what that girl sees in you boy, wiping your snot on your clothes. Ach, you're filth!"

This time Balzor's laugh was a lot stronger. Picking up both bowls with the plate of bread on top of them, he walked out with a wink thrown over his shoulder at her. Nerva never changed, and that felt right somehow – one constant in a life of chaos.

Aria was up and out of bed when he'd returned, declaring she was going to honour the dead, then relenting after smelling the soup and decided hunger couldn't wait. The consoling and the revelations later, and they were here, walking down the path to Aria's home, just like any other night from the tavern - if the tavern wasn't burnt down and two of the town's most revered inhabitants dead.

Hearing Alnor had died brought a sense of victory to Balzor, one he struggled to suppress for Alkor's sake; he would have gotten away with his deeds otherwise, the words 'prison' or 'hanging' didn't apply to nobles, instead being confined to their estates to live an easy life. Death was the only choice in his eyes.

Muffled wings flapped above their heads, his keen eyesight picking out the leather-like wings of the earliest bats around the grasping branches. Even in the dim light, the wood seemed vibrant to him, more than it had ever done before. Shadowed areas were no longer dark, the sun's rays barely blinded him; he could feel the moisture in the air from the stream, though it lay a fair distance beyond the wall. He could pinpoint a bird's call from further than he'd ever thought possible, hear hooves of the horses in the stables. Though the pulsing had gone after he'd let it loose, a lot of the perks had stayed, albeit not as strongly.

Grouped with the raw power coursing through his body, Balzor was inclined to believe what Alkor had said, despite it being the craziest thing to ever leave his brother's mouth. Feeling Aria tense beside him, he froze, scanning the area for the threat whilst putting himself in front of her.

"Relax. Everything's fine," she joked, though Balzor could hear the way she forced those final two words.

He turned to look into her eyes, seeing the depth of the worry and sadness in them. "We don't know what we'll find yet."

"She's dead Balzor! I wouldn't be alive otherwise. That's how the bond works," she said harshly, shutting down his attempt at consolation.

Pushing past him, she began to walk with more strength towards the end of the path, a thin block of sunshine the only sign of light still left, flashing across Aria's face as she left the trees and stopped at her grandmother's gate. He hurried beside her, loathe to let her face this alone, and stopped as he saw the familiar house. Nothing seemed out of place – potted herbs on the windowsill still lording themselves over the garden plants, which danced lightly in the breeze; shutters open on the windows and a cup sitting just beside the herbs, giving Balzor a picture of the Seeress standing there drinking her regular tea, enjoying the view. But there were no flickering candles inside, no wood smoke climbing lazily through the chimney, no impatient shout of, 'Girl, get inside,' as they waited by the gate.

He glanced at Aria. She was trembling, one hand on the gate to steady herself as the other covered her mouth as her eyes glistened. Taking that hand, he placed his other on the gate, pushing it open slowly.

"Come on," he said gently. "I'll be here with you, always."

A grateful look was her only response. They began to stalk towards the house, Balzor feeling like an intruder despite it being Aria's home. Not hesitating this time, Aria pushed open the door quickly, flicking her wrist as she did so. A flare of light made Balzor flinch, then prepare to step into harm's way yet again. This time, Aria chuckled.

"Seems controlling my power isn't as much of a problem anymore."

Candles had lit around the room, half burnt logs in the fireplace re-igniting from their slumber. The glumness that the house held evaporated slightly with the warmth and light, though Aria's darting eyes kept Balzor on edge. The couch and all the chairs were empty. Balzor scanned the kitchen quickly to make sure there wasn't a prone form on the ground. *A corpse,* he thought grimly, dreading Aria's strangled cry that he was sure would come.

She emerged from the bedroom with a small, sad smile on her face, clutching a bracelet. She wiped a tear from her cheek as he enveloped her in a hug, burning to ask the question but scared to bring her more pain.

"Don't worry, we won't find her. It seems giving your life for another guarantees not only your soul to the Gods, but your body too. She's moved on to a better place, all of her."

Confusion was his only reaction to what she said, though as she disengaged and sat at the table, she tore open an envelope. He moved into the room and found nothing. A crawling sensation washed over his skin, the result of starting to believe Aria's comment; he'd never heard of the God's taking somebody in life, but who was he to argue with a Seeress? Checking everywhere whilst attempting to be subtle was hard, but he thought he managed it, though the letter she was reading took most of the credit – she was engrossed, eyebrows furrowed as her lips mouthed soundlessly what she was reading.

After a few moments of watching her, he sat on the other side of the table waiting patiently. She stood abruptly from the table, breathing heavily as the chair clattered to the ground and making Balzor leap out of his skin. He rushed up from his side and dashed to her, putting a hand on her shoulder.

"Aria, what? What is it?" he exclaimed, but she just kept staring at the letter, one hand on her stomach and disbelief on her face.

Not getting an answer, he picked up the paper and began to read.

"Aria, If you're reading this, then I have passed onto the afterlife, a payment so you may live. I saw my death mere days ago and knew the events that led up to it. I also know that to stop it, I would have to stop the ascension of one of the most powerful Annarites this world has seen, who will fight the insatiable coming darkness. Something is coming, girl, and it's not as trivial as Annar verses Kerazar. Somebody is pulling the strings, and the Gods are in a rage at their actions. I cannot speak for you, but the aura I see around you and the boy is chaotic apart, but serene together. The connection between you is no mere coincidence, it is the will of the Gods. Do not mourn me, I will watch over you and my great-grandchild from Ezimat's hall and await the day where I finally see you again.
All my love, Gran.

PS. If you let my garden die, I will haunt your dreams."

He read it again, not understanding the reason for Aria's numb state. She'd moved slowly to the couch and sat down whilst he read, her hand still resting on her stomach as she hyperventilated. He sighed exasperatedly.

"Unless you plan on giving me a heart attack, do you mind telling me what in Ezimat's balls is wr – "

Then it fell into place, and he froze too. "Aria..." he said hesitantly. She looked directly into his eyes and he felt a pure feeling of adoration inside of him. *"I will watch over you and my great grandchild from Ezimat's hall."* Those words etched into his mind as he felt heat suffuse his cheeks and an unbidden smile break through his shock.

"I'm pregnant."

Epilogue

The sound of steady hooves had been Krinar's constant companion for days now, a grim silence settling over the group as they rode, sensing their King's mood. The chatter continued in the camp, some still boasting over kills from that night, as though his father's men weren't taken by surprise as they were slaughtered by their friends. Sickening sycophants, but they'd played their part.

Sending Varnan with Alnor seemed like the logical choice at the time, though since then he'd been unpleasantly surprised by his realisation that he relied heavily on the man. Despite his incessant dark humour, he was loyal to the core and wasn't afraid to give his true opinion, regardless of the difference in rank. He missed the ugly brute, though he'd never say it aloud. Engrossed in his thoughts, for a time he forgot about the building anticipation in his chest as they came closer to the Buccai pass, the bulwark of the Annar against the Kerazar. Years of planning finally ending, the bulwark would be willingly opened.

A thrill ran through Krinar for what felt like the hundredth time that day, the thought of meeting his uncle in the flesh had him on edge. They had only corresponded with messengers that had braved the seas and entered Annar to find him in secret. Starting small, he built his trust as his Uncle Elart's plans worked time and time again. Riling up the General all those years ago, forcing him to focus his efforts on the 'Hounds', when in reality, the Kerazar were amassing strength and biding their time. Aldred and his father had been a bane to the Kerazar before that, repeatedly leading raiding parties into the tribe lands, keeping their numbers low to avoid a full-scale war. Having their attention focused inland was essential, and Krinar had assured it beautifully. Regret was a feeling he constantly kept down, thoughts of his mother's disappointment and anguish hurting in a way nothing else could. Throughout it all, she was the only one that had truly loved him. He would keep to the ruse that his father died in battle, a futile hope that she'd never know the truth and disown him forever.

Feeling a touch on his shoulder as he rode, he snapped out of his trance and spun in his saddle before seeing the red cloak beside him. Having no clue of his name, he acted every bit the arrogant royal.

"Speak," he commanded.

The man blanched at his King's evident slight but spoke. "We'll be able to see the fort within the hour, sire. I know these lands well. My father was born on a farm around here, just outside Foundisium."

Krinar couldn't bring himself to care, but he plastered what he hoped was a charming smile on his face before he replied. "Your father must be a rare kind of man to produce a son such as you! Have you ever seen the fort?"

The man instantly brightened at his King's interest. Krinar listened in disdain as the man babbled on about his father and the things they did as children, all the while keeping that fake smile, an image of the doting King to his men. Gods! He couldn't wait for this façade to end and be surrounded by his equals; he was keen to meet his cousin, who he'd never had any liaison with besides grilling the shifty messengers for every bit of information before sending them back with a reply. Most of all though, it was his Uncle Elart he craved to meet. The man had forged a kingdom out of nothing, braving the harsh winters and blistering summers of the tribe lands to bring the roaming nomads under one banner. *That* was a real King, not his father who grew fat and jumped at every shadow towards the end.

"Sire!" the blabbering man exclaimed, once again knocking him away from his comforting thoughts. This time, however, it was worth the interruption, the man's quivering finger pointing at the reason for his journey: Buccai pass. In the space of a moment his irritation evaporated, a whoop of joy escaping his lips at the sight.

"Well, what are we waiting for man? Let's go!" he yelled.

Digging his heels in, he shot forward with a whoop, surprising the rest of the red cloaks who were trundling along in their daydreams. He felt a kindling of begrudging admiration for the chatty man beside him as he kept pace with Krinar. Maybe he should learn his name, subtly of course, lest he give away the fact that he didn't have a clue. None of that mattered for now, with the dry wind slapping his face; miniscule pieces of sand doing their utmost to foul his vision, teaming up with the harsh sun to hinder his progress the best they could. Nothing would slow him now; he was over a day late already.

Hearing the warning horns blaring in the distance, he increased his pace to one bordering on reckless, yet still the man kept up with him. *I definitely have to learn his name,* Krinar thought. Making him race horses wouldn't be a bad idea. Varnan could set up a gambling ring to take easy money, a sure way to beggar merchants in a single day.

Laughing aloud, he earned himself a quizzical glance from the future racer, which he again ignored. As the walls came closer, he began to see specks atop them, milling around in confusion as the group galloped at differing speeds, all cohesion disintegrated with their new King's excitement.

The specks, Krinar noticed as he came closer still, held something poised in their arms, aimed at the approaching group. *Crossbows*, he thought. Slowing considerably, he raised his right fist to alert his men to do the same. It wouldn't do to get shot with a stray quarrel so close to his dream. They slowed within moments, some slightly later than others, their mounts carrying them a few steps further than the vanguard before finally coming to a slow trot, allowing their King to move ahead once more. They moved like that for the rest of the way, horses' flanks heaving as they struggled to regain breath from the impulsive charge.

The casual trot must have brought considerable confusion in the sentries, which kept Krinar's jovial mood high as they came within earshot of the fort. Many-a-time Krinar had passed through the fort, either with his father on their raids, or alone to keep up the morale of the frontier men; not a single time had he not marvelled at the gargantuan defence that provided safety from the Kerazar. It consisted of only two walls; one faced them now, easily the height of six men, and he knew it could hold as many as that abreast, a thick, oak gate in its centre. The other wall was larger still, putting even the walls of Grea to shame with its height. A bit excessive to keep out rabid tribesmen in Krinar's opinion, but probably needed since his uncle had taken control.

Natural obstacles prevented access from the north and the south, leaving the building of walls a wasteful enterprise. Steep, towering mountains lay to the north, ones that even a spider would struggle to traverse without risk. To the south, a sheer cliff dropped down to the Vastial sea, promising a watery death to anyone stupid enough to attempt it's climb - not to mention the mounted siege engines aiming out to sea, daring any ships to brave their wrath. The Annar had controlled the seas in the area for decades, but you could never be too careful. Within a few hours, protection from them would be unnecessary – they would be allies. Holding up a closed fist high in the air, Krinar halted his group, glancing to the still unnamed man beside him. He took the hint. Drawing himself up to full height, he bellowed his challenge.

"Why do the gates stand shut for the King of the Annar?"

Swift movement ensued atop the wall, certain men gesturing furiously below to the gate, others holding up their palms to calm that the comment had broken. One of the men from the latter group shouted back.

"We have had no news of a royal arrival. The last we heard, Malker was to the East, dealing with the rebels that plague us. How come you to be here, without said King to show?"

Despite the impudence, Krinar didn't have an ounce of anger for the speaker, instead sort of glad that the man was taking his role so seriously at the frontier. Laying a hand on no-name's arm, Krinar rode forward alone.

"Sire!" no-name hissed, but Krinar paid no heed.

If he couldn't walk unhindered within his own realm, he deserved to be shot down where he stood. "Good man! The news you have so artfully stated is weeks late. My beloved father was slain by the very rebels he tried to vanquish. In his place, you now see his son, the Prince of Annar: Krinar. I have not yet assumed my father's role, my grief is too raw yet for such things, but I also need to ensure that his legacy is still protected by these great walls. Ask the men beside you, at least some must recognise my face! Come, friend, allow us inside."

Krinar stood apart from his war band, refusing to swat at the flies which infuriatingly buzzed around his face, as the gesturing and raised voices began again from the ramparts. The speaker turned yet again, opening his arms wide.

"Enter, sire, and welcome!"

Krinar inclined his head, unsure if the man could even see at that distance, and clicked twice to his steed, urging it forwards at a slow pace. His men were slow to follow, leaving him moving alone for a few moments before he heard the bustle behind him. This was how he'd imagined it, the first entering of the fort with his men behind him, welcomed with open arms. A blessed shadow graced his scalp as he passed under the gate, barely glancing left and right to see the awestruck guards gawping at a member of the royal family. He'd really taken for granted his men's indifference to him but found that he basked in the attention as he passed back into the stifling sun. He could hear the sea's waves clearer once inside the walls, their soothing crashing against the cliff nectar to his ears after so long.

He closed his eyes, revelling in the serene feeling that had spread through his body, the anticipation buried only slightly beneath. The slam of the gate closing caused him to open his eyes, though the feeling remained. Soon, the feeling would be all that he felt. Dismounting swiftly and handing his reins to a waiting squire, he took a deep breath of the coastal air before turning towards the gate, and the men hurrying quickly down the stairs beside it.

Recognising over half of them, he nodded and clasped hands like old friends, just as they'd planned months before. Squires rushed around them taking the horses, some much older than usual, again planted months in advance. If it came to it, Krinar had enough men here to force his will, though he didn't think it would come to that. Wringing his hands nervously, the speaker from the wall approached.

"Sire, I apologise profusely for the delay. You must understand, bandits from the desert attempt to gain entry here frequently, so protocols must be kept," he almost pleaded.

Krinar, for once remembering the name of a man, responded. "Harrison Munat, you dog! I hadn't heard you'd been sent to the frontier! How fares your family? I passed Torizo on our way to the fight the rebels but didn't have to chance to sample its wares. Come, show me around, old friend."

Harrison beamed at being remembered, only a lowly cousin to the actual noble family in Torizo. Fiercely loyal, if Krinar remembered rightly, one who hated the Kerazar in his bones. He'd have to keep this one close, until the deed was done. Unaware of his King's inner thoughts, Harrison proceeded with his tour, pompously describing each aspect of the fort, as though Krinar had never been there before. Soon, he was pleasantly surprised by aspects that had sprung up within its walls – a small tavern being held in the highest regard. He dismissed his men instantly upon seeing this, the tavern's owner almost teary eyed at the amount of custom he would soon receive. Only no-name remained with him, though he whispered furiously to one of the others to bring him and Krinar wine. Krinar pretended not to notice, though inside he was grateful for the man. After remembering the Munat's name, it felt wrong somehow not to know his travelling partner's. He would have to remedy that, and soon.

Unperturbed by the dismissal of the red cloaks, Harrison continued without pause, bragging about the extra forge that he himself had commissioned, the extension to the barracks block, with additional bath houses to accommodate. If Krinar would have

336

cared at all about the fort, he might have taken more notice of what the incessant man was saying. As it was, he made sure he nodded in all the right places, throwing in a clap on the shoulder if the man looked like he needed more praise.

No-name followed in their wake, keeping them supplied with wine from his hastily procured skin and soothing their parched throats as the sun baked them. It had seemed like the rays were against them earlier, but as he crested the western wall and gazed across the plains of the tribe lands, it lent a warm hand to his neck, Ezimat's thanks to a faithful servant.

Krinar smiled and enjoyed the heat, taking delight in its orange glow that happily illuminated the brushes and dirt for miles ahead. Seeing a batch of trees beside the lazy sun, his smile became broader.

"If only time could speed up, setting the sun ahead of itself," Krinar murmured.

No-name chuckled enthusiastically, though Harrison looked uneasy. "Sire?" he asked.

"You will see, soon enough."

Minutes passed. The sound of the waves eclipsed by the carousing of his men, released after weeks in the field. He began to hear drums from the inn, and he could contain himself no longer, yelling in delight.

"Listen, my faithful Munat. Listen to the dawn of a new age!" Harrison looked nonplussed at his King's glee, doing his best to mimic it, whilst simultaneously looking towards the inn. The drums were getting louder by the second, the doors thrown open to allow the sound to carry. No singing ensued, just the steady beating of the drum, perfectly in time. Keeping his eyes fixed outwards, Krinar tapped the beat on his leg with his fingers, no-name crying aloud in triumph, whilst Harrison did the same in utter fear. Because to the sound of the drums, a long line of savage men had appeared at the trees that hugged the sun's final rest.

"To arms! The Kerazar approach, to ar- " Harrison began.

His orders were muffled as no-name's fist crunched into his teeth, sending him screaming off the edge of the wall and landing in a heap at the stair's base, blood creeping from his ears as his eyes gazed listlessly to the skies. A few exclamations accompanied the untimely demise, all quickly silenced.

Not bothering to look behind, knowing his men knew their trade, he stared in wonder at the horde approaching. Never in his wildest dreams could he have imagined his Uncle Elart would have mustered so many men, the whole plain filling up like a colony of ants; they could conquer the world with this. A fleeting thought crossed his mind that barely any horses were present, just thousands of foot soldiers. *No matter,* he thought. *The Annar can be the cavalry, the Kerazar the hammer.*

Beating louder, the drums continued their mantra, eclipsing all other sounds as the sun crept slowly beneath the skyline. Waves picked up their pace as the sun disappeared, bringing with it a wind that howled with feeling, adding to the drumming with an orchestra of sound. As if feeling the mood of the fort, a steady patter of rain began, ricocheting off the wall as it picked up the tempo.

Individual men soon became clear to Krinar, two specifically in the centre of the line – the only two on horseback. Knowing in his soul that these were the men that he'd longed to see, he bellowed the words that the Buccai pass fort hadn't heard in years.

"OPEN THE GATES!"

Drumming stopped. The waves continued their angry crashing against the cliffs, egged on by the raging wind and the present rumble of thunder. The thunder continued for longer than usual, making the wall he stood on shake uncontrollably, causing even him to look startled, before he realised the obvious and turned to no-name who was gazing fearfully at the skies.

"It's not thunder man, it's the gates! Come on."

Making their way down the now slippery steps, Krinar and no name planted themselves within the crowd of drummers, stood in the eerie silence, their instruments forgotten as the magnitude of what they'd finally done hit home.

The first ranks of Kerazar walked slowly through the gates, cheering madly at the honour of being the first to do something that before had only seemed a dream. They jeered at the waiting red cloaks, who shifted with unease despite knowing the truce that held between them.

Krinar, however, kept his eyes on the two men in the centre, dismounting silently from their barely serviceable mounts and passing over the reins. The younger of them made a wordless shout, chopping with his hand and bringing instant silence to the others.

Krinar steeled his nerve, stopping his hand from drawing the circle on his head as even the elements fell silent to the man's barked command. Standing with only the sound of rain piercing the veil, Krinar grinned and spread his arms wide, acting out a feeling he most certainly didn't feel. The men who he could only guess were his uncle and his cousin stepped forward, their faces a mirror of his own as they approached, the horde shifting closer as they did.

"It can't finally be my dear nephew. Is that you, Krinar?" the larger man said, face still hidden by the shroud of darkness that covered the fort. The other man didn't make a sound.

"Speak, nephew. Do not leave an old man out in the rain for a courtesy." Krinar knew as soon as he spoke who he was, having heard his father's voice constantly for years, the similarity too obvious to ignore. Keeping on his grin and hoping it hid his nerves, he stepped forward with his arms still spread.

"Uncle Elart!" he exclaimed. "It is an honour to finally meet – "

The rest of his greeting was cut short, the bear hug from his uncle crushing the air from his lungs. Krinar gasped in relief, which he hoped sounded better than he'd thought as his uncle released him. He tried to keep the smile plastered on his face whilst catching his breath, coughing slightly as he found he was unable to do so. Another cough followed and he covered his mouth with his hand to avoid humiliation.

Behind him he could hear shouts and the sound of metal clashing, but his brain couldn't register the tell-tale sounds of a battle unfolding. Raising his hand away from his mouth, he saw a bright red stain in his palm. Feeling his legs weaken, the strength began to leave his body.

Shadows darted around the edge of his vision, the dreaded tribesmen falling onto his red cloaks with howls and screams, and still Krinar didn't believe the turn of fate. Only when he dropped to his knees with his uncle still holding him, did he register the horrible truth.

"I'm sorry, my nephew. It's just the way it works," he rasped into his ear, pushing him savagely down in to the soaking mud, face to face with no-name, who's eyes were glazed and long dead.

Grady, Krinar thought triumphantly. That's his fucking name!

His triumph was short lived, as the dim edges began to close on his vision. Attempting to scream his defiance, it instead came out as a pitiful gurgling as his hand attempting to grasp onto Grady's, loyal until the end.

Elart watched in disdain as his family died with ease below him, stamping on

Krinar's hand as it reached for a final rest. He basked in the sound of his nephew's agony as he died in the mud, enjoying watching his brother's son die. He watched his own son with pride as he dispatched three of the Annar within seconds, Ezimat chosen to his bones, like the rest of his children. Those, he would get back off the priest in time.

Rain increased its pace above them, battering the bodies of the slain and dripping down Elart's nose as his son came closer. He was grinning maniacally, with streams of blood staining his teeth as he clasped hands with his father.

Elart grasped with all the fervour of a man possessed, staring directly into his son's eyes.

"We're in."

END OF BOOK ONE

Acknowledgements

And that's the end of book one! If you've made it this far, thank you for taking the time to read Annarite Born, and I hope you'll stick around for the remainder of the trilogy. This story has been a pocket of words in my brain for many years, so to finally get it out to the world has been a surreal feeling and I'm still riding the high of it all. Firstly, I'd like to thank Herman. He became a close friend through an online game we played at the time, and he read each chapter as it was written, giving me the confidence to keep going with his encouragement. Without you my friend, Annarite Born would never have been finished, discarded like the countless other times I've tried.

Next, to my amazing editor, Jonathan Creer. His insight into not only the development of the story, but the tidying up of my shoddy lines after, made the book what it is now. Thank you for all your help, and I'd recommend his services to anybody looking for an editor.

To the best beta readers: Laura, Virginia, Flaka and my Uncle Darren! The comments and insight into something that hadn't long since finished drafting brought it up to a level I was happy with, and definitely kept me sane through the editing phases. Also, to Bryan Wilson and Andrew Watson, who have endured countless questions from me about publishing. It can't have been easy!

Last – but most definitely not least – to you, the reader! Without you, none of this is possible, especially for us indies. If I could trouble you to leave a review on Amazon, Goodreads, or any other platform you're on, it would mean the world to me. It's the only thing that gets Annarite Born out there to more of you, and I would appreciate it greatly.

Thank you to you all and see you in Book 2!

Ben

www.ingramcontent.com/pod-product-compliance
Ingram Content Group UK Ltd.
Pitfield, Milton Keynes, MK11 3LW, UK
UKHW040826061025
8242UKWH00038B/645

9 781068 264610